# MANNA FR

## ALSO BY ROGER ZELAZNY

*The Dream Master*
*This Immortal*
*Four for Tomorrow*
*Lord of Light*
*Creatures of Light and Darkness*
*Damnation Alley*
*Isle of the Dead*
*Nine Princes in Amber*
*The Doors of His Face, the Lamps of His Mouth*
*Jack of Shadows*
*The Guns of Avalon*
*To Die in Italbar*
*Sign of the Unicorn*
*Deus Irae* (with Philip K. Dick)
*Doorways in the Sand*
*The Hand of Oberon*
*My Name Is Legion*
*The Courts of Chaos*
*Roadmarks*
*Changeling*
*The Last Defender of Camelot*
*The Changing Land*
*Madwand*
*To Spin is Miracle Cat*
*Dilvish the Damned*
*Eye of Cat*
*Unicorn Variations*
*Trumps of Doom*
*Blood of Amber*
*A Dark Traveling*
*Sign of Chaos*
*Frost and Fire*
*Knight of Shadows*
*Prince of Chaos*
*A Night in the Lonesome October*
*A Farce to be Reckoned With*
*Forever After*
*Warriors of Blood and Dream*
*Wheel of Fortune*
*Donnerjack*
*PsychoShop* (with Alfred Bester)

# MANNA FROM HEAVEN

## ROGER ZELAZNY

### Introduction by
### Steven Brust

### Edited by
### Scott Zrubeck

DNA PUBLICATIONS/WILDSIDE PRESS ❈ 2003

# MANNA FROM HEAVEN

Published by
DNA Publications and Wildside Press.

For more information, contact:

DNA Publications & Wildside Press
The Fantastic Book Club
P.O. Box 2988
Radford VA 24141

# CONTENTS

# INTRODUCTION

I was at Roger's memorial service, surrounded by his family and his friends, and we were sharing memories and stories and reading passages from his work. Gradually, I got the panicky feeling that Paul had in Frank Herbert's *Dune* when he realized that circumstances required him to speak, and he had no idea what to say. In my case, it was because everything that formed in my head was about me, not Roger—how I felt when he wrote an introduction to one of my books. How I felt when I first read his work. What it was like talking to him on the phone when I was supposed to be working. My first in-person meeting with him. What his letters were like, and how it felt to receive them.

Me. But I didn't want to talk about me, I wanted to talk about him, and so I kept drawing a blank.

Eventually I muttered a few inanities, and, naturally, a few days later I thought of the passage of his I ought to have read. More on that later.

My point now is that I find myself in the same situation. I want to talk about Roger, but all I can think of to say is about me, and I'm not what this is supposed to be about. For example...

In 1971 I decided that I wanted to write.

I'd been writing, of course, for about as long as I could read, but I got serious about it in 1971, because that was when a friend introduced me to *Lord of Light* by Roger Zelazny. I remember putting the book down, staring off into space (I do that a lot during and after reading something by Roger), and realizing that what I wanted to do with my life was to make other people feel the way that book had made me feel.

It goes without saying that I immediately went out and grabbed everything of his I could get my hands on, and continued to do so until he passed away in 1995. His novels have always been to me a source of inspiration, making me want to go out and do something cool—something in which there is the perfect match between the story and how the story is told, in which there is as much depth of meaning as the reader chooses to look for, and as much sheer kick-back-and-enjoy fun stuff as anyone could want. I'd put down one of his novels, re-read for the tenth or eleventh time, with the feeling, "Yep. That's how you do that."

His short fiction, on the other hand, has been a source of frustration to me. I read "He Who Shapes" and thought, "I can never do something like that." I read "For a Breath I Tarry" and thought, "I'll stick to novels." I read "A Rose for Ecclesiastes," and started checking the want-ads for bar-tending positions.

I've tried to figure out what I've learned from him. I'm not really sure if I've exactly *learned* anything. My friend Will Shetterly has pointed out that you can learn more easily from someone who almost gets it right than from a master who makes everything appear so seamless and effortless that you're never sure how he carried it off.

Roger was a master.

One of the truisms about writing that I quite like is the one that goes, "An editor isn't really buying a story, he's buying the way the story is told." This is nowhere more obvious than in Roger Zelazny's short fiction. In this volume you'll find "The Furies," one of my favorites. Consider what actually takes place during the story, then consider how you, the reader, discover it, how you're led there, and the emotional punch, that elevator-dropping sensation as the pieces come together. It isn't where you're going that counts, it's how you get there. And who is going along with you.

I think I have, in one way or another, fallen in love with just about every character Roger has created. When someone refers to "so and so is good with characterization," he might mean one of three things: The characters are easily distinguished from one another; the reader knows and understands the characters at a deep and profound level; or simply, these people are cool and I want to follow them around and see what they do. Roger, in my opinion, wrote strong characters by any of those standards, but especially by the third. From Kalifriki of the Thread to that feisty Ford convertible in "Auto-da-Fé" I've always been grabbed by the people Roger has created who pass through my world.

And another thing is that rare ability to simultaneously confuse and reassure you: Yes, he seems to be saying, I know this makes no sense. But trust me, it's that way for a reason, hang with me. And you do, and you're glad you did. I've tried to analyze this, to figure out how he does it. I've failed. Now I just enjoy. Find his story, "No Award," or read the prologue to *Bridge of Ashes*. See what I mean? It may be that this is what I value the most—that, "Oh, now I get it!" moment of epiphany about what the story is doing that, at its best, parallels some epiphany about life, and at its worst, merely (merely?) brings a moment of delight.

But over and above everything else, there is one thing in a writer that either captures your heart or leaves you cold, and, really, takes precedence over everything else: the way he uses words.

*Pain made his mouth a bow. His teeth, the arrows, clenched.*

Oh, yeah.

He put together sentences that still take my breath away. Now, I ask you: am I speaking of him, or of me?

Well, both, I guess. If there is anything in life that is purely subjective, it is the way one responds to a work of art. Those responses are mine, and I treasure them, and I find reason to treasure them anew each time I reread his work. That's what we've been left with: treasure. And that is what is in these pages: treasure.

And speaking of what we've been left with, here is that passage I should have read at his memorial. Jane? Trent? Walter Jon? Neil? George? The rest of you? Here's what I ought to have said, from *Isle of the Dead*:

> For some stupid reason my eyes filled with tears at this passage. Every world I had designed and built moved by me. I had forgotten the glory.
> The feeling that had filled me with the creation of each of them came over me then. I had hurled something into the pit. Where there had been darkness, I had hung my worlds. They were my answer. When I finally walked that Valley, they would remain after me. Whatever the Bay claimed, I had made some replacements, to thumb my nose at it. I had done something, and I knew how to do more.

Now I'm going to shut up and let you read the stories.

Steven Brust
Las Vegas, NV
August, 2003

# GODSON

The first time I saw Morris Leatham, at the baptismal font where he became my godfather, I was too small for the memory to stick. Thereafter he visited me every year on my birthday, and this year was no exception.

"Morrie," I said, knuckling my right eye and then my left. I opened them and stared through the predawn light of my bedroom to the chair beside the window with the dead geranium on the sill, where he sat, tall and thin, almost anorectic-looking.

He rose, smiling, and crossed to the side of the bed. He extended a hand, drew me to my feet, and passed me my robe. "Put it on," he said, as he led me out of the room. My Aunt Rose and Uncle Matt were still asleep. Moments later, it seemed, Morrie and I were walking inside the local mall. It was dimly lit, and there was no one about.

"What are we doing here?" I asked.

"I'd like you to walk through, look around, and tell me what you'd like for a birthday present."

"I know right where it is," I said. "Come on."

I led him past the bench where the night watchman lay unmoving, a wet spot at the crotch of his uniform trousers. I stopped before a store window and pointed.

"Which one?" Morrie asked.

"The black one," I said.

He chuckled.

"One black bicycle for David," he said. "I'll get you one like that, only better. It'll be delivered later today."

"Thank you," I said, turning and hugging him. Then, "Don't you think we ought to wake that guard up? His boss might come by."

"He's been dead for some time, David. Myocardial infarct. Died in his sleep."

"Oh."

"That's how most people say they'd like to go, so he had it good," Morrie told me. "Just turned seventy-three last month. His boss thought he was younger. Name's William Strayleigh—'Bill,' to his friends."

"Gee, you know a lot of people."

"You meet everybody in my line of work."

I wasn't sure what Morrie's line of work was, exactly, but I nodded as if I were.

I woke up again later and cleaned up and dressed and went downstairs for breakfast. There was a birthday card beside my plate, and I opened it and read it and said, "Thanks, Aunt Rose."

"Just wanted you to know we hadn't forgotten," she said.

"My godfather Morrie remembered, too. He was by earlier, and he took me to the mall to pick out a present and—"

She glanced at the clock.

"The mall doesn't open for another half hour."

"I know," I said. "But he got me in anyway. Too bad about the night watchman, though. Died in his sleep on a bench. I'm getting a black ten-speed that'll be sent over this afternoon."

"Don't start on that business again, David. You know it bothers Uncle Matt."

"Just wanted you to know the bike was coming."

"Nobody's been here this morning. Nobody's been out and back in. You miss your folks. It's natural you have these dreams around your birthday."

"And I get presents."

"Hard for us to know, since you weren't with us last year."

"Well, it's true. Morrie always gives me something. Dad could have told you."

"Maybe," she said. "But it's strange that Morris has never gotten in touch with us."

"He travels a lot."

She turned away, began making French toast.

"Just don't mention him around Matt."

"Why not?"

"Because I asked you not to, okay?"

I nodded when she glanced my way.

The doorbell rang that afternoon, and when I opened the door it was there: a bike with a paint job so dark and shiny that it looked like a series of black mirrors. I couldn't find a manufacturer's name on it, just a silver-edged plate on the handlebar post in the shape of a small black heart. The note tied to the bar said, "Happy Birthday, David. His name is Dorel. Treat him well and he will serve you well.—M."

It was a long time before I knew exactly what that meant. But the first thing I did, of course—after removing the tag and handing it to Uncle Matt—was to take it down the steps, mount, and ride off.

"Dorel," I said softly. "He told me you're called Dorel." Was it my imagination, or did a brief vibration pass through that midnight frame just then?

Everything Morrie gave me had a special character to it—like the Magic Kit I had gotten last year, with the Indian Rope Trick I never used (I'm not a good climber) and the Five-Minute Time Warp which I never found any use for. I keep it in my pocket.

"My name's David," I continued. "You're beautiful and you're fast and you're easy to steer. I like you a lot."

It was as if I were going downhill all the way to the corner and back.

When I parked Dorel on the porch again, Uncle Matt was waiting right inside the door. "I just heard on the news," he said, "that the night watchman at the mall was found dead this morning, of a heart attack."

"I know," I said. "I told Aunt Rose about it earlier."

"How did you know about it?"

"I was over there, before the mall opened, with Morrie. He got us in, and I picked out the kind of bike I wanted."

"How did he get you in?"

"Uh, I don't really remember the details."

Uncle Matt scratched his chin through his beard and narrowed his gray eyes behind his thick glasses. They looked a lot like my eyes, and—I suddenly remembered—my dad's.

"What's he look like, anyway—your godfather?" he asked.

I shrugged. It was hard to remember just what he looked like. "Kind of thin. He has dark hair, I think. And a real nice voice. Makes you want to do whatever he says."

"That's all?"

"I guess so."

"Damn! That's no description, David. That could be almost anybody."

"I'm sorry."

He reached out and squeezed my shoulder as I began to draw back.

"I didn't mean to yell at you," he said. "It's just that the whole business is kind of—unusual. Not to speak ill of my own brother, but it's no secret that your father was a heavy drinker. Especially there at the end. It's why your mother left him. Probably what killed him, too."

I nodded. I'd heard—or overheard—all this before.

"He told a bizarre story of the way he met your godfather. Sounded like something a paranoid Trotskyite drunk might come up with, and I didn't believe a word of it. Still don't."

I stared at him. I knew what a paranoid was, also. And two out of three wasn't bad.

"I don't remember the story," I said, "if I ever knew."

Uncle Matt sighed, and told me the tale.

My father met Morrie at a crossroads, pursuant to a dream. He'd dreamed that a voice came to him out of a thundercloud limned with lightning, and it said, "I am God. You have alienated everyone close to you and I pity you. I shall stand for your son in my own church and make him happy in life." My father said,

"You give to the rich and leave the poor working stiffs to hunger. I do not want you for my son's godfather." And there was a clap of thunder and the cloud went away, and the earth split and a flame rose up out of the crack and a voice spoke from it, saying, "I am Satan. Have me. I will make him rich. I will see that he gets on well in the world."

My father said, "You are the Prince of Bullshitters. I do not want you either, for I do not trust you." And fire flared, and Satan was gone, also. Later then he was halfway to wakefulness, a shadowy figure passed near and told him, "'When you awaken walk outside. Stop at the first crossroads you come to. I will meet you there."

"Who are you?" my father asked. "I am he who makes all equal," came the reply, "in a most democratic fashion." And my father got up, dressed, went out into the darkness, and waited at the crossroads. There he met Morris, and he invited him to be my godfather, for he said that one who had him for a friend would lack nothing.

"Do you know what that means?" Uncle Matt asked me.

"Yeah. It's a good thing that he went to the crossroads, or I wouldn't have my bike."

He stared at me for several moments. "Rose and I weren't present at your christening. We'd had a disagreement with Sam earlier. So neither of us got to meet Morris."

"I know."

"The next time you see him, tell him it had nothing to do with him, or with you. Tell him we wish he'd stop by sometime."

"You will get to see him," I told him. "He says everyone does. I'll ask him to name a date next time—"

"Never mind," he said, suddenly.

Later, that evening, after my birthday party, I went out on my new bike again. Lacking an address for a thank-you note, I resolved to go visit Morrie and say it aloud. In the past, when I'd wanted to see him between birthdays I would wander about trying to figure out how to do it and before long I always encountered him—most recently as part of the crowd at an auto accident, and once at the beach, where I was watching the guard give mouth-to-mouth resuscitation to a guy. This time, though, I'd go in style.

I pedaled hard till I got to the outskirts of town, coasted downhill to a wooded area, turned onto an old logging road now mainly used by hunters, fishermen, hikers, and kids from the high school following dances and movies. It was darker down here than it was up on the hill, and I bore to the left, coming onto a long, winding stretch under summer foliage.

"Dorel," I said, "I'm really happy with you, and I want to go and thank Morrie for such a great birthday present. I don't know where to find him but I've got a feeling you do. I'd like you to help me get to him—now."

A throbbing seemed to begin within the dark vehicle, and as we rounded the next corner a kind of stroboscopic effect began. At first it seemed that it might simply have been from the angle of the light and the trees' spacing. But after a while each period of darkness seemed more intense, lasted a little longer; and each time the light returned it came more dimly, came for a shorter bit of time.

Soon, I coasted down a dark tunnel—for I noted that I need no longer pedal but only steer in the direction of a distant light which now came into view. Dorel vibrated, and we picked up speed. After a time, the light grew brighter and I entered a gallery of stalactites and still pools. The place was a blaze of light, for there were candles everywhere I looked on every ledge, in every niche, atop every flat surface. They varied in size, they burned with a still intensity. There were no drafts here, save for the rush of air from my own passage, and we were slowing, slowing.... I put my foot down, halted, and stared. I had never seen so many candles before in my life.

"Thanks, Dorel," I whispered.

I set the kickstand and walked about. There were tunnels leading off in all directions from the grotto, all of them blazing for as far as I could see with multitudes of candles. Every now and then a burntdown candle stub would gutter and go out. Shadows darted about these like black butterflies as they died.

Wandering, I was suddenly concerned about finding my way back out. I halted and looked about for Dorel. Once I was back upon my bike, I was sure I could retrace my route.

A shadow glided around boulder, plinth, stalactite. It was my bike, with my godfather seated upon it and pedaling slowly, grinning. He wore what appeared to be a dark cloak. He waved and made his way in my direction.

"How good of you to come and visit," he called out.

"Wanted to say thanks for the present," I told him. "Dorel's really neat."

"Glad you like him." He drew up before me, braked, and dismounted, setting the stand.

"I never knew a bike to have a name before."

He ran a bony finger along the handlebars.

"He is something that owes me a great debt. He is paying it off in this fashion," he said. "Would you care for a cup of tea or hot chocolate?"

"I'd like a hot chocolate," I said.

He led me around a corner and into a niche where a slab of stone bore a red-and-white calico tablecloth. Two cups and saucers were laid upon it, along with napkins and spoons. Sounds of classical music were in the air, and I could not determine their source. We seated ourselves and he reached for a carafe which stood within a wire frame above one of the ubiquitous candles. Raising it, he filled our cups.

"What is that music?" I asked.

"Schubert's Quartet in D Minor, a favorite piece of mine," he said. "Marshmallow?"

"Yes, please."

He added marshmallows. It was hard to see his face, the way the shadows danced about him.

"Is this where you work, Morrie, or where you live?"

He handed me my cup, leaned back, and commenced cracking his knuckles, one by one, a talent I mightily envied him.

"I do a lot of my work in the field," he said. "But you might consider this my office, and I do keep an apartment here. Yes, it is both."

"I see," I said. "It's certainly well lit."

He chuckled. He gestured broadly, and the nearby flames flickered wildly.

"She'll think it a fainting spell," he remarked.

"Who?" I asked.

"The lady who belongs to that candle. Name's Luisa Trujillo. She's forty-eight years old and lives in New York City. She's got another twenty-eight years to go. *Bueno.*"

I lowered my cup, turned slowly, and regarded the immense cavern and all of the side chambers and tunnels.

"Yes," he said after a time. "All there, all of them. There's one for each of them."

"I read that there are several billion people in the world."

He nodded.

"Lot of wax," he observed.

"Good chocolate," I said.

"Thanks. The Big Ten's really come upon bad days."

"Huh?"

"Everything interesting's happening in the West," he said.

"Oh," I said. "Football. You're talking college football, aren't you?"

"Yes, but I like pro football, too. What about you?"

"I don't know enough about it," I said, "but I'd like to," and he commenced telling me.

Much later, we simply sat, watching the candles flicker. At length, he refilled our cups.

"You given any thought to what you want to be when you grow up?" he asked.

"Not really," I said.

"Consider being a physician. You'd have a knack for it. I'd see to that," he said. "'Do you play chess?"

"No."

"Good game, too. You ought to learn. I've a mind to teach you."

"All right."

I don't know how long we sat there, using the squares on the tablecloth for our board. The pieces were of bone—the clean white of fresh, the almost-brown of aged, bone—which were quite elegant. As we played, I realized that I liked the game.

"A physician," I remarked after a time.

"Yes, think about it."

"I will," I agreed.

And so I did. It was good to have some sort of goal. I made it a point to study extra hard for math, chemistry, and biology classes. College wasn't particularly difficult, and while I worried as to where the money for med school would come from, a distant relative died at just the right time and left me enough to take care of it.

Even after I'd gone away to college I still rode Dorel—as sleek and shiny as ever—to Morrie's office every year on my birthday, where we drank hot chocolate, played chess, and talked football.

"You graduate in June," he remarked. "Then you do an internship and a residency."

"That's right."

"You've thought about the area in which you would like to specialize?"

"I was thinking of dermatology. I figure nobody will ever call me in the middle of the night with a dermatological emergency."

"Hm," Morrie said, stirring his chocolate with a delicate bone which served us as a spoon. "When I suggested the medical profession I had something a little more basic in mind. Internal medicine, perhaps."

A bat darted by, caught hold of Morrie's cloak, crawling inside, and hanging upside down from a seam. I took a sip of chocolate, moved my bishop.

"A lot of hard work there," I finally said. "'Dermatologists make pretty good money."

"Bah!" Morrie said. He moved a knight. "Check," he added. "As an internist you will become the greatest consulting physician in the world."

"Really?" I asked, and I studied the chess pieces.

"Yes. You will manage some miraculous-seeming cures."

"Are you sure you've considered all the ramifications? If I get that good, I could be cutting into your business."

Morrie laughed. "There is a balance between life and death, and in this we play our parts. For mine, really, is the power over life, as yours will be the power over death. Think of it as a family business."

"All right. I'll give it a shot," I said. "By the way, I resign. You've got me in four moves."

"Three."

"Whatever you say. And thanks for the present, those diagnostic tools. I've never seen anything like them."

"I'm sure they'll come in handy. Happy Birthday," he said.

⋆　　⋆　　⋆

And so I went off to a big hospital in a big city in the Northwest, to do my time. I saw Morrie more than ever there. Usually, he'd stop by when I was on the night shift.

"Hi, Dave. That one in Number Seven. She'll be checking out at 3:12 A.M.," he said, seating himself beside me. "Too bad about the fellow in Number Sixteen."

"Ah, he was fading fast. We knew it was just a matter of time."

"You could have saved that one, Dave."

"We tried everything we knew."

He nodded. "Guess you're going to have to learn a few more things, then."

"If you're teaching, I'll take notes," I said.

"Not yet, but soon," he responded. He reached out and touched my cup of coffee, which had long ago gone cold. It began to steam again. He rose and faced the window. "About time," he said, and a moment later there came the blaring of a horn from the highway below, followed by the sound of a collision. "I'm needed," he said. "Good night." And he was gone.

He did not mention it again for a long while, and I almost thought he had forgotten. Then, one day the following spring—a sunny and deliciously balmy occasion—I went walking in the park. Suddenly, it seemed that I cast two shadows. Then one of them spoke to me:

"Lovely day, eh, Dave?"

I looked about. "Morrie, you're very quiet when you come up on a person."

"Indeed," he said.

"You're dressed awfully solemnly for such a fine, bright morning."

"Working clothes," he said.

"That's why you're carrying a long, sharp tool?"

"Right."

We walked in silence for a time, passing through a field and into a grove of trees. Abruptly, he dropped to his knees at the foot of a small rise, extended his hands amid grasses, and spread them. Two small flowering plants lay between his extended forefingers and thumbs. No, what had seemed a pair of plants could now be seen as but one. What had misled me was that it bore both blue and yellow flowers. I regarded the leaves. I recalled a botany class I had once taken. . . .

"Yes, study it," he said.

"I can't identify it," I told him.

"I would be most surprised if you could. It is quite rare, and the only sure way to know it and to find it when you need it is by means of introduction and by words of summoning, which I shall teach you."

"I see."

"And in your case it will be necessary to place samples under cultivation in your apartment. For you must learn its usages more deeply than any other who knows of it. Roots, leaves, stalks, flowers: each part has a separate virtue, and they can be made to work in a wide variety of combinations."

"I do not understand. I've spent all this time getting a first-rate medical education. Now you want me to become an herbalist?"

He laughed.

"No, of course not. You need your techniques as well as your credentials. I am not asking you to abandon the methods you have learned for helping people, but merely to add another for . . . special cases."

"Involving that little flower?"

"Exactly."

"What is it called?"

"Bleafage. You won't find it in any herbal or botany text. Come here and let me introduce you and teach you the words. Then you will remove it and take it to your home, to cultivate and become totally familiar with."

I ate, drank, and even slept with the bleafage. Morrie stopped by periodically and instructed me in its use. I learned to make tinctures, poultices, salves, plasters, pills, wines, oils, liniments, syrups, douches, enemas, electuaries, and fomentations of every part and combination of parts of the thing. I even learned how to smoke it. Finally, I began taking a little of it to work with me every now and then and tried it on a number of serious cases, always with remarkable results.

My next birthday, Morrie took me to a restaurant in town, and afterward an elevator in the parking garage seemed to keep descending, finally releasing us in his office.

"Neat trick, that," I said.

I followed him along a bright, winding tunnel, his invisible servants moving about us, lighting fresh candles and removing the remains of those which had expired. At one point, he stopped and removed a stump of a candle from a case, lit it from the guttering flame of one upon a ledge, and replaced the old one with the new one, just as the former went out.

"What did you just do, Morrie?" I asked. "I've never seen you replace one before."

"I don't do it often," he answered. "But that woman you fed the bleafage to this afternoon—the one in 465—she's just rallied." He measured the candle stump between thumb and forefinger. "Six years, eight months, three days, seven hours, fourteen minutes, twenty-three seconds," he observed. "That's how much life you have bought her."

"Oh," I said, trying to study his face and failing, within the darting shadows.

"I'm not angry, if that's what you're looking for," he said. "You must try the bleafage out if you're to understand its power."

"Tell me," I said, "is it a power over life or a power over death that we are discussing?"

"That's droll," he said. "Is it one of those Zen things? I rather like it."

"No, it was a serious question."

"Well, mine is a power over life," he said, "and vice versa. We're sort of 'yin-yang' that way."

"But you're not restricted to your specialty, not when you have this bleafage business going for you, too."

"David, I can't use the herb. I can only teach you about it. I require a human master of bleafage to use it for me."

"Oh, I see."

"Not entirely, I'm certain. Go ahead and experiment. It may seem that the people you treat with it all come to you by chance, but this will not always be the case."

I nodded and studied the flowers.

"You have a question?" he asked.

"Yes. That candle stub you used for purposes of extending Mrs. Emerson, of Room 465, for six years, plus—How did it come to be snuffed out at just that point, rather than having burned itself all the way down? It's almost as if you'd—snuffed someone prematurely."

"It is, isn't it?" he said, grinning broadly. "As I mentioned, death *is* a power over life. Let's have some coffee and our brandy now, shall we?"

I was more than a little puzzled by the way Morrie ran his business. But it was his show and he'd always been kind to me. He'd given me a whole new wardrobe for a birthday present, and when I completed my residency he gave me a new car. Dorel was still in fine fettle, but I needed a car once I began my practice. I moved Dorel to the rear of the garage and rode him only on the weekends. But I found myself going out there more and more, evenings, sitting on the high stool beside the workbench, popping the tab on a cold one and talking to my bike the way I had when I was a kid.

"Funny," I said, "that *he* should give me a wonder drug for saving lives. On the other hand," I reflected, "it's obvious that he did sort of push me into medicine. Could it be that he wants control over the life-*giving* half of the yin-yang? Not just letting someone live, but assuring quality time by removing causes of suffering?"

Dorel's frame creaked as he leaned slightly in my direction. His headlight blinked on, blinked off.

"Is that an affirmative?" I asked.

The blinking was repeated.

"Okay, I'll take that as 'yes,'" I said, "and two for 'no.'"

One blink followed.

"It would make a kind of sense," I said, "for two reasons: First, back when I was still at the hospital, I gave a sample of bleafage to Dr. Kaufman, a biochemist, and asked him whether he could determine its major constituents. He died in the lab the next day, and a fire destroyed whatever he was working on. Later, I ran into Morrie in the morgue, and he told me that synthesizing bleafage was a no-no. He did not want it to become as common as aspirin or antibiotics. That would make it seem he only wanted certain persons to benefit.

"Second," I continued, "I believe this guess was confirmed by the instructions he gave me when I set up in private practice."

Morrie told me that I would get calls from all over for consultations. He never said where they'd get my name or number or why they'd want me, but he was right. They did start coming in. He told me to take my bleafage with me whenever I went, and my special diagnostic tools, but that the entire diagnosis and treatment—or lack of it—would be governed solely by a matter of personal perception. I can see Morrie when other people can't. He said that in those special cases where I'm called in to consult he would enter the room. If he were to stand at the head of the bed, I was to diagnose and treat, and the patient would live. But if he stood at the foot, I was to perform a few routine tests and pronounce it a hopeless case.

"It almost seems as if there were an agenda, as if he had a special deal with some of my patients or a plan into which they fit."

The light blinked once.

"Ah, you think so, too! Do you know what it is?"

It blinked twice, then a third time.

"Yes and no? You have some guesses, but you're not sure?"

It blinked once.

"Of course, no matter what the reasons, I'm helping a lot of people who wouldn't be helped otherwise."

A single blink.

"Morrie once said that you're working off a debt by being a bicycle."

A single blink.

"I didn't understand what he meant then, and I still don't. Is there a way you could tell me?"

Again, a single blink.

"Well, what is it?"

Abruptly, Dorel rolled across the garage, leaned against the wall, and grew still and lightless. I gathered that meant that I had to figure it out for myself. I tried, too, but was interrupted by a phone call. Emergency. Not at the hospital, but one of those special emergency cases.

"This is Dr. Puleo, Dan Puleo. We met at that ER seminar this spring."

"I remember," I said.

"Speaking of emergencies . . ."

"You got one?"

"There's a limousine on the way to pick you up."

"To take me where?"

"The governor's mansion."

"This involves Caisson himself?"

"Yes."

"How come he's not in the hospital?"

"He will be, but you're near and I think you can beat the ambulance."

"I think I can beat the limo, too," I said, "if I take the bike trail through the park."

I hung up, snatched my med kit, ran back to the garage.

"We've got to get to the governor's mansion fast," I said to Dorel as I wheeled him out and mounted.

What followed was a blur. I remember dismounting and making my way shakily to the door. Somehow I was inside then, shaking hands with Puleo and being escorted into a bedroom—as the doctor said something about a bad bout of flu recently, kidney stones last year, and no history of heart problems. No vital signs at the moment either.

I stared at the figure on the bed—Lou Caisson, a reform governor who was doing a great job on a number of fronts his predecessor had let slide, as well as maintaining the previous administration's gains. All that, and having an attractive, talented daughter like Elizabeth, as well. I had not seen her since we'd broken up back in school and headed for different parts of the country. As I moved forward to begin my examination, I felt a guilty pang. I had let Morrie break us up, with his insistence that I attend a West Coast med school after I'd been accepted at the one with the Eastern university she was to attend.

Speaking of Morrie . . .

A shadow slid forward and Morrie stood at the foot of the bed. He was shaking his head.

I checked for a carotid pulse. There was none. I raised an eyelid. . . .

Suddenly, I was mad. As I heard the sirens in the distance, I was swept by a wave of anger over every decision in my life that Morrie had influenced. In an instant looking back, I saw just how manipulated I had been with all his little bribes and attentions. I opened my med kit and placed it on the bed.

"Are you going to treat him?" Puleo asked.

I leaned forward, slid my arms beneath Caisson, picked him up. I backed away then, walked around the foot of the bed behind Morrie, and laid him back down again, this time with Morrie standing at his head. I reached across and picked up my kit.

"I can't take any responsibility—" Puleo began.

I filled the long syringe.

"If I treat him right now, he'll live," I said. "If I don't, he'll die. It's as simple as that."

I unbuttoned Caisson's pajama top and opened it.

"David, don't do it!" Morrie said.

I did it—3 cc's of tincture of bleafage, intracardially. I heard the ambulance pull up out front.

When I straightened, Morrie was glaring at me. He turned away then and walked out of the room without even bothering to use the door. I heard Caisson gasp. When I checked his carotid again the pulse was present. A moment later he opened his eyes. I put my kit away and buttoned his shirt.

"You'll be all right," I said to him.

"What course of treatment is indicated now?" Puleo asked.

"Put him in the ICU and watch him for twenty-four hours. If he's okay after that, you can do whatever you want with him."

"What about continuing medication?"

"Negative," I said. "Excuse me. I have to go now."

When I turned away she was standing there.

"Hi, Betty," I said.

"David," she said, "is he going to be all right?"

"Yes." I paused, then, "How've you been?"

"Oh, pretty well."

I started toward the door, then stopped.

"Could we talk for a minute, in private?" I asked.

She led me to a little sitting room, where we sat.

"I wanted you to know I've been missing you for a long time," I said, "and I'm sorry about the way I broke up with you. I suppose you've got a boyfriend now?"

"I take it that means you're unencumbered yourself?"

"That's right."

"And if I am, too?"

"'I'd like to go out with you again. Get to know you again. Is there any possibility? Might you be interested?"

"I could tell you that I'm going to have to think about it. But that wouldn't be true. I have thought about it, and the answer is yes, I will go out with *you*."

When I reached out and squeezed her hand, she returned the pressure. We sat and talked for the next two hours and made a date to go out the next night.

Riding back through the park, in the dark, I switched on Dorel's headlight and was reminded of our earlier "conversation."

"Talk! Damn you!" I said. "I want your opinion!"

"All right."

"What?"

"I said, 'All right.' What do you want to know?"

"How come you wouldn't talk to me earlier?"

"I could only talk if you ordered me to. This is the first time you have."

"What are you—really?"

"I was a physician he'd trained in early nineteenth-century Virginia. Name's Don Laurel. I did something he didn't like. Manufactured and sold a patent medicine—Laurel's Bleafage Tonic."

"Must have helped some people he didn't want helped."

"Aye, and maybe a few horses, too."

"I just saved someone he didn't want saved."

"I don't know what to tell you—except that I was arrogant and insolent when he confronted me concerning the medicine, and I wound up as transportation. You might want to try a different tack."

"Thanks," I said, plucking a quarter from under the headlight and flipping it. "Tails. I will."

Of course, Morrie came by later.

"Evening," I said. "Care for a cup of tea?"

"David, how could you?" he asked. "I've been good to you, haven't I? How could you go against my express wishes that way?"

"I'm sorry, Morrie," I said. "I did it because I felt sorry for the guy— starting off with such a great year in office, particularly those health care programs, putting all those fat-cat business interests in their place, and being taken out of the game so suddenly. And—well, I used to date his daughter. I still like her, as a matter of fact, and I felt sorry for her, too. That's why I did it."

He put his hand on my shoulder and squeezed it.

"David, you're a good-hearted boy," he said. "It's hard to fault a man for compassion, but in my line of work it can be a liability. You're going to have to be ruled by your head, not your heart, when you're working my cases, you understand?"

"Yes, Morrie."

"Okay, let's have that cup of tea and talk football."

Three days later I was doing some work around the house when the phone rang. I recognized the governor's voice immediately.

"How are you feeling, sir?" I asked.

"Fine, and I know I owe you a lot, but that's not why I'm calling," he said.

I knew it. Before he said another word, I could feel it coming: Morrie's revenge. My test.

"Emergency?" I said.

"That's right. It's Betty, and from what Puleo told me about my seizure this sounds like the same thing. He didn't say anything about its being contagious."

"I'll be right over."

"Should I call an ambulance?"

"No."

I hung up, got my kit, went for Dorel. As we headed through the park, I told him what had happened.

"What are you going to do?" he asked,.

"You know what I'm going to do."

"I was afraid of that."

And so, as I checked her over, Morrie entered the room and stood at the foot of the bed. I drew 3 cc's into the syringe, then I turned her around.

"David, I forbid it," he said.

"Sorry, Morrie," I told him, and I administered the injection.

When she opened her eyes, I leaned down and kissed her, at about the same time that I felt Morrie's hand upon my shoulder. This time his grip was icy.

"Me, too," he said.

. . . And then we were walking in total silence through a dim place of constantly shifting shadows.

I seem to recall moving amid pieces of my world, in monochrome, as well as the way into his, down under the ground, of caves, tunnels, still pools. I knew we were arrived when we entered a tunnel lined with candles and followed it to that bright and massive central grotto where we had played so long at chess and drunk so much chocolate.

Passing through that vast gallery I seemed to acquire solidity once more. My footfalls created echoes. I felt again that cold grip which steered me. Some of the shadows fell aside, like drawn curtains.

Morrie took me through the grotto, up a corridor, then down a small, chilly tunnel off to its left which I had never visited before. I was too proud to ask him where we were headed and so be the first to speak.

At length, we halted, and he released my arm and gestured.

Jamming my cold hands into my pockets, I followed the gesture but could not at first tell what he was indicating, as we stood in a fairly average area of his office, ledges and niches full of candles. Then I saw that one of them was much lower than all of the others and was flickering now, preparatory to guttering. Assuming it to be Betty's, I waited to see it replaced by the action of one of the invisible entities.

"It was worth it," I said. "I love her, you know."

He turned and stared at me. Then he chuckled.

"Oh, no," he said. "You think that that's her candle? No. You don't understand. She'll live. You've seen to that. Her candle is already in good shape. This is *your* candle. You started out kind of handicapped in that regard. Sorry."

I withdrew a hand from my pocket, reached out, touched it gently.

"You mean that's all I have? Maybe a few minutes? And you didn't mess with it because you're mad at me? That's *really* the way it is?"

"That's right," he said.

I licked my lips.

"Any—uh—chance of an—extension?" I asked.

"When you've crossed my will a second time, after I'd warned you?"

"I didn't do it lightly," I said. "I told you I'd known Betty years ago, and I cared about her then. I didn't realize how much until just recently, when it was almost too late. There was no real choice then. I had to save her. Perhaps such emotions are something you cannot quite understand—"

He laughed again.

"Of course I can understand caring about something," he said. "Why do you think I'd decided to take Governor Caisson right when I did? The son of a bitch's business policies had just cost the town a pro football franchise—for my favorite team. And I'd been angling to get them here for over a generation."

"So you *were* grabbing him off early?"

"You bet I was. Then you had to butt in for the first time in your life."

"I begin to understand. . . . Say, Morrie, you know it's not too late to transfer my flame to a fresh candle."

"True," he acknowledged, "and you are my *godson*. That still counts for something.

He stared a moment longer at the candle.

"Probably should," he said. "Shouldn't stay mad forever. Family counts for something . . ." and he stooped and reached into an opened case back in a recess in the wall.

Drawing forth a candle, he stood and reached for ward with his other hand toward my sputtering taper. He touched it, began to raise it. Then I saw it slip from his fingers and plunge groundwards.

"Shit!" I heard Morrie say as it fell. "Sorry, David—"

Lying on the floor, watching a tiny spark, feeling that something had worked properly, not recalling what. . . . And my cheekbone was sore where I'd hit it when I fell.

I lay amid countless lights. There were things I had to do, and do quickly. What were they?

I raised my head and looked about. Morrie was gone. . . .

Ah, yes. Morrie, my godfather. Gone. . . .

I placed my palms upon the floor and pushed myself up. Nobody there but me, a guttering candle, and a black bicycle. What was it I was supposed to remember? My mind felt heavy and slow.

"Get a candle out of the box, David! Hurry!" Dorel told me. "You've got to take the flame from the other before it dies again."

Dies again. . . .

Then I remembered and shuddered. That's what I had done—died. And I would do it again and for keeps if I didn't act quickly. Fearing the worst, I had been able to buy this brief recurrence of the light, finally finding a use for the Five-Minute Time Warp I kept in my pocket. But how long it would last, lying there, sputtering, upon the floor, I could not tell.

I moved with accelerated deliberation—that is to say, as fast as I felt I could without disturbing the air to the point of ending the enterprise. It was just a piece of wick in an irregular puddle of wax now.

I groped in the carton, took out a candle, moved it to a position above the failing flame, held it there. For a second, the first one nearly died and my vision darkened and a numbness passed over me. But it caught, and these symptoms vanished. I turned it upright then and rose to my feet, groping once again in my pocket. I carried dried stems, flowers, roots, and leaves of bleafage wrapped in a handkerchief.

I placed the handkerchief on Dorel's seat and unfolded it.

"Good idea," he suggested as I began eating the specimens. "But as soon as you're finished I want to lead you to another tunnel where we can hide your candle amid many. We ought to hurry, though, in case he's still in the area."

I stuffed the last of the bleafage into my mouth and set off walking beside him, carrying my candle.

"Could you locate Betty's candle and hide it, too?" I asked.

"Given the time, the appropriate form, and the access," he said.

I followed him down another tunnel.

"I used to work here," he went on. "I was an invisible entity before he made me a bike. If I were an invisible entity here again I could keep moving your candle and Betty's so that he'd never know. I could correct any number of his petty abuses the way I used to. Might keep lighting you new ones, too, if you got into bleafage research."

"I could be persuaded," I said. "What would it take to make you an invisible entity again?"

"I'm not permitted to say."

"Even if I order you?"

"Even then. This is a different category of restriction. I can't think of a way to tell you how to get around this one."

We moved a little farther down the tunnel and he halted.

"To your left," he said, "in that low niche where several others are burning."

I dribbled a little wax to anchor it, set it upon that spot, held it in place till it was fixed.

"Mount," Dorel said then.

I climbed onto the seat, and we coasted through a series of chambers. Soon the stroboscopic effect began again.

"Back to where you were?" Dorel asked.

"Yes."

After a time, the upper world flashed into being for longer and longer intervals, as the underworld diminished.

Then we were slowing before the governor's mansion. Then we were halted there. I was dismounting. There was still some daylight, though the sun hovered just above the western horizon. As I was setting the kickstand, I heard the front door open.

"Dave!" she called.

I looked up, watched her approach down the stair. I realized again how lovely she was, how much I wanted to protect her. In a moment, she was in my arms.

"Dave, what happened? You just sort of faded away."

"My godfather, Morrie, took me. I'd done something he didn't like."

"Your godfather? You never mentioned him before. How could he do that?"

"He is a person of great power over life," I said, "who is responsible for whatever power I possess over death. Fortunately, he thinks I'm dead now. So I believe I'll have some reconstructive surgery, change the spelling of my name, grow a beard, move to another state, and run a small, low-key practice to cover the expense of my bleafage research. I love you. Will you marry me and come along?"

Dorel said, "I hate to tell you that you sound a little crazy, Dave, but you do."

She stared at my bike.

"Are you a ventriloquist, too?" she asked me.

"No, that was Dorel talking. He just saved my life. He's a rebel spirit doing time as a bicycle, and he's been with me since I was a kid. Saved my life a couple of times then, too." I reached out and patted his seat.

Descending the steps, she leaned forward and kissed the top of the handlebars.

"Thanks, Dorel," she said, "whatever you are."

Whatever he was, it was no longer a bicycle. He fell apart in the day's-end light into a swirling collection of golden motes. I watched, fascinated, as the phenomenon resolved itself into a tower about six feet in height, narrowing as it grew.

I heard Betty draw in a long breath.

"What did I just set off?" she asked.

"Beats me," I said. "But since there was no frog I don't think you get a prince."

"Guess I'm stuck with you then," she said, and we watched the bright whirlwind assemble itself into a human shape—that of a tall, bewhiskered man in buckskins.

He bowed to Betty.

"Don Laurel," he said. "At your service, ma'am."

Then he turned and shook my hand.

"Sorry to deprive you of transportation, Dave," he said. "But I just got my enchantment broken."

"Calls for a celebration," I said.

He shook his head.

"Now that I'm unbiked I have to find a niche quick,"' he said, "or I'll fade to airy nothingness. So I'll be heading back below, and I'll take up residence in the caves. He'll never spot an extra invisible entity. And I'll keep moving both of your candles out of his way. Good luck with the bleafage work. I'll be in touch."

With that, he turned once more into a tower of light. The motes darted like fireflies and were gone.

"That's a relief," I said, moving once more to embrace her. "But I wish things had gone differently with Morrie. I like him. I'm going to miss him."

"He doesn't exactly sound like a nice guy," she observed.

"His line of work hardens him a bit," I explained. "He's actually quite sensitive."

"How can you tell?"

"He likes football and chess."

"They both represent violence—physical, and abstract."

". . . And hot chocolate. And Schubert's Quartet in D Minor. And he does care about the balance between life and death, most of the time."

She shook her head.

"I know he's family," she said. "But he scares me."

"Well, we're going incognito now. He shan't be a problem."

I was able to leave it at that for a long time. Betty and I were married, and I did change my name and move to a small town in the South—though I opted against cosmetic surgery. The beard and tinted glasses and a different hairstyle altered my appearance considerably, or so I thought. I built up a satisfactory practice, had a greenhouse full of bleafage, and set up a small home laboratory. For over a year I managed not to be present at life-and-death crises, and when visiting my patients in hospital I was able to avoid other patients at terminal moments which might have resulted in an undesired family reunion. You might say I was pathologically circumspect in this regard; even so, I did glimpse Morrie going around corners on a few occasions.

I kept wondering, though, given my line of work, when—not if—we would meet, and whether I would be able to carry the encounter with sufficient aplomb so as not to reveal that I possessed the ability to see him. When it did occur, of course, it was nowhere near the hospital, and I was not even thinking of these matters.

It was a Saturday evening in October and I heard the squeal of brakes followed by the sound of a heavy impact up the street from our home. I grabbed my bag and a flashlight and was out the door in moments. Betty followed me as I hurried to the corner where two cars had collided. Broken glass was everywhere and the smell of gasoline was strong.

Each vehicle had but a driver. One was obviously dead, and the other— a younger man—was badly injured, but still breathing.

"Go call 911!" 1 shouted to Betty as I moved to succor the second man. He had been thrown from the car and lay upon the pavement, a massive, well muscled individual with a bubbly pneumothorax, heavy arterial bleeding, numerous lesser lacerations, a possibly broken back, and fractured skull.

As I slapped a cover on the pneumothorax and moved to deal with the bleeding a familiar figure was suddenly beside me. I forgot to pretend to be unseeing. In the press of the moment, I simply nodded, and said, "Can't argue with you about this one. Take him if you must."

"No," he said. "Save him for me, Dave. Shoot him up with bleafage. You've got all the time you need."

"What's so special about him, Morrie? I haven't forgotten how you treated me when I wanted to make an exception."

"All right. I'll forgive and forget if you'll do the same—and save this guy. My power, as I've often said, is not over death."

"Then how's about you promise to let me save whom I can, and do whatever I would with the bleafage?"

"Looks like you're doing that, anyway. But all right, I'll make it formal."

"I wish you could have been at my wedding, Morrie."

"I was there."

"You were? I didn't see you."

"I was in the back. I wore bright colors so you wouldn't notice."

"That guy in the Hawaiian shirt?"

"Yes, that was me."

"I'll be damned."

"And I sent you the microwave oven."

"There was no card with it."

"Well, we weren't talking."

"I did wonder about the Heat of Hell brand name. Good oven, though, I'll give you that. Thanks."

My patient moaned.

"About this guy, Morrie—Why are you so dead set against taking him?"

"You don't recognize him?"

"Too much blood on his face."

"That's the new quarterback for the Atlanta Falcons."

"No kidding. But what about the balance between life and death and all that?"

"They're really going to need him this season."

"I forgot you were a Falcons fan."

"The bleafage, boy, the bleafage."

And so . . . The Falcons are doing well this season, not the least because of their new quarterback. Not too many people die during Falcons' games, because Morrie comes by for beer and pizza and we watch them on the tube together. He collects with a vengeance afterward, though, if the Falcons don't do well. Read the obits.

Morrie hints strongly that he'd like to know what I did with the candles. But he can keep on wondering.

Don Laurel and I stay in touch. He comes by every Halloween for a glass of blood and we bring each other up to date on everything from bleafage to candles. And sometimes he changes into a bicycle for old times' sake, and we ride between the worlds.

This morning I walked back to the crossroads where the accident had occurred. Morrie was standing beside a lamppost petting a dead cat.

"Morning, Dave."

"Morning. You're up bright and early."

"Thought you might be coming by. When's she due?"

"In the spring."

"You really want me for godfather?"

"Can't think of anyone I'd rather have. Was that the same dream you sent my dad?"

"No. It's a remake. I updated it. Been watching some MTV."

"Kind of thought so. Care for a cup of coffee?"

"Don't mind if I do."

We walked home as the morning shadows fled. Whoever catches them may make himself a cloak of darkness.

# MANA FROM HEAVEN

I felt nothing untoward that afternoon, whereas, I suppose, my senses should have been tingling. It was a balmy, sun-filled day with but the lightest of clouds above the ocean horizon. It might have lulled me within the not unpleasant variations of my routine. It was partly distraction, Then, of my subliminal, superliminal perceptions, my early-warning system, whatever. . . . This, I suppose, abetted by the fact that there had been no danger for a long while, and that I was certain I was safely hidden. It was a lovely summer day.

There was a wide window at the rear of my office, affording an oblique view of the ocean. The usual clutter lay about—opened cartons oozing packing material, a variety of tools, heaps of rags, bottles of cleaning compounds and restoratives for various surfaces. And of course the acqui-sitions: Some of them still stood in crates and cartons; others held ragged rank upon my workbench, which ran the length of an entire wall—a rank of ungainly chessmen awaiting my hand. The window was open and the fan purring so that the fumes from my chemicals could escape rapidly. Bird songs entered, and a sound of distant traffic, sometimes the wind.

My Styrofoam coffee cup rested unopened upon the small table beside the door, its contents long grown cold and unpalatable to any but an oral masochist. I had set it there that morning and forgotten it until my eyes chanced to light upon it. I had worked through coffee break and lunch, the day had been so rewarding. The really important part had been completed, though the rest of the museum staff would never notice. Time now to rest, to celebrate, to savor all I had found.

I raised the cup of cold coffee. Why not? A few words, a simple gesture . . .

I took a sip of the icy champagne. Wonderful.

I crossed to the telephone then, to call Elaine. This day was worth a bigger celebration than the cup I held. Just as my hand was about to fall upon the instrument, however, the phone rang. Following the startle response, I raised the receiver.

"Hello," I said.

Nothing.

"Hello?"

Nothing again. No . . . Something.

Not some weirdo dialing at random either, as I am an extension. . . .

"Say it or get off the pot," I said

The words came controlled, from back in the throat, slow, the voice unidentifiable:

"Phoenix—Phoenix—burning—bright," I heard.

"Why warn me, asshole?"

"Tag. You're—it."

The line went dead.

I pushed the button several times, roused the switchboard.

"Elsie," I asked, "the person who just called me—what were the exact words—"

"Huh?" she said. "I haven't put any calls through to you all day, Dave."

"Oh."

You okay?"

"Of course."

"Short circuit or something," I said. "Thanks."

I cradled it and tossed off the rest of the champagne. It was no longer a pleasure, merely a housecleaning chore. I fingered the tektite pendant I wore, the roughness of my lava-stone belt buckle, the coral in my watchband. I opened my attaché case and replaced certain items I had been using. I removed a few, also, and dropped them into my pockets.

It didn't make sense, but I knew that it had been for real because of the first words spoken. I thought hard. I still had no answer, after all these years. But I knew that it meant danger. And I knew that it could take any form.

I snapped the case shut. At least it had happened today, rather than, say, yesterday. I was better prepared.

I closed the window and turned off the fan. I wondered whether I should head for my cache. Of course, that could be what someone expected me to do.

I walked up the hall and knocked on my boss's half-open door.

"Come in, Dave. What's up?" he asked.

Mike Thorley, in his late thirties, mustached, well dressed, smiling, put down a sheaf of papers and glanced at a dead pipe in a big ashtray.

"A small complication in my life," I told him. "Is it okay if I punch out early today?"

"Sure. Nothing too serious, I hope?"

I shrugged.

"I hope not, too. If it gets in the way, though, I'll probably need a few days."

He moved his lips around a bit, then nodded.

"You'll call in?"

"Of course."

"It's just that I'd like all of that African stuff taken care of pretty soon."

"Right," I said. "Some nice pieces there."

He raised both hands.

"Okay. Do what you have to do."

"Thanks.

I started to turn away. Then, "One thing," I said.

"Yes?"

"Has anybody been asking about me—anything?"

He started to shake his head, then stopped.

"Unless you count that reporter," he said.

"What reporter?"

"The fellow who phoned the other day, doing a piece on our new acquisitions. Your name came up, of course, and he had a few general questions—the usual stuff, like how long you've been with us, where you're from. You know."

"What was his name?"

"Wolfgang or Walford. Something like that."

"What paper?"

"The *Times*."

I nodded.

"Okay. Be seeing you."

"Take care."

I used the pay phone in the lobby to call the paper. No one working there named Wolfgang or Walford or something like that, of course. No article in the works either. I debated calling another paper, just in case Mike was mistaken, when I was distracted by a tap upon the shoulder. I must have turned too quickly, my expression something other than composed, for her smile faded and fear arced across her dark brows, slackened her jaw.

"Elaine!" I said. "You startled me. I didn't expect . . ."

The smile found its way back.

"You're awfully jumpy, Dave. What are you up to?"

"Checking on my dry cleaning," I said. "You're the last person—"

"I know. Nice of me, isn't it? It was such a beautiful day that I decided to knock off early and remind you we had a sort of date."

My mind spun even as I put my arms about her shoulders and turned her toward the door. How much danger might she be in if I spent a few hours with her in full daylight? I was about to go for something to eat anyway, and I could keep alert for observers. Also, her presence might lull anyone watching me into thinking that I had not taken the call seriously, that perhaps I was not the proper person after all. For that matter, I realized that I wanted some company just then. And if my sudden departure became necessary, I also wanted it to be her company this one last time.

"Yes," I said. "Great idea. Let's take my car."

"Don't you have to sign out or something?"

"I already did. I had the same feeling you did about the day. I was going to call you after I got my cleaning."

"It's not ready yet," I added, and my mind kept turning.

A little trickle here, a little there. I did not feel that we were being observed.

"I know a good little restaurant about forty miles down the coast. Lots of atmosphere. Fine sea food," I said as we descended the front stairs. "And it should be a pleasant drive."

We headed for the museum's parking lot, around to the side.

"I've got a beach cottage near there too," I said.

"You never mentioned that."

"I hardly ever use it."

"Why not? It sounds wonderful."

"It's a little out of the way."

"Then why'd you buy it?"

"I inherited it," I said.

I paused about a hundred feet from my car and jammed a hand into my pocket.

"Watch," I told her.

The engine turned over, the car vibrated.

"How . . . ?" she began.

"A little microwave gizmo. I can start it before I get to it."

"You afraid of a bomb?"

I shook my head.

"It has to warm up. You know how I like gadgets."

Of course I wanted to check out the possibility of a bomb. It was a natural reaction for one in my position. Fortunately, I had convinced her of my fondness for gadgets early in our acquaintanceship—to cover any such contingencies as this. Of course, too, there was no microwave gizmo in my pocket. Just some of the stuff.

We continued forward then, I unlocked the doors and we entered it.

I watched carefully as I drove. Nothing, no one, seemed to be trailing us. "Tag. You're it," though. A gambit. Was I supposed to bolt and run? Was I supposed to try to attack? If so, what? Who?

Was I going to bolt and run?

In the rear of my mind I saw that the bolt-and-run pattern had already started taking shape.

How long, how long, had this been going on? Years. Flight. A new identity. A long spell of almost normal existence. An attack. . . . Flee again. Settle again.

If only I had an idea as to which one of them it was, then I could attack. Not knowing, though, I had to avoid the company of all my fellows—the only ones who could give me clues.

"You look sicklied o'er with the pale cast of thought, Dave. It can't be your dry cleaning, can it?"

I smiled at her.

MANA FROM HEAVEN ✤ 35

"Just business," I said. "All of the things I wanted to get away from. Thanks for reminding me."

I switched on the radio and found some music. Once we got out of city traffic, I began to relax. When we reached the coast road and it thinned even further, it became obvious that we were not being followed. We climbed for a time, then descended. My palms tingled as I spotted the pocket of fog at the bottom of the next dip. Exhilarated, I drank its essence. Then I began talking about the African pieces, in their mundane aspects. We branched off from there. For a time, I forgot my problem. This lasted for perhaps twenty minutes, until the news broadcast. By then I was projecting goodwill, charm, warmth, and kind feelings. I could see that Elaine had begun enjoying herself. There was feedback. I felt even better. There—

". . . new eruptions which began this morning," came over the speaker. "The sudden activity on the part of El Chinchonal spurred immediate evacuation of the area about—"

I reached over and turned up the volume, stopping in the middle of my story about hiking in the Alps.

"What—?" she said.

I raised a finger to my lips.

"The volcano," I explained.

"What of it?"

"They fascinate me," I said.

"Oh."

As I memorized all of the facts about the eruption I began to build feelings concerning my situation. My having received the call today had been a matter of timing. . . .

"There were some good pictures of it on the tube this morning," she said as the newsbrief ended.

"I wasn't watching. But I've seen it do it before, when I was down there."

"You visit volcanos?"

"When they're active, yes."

"Here you have this really oddball hobby and you've never mentioned it," she observed. "How many active volcanos have you visited?"

"Most of them," I said, no longer listening, the lines of the challenge becoming visible—the first time it had ever been put on this basis. I realized in that instant that this time I was not going to run.

"Most of them?" she said. "I read somewhere that there are hundreds, some of them in really out-of-the-way places. Like Erebus—"

"I've been in Erebus," I said, "back when—" And then I realized what I was saying. "—back in some dream," I finished. "Little joke there."

I laughed, but she only smiled a bit.

It didn't matter, though. She couldn't hurt me. Very few mundanes could. I was just about finished with her anyway. After tonight I would forget her. We would never meet again. I am by nature polite, though; it is a thing I value above sentiment. I would not hurt her either: It might be easiest simply to make her forget.

"Seriously, I do find certain aspects of geophysics fascinating."

"I've been an amateur astronomer for some time," she volunteered. "I can understand."

"Really? Astronomy? You never told me."

"Well?" she said.

I began to work it out, small talk flowing reflexively.

After we parted tonight or tomorrow morning, I would leave. I would go to Villahermosa. My enemy would be waiting—of this I felt certain. "Tag. You're it." "This is your chance. Come and get me if you're not afraid."

Of course, I was afraid.

But I'd run for too long. I would have to go, to settle this for good. Who knew when I'd have another opportunity? I had reached the point where it was worth any risk to find out who it was, to have a chance to retaliate. I would take care of all the preliminaries later, at the cottage, after she was asleep. Yes.

"You've got beach?" she asked.

"Yes."

"How isolated?"

"Very. Why?"

"It would be nice to swim before dinner."

So we stopped by the restaurant, made reservations for later and went off and did that. The water was fine.

The day turned into a fine evening. I'd gotten us my favorite table, on the patio, out back, sequestered by colorful shrubbery, touched by flower scents, in the view of mountains. The breezes came just right. So did the lobster and champagne. Within the restaurant, a pleasant music stirred softly. During coffee, I found her hand beneath my own. I smiled. She smiled back.

Then, "How'd you do it, Dave?" she asked.

"What?"

"Hypnotize me."

"Native charm, I guess," I replied, laughing.

"That is not what I mean."

"What, then?" I said, all chuckles fled.

"You haven't even noticed that I'm not smoking anymore."

"Hey, you're right! Congratulations. How long's it been?"

"Acouple of weeks," she replied. "I've been seeing a hypnotist."

"Oh, really?"

"Mm-hm. I was such a docile subject that he couldn't believe I'd never been under before. So he poked around a little, and he came up with a description of you, telling me to forget something."

"Really?"

"Yes, really. You want to know what I remember now that I didn't before?"

"Tell me."

"An almost-accident, late one night, about a month ago. The other car didn't even slow down for the stop sign. Yours levitated. Then I remember us parked by the side of the road, and you were telling me to forget. I did."

I snorted.

"Any hypnotist with much experience will tell you that a trance state is no guarantee against fantasy—and a hallucination recalled under hypnosis seems just as real the second time around. Either way—"

"I remember the *ping* as the car's antenna struck your right rear fender and snapped off."

"They can be vivid fantasies too."

"I looked, Dave. The mark is there on the fender. It looks just as if someone had swatted it with an antenna."

Damn! I'd meant to get that filled in and touched up. Hadn't gotten around to it, though.

"I got that in a parking lot," I said.

"Come on, Dave."

Should I put her under now and make her forget having remembered? I wondered. Maybe that would be easiest.

"I don't care," she said then. "Look, I really don't care. Strange things sometimes happen. If you're connected with some of them, that's okay. What bothers me is that it means you don't trust me . . ."

Trust? That is something that positions you as a target. Like Proteus, when Amazon and Priest got finished with him. Not that he didn't have it coming. . . .

". . . and I've trusted you for a long time."

I removed my hand from hers. I took a drink of coffee. Not here. I'd give her mind a little twist later. Implant something to make her stay away from hypnotists in the future too.

"Okay," I said. "I guess you're right. But it's a long story. I'll tell you after we get back to the cottage."

Her hand found my own, and I met her eyes.

"Thanks," she said.

We drove back beneath a moonless sky clotted with stars. It was an unpaved road, dipping, rising, twisting amid heavy shrubbery. Insect noises came in through our open windows, along with the salt smell of the sea. For a moment, just for a moment, I thought that I felt a strange tingling, but it could have been the night and the champagne And it did not come again.

Later, we pulled up in front of the place, parked and got out. Silently, I deactivated my invisible warden. We advanced, I unlocked the door, I turned on the light.

"You never have any trouble here, huh?" she asked.

"What do you mean?"

"People breaking in, messing the place up, ripping you off?"

"No," I answered.

"Why not?"

"Lucky, I guess."

"Really?"

"Well . . . it's protected, in a very special way. That's a part of the story too. Wait till I get some coffee going."

I went out to the kitchen, rinsed out the pot, put things together and set it over a flame. I moved to open a window, to catch a little breeze.

Suddenly, my shadow was intense upon the wall. I spun about.

The flame had departed the stove, hovered in the air and begun to grow. Elaine screamed just as I turned, and the thing swelled to fill the room. I saw that it bore the shifting features of a fire elemental, just before it burst apart to swirl tornadolike through the cottage. In a moment, the place was blazing and I heard its crackling laughter.

"Elaine!" I called, rushing forward, for I had seen her transformed into a torch.

All of the objects in my pockets plus my belt buckle, I calculated quickly, probably represented a sufficient accumulation of power to banish the thing. Of course the energies were invested, tied up, waiting to be used in different ways. I spoke the words that would rape the power-objects and free the forces. Then I performed the banishment.

The flames were gone in an instant. But not the smoke, not the smell.

. . . And Elaine lay there sobbing, clothing and flesh charred, limbs jerking convulsively. All of her exposed areas were dark and scaly, and blood was beginning to ooze from the cracks in her flesh.

I cursed as I reset the warden. I had created it to protect the place in my absence. I had never bothered to use it once I was inside. I should have.

Whoever had done this was still probably near. My cache was located in a vault about twenty feet beneath the cottage—near enough for me to use a number of the power things without even going after them. I could draw out their mana as I just had with those about my person. I could use it against my enemy. Yes. This was the chance I had been waiting for.

I rushed to my attaché case and opened it. I would need power to reach the power and manipulate it. And the mana from the artifacts I had drained was tied up in my own devices. I reached for the rod and the sphere. At last, my enemy, you've had it! You should have known better than to attack me here!

Elaine moaned. . . .

I cursed myself for a weakling. If my enemy were testing me to see whether I had grown soft, he would have his answer in the affirmative. She was no stranger, and she had said that she trusted me. I had to do it. I began the spell that would drain most of my power-objects to work her healing.

It took most of an hour. I put her to sleep. I stopped the bleeding. I watched new tissues form. I bathed her and dressed her in a sport shirt and rolled-up pair of slacks from the bedroom closet, a place the flames had not reached. I left her sleeping a little longer then while I cleaned up, opened the windows and got on with making the coffee.

At last, I stood beside the old chair—now covered with a blanket—into which I had placed her. If I had just done something decent and noble, why did I feel so stupid about it? Probably because it was out of character. I was reassured, at least, that I had not been totally corrupted to virtue by reason of my feeling resentment at having to use all of that mana on her behalf.

Well . . . Put a good face on it now the deed was done.

How?

Good question. I could proceed to erase her memories of the event and implant some substitute story—a gas leak, perhaps—as to what had occurred, along with the suggestion that she accept it. I could do that. Probably the easiest course for me.

My resentment suddenly faded, to be replaced by something else, as I realized that I did not want to do it that way. What I did want was an end to my loneliness. She trusted me. I felt that I could trust her. I wanted someone I could really talk with.

When she opened her eyes, I put a cup of coffee into her hands.

"Cheerio," I said.

She stared at me, then turned her head slowly and regarded the still-visible ravages about the room. Her hands began to shake. But she put the cup down herself, on the small side table, rather than letting me take it back. She examined her hands and arms. She felt her face.

"You're all right," I said.

"How?" she asked.

"That's the story," I said. "You've got it coming."

"What was that thing?"

"That's a part of it."

"Okay," she said then, raising the cup more steadily and taking a sip. "Let's hear it."

"Well, I'm a sorcerer," I said, "a direct descendant of the ancient sorcerers of Atlantis."

I paused. I waited for the sigh or the rejoinder. There was none.

"I learned the business from my parents," I went on, "a long time ago. The basis of the whole thing is mana, a kind of energy found in various things and places. Once the world was lousy with it. It was the basis of an entire culture. But it was like other natural resources. One day it ran out. Then the magic went away. Most of it. Atlantis sank. The creatures of magic faded, died. The structure of the world itself was altered, causing it to appear much older than it really is. The old gods passed. The sorcerers, the ones who manipulated the mana to produce magic, were pretty much out of business. There followed the real dark ages, before the beginnings of civilization as we know it from the history books."

"This mighty civilization left no record of itself?" she asked.

"With the passing of the magic, there were transformations. The record was rewritten into natural—seeming stone and fossil-bed, was dissipated, underwent a sea change."

"Granting all that for a moment," she said, sipping the coffee, "if the power is gone, if there's nothing left to do it with, how can you be a sorcerer?"

"Well, it's not all gone," I said. "There are small surviving sources, there are some new sources, and—"

"—and you fight over them? Those of you who remain?"

"No . . . not exactly," I said. "You see, there are not that many of us. We intentionally keep our numbers small, so that no one goes hungry."

"'Hungry'?"

"A figure of speech we use. Meaning to get enough mana to keep body and soul together, to stave off aging, keep healthy and enjoy the good things."

"You can rejuvenate yourselves with it? How old are you?"

"Don't ask embarrassing questions. If my spells ran out and there was no more mana, I'd go fast. But we can trap the stuff, lock it up, hold it, whenever we come across a power-source. It can be stored in certain objects—or, better yet, tied up in partial spells, like dialing all but the final digit in a phone number. The spells that maintain one's existence always get primary consideration."

She smiled.

"You must have used a lot of it on me."

I looked away.

"Yes," I said.

"So you couldn't just drop out and be a normal person and continue to live?"

"No."

"So what was that thing?" she asked. "What happened here?"

"An enemy attacked me. We survived."

She took a big gulp of the coffee and leaned back and closed her eyes. Then, "Will it happen again?" she asked.

"Probably. If I let it."

"What do you mean?"

"This was more of a challenge than an all-out attack. My enemy is finally getting tired of playing games and wants to finish things off."

"And you are going to accept the challenge?"

"I have no choice. Unless you'd consider waiting around for something like this to happen again, with more finality."

She shuddered slightly.

"I'm sorry," I said.

"I've a feeling I may be too," she stated, finishing her coffee and rising, crossing to the window, looking out, "before this is over."

"What do we do next?" she asked, turning and staring at me.

"I'm going to take you to a safe place and go away," I said, "for a time." It seemed a decent thing to add those last words, though I doubted I would ever see her again.

"The hell you are," she said.

"Huh? What do you mean? You want to be safe, don't you?"

"If your enemy thinks I mean something to you, I'm vulnerable—the way I see it," she told me.

"Maybe . . ."

The answer, of course, was to put her into a week-long trance and secure her down in the vault, with strong wards and the door openable from the inside. Since my magic had not all gone away, I raised one hand and sought her eyes with my own.

What tipped her off, I'm not certain. She looked away, though, and suddenly lunged for the bookcase. When she turned again she held an old bone flute that had long lain there.

I restrained myself in mid-mutter. It was a power-object that she held, one of several lying about the room, and one of the few that had not been drained during my recent workings. I couldn't really think of much that a nonsorcerer could do with it, but my curiosity restrained me.

"What are you doing?" I asked.

"I'm not sure," she said. "But I'm not going to let you put me away with one of your spells."

"Who said anything about doing that?"

"I can tell."

"How?"

"Just a feeling."

"Well, damn it, you're right. We've been together too long. You can psych me. Okay, put it down and I won't do anything to you."

"Is that a promise, Dave?"

"Yeah. I guess it is."

"I suppose you could rat on it and erase my memory."

"I keep my promises."

"Okay." She put it back on the shelf. "What are we going to do now?"

"I'd still like to put you someplace safe."

"No way."

I sighed.

"I have to go where that volcano is blowing."

"Buy two tickets," she said.

It wasn't really necessary. I have my own plane and I'm licensed to fly the thing. In fact, I have several located in different parts of the world. Boats, too.

"There is mana in clouds and in fogbanks," I explained to her. "In a real pinch, I use my vehicles to go chasing after them."

We moved slowly through the clouds. I had detoured a good distance, but it was necessary. Even after we had driven up to my apartment and collected everything I'd had on hand, I was still too mana-impoverished for the necessary initial shielding and a few strikes. I needed to collect a little more for this. After that it wouldn't matter, the way I saw things. My enemy and I would be plugged into the same source. All we had to do was reach it.

So I circled in the fog for a long while, collecting. It was a protection spell into which I concentrated the mana.

"What happens when it's all gone?" she asked, as I banked and climbed for a final pass before continuing to the southeast.

"What?" I said.

"The mana. Will you all fade away?"

I chuckled.

"It can't," I said. "Not with so few of us using it. How many tons of meteoritic material do you think have fallen to earth today. They raise the background level almost imperceptibly—constantly. And much of it falls into the oceans. The beaches are thereby enriched. That's why I like to be near the sea. Mist-shrouded mountaintops gradually accumulate it. They're good places for collecting too. And new clouds are always forming. Our grand plan is more than simple survival. We're waiting for the day when it reaches a level where it will react and establish fields over large areas. Then we won't have to rely on accumulators and partial spells for its containment. The magic will be available everywhere again."

"Then you will exhaust it all and be back where you started again."

"Maybe," I said. "If we've learned nothing, that may be the case. We'll enter a new golden age, become dependent upon it, forget our other skills, exhaust it again and head for another dark age. Unless . . ."

"Unless what?"

"Unless those of us who have been living with it have also learned something. We'd need to figure the rate of mana exhaustion and budget ourselves. We'd need to preserve technology for things on which mana had been used the last time around. Our experience in this century with physical resources may be useful. Also, there is the hope that some areas of space may be richer in cosmic dust or possess some other factor that will increase the accumulation. Then, too, we are waiting for the full development of the space program—to reach other worlds rich in what we need."

"Sounds as if you have it all worked out."

"We've had a lot of time to think about it."

"But what would be your relationship with those of us who are not versed in magic?"

"Beneficent. We all stand to benefit that way."

"Are you speaking for yourself or for the lot of you?"

"Well, most of the others must feel the same way. I just want to putter around museums. . . ."

"You said that you had been out of touch with the others for some time."

"Yes, but—"

She shook her head and turned to look out at the fog.

"Something else to worry about," she said.


I couldn't get a landing clearance, so I just found a flat place and put it down and left it. I could deal later with any problems this caused.

I unstowed our gear; we hefted it and began walking toward that ragged, smoky quarter of the horizon.

"We'll never reach it on foot," she said.

"You're right," I answered. "I wasn't planning to, though. When the time is right something else will present itself."

"What do you mean?"

"Wait and see."

We hiked for several miles, encountering no one. The way was warm and dusty, with occasional tremors of the earth. Shortly, I felt the rush of mana, and I drew upon it.

"Take my hand," I said.

I spoke the words necessary to levitate us a few feet above the rocky terrain. We glided forward then, and the power about us increased as we advanced upon our goal. I worked with more of it, spelling to increase our pace, to work protective shields around us, guarding us from the heat, from flying debris.

The sky grew darker, from ash, from smoke, long before we

commenced the ascent. The rise was gradual at first but steepened steadily as we raced onward. I worked a variety of partial spells, offensive and defensive, tying up quantities of mana just a word, just a fingertip gesture away.

"Reach out, reach out and touch someone," I hummed as the visible world came and went with the passage of roiling clouds.

We sped into a belt where we would probably have been asphyxiated but for the shield. The noises had grown louder by then. It must have been pretty hot out there too. When we finally reached the rim, dark shapes fled upward past us and lightning stalked the clouds. Forward and below, a glowing, seething mass shifted constantly amid explosions.

"All right!" I shouted. "I'm going to charge up everything I brought with me and tie up some more mana in a whole library of spells! Make yourself comfortable!"

"Yeah," she said, licking her lips and staring downward. "I'll do that. But what about your enemy?"

"Haven't seen anybody so far—and there's too much free mana around for me to pick up vibes. I'm going to keep an eye peeled and take advantage of the situation. You watch too."

"Right," she said. "This is perfectly safe, huh?"

"As safe as L.A. traffic."

"Great. Real comforting," she observed as a huge rocky mass flew past us.

We separated later. I left her within her own protective spell, leaning against a craggy prominence, and I moved off to the right to perform a ritual that required greater freedom of movement.

Then a shower of sparks rose into the air before me. Nothing especially untoward about that, until I realized that it was hovering for an unusually long while. After a time, it seemed that it should have begun dispersing. . . .

"Phoenix, Phoenix, burning bright!" The words boomed about me, rising above the noises of the inferno itself.

"Who calls me?" I asked.

"Who has the strongest reason to do you harm?"

"If I knew that, I wouldn't ask."

"Then seek the answer in hell!"

A wall of flame rushed toward me. I spoke the words that strengthened my shield. Even so, I was rocked within my protective bubble when it hit. Striking back was going to be tricky, I could see, with my enemy in a less-than-material form.

"All right, to the death!" I cried, calling for a lightning stroke through the space where the sparks spun.

I turned away and covered my eyes against the brilliance, but I still felt its presence through my skin.

My bubble of forces continued to rock as I blinked and looked forward. The air before me had momentarily cleared, but everything seemed somehow darker, and—

A being—a crudely man-shaped form of semisolid lava—had wrapped its arms as far as they would go about me and was squeezing. My spell held, but I was raised above the crater's rim.

"It won't work!" I said, trying to dissolve the being.

"The hell you say!" came a voice from high overhead.

I learned quickly that the lava-thing was protected against the simple workings I threw at it. All right, then hurl me down. I would levitate out. The Phoenix would rise again. I—

I passed over the rim and was falling. But there was a problem. A heavy one.

The molten creature was clinging to my force-bubble, Magic is magic and science is science, but there are correspondences. The more mass you want to move, the more mana you have to expend. So, taken off guard, I was dropping into the fiery pit despite a levitation spell that would have borne me on high in a less encumbered state. I immediately began a spell to provide me with additional buoyancy.

But when I had finished, I saw that something was countering me— another spell, a spell that kept increasing the mass of my creature-burden by absorption as we fell. Save for an area between my feet through which I saw the roiling lake of fire, I was enclosed by the flowing mass of the thing. I could think of only one possible escape, and I didn't know whether I had time for it.

I began the spell that would transform me into a spark-filled vortex similar to that my confronter had worn. When I achieved it, I released my protective spell and flowed.

Out through the nether opening then, so close to that bubbling surface I would have panicked had not my mind itself been altered by the transformation, into something static and poised.

Skimming the heat-distorted surface of the magma, I swarmed past the heavily weighted being of animated rock and was already rising at a rapid rate, buffeted, borne aloft by heat waves, when it hit a rising swell and was gone. I added my own energy to the rising and fled upward, through alleys of smoke and steam, past flashes of lava bullets.

I laid the bird-shape upon my glowing swirls, I sucked in mana, I issued a long, drawn-out rising scream. I spread my wings along expanding lines of energy, seeking my swirling adversary as I reached the rim.

Nothing. I darted back and forth, I circled. He/she/it was nowhere in sight.

"I am here!" I cried. "Face me now!"

But there was no reply, save for the catastrophe beneath me from which fresh explosions issued.

"Come!" I cried. "I am waiting!"

So I sought Elaine, but she was not where I had left her. My enemy had either destroyed her or taken her away.

I cursed then like thunder and spun myself into a large vortex, a rising tower of lights. I drove myself upward then, leaving the earth and that burning pimple far beneath me.

For how long I rode the jet streams, raging, I cannot say. I know that I circled the world several times before any semblance of rational thinking returned to me, before I calmed sufficiently to formulate anything resembling a plan.

It was obviously one of my fellows who had tried to kill me, who had taken Elaine from me. I had avoided contact with my own kind for too long. Now I knew that I must seek them out, whatever the risk, to obtain the knowledge I needed for self-preservation, for revenge.

I began my downward drift as I neared the Middle East. Arabia. Yes. Oil fields, places of rich, expensive pollutants, gushing mana-filled from the earth. Home of the one called Dervish.

Retaining my Phoenix-form, I fled from field to field, beelike, tasting, using the power to reinforce the spell under which I was operating. Seeking . . .

For three days I sought, sweeping across bleak landscapes, visiting field after field. It was like a series of smorgasbords. It would be so easy to use the mana to transform the countryside. But of course that would be a giveaway, in many respects.

Then, gliding in low over shimmering sands as evening mounted in the East, I realized that this was the one I was seeking. There was no physical distinction to the oil field I approached and then cruised. But it stood in the realm of my sensitivity as if a sign had been posted. The mana level was much lower than at any of the others I had scanned. And where this was the case, one of us had to be operating.

I spread myself into even more tenuous patterns. I sought altitude. I began circling.

Yes, there was a pattern. It became clearer as I studied the area. The low-mana section described a rough circle near the northwest corner of the field, its center near a range of hills.

He could be working in some official capacity there at the field. If so, his duties would be minimal and the job would be a cover. He always had been pretty lazy.

I spiraled in and dropped toward the center of the circle as toward the eye of a target. As I rushed to it, I became aware of the small, crumbling adobe structure that occupied that area, blending almost perfectly with its surroundings. A maintenance or storage house, a watchman's quarters. . . . It did not matter what it seemed to be. I knew what it had to be.

I dived to a landing before it. I reversed my spell, taking on human form once again. I pushed open the weather-worn, unlatched door and walked inside.

The place was empty, save for a few sticks of beaten furniture and a lot of dust. I swore softly. This had to be it.

I walked slowly about the room, looking for some clue.

It was nothing that I saw, or even felt, at first. It was memory—of an obscure variant of an old spell, and of Dervish's character—that led me to turn and step back outside.

I closed the door. I felt around for the proper words. It was hard to remember exactly how this one would go. Finally, they came flowing forth and I could feel them falling into place, mortise and tenon, key and lock. Yes, there was a response. The subtle back-pressure was there. I had been right.

When I had finished, I knew that things were different, I reached toward the door, then hesitated. I had probably tripped some alarm. Best to have a couple of spells at my fingertips, awaiting merely guide-words. I muttered them into readiness, then opened the door.

A marble stairway as wide as the building itself led downward, creamy jewels gleaming like hundred-watt bulbs high at either hand.

I moved forward, began the descent. Odors of jasmine, saffron and sandalwood came to me. As I continued I heard the sounds of stringed instruments and a flute in the distance. By then I could see part of a tiled floor below and ahead—and a portion of an elaborate design upon it.

I laid a spell of invisibility over myself and kept going.

Before I reached the bottom, I saw him, across the long, pillared hall.

He was at the far end, reclined in a nest of cushions and bright patterned rugs. An elaborate repast was spread before him. A narghile bubbled at his side. A young woman was doing a belly dance nearby.

I halted at the foot of the stair and studied the layout. Archways to both the right and the left appeared to lead off to other chambers. Behind him was a pair of wide windows, looking upon high mountain peaks beneath very blue skies—representing either a very good illusion or the expenditure of a lot of mana on a powerful space-bridging spell. Of course, he had a lot of mana to play around with. Still, it seemed kind of wasteful.

I studied the man himself. His appearance was pretty much unchanged—sharp-featured, dark-skinned, tall, husky running to fat.

I advanced slowly, the keys to half a dozen spells ready for utterance or gesture.

When I was about thirty feet away he stirred uneasily. Then he kept glancing in my direction. His power-sense was still apparently in good shape.

So I spoke two words, one of which put a less-than-material but very potent magical dart into my hand, the other casting aside my veil of invisibility.

"Phoenix!" he exclaimed, sitting upright and staring. "I thought you were dead!"

I smiled.

"How recently did that thought pass through your mind?" I asked him.

"I'm afraid I don't understand. . . ."

"One of us just tried to kill me, down in Mexico."

He shook his head.

"I haven't been in that part of the world for some time."

"Prove it," I said.

"I can't," he replied. "You know that my people here would say whatever I want them to—so that's no help. I didn't do it, but I can't think of any way to prove it. That's the trouble with trying to demonstrate a negative. Why do you suspect me, anyway?"

I sighed.

"That's just it. I don't—or, rather, I have to suspect everyone. I just chose you at random. I'm going down the list."

"Then at least I have statistics on my side."

"I suppose you're right, damn it."

He rose, turned his palms upward.

"We've never been particularly close," he said. "But then, we've never been enemies either. I have no reason at all for wishing you harm."

He eyed the dart in my hand. He raised his right hand, still holding a bottle.

"So you intend to do us all in by way of insurance?"

"No, I was hoping that you would attack me and thereby prove your guilt. It would have made life easier."

I sent the dart away as a sign of good faith.

"I believe you," I said.

He leaned and placed the bottle he held upon a cushion.

Had you slain me that bottle would have fallen and broken," he said. "Or perhaps I could have beaten you on an attack and drawn the cork. It contains an attack djinn."

"Neat trick."

"Come join me for dinner," he suggested. "I want to hear your story. One who would attack you for no reason might well attack me one day."

"All right," I said.

The dancer had been dismissed. The meal was finished. We sipped coffee. I had spoken without interruption for nearly an hour. I was tired, but I had a spell for that.

"More than a little strange," he said at length. "And you have no recollection, from back when all of this started, of having hurt, insulted or cheated any of the others?"

"No."

I sipped my coffee.

"So it could be any of them," I said after a time. "Priest, Amazon, Gnome, Siren, Werewolf, Lamia, Lady, Sprite, Cowboy . . ."

"Well, scratch Lamia," he said. "I believe she's dead."

"How?"

He shrugged, looked away.

"Not sure," he said slowly. Then, "Well, the talk at first was that you and she had run off together. Then, later, it seemed to be that you'd died together somehow."

"Lamia and me? That's silly. There was never anything between us."

He nodded.

"Then it looks now as if something simply happened to her."

"Talk . . ." I said. "Who was doing the talking?"

"You know. Stories just get started. You never know exactly where they come from."

"Where'd you first hear it?"

He lowered his eyelids, stared off into the distance.

"Gnome. Yes. It was Gnome mentioned the matter to me at Starfall that year."

"Did he say where he'd heard it?"

"Not that I can recall."

"Okay," I said. "I guess I'll have to go talk to Gnome. He still in South Africa?"

He shook his head, refilled my cup from the tall, elegantly incised pot.

"Cornwall," he said. "Still a lot of juice down those old shafts."

I shuddered slightly.

"He can have it. I get claustrophobia just thinking about it. But if he can tell me who—"

"There is no enemy like a former friend," Dervish said. "If you dropped your friends as well as everyone else when you went into hiding, it means you've already considered that. . . ."

"Yes, as much as I disliked the notion. I rationalized it by saying that I didn't want to expose them to danger, but—"

"Exactly."

"Cowboy and Werewolf were buddies of mine. . . ."

". . . And you had a thing going with Siren for a long while, didn't you?"

"Yes, but—"

"A woman scorned?"

"Hardly. We parted amicably."

He shook his head and raised his cup.

"I've exhausted my thinking on the matter."

We finished our coffee. I rose then.

"Well, thanks. I guess I'd better be going. Glad I came to you first."

He raised the bottle.

"Want to take the djinn along?"

"I don't even know how to use one."

"The commands are simple. All the work's already been done."

"Okay. Why not?"

He instructed me briefly, and I took my leave. Soaring above the great oil field, I looked back upon the tiny, ruined building. Then I moved my wings and rose to suck the juice from a cloud before turning west.

Starfall, I mused, as earth and water unrolled like a scroll beneath me. Starfall—The big August meteor shower accompanied by the wave of mana called Starwind, the one time of year we all got together. Yes, that was when gossip was exchanged. It had been only a week after a Starfall that I had first been attacked, almost slain, had gone to ground. . . . By the following year the stories were circulating. Had it been something at that earlier Starfall—something I had said or done to someone—that had made me an enemy with that finality of purpose, that quickness of retaliation?

I tried hard to recall what had occurred at that last Starfall I had attended. It had been the heaviest rush of Starwind in memory. I remembered that. "Mana from heaven," Priest had joked. Everyone had been in a good mood. We had talked shop, swapped a few spells, wondered what the heightened Starwind portended, argued politics—all of the usual things. That business Elaine talked about had come up. . . .

Elaine. . . . Alive now? I wondered. Someone's prisoner? Someone's insurance in case I did exactly what I was doing? Or were her ashes long since scattered about the globe? Either way, someone would pay.

I voiced my shrill cry against the rushing winds. It was fled in an instant, echoless. I caught up with the night, passed into its canyons. The stars came on again, grew bright.

The detailed instructions Dervish had given me proved exactly accurate. There was a mineshaft at the point he had indicated on a map hastily sketched in fiery lines upon the floor. There was no way I would enter the thing in human form, though. A version of my Phoenix-aspect would at least defend me against claustrophobia. I cannot feel completely pent when I am not totally material.

Shrinking, shrinking, as I descended, I called in my tenuous wings and tail, gaining solidity as I grew smaller. Then I bled off mass-energy, retaining my new dimensions, growing ethereal again.

Like a ghost-bird, I entered the adit, dropping, dropping. The place was dead. There was no mana anywhere about me. This, of course, was to be expected. The upper levels would have been the first to be exhausted.

I continued to drop into dampness and darkness for a long while before I felt the first faint touch of the power. It increased only slowly as I moved, but it did begin to rise.

Finally, it began to fall off again and I retraced my route. Yes, that side passage . . . Its source. I entered and followed.

As I worked my way farther and farther, back and down, it continued to increase in intensity. I wondered briefly whether I should be seeking the weaker area or the stronger. But this was not the same sort of setup as Dervish enjoyed. Dervish's power source was renewable, so he could remain stationary. Gnome would have to move on once he had exhausted a local mana supply.

I spun around a corner into a side tunnel and was halted. Frozen. Damn.

It was a web of forces holding me like a butterfly. I ceased struggling almost immediately, seeing that it was fruitless in this aspect.

I transformed myself back into human form. But the damned web merely shifted to accommodate the alteration and continued to hold me tightly.

I tried a fire spell, to no avail. I tried sucking the mana loose from the web's own spell, but all I got was a headache. It's a dangerous measure, only effective against sloppy workmanship—and then you get hit with a backlash of forces when it comes loose. The spell held perfectly against my effort, however. I had had to try it, though, because I was feeling desperate, with a touch of claustrophobia tossed in. Also, I thought I'd heard a stone rattle farther up the tunnel.

Next I heard a chuckle, and I recognized the voice as Gnome's.

Then a light rounded a corner, followed by a vaguely human form.

The light drifted in front of him and just off to his left—a globe, casting an orange illumination—touching his hunched, twisted shape with a flamelike glow as he limped toward me. He chuckled again.

"Looks as if I've snared a Phoenix," he finally said.

"Very funny. How about unsnaring me now?" I asked.

"Of course, of course," he muttered, already beginning to gesture.

The trap fell apart. I stepped forward.

"I've been asking around," I told him. "What's this story about Lamia and me?"

He continued his gesturing. I was about to invoke an assault or a shielding spell when he stopped, though. I felt none the worse and I assumed it was a final cleanup of his web.

"Lamia? You?" he said. "Oh. Yes I'd heard you'd run off together. Yes. That was it."

"Where'd you hear it?"

He fixed me with his large, pale eyes.

"Where'd you hear it?" I repeated.

"I don't remember."

"Try."

"Sorry."

"Sorry, hell!" I said , taking a step forward. "Somebody's been trying to kill me and—"

He spoke a word that froze me in mid-step. Good spell that.

"—and he's been regrettably inept," Gnome finished.

"Let me go, damn it!" I said.

"You came into my house and assaulted me."

"Okay, I apologize. Now—"

"Come this way."

He turned his back on me and began walking. Against my will, my body made the necessary movements. I followed.

I opened my mouth to speak a spell of my own. No words came out. I wanted to make a gesture. I was unable to begin it.

"Where are you taking me?" I tried.

The words came perfectly clear. But he didn't bother answering me for a time. The light moved over glistening of some metallic material within the sweating walls.

Then, "To a waiting place," he finally said, turning into a corridor to the right, where we splashed through puddles for a time.

"Why?" I asked him. "What are we waiting for?"

He chuckled again. The light danced. He did not reply.

We walked for several minutes. I began finding the thought of all those tons of rocks and earth above me very oppressive. A trapped feeling came over me. But I could not even panic properly under the confines of that spell. I began to perspire profusely, despite a cooling draft from ahead.

Then Gnome turned suddenly and was gone, sidling into a narrow cleft I would not have seen or noticed had I been coming this way alone.

"Come," I heard him say.

My feet followed the light, moved to drift between us here. I sidled after him for a good distance before the way widened. The ground dropped roughly, abruptly, and the walls retracted and the light shot on ahead, gaining altitude.

Gnome raised a broad hand and halted me. We were in a small, irregularly shaped chamber—natural, I guessed. The weak light filled it. I looked about. I had no idea why we had stopped here. Gnome's hand moved and he pointed.

I followed the gesture but still could not tell what it was that he was trying to indicate. The light drifted forward then, hovered near a shelflike niche.

Angles altered, shadows shifted. I saw it.

It was a statue of a reclining woman, carved out of coal.

I moved a step nearer. It was extremely well executed and very familiar.

"I didn't know you were an artist . . ." I began, and the realization struck me even as he laughed.

"It is—art," he said. "Not the mundane kind."

I had reached forward to touch the dark cheek. I dropped my hand, deciding against it.

"It's Lamia, isn't it?" I asked. "It's really her. . . ."

"Of course."

"Why?"

"She has to be someplace, doesn't she?"

"I'm afraid I don't understand."

He chuckled again.

"You're a dead man, Phoenix, and she's the reason. I never thought I'd have the good fortune to have you walk in this way. But now that you have, all of my problems are over. You will rest a few corridors away from here, in a chamber totally devoid of mana. You will wait, while I send for Werewolf to come and kill you. He was in love with Lamia, you know. He is convinced that you ran off with her. Some friend you are. I've been waiting for him to get you for some time now, but either he's clumsy or you're lucky. Perhaps both."

"So it's been Werewolf all along."

"Yes."

"Why? Why do you want him to kill me?"

"It would look badly if I did it myself. I'll be sure that some of the others are here when it happens. To keep my name clean. In fact, I'll dispatch Werewolf personally as soon as he's finished with you. A perfect final touch."

"Whatever I've done to you, I'm willing to set it right."

Gnome shook his head.

"What you did was to set up an irreducible conflict between us," he said. "There is no way to set it right."

"Would you mind telling me what it is that I did?" I asked.

He made a gesture, and I felt a compulsion to turn and make my way back toward the corridor. He followed, both of us preceded by his light.

As we moved, he asked me, "Were you aware that at each Starfall ceremony for the past ten or twelve years the mana content of the Starwind has been a bit higher?"

"It was ten or twelve years ago that I stopped attending them," I answered. "I recall that it was very high that year. Since then, when I've thought to check at the proper time, it has seemed high, yes."

"The general feeling is that the increase will continue. We seem to be entering a new area of space, richer in the stuff."

"That's great," I said, coming into the corridor again. "But what's that got to do with your wanting me out of the way, with your kidnaping Lamia and turning her to coal, with your siccing Werewolf on me?"

"Everything," he said, conducting me down a slanting shaft where the mana diminished with every step. "Even before that, those of us who had been doing careful studies had found indications that the background level of mana is rising."

"So you decided to kill me?"

He led me to a jagged opening in the wall and indicated that I should enter there. I had no choice. My body obeyed him. The light remained outside with him.

"Yes," he said then, motioning me to the rear of the place. "Years ago it would not have mattered—everyone entitled to any sort of opinion they felt like holding. But now it does. The magic is beginning to return, you fool. I am going to be around long enough to see it happen, to take advantage of it. I could have put up with your democratic sentiments when such a thing seemed only a daydream—"

And then I remembered our argument, on the same matter Elaine had brought up during our ride down the coast.

"—but knowing what I knew and seeing how strongly you felt, I saw you as one who would oppose our inevitable leadership in that new world. Werewolf was another. That is why I set it up for him to destroy you, to be destroyed, in return, by myself."

"Do all of the others feel as you do?" I asked.

"No, only a few—just as there were only a few like you, Cowboy and the Wolf. The rest will follow whoever takes the lead, as people always do."

"Who are the others?"

He snorted.

"None of your business now," he said.

He began a familiar gesture and muttered something. I felt free of whatever compulsion he had laid upon me, and I lunged forward. The entrance had not changed its appearance, but I slammed up against something—as if the way were blocked by an invisible door.

"I'll see you at the party," he said, inches away, beyond my reach. "In the meantime, try to get some rest." I felt my consciousness ebbing. I managed to lean and cover my face with my arms before I lost all control. I do not remember hitting the floor.

*     *     *

How long I lay entranced I do not know. Long enough for some of the others to respond to an invitation, it would seem. Whatever reason he gave them for a party, it was sufficient to bring Knight, Druid, Amazon, Priest, Siren and Snowman to a large hall somewhere beneath the Cornish hills. I became aware of this by suddenly returning to full consciousness at the end of a long, black corridor without pictures. I pushed myself into a seated position, rubbed my eyes and squinted, trying to penetrate my cell's gloom. Moments later, this was taken care of for me. So I knew that my awakening and the happening that followed were of one piece.

The lighting problem was taken care of for me by the wall's beginning to glow, turning glassy, then becoming a full-color 3-D screen, complete with stereo. That's where I saw Knight, Druid, Amazon, etc. That's how I knew it was a party: There were food and a sound track, arrivals and departures. Gnome passed through it all, putting his clammy hands on everybody, twisting his face into a smile and being a perfect host.

Mana, mana, mana. Weapon, weapon, weapon. Nothing. Shit.

I watched for a long while, waiting. There had to be a reason for his bringing me around and showing me what was going on. I searched all of those familiar faces, overheard snatches of conversation, watched their movements. Nothing special. Why then was I awake and witnessing this? It had to be Gnome's doing, yet . . .

When I saw Gnome glance toward the high archway of the hall's major entrance for the third time in as many minutes, I realized that he, too, was waiting.

I searched my cell. Predictably, I found nothing of any benefit to me. While I was looking, though, I heard the noise level rise and I turned back to the images on the wall.

Magics were in progress. The hall must have been mana-rich. My colleagues were indulging themselves in some beautiful spellwork— flowers and faces and colors and vast, exotic, shifting vistas filled the screen now—just as such things must have run in ancient times. Ah! One drop! One drop of mana and I'd be out of here! To run and return? Or to seek immediate retaliation? I could not tell. If there were only some way I could draw it from the vision itself . . .

But Gnome had wrought too well. I could find no weak spot in the working before me. I stopped looking after a few moments, for another reason as well. Gnome was announcing the arrival of another guest.

The sound died and the picture faded at that point. The corridor beyond my cell seemed to grow slightly brighter. I moved toward it. This time my way was not barred, and I continued out into the lighter area. What had happened? Had some obscure force somehow broken Gnome's finely wrought spells?

At any rate, I felt normal now and I would be a fool to remain where he had left me. It occurred to me that this could be part of some higher trap or torture, but still—I had several choices now, which is always an improvement.

I decided to start back in the direction from which we had come earlier, rather than risk blundering into that gathering. Even if there was a lot of mana about there. Better to work my way back, I decided, tie up any mana I could find along the way in the form of protective spells and get the hell out.

I had proceeded perhaps twenty paces—while formulating this resolution. Then the tunnel went through an odd twisting that I couldn't recall. I was still positive we had come this way, though, so I followed it. It grew a bit brighter as I moved along, too, but that seemed all for the better. It allowed me to hurry.

Suddenly, there was a sharp turning that I did not remember at all. I took it and I ran into a screen of pulsing white light, and then I couldn't stop. I was propelled forward, as if squeezed from behind. There was no way that I could halt. I was temporarily blinded by the light. There came a roaring in my ears.

And then it was past, and I was standing in the great hall where the party was being held, having emerged from some side entrance, in time to hear Gnome say, ". . . And the surprise guest is our long-lost brother Phoenix!"

I stepped backward, to retreat into the tunnel from which I had emerged, and I encountered something hard. Turning, I beheld only a blank wall of rock.

"Don't be shy, Phoenix. Come and say hello to your friends," Gnome was saying.

There was a curious babble, but above it from across the way came an animallike snarl and I beheld my old buddy Werewolf, lean and swarthy, eyes blazing, doubtless the guest who was just arriving when the picture had faded.

I felt panic. I also felt mana. But what could I work in only a few seconds' time?

My eyes were pulled by the strange movement in a birdcage on the table beside which Werewolf stood. The others' attitudes showed that many of them had just turned from regarding it.

It registered in an instant.

Within the cage, a nude female figure no more than a hand high was dancing. I recognized it as a spell of torment: The dancer could not stop. The dancing would continue until death, after which the body would still jerk about for some time.

And even from that distance I could recognize the small creature as Elaine.

The dancing part of the spell was simple. So was its undoing. Three words and a gesture. I managed them. By then Werewolf was moving toward me. He was not bothering with a shapeshift to his more fearsome form. I sidestepped as fast as I could and sought for a hold involving his arm and shoulder. He shook it off. He always was stronger and faster than me.

He turned and threw a punch, and I managed to duck and counter-punch to his midsection. He grunted and hit me on the jaw with a weak left. I was already backing away by then. I stopped and tried a kick and he batted it aside, sending me spinning to the floor. I could feel the mana all about me, but there was no time to use it.

"I just learned the story," I said, "and I had nothing to do with Lamia—"

He threw himself upon me. I managed to catch him in the stomach with my knee as he came down.

"Gnome took her . . ." I got out, getting in two kidney punches before his hands found my throat and began to tighten. "She's coal—"

I caught him once, high on the cheek, before he got his head down.

"Gnome—damn it!" I gurgled.

"It's a lie!" I heard Gnome respond from somewhere nearby, not missing a thing.

The room began to swim about me. The voices became a roaring, as of the ocean. Then a peculiar thing happened to my vision as well: Werewolf's head appeared to be haloed by a coarse mesh. Then it dropped forward, and I realized that his grip had relaxed.

I tore his hands from my throat and struck him once, on the jaw. He rolled away. I tried to also, in the other direction, but settled for struggling into a seated, then a kneeling, then a crouched, position.

I beheld Gnome, raising his hands in my direction, beginning an all-too-familiar and lethal spell. I beheld Werewolf, slowly removing a smashed birdcage from his head and beginning to rise again. I beheld the nude, fullsize form of Elaine rushing toward us, her face twisted. . . .

The problem of what to do next was settled by Werewolf's lunge.

It was a glancing blow to the midsection because I was turning when it connected. A dark form came out of my shirt, hovered a moment and dropped floorward: It was the small bottle of djinn Dervish had given me.

Then, just before Werewolf's fist exploded in my face, I saw something slim and white floating toward the back of his neck. I had forgotten that Elaine was second *kyu* in Kyokushinkai.

Werewolf and I both hit the floor at about the same time, I'd guess.

. . . Black to gray to full-color; bumblebee hum to shrieks. I could not have been out for too long. During that time, however, considerable change had occurred.

For one, Elaine was slapping my face.

"Dave! Wake up!" she was saying. "You've got to stop it!"

"What?" I managed.

"That thing from the bottle!"

I propped myself on an elbow—jaw aching, side splitting—and I stared.

There were smears of blood on the nearest wall and table. The party had broken into knots of people, all of whom appeared to be in retreat in various stages of fear or anger. Some were working spells; some were simply fleeing. Amazon had drawn a blade and was holding it before her while gnawing her lower lip. Priest stood at her side, muttering a death spell, which I knew was not going to prove effective. Gnome's head was on the floor near the large archway, eyes open and unblinking. Peals of thunderlike laughter rang through the hall.

Standing before Amazon and Priest was a naked male figure almost ten feet in height, wisps of smoke rising from its dark skin, blood upon its upraised right fist.

"Do something!" Elaine said.

I levered myself a little higher and spoke the words Dervish had taught me, to put the djinn under my control. The fist halted, slowly came unclenched. The great bald head turned toward me, the dark eyes met my own.

"Master . . . ?" it said softly.

I spoke the next words, of acknowledgment. Then I climbed to my feet and stood, wavering.

"Back into the bottle now—my command."

Those eyes left my own, their gaze shifting to the floor.

"The bottle is shattered, master," it said.

"So it is. Very well . . ."

I moved to the bar. I found a bottle of Cutty Sark with just a little left in the bottom. I drank it.

"Use this one, then," I said, and I added the words of compulsion.

"As you command," it replied, beginning to dissolve.

I watched the djinn flow into the Scotch bottle and then I corked it.

I turned to face my old colleagues.

"Sorry for the interruption," I said. "Go ahead with your party."

I turned again.

"Elaine," I said. "You okay?"

She smiled.

"Call me Dancer," she said. "I'm your new apprentice."

"A sorcerer needs a feeling for mana and a natural sensitivity to the way spells function," I said.

"How the hell do you think I got my size back?" she asked. "I felt the power in this place, and once you turned off the dancing spell I was able to figure how to—"

"I'll be damned," I said. "I should have guessed your aptitude back at the cottage, when you grabbed that bone flute."

"See, you need an apprentice to keep you on your toes."

Werewolf moaned, began to stir. Priest and Amazon and Druid approached us. The party did not seem to be resuming. I touched my finger to my lips in Elaine's direction.

"Give me a hand with Werewolf," I said to Amazon. "He's going to need some restraining until I can tell him a few things."

The next time we splashed through the Perseids we sat on a hilltop in northern New Mexico, my apprentice and I, regarding the crisp, post-midnight sky and the occasional bright cloud-chamber effect within it. Most of the others were below us in a cleared area, the ceremonies concluded now. Werewolf was still beneath the Cornish hills, working with Druid, who recalled something of the ancient flesh-to-coal spell. Another month or so, he'd said, in the message he'd sent.

"'Flash of uncertainty in sky of precision,'" she said.

"What?"

"I'm composing a poem."

"Oh." Then, after a time, I added, "What about?"

"On the occasion of my first Starfall," she replied, "with the mana gain apparently headed for another record."

"There's good and there's bad in that."

". . . And the magic is returning and I'm learning the Art."

"Learn faster," I said.

". . . And you and Werewolf are friends again."

"There's that."

". . . You and the whole group, actually."

"No.

"What do you mean?"

"Well, think about it. There are others. We just don't know which of them were in Gnome's corner. They won't want the rest of us around when the magic comes back. Newer, nastier spells—ones it would be hard to imagine now—will become possible when the power rises. We must be ready. This blessing is a very mixed thing. Look at them down there—the ones we were singing with—and see whether you can guess which of them will one day try to kill you. There will be a struggle, and the winners can make the outcome stick for a long time."

She was silent for a while.

"That's about the size of it," I added.

Then she raised her arm and pointed to where a line of fire was traced across the sky. "There's one!" she said. "And another! And another!"

Later, "We can count on Werewolf now," she suggested, "and maybe

Lamia, if they can bring her back. Druid, too, I'd guess."

"And Cowboy."

"Dervish?"

"Yeah, I'd say. Dervish."

". . . And I'll be ready."

"Good. We might manage a happy ending at that."

We put our arms about each other and watched the fire fall from the sky.

# CORRIDA

He awoke to an ultrasonic wailing. It was a thing that tortured his eardrums while remaining just beyond the threshhold of the audible.

He scrambled to his feet in the darkness.

He bumped against the walls several times. Dully, he realized that his arms were sore, as though many needles had entered there.

The sound maddened him. . . .

Escape! He had to get away!

A tiny patch of light occurred to his left.

He turned and raced toward it and it grew into a doorway.

He dashed through and stood blinking in the glare that assailed his eyes.

He was naked, he was sweating. His mind was full of fog and the rag-ends of dreams.

He heard a roar, as of a crowd, and he blinked against the brightness.

Towering, a dark figure stood before him in the distance. Overcome by rage, he raced toward it, not quite certain why.

His bare feet trod hot sand, but he ignored the pain as he ran to attack.

Some portion of his mind framed the question "Why?" but he ignored it.

Then he stopped.

A nude woman stood before him, beckoning, inviting, and there came a sudden surge of fire within his loins.

He turned slightly to his left and headed toward her.

She danced away.

He increased his speed. But as he was about to embrace her, there came a surge of fire in his right shoulder and she was gone.

He looked at his shoulder and an aluminum rod protruded from it, and the blood ran down along his arm. There arose another roar.

. . . And she appeared again.

He pursued her once more and his left shoulder burned with sudden fires. She was gone and he stood shaking and sweating, blinking against the glare.

"It's a trick," he decided. "Don't play the game!"

She appeared again and he stood stock still, ignoring her.

He was assailed by fires, but he refused to move, striving to clear his head.

The dark figure appeared once more, about seven feet tall and possessing two pairs of arms.

It held something in one of its hands. If only the lightning weren't so crazy, perhaps he . . .

But he hated that dark figure and he charged it. Pain lashed his side . Wait a minute! Wait a minute!

Crazy! It's all crazy! he told himself, recalling his identity. This is a bullring and I'm a man, and that dark thing isn't. Something's wrong.

He dropped to his hands and knees, buying time. He scooped up a double fistful of sand while he was down.

There came proddings, electric and painful. He ignored them for as long as he could, then stood.

The dark figure waved something at him and he felt himself hating it.

He ran toward it and stopped before it. He knew it was a game now. His name was Michael Cassidy. He was an attorney. New York. Of Johnson, Weems, Daugherty and Cassidy. A man had stopped him, asking for a light. On a street corner. Late at night. That he remembered.

He threw sand at the creature's head.

It swayed momentarily, and its arms were raised toward what might have been its face.

Gritting his teeth, he tore the aluminum rod from his shoulder and drove its sharpened end into the creature's middle.

Something touched the back of his neck, and there was darkness and he lay still for a long time.

When he could move again, he saw the dark figure and he tried to tackle it.

He missed, and there was pain across his back and something wet.

When he stood once more, he bellowed, "You can't do this to me! I'm a man! Not a bull!"

There came a sound of applause.

He raced toward the dark thing six times, trying to grapple with it, hold it, hurt it. Each time, he hurt himself.

Then he stood, panting and gasping, and his shoulders ached and his back ached, and his mind cleared a moment and he said, "You're God, aren't you? And this is the way You play the game . . ."

The creature did not answer him and he lunged.

He stopped short, then dropped to one knee and dove against its legs.

He felt a terrible fiery pain within his side as he brought the dark one to earth. He struck at it twice with his fists, then the pain entered his breast and he felt himself grow numb.

"Or are you?" he asked, thick-lipped. "No, you're not . . . Where am I?"

His last memory was of something cutting away at his ears.

# PRINCE OF THE POWERS OF THIS WORLD

"God's balls!" said the first gravedigger, driving his spade into the earth, the better to lean upon it, to watch the bloody glow of the dying sun. "We'll be at this all night!"

"God damned ground's harder nor a stone," said the second. "Just like the old bastard to die midwinter and us to have the buryin' of 'im."

The third paused to blow upon his hands.

"Sooner the damned better he's underground. Out of sight, out of mind," he observed. "'Twas good watchin' his church burn. By the Old One's split feet! We could use some of that warm now, sure!"

The others chuckled.

"Aye!"

"True!"

They watched the sun slip away, the shadows rush to fill its place.

"Hark! What star is that, on high?" asked the first, pointing.

The others looked in the direction of his gesture.

"He's a right bright ruddy bastard," said the second. "But he ain't big-balled Mars. I don't know. . . . Never seen his like afore."

"Son of a bitch seems to be movin'," said the third, "off to the north."

"Aye," said the first.

"What's this?" asked the second. "Music? D'you hear it?"

"Music? Yer daft," said the third. "Y'd too much ale a' Mistress Doll's."

"Yer bloody deaf! Get the shit outen yer ears and give a listen!"

"He's right," said the first. "It seems to be comin' up outen the ground." With that, he pushed upon his spade with his foot and removed a clod of earth. He leaned then. "Pay heed," he said after a moment. "'Tis down there."

The others bent forward, listening.

"By Holy Joe's holy horns!" said the second. "'Tis pipes and some stringy thing and a drum, risin' like a fart outen the bowels of the earth—"

"Lads," said the third, dropping his spade and climbing out of the hole, "I've a mind not to be about when that wind breaks."

The others quickly retreated, also.

As they drew back from the half-dug grave the music came louder and the earth began to vibrate beneath their feet. Then, a dozen paces from their work, they were cast to the ground by a spasm that rippled through it like a wave through water. They shaded their eyes against the sudden illumination of flames which burst from the grave.

"Lords of the year! We're undone!" cried the first. "Behold what elevates from the Pit!"

Like a statue carved from old night, the horned, bat-winged figure rose amid the flames to tower above them. Its great yellow eyes moved from side to side, then fixed upon them where they lay quivering. The music throbbed and skirled about it as it raised a leg to place a hoof the size of a bread loaf upon the grave's edge. Suddenly, its voice sounded, flute-like, above the tune from the earth:

"Rejoice, you miserable motherfuckers, for tonight is the night of your lord's birth!"

"Glad to hear that," said the first.

"I'm rejoicin' a'ready," said the second.

"Me, too," said the third, eyes darting toward the cover of a nearby thicket.

"This night he is born to a former virgin tupped screamin' by the Lord of Darkness in the convent where she dwelled," the dark creature went on. "Cast out by the nuns, refused shelter by the fearful country folk, she wandered, halfmad, till this night when she gives birth in a cave occasionally used for the quartering of animals. Her son is the Messiah of Hell, and I, Asmodeus, proclaim his reign to you! Now get your asses over to the cave and pay him homage!"

The music had risen as he spoke, retreated now as he concluded.

"Aye, Lord Asmodeus," said the first. "But—uh—where shall we find this cave with the babe in it?"

Asmodeus raised his right hand, pointing a talon on high.

"Follow the damned star," he said, "'Tis really a demon in a fiery chariot. He'll halt it above the cave so there can be no mistake."

"Yes, sir!" said the second.

"We're on our way!" said the third.

Asmodeus leapt from the grave and began to dance. The earth shook again, and from somewhere a chorus of childlike voices accompanied him as he sang:

> *What child is this that is brought to birth*
> *With eyes like coals a-blazing?*
> *This, this is the Prince of Earth,*
> *Who'll take it to its ending.*

When the first gravedigger looked back he saw that the other two were not far behind him.

Coming at length to a cave from which a faint glow emerged, the gravediggers halted, then advanced slowly, to peer within.

They beheld a mother and child, reclining on a bed of straw, huddled amid pigs, rats, ravens, and a pair of strange furry creatures.

"What are the two big'uns?" whispered the second gravedigger.

"Jackals," said the first. "I saw their like one time in a book at the castle. The lord was readin' on the eve of a hunt, and he'd a mind to show us pictures of animals from other lands. Don't know what these two might be doin' here, though."

"P'raps they're someone's pets as got free."

"P'raps."

The third gravedigger cleared his throat.

"We'd best be payin' our respects," he said. "Wouldn't want to have Asmodeus mad at us."

"You're right," said the first.

Simultaneously then, all three of them cleared their throats.

The woman, almost a child herself, turned her head in their direction.

"Who's there?" she asked.

"Just—just some gravediggers," said the first, entering. "We were told to follow a star and we'd find this place. We came to pay our respects—to your child." The others followed him into the cave. The jackals raised their heads and regarded the men with yellow, unblinking eyes. It was difficult to tell where the light—a pale red glow—came from. Perhaps from the child himself. Silently, the mother began to weep.

"Well, here he is," she finally said, indicating the small black figure at her side. "He's sleeping just now."

The men dropped to their knees.

"'Tis good you'd a warm furry robe to wrap 'im in," said the second.

She laughed, though her tears continued to flow.

"'Tis not a robe. 'Tis his own hairy hide," she said.

"Oh," said the third. "Seein' as you're not so fortunate, let me give you my cloak."

"I can't take your cloak. It's cold out there."

"I've another at home. Take it," he said. "Even with your animal friends you'll be needin' it."

He extended it, let it fall upon her.

"I hope he brings you some kind of joy," said the second.

She bit her lip.

"Who knows? He might take more after me than after his da. 'Tis possible, you know."

"Of course," said the first, turning away. "I wish you good fortune—and that the young 'un will love you and honor you and care for you."

"Why should I?" came a tiny voice.

He looked back, and the child's strange eyes (he could never recall their color) were open and fixed upon him.

"He has been able to speak since the moment of his birth," the mother stated.

"Why should I?" the child repeated.

"Because she loves you and tends to you and has suffered for you and will suffer for you," the first replied.

The child turned his gaze upward.

"Mother, is this true?" he asked.

"Yes," she answered.

"I do not want you to suffer," he said.

"There is little you can do about it," she told him.

"We shall see," he stated.

"I guess we'd best be going now," said the first gravedigger.

She nodded.

"Thank you for the cloak," she said to the third.

"Bide a moment," said the child. "Who told you to follow the star to this place?"

"A demon named Asmodeus," said the second. "He came up out of the ground and so bade us."

"And why did you do as he told you?"

"Why, we feared him, sir," said the first.

"I see. Thank you. Good night to you."

The gravediggers backed out of the cave, were gone into the night.

"Those men," the child said then, "do not love me or tend to me as you do. They came because they feared that they would suffer if they did not obey my uncle. Is that not correct?"

"Yes," his mother said. "That is correct."

"Then which is stronger, love or fear?"

"I do not know," she said. "But the one did not give me his cloak out of fear, and he will suffer from the cold because of it."

"Does that mean that he loves you?"

"It is a kind of love to tend to another when you do not have to. But it is more a friendly thing than a lovely thing. With fear, you do things because you must or you will be hurt."

"I see," said the furry child, snuggling against her. "The man is a friend."

Later, as they dozed, three more figures approached the cave and begged permission to enter. They were three kings who had traveled far and over the sea out of the East and the South, bearing gifts of opium, strychnine, and silver, each of which gave power over people by different means. They desired that their kingdoms be spared when the days of the conflagration arrived—and that, as future allies, they might benefit from the destruction of their neighbors who resisted.

"I begin to understand," the child said after they had left. "They do not love me, they fear me."

"That is right," she said.

"They are not even friends."

"No, they are not."

At midnight a great rush of fire occurred beyond the cave mouth, filling the entire enclosure with baleful brilliance. The mother gasped and shielded her eyes, but the child stared into the flames, where a dark, brooding, masculine form took shape. With a laugh, the figure strode forward, to regard them. Then he stooped, snatched the gravedigger's cloak away from the woman and cast it back over his shoulder, where it burst into flames. Then he threw an ermine robe atop her and the child.

"You!" she gasped.

"Yes," he replied. "My son and my mare deserve the best of garments." Reaching behind him, he produced a stack of shirts, skirts, and swaddling clothes which he laid nearby. "And good meats, fresh fruits, bread, vegetables, herbs, wine." He placed a massive basket upon the floor. Then he leaned to examine the opium, the strychnine, the thirty pieces of silver. "Ah, the kings have been by to plead for their pathetic realms," he said. "Well, do with them as you would, when your time comes."

"I shall," said the child.

"Do you know who you are, boy?" the dark one asked.

"I am her son, and yours."

"That is right, and you can summon a legion of demons to do your bidding simply by naming them. If you think about it, you will see that you know all of their names."

"It seems that I do."

"Do you know what it is that I want of you?"

"Something involving blood and fire and destruction, I believe. Someone may have referred to it as the final conflagration."

"That is close enough. The details will become clearer to you as you grow older. And you can always call upon me for a consultation if you are in doubt."

"Thank you."

"The means will be a young man who would be king. You will meet him one day, make him your slave, help him to his kingship, see him unite this realm, then have him cross the Channel to kick down the remaining holdings of the Roman Empire, take it for his own, and forge it into a new power under his command. Then you will be in position to execute the next phase of my plan—"

"Father, what will his name be, this young king?"

"I cannot see that deeply into things that are yet to be. There is always a cloud about major events."

"Will this man love me, or will he fear me?"

"Neither, if you use your powers properly. Think upon the lessons of your gifts. The silver teaches that people will betray others, and that everything has a price. The strychnine teaches that those who are too trouble-some can be eliminated. The opium teaches that people may be placed in thrall, may be led as you choose, by a dulling of their senses and a laying on of glamour. That may be the easiest route with your king. You will know what is best when the time comes.

"I understand you," said the child. "How am I to know this man?"

"A fair question, my son. Behold!" With that, the dark one turned to his rear. When he turned back, he held a blade in his hand. He brandished it on high and it took fire with a roaring sound. Then, with a single step, he crossed the cave and plunged the weapon into a stone. "There," he answered. "He will be the only man capable of drawing that sword from that stone."

"I see," said the child. "Yes, I, too, see these things that are yet to be, through a cloud, dimly. I understand how I may use it."

"Very well, lad. If you need anything, call upon my minions. They will obey you as they would me."

"I shall, father."

The dark one turned, retreated into the flames beyond the cave mouth, and was gone. Moments later, the flames died.

The child yawned and snuggled against his mother once again. "Tell me, son," she asked. "Can you really see the future, like your father?"

"Better," he replied, yawning again. "Arthur shall be my friend."

# THE FURIES

As an afterthought, Nature sometimes tosses a bone to those it maims and casts aside. Often, it is in the form of a skill, usually useless, or the curse of intelligence.

When Sandor Sandor was four years old he could name all the one hundred forty-nine inhabited worlds in the galaxy. When he was five he could name the principal land masses of each planet and chalk them in, roughly, on blank globes. By the time he was seven years old he knew all the provinces, states, countries and major cities of all the main land masses on all one hundred forty-nine inhabited worlds in the galaxy. He read Landography, History, Landology and popular travel guides during most of his waking time; and he studied maps and travel tapes. There was a camera behind his eyes, or so it seemed, because by the time he was ten years old there was no city in the galaxy that anyone could name about which Sandor Sandor did not know *something*.

And he continued.

Places fascinated him. He built a library of street guides, road maps. He studied architectural styles and principal industries, and racial types, native life forms, local flora, landmarks, hotels, restaurants, airports and seaports and spaceports, styles of clothing and personal ornamentation, climatic conditions, local arts and crafts, dietary habits, sports, religions, social institutions, customs.

When he took his doctorate in Landography at the age of fourteen, his oral examinations were conducted via closed circuit television. This is because he was afraid to leave his home—having done so only three times before in his life and having met with fresh trauma on each occasion. And *this* is because on all one hundred forty-nine inhabited worlds in the galaxy there was no remedy for a certain degenerative muscular disease. This disease made it impossible for Sandor to manipulate even the finest prosthetic devices for more than a few minutes without suffering fatigue and great pain; and to go outside he required three such devices—two legs and a right arm—to substitute for those which he had missed out on receiving somewhere along the line before birth.

Rather than suffer this pain, or the pain of meeting persons other than his Aunt Faye or his nurse, Miss Barbara, he took his oral examinations via closed circuit television.

The University of Brill, Dombeck, was located on the other side of that small planet from Sandor's home, else the professors would have come to see *him*, because they respected him considerably. His 855-page dissertation, "Some Notes Toward a Gravitational Matrix Theory Governing the Formation of Similar Land Masses on Dissimilar Planetary Bodies," had drawn attention from Interstel University on Earth itself. Sandor Sandor, of course, would never see the Earth. His muscles could only sustain the gravitation of smaller planets, such as Dombeck.

And it happened that the Interstel Government, which monitors everything, had listened in on Sandor's oral examinations and his defense of his dissertation.

Associate Professor Baines was one of Sandor's very few friends. They had even met several times in person, in Sandor's library, because Baines often said he'd wanted to borrow certain books and then came and spent the afternoon. When the examinations were concluded, Associate Professor Baines stayed on the circuit for several minutes, talking with Sandor. It was during this time that Baines made casual reference to an almost useless (academically, that is) talent of Sandor's.

At the mention of it, the government man's ears had pricked forward (he was a Rigellian). He was anxious for a promotion and he recalled an obscure memo. . . .

Associate Professor Baines had mentioned the fact that Sandor Sandor had once studied a series of thirty random photos from all over the civilized galaxy, and that the significant data from these same photos had also been fed into the Department's L-L computer. Sandor had named the correct planet in each case, the land mass in 29, the county or territory in twenty-six, and he had correctly set the location itself within fifty square miles in twenty-three instances. The L-L comp had named the correct planet for twenty-seven.

It was not a labor of love for the computer.

So it became apparent that Sandor Sandor knew just about every damn street in the galaxy.

Ten years later he knew them all.

But three years later the Rigellian quit his job, disgusted, and went to work in private industry, where the pay was better and promotions more frequent. *His* memo, and the tape, had been filed, however. . . .

Benedick Benedict was born and grew up on the watery world of Kjum, and his was an infallible power for making enemies of everyone he met.

The reason why is that while some men's highest pleasure is drink, and others are given to gluttony, and still others are slothful, or lechery is their chief delight, or *Phrinn*-doing, Benedick's was gossip—He was a loudmouth.

Gossip was his meat and his drink, his sex and his religion. Shaking hands with him was a mistake, often a catastrophic one. For, as he clung to your hand, pumping it and smiling, his eyes would suddenly grow moistened, the tears would dribble down his fat cheeks.

He wasn't sad when this happened. Far from it. It was a somatic conversion from his paranorm reaction.

He was seeing your past life.

He was selective, too; he only saw what he looked for. And he looked for scandal and hate, and what is often worse, love; he looked for lawbreaking and unrest, for memories of discomfort, pain, futility, weakness. He saw everything a man wanted to forget, and he talked about it.

If you are lucky he won't tell you of your own. If you have ever met someone else whom he has also met in this manner, and if this fact shows, he will begin talking of *that* person. He will tell you of that man's or woman's life because he appreciates this form of social reaction even more than your outrage at yourself. And his eyes and voice and hand will hold you, like the clutch of the Ancient Mariner, in a sort of half dream-state; and you will hear him out and you will be shocked beneath your paralysis.

Then he will go away and tell others about you.

Such a man was Benedick Benedict. He was probably unaware how much he was hated, because this reaction never came until later, after he had said "Good day," departed, and been gone for several hours. He left his hearers with a just-raped feeling—and later fear, shame, or disgust forced them to suppress the occurrence and to try to forget him. Or else they hated him quietly, because he was dangerous. That is to say, he had powerful friends.

He was an extremely social animal: he loved attention; he wanted to be admired; he craved audiences.

He could always find an audience too, somewhere. He knew so many secrets that he was tolerated in important places in return for the hearing. And he was wealthy too, but more of that in a moment.

As time went on, it became harder and harder for him to meet new people. His reputation spread in geometric proportion to his talking, and even those who would hear him preferred to sit on the far side of the room, drink enough alcohol to partly deaden memories of themselves, and to be seated near a door.

The reason for his wealth is because his power extended to inanimate objects as well. Minerals were rare on Kjum, the watery world. If anyone brought him a sample he could hold it and weep and tell them where to dig to hit the main lode.

From one fish caught in the vast seas of Kjum, he could chart the course of a school of fish.

Weeping, he could touch a native rad-pearl necklace and divine the location of the native's rad-pearl bed.

Local insurance associations and loan companies kept Benedict Files— the pen a man had used to sign his contract, his snubbed-out cigarette butt, a plastex hanky with which he had mopped his brow, an object left in security, the remains of a biopsy or blood test—so that Benedick could use his power against those who renege on these companies and flee, on those who break their laws.

He did not revel in his power either. He simply enjoyed it. For he was one of the nineteen known paranorms in the one hundred forty-nine inhabited worlds in the galaxy, and he knew no other way.

Also, he occasionally assisted civil authorities, if he thought their cause a just one. If he did not, he suddenly lost his power until the need for it vanished. This didn't happen too often though, for an humanitarian was Benedick Benedict, and well-paid, because he was laboratory-tested and clinically-proven. He could psychometrize. He could pick up thought-patterns originating outside his own skull. . . .

Lynx Links looked like a beachball with a beard, a fat patriarch with an eyepatch, a man who loved good food and drink, simple clothing, and the company of simple people; he was a man who smiled often and whose voice was soft and melodic.

In his earlier years he had chalked up the most impressive kill-record of any agent ever employed by Interstel Central Intelligence. Forty-eight men and seventeen malicious alien life-forms had the Lynx dispatched during his fifty-year tenure as a field agent. He was one of the three men in the galaxy to have lived through half a century's employment with ICI. He lived comfortably on his government pension despite three wives and a horde of grandchildren; he was recalled occasionally as a consultant; and he did some part-time missionary work on the side. He believed that all life was one and that all men were brothers, and that love rather than hate or fear should rule the affairs of men. He had even killed with love, he often remarked at Tranquility Session, respecting and revering the person and the spirit of the man who had been marked for death.

This is the story of how he came to be summoned back from Hosanna, the World of the Great and Glorious Flame of the Divine Life, and was joined with Sandor Sandor and Benedick Benedict in the hunt for Victor Corgo, the man without a heart.

Victor Corgo was captain of the *Wallaby*. Victor Corgo was Head Astrogator, First Mate, and Chief Engineer of the *Wallaby*. Victor Corgo was the *Wallaby*.

One time the *Wallaby* was a proud Guardship, an ebony toadstool studded with the jewel-like warts of fast-phase projectors. One time the *Wallaby* skipped proud about the frontier worlds of Interstel, meting out the unique justice of the Uniform Galactic Code—in those places where there was no other law. One time the proud *Wallaby*, under the command of Captain Victor Corgo of the Guard, had ranged deep space and become a legend under legendary skies.

A terror to brigands and ugly aliens, a threat to Code-breakers, and a thorn in the sides of evildoers everywhere, Corgo and his shimmering fungus (which could burn an entire continent under water level within a single day) were the pride of the Guard, the best of the best, the cream that had been skimmed from all the rest.

Unfortunately, Corgo sold out.

He became a heel.

. . . A traitor.

A hero gone bad. . . .

After forty-five years with the Guard, his pension but half a decade away, he lost his entire crew in an ill-timed raid upon a pirate stronghold on the planet Kilsh, which might have become the hundred-fiftieth inhabited world of Interstel.

Crawling, barely alive, he had made his way half across the great snowfield of Brild, on the main land mass of Kilsh. At the fortuitous moment, Death making its traditional noises of approach, he was snatched from out of its traffic lane, so to speak, by the Drillen, a nomadic tribe of ugly and intelligent quadrapeds, who took him to their camp and healed his wounds, fed him, and gave him warmth. Later, with the cooperation of the Drillen, he recovered the *Wallaby* and all its arms and armaments, from where it had burnt its way to a hundred feet beneath the ice.

Crewless, he trained the Drillen.

With the Drillen and the *Wallaby* he attacked the pirates.

He won.

But he did not stop with that.

No.

When he learned that the Drillen had been Marked for death under the Uniform Code he sold out his own species. The Drillen had refused relocation to a decent Reservation World. They had elected to continue occupancy of what was to become the hundred-fiftieth inhabited world in the galaxy (that is to say, in Interstel).

Therefore, the destruct-order had been given.

Captain Corgo protested, was declared out of order.

Captain Corgo threatened, was threatened in return.

Captain Corgo fought, was beaten, died, was resurrected, escaped restraint, became an outlaw.

He took the *Wallaby* with him. The *Happy Wallaby*, it had been called in the proud days. Now, it was just the *Wallaby*.

As the tractor beams had seized it, as the vibrations penetrated its ebony hull and tore at his flesh, Corgo had called his six Drillen to him, stroked the fur of Mala, his favorite, opened his mouth to speak, and died just as the words and the tears began.

"I am sorry . . ." he had said.

They gave him a new heart, though. His old one had fibrillated itself to pieces and could not be repaired. They put the old one in a jar and gave him a shiny, antiseptic egg of throbbing metal, which expanded and contracted at varying intervals, dependent upon what the seed-sized computers they had planted within him told of his breathing and his blood sugar and the output of his various glands. The seeds and the egg contained his life.

When they were assured that this was true and that it would continue, they advised him of the proceedings of the courts-martial.

He did not wait, however, for due process. Breaking his parole as an officer, he escaped the Guard Post, taking with him Mala, the only remaining Drillen in the galaxy. Her five fellows had not survived scientific inquiry as to the nature of their internal structures. The rest of the race, of course, had refused relocation.

Then did the man without a heart make war upon mankind.

Raping a planet involves considerable expense. Enormous blasters and slicers and sluicers and refiners are required to reduce a world back almost to a state of primal chaos, and then to extract from it its essential (*i.e.*, commercially viable) ingredients. The history books may tell you of strip-mining on the mother planet, back in ancient times. Well, the crude processes employed then were similar in emphasis and results, but the operations were considerably smaller in size.

Visualize a hundred miles of Grand Canyon appearing overnight; visualize the reversal of thousands of Landological millennia in the twinkling of an eye; consider all of the Ice Ages of the Earth, and compress them into a single season. This will give you a rough idea as to time and effect.

Now picture the imported labor—the men who drill and blast and slice and sluice—for the great mining combines: Not uneducated, these men; willing to take a big risk, certainly though, these men—maybe only for one year, because of the high pay; or maybe they're careerists, because of the high pay—these men, who hit three worlds in a year's time, who descend upon these worlds in ships full of city, in space-trailer mining camps, out of the sky; coming, these men, from all over the inhabited galaxy, bringing with them the power of the tool and the opposed thumb, bearing upon their brows the mark of the Solar Phoenix and in their eyes the cold of the spaces they have crossed over, they know what to do to make the domes of atoms rise before them and to call down the probosci of suck-vortices from the freighters on the other side of the sky; and they do it thoroughly and efficiently, and not without style, tradition, folk-songs, and laughter—for they are the sweat-crews, working against time (which is money), to gain tonnage (which is money), and to beat their competitors to market (which is important, inasmuch as one worldsworth influences future sales for many months); these men, who bear in one hand the flame and in the other the whirlwind, who come down with their families and all their possessions, erect temporary metropoli, work their magic act, and go—after the vanishing trick has been completed

Now that you've an idea as to what happens and who is present at the scene, here's the rub:

Raping a planet involves considerable expense.

The profits are more than commensurate, do not misunderstand. It is just that they could be even greater. . . .

How?

Well—For one thing, the heavy machinery involved is quite replaceable, in the main. That is, the machinery which is housed within the migrant metropoli.

Moving it is expensive. Not moving it isn't. For it is actually cheaper, in terms of material and labor, to manufacture new units than it is to fast-phase the old ones more than an average of 2.6 times.

Mining combines do not produce them (and wouldn't really want to); the mining manufacturing combines like to make new units as much as the mining combines like to lose old ones.

And of course it is rented machinery, or machinery on which the payments are still being made, to the financing associations, because carrying payments makes it easier to face down the Interstel Revenue Service every fiscal year.

Abandoning the units would be criminal, violating either the lessor-lessee agreement or the Interstel Commercial Code.

But accidents do happen.

Often, too frequently to make for comfortable statistics . . .

Way out there on the raw frontier.

Then do the big insurance associations investigate, and they finally sigh and reimburse the lienholders.

And the freighters make it to market ahead of schedule, because there is less to dismantle and march-order and ship.

Time is saved, commitments are met in advance, a better price is generally obtained, and a head start on the next worldsworth is supplied in this manner.

All of which is nice.

Except for the insurance associations.

But what can happen to a transitory New York full of heavy equipment?

Well, some call it sabotage.

. . . Some call it mass-murder.

. . . Unsanctioned war.

. . . Corgo's lightning.

But it is written that it is better to burn one city than to curse the darkness.

Corgo did not curse the darkness.

. . . Many times.

The day they came together on Dombeck, Benedick Benedict leaned forward in his chair and pressed the held-forth hand, smiled, said: "Mister Sandor . . ."

As his hand was shaken, his smile reversed itself. Then it went away from his face. He was shaking an artificial hand.

". . . And you are the Lynx?"

"That is correct, my brother. You must excuse me if I do not shake hands. It is against my religion. I believe that life does not require reassurance as to its oneness."

"Of course," said Benedick. "I once knew a man from Dombeck. He was a *gnil* smuggler, named Worten Wortan—"

He is gone to join the Great Flame," said the Lynx. "That is to say, he is dead now. ICI apprehended him two years ago. He passed to Flame while attempting to escape restraint."

"Really?" said Benedick. "He was at one time a *gnil* addict himself—"

"I know. I read his file in connection with another case."

"Dombeck is full of *gnil* smugglers"—Sandor.

"Oh. Well, then let us talk of this man Corgo."

"Yes"—the Lynx.

"Yes"—Sandor.

"The ICI man told me that many insurance associations have lodged protests with their Interstel representatives."

"That is true"—Lynx.

"Yes"—Sandor, biting his lip. "Do you gentlemen mind if I remove my legs?"

"Not at all"—the Lynx. "We are co-workers, and informality should govern our gatherings."

"Please do," said Benedick.

Sandor leaned forward in his chair and pressed the coupling controls. There followed two thumps from beneath his desk. He leaned back then and surveyed his shelves of globes.

"Do they cause you pain?" asked Benedick.

"Yes—" Sandor.

"Were you in an accident?"

"Birth"—Sandor.

The Lynx raised a decanter of brownish liquid to the light. He stared through it.

"It is a local brandy"—Sandor. "Quite good. Somewhat like the *xmili* of

Bandla, only nonaddictive. Have some."

The Lynx did, keeping it in front of him all that evening.

"Corgo is a destroyer of property," said Benedick.

Sandor nodded.

". . . And a defrauder of insurance associations, a defacer of planetary bodies, a deserter from the Guard—"

"A murderer"—Sandor.

". . . And a zoophilist," finished Benedick.

"Aye"—the Lynx, smacking his lips.

"So great an offender against public tranquility is he that he must be found."

". . . And passed back through the Flame for purification and rebirth."

"Yes, we must locate him and kill him," said Benedick.

"The two pieces of equipment . . . Are they present?"—the Lynx.

"Yes, the phase-wave is in the next room."

". . . And?" asked Benedick.

"The other item is in the bottom drawer of this desk, right side."

"Then why do we not begin now?"

"Yes. Why not now?"—the Lynx.

"Very well"—Sandor, "One of you will have to open the drawer, though. It is in the brown-glass jar, to the back."

"I'll get it," said Benedick.

A great sob escaped him after a time, as he sat there with rows of worlds at his back, tears on his checks, and Corgo's heart clutched in his hands.

It is cold and dim.

"Where?"—the Lynx.

"It is a small place. A room? Cabin? Instrument panels . . . A humming sound . . . Cold, and crazy angles everywhere . . . Vibration . . . Hurt!"

"What is he doing?"—Sandor.

". . . Sitting, half-lying—a couch, webbed, about him. Furry one at his side, sleeping. Twisted—angles—everything—wrong. Hurt!"

"The *Wallaby*, in transit."—Lynx.

"Where is he going?"—Sandor.

"*Hurt!*" shouted Benedick.

Sandor dropped the heart into his lap.

He began to shiver. He wiped at his eyes with the backs of his hands.

"I have a headache," he announced.

"Have a drink."—Lynx.

He gulped one, sipped the second.

"Where was I?"

The Lynx raised his shoulders and let them fall.

"The *Wallaby* was fast-phasing somewhere, and Corgo was in phase-sleep. It is a disturbing sensation to fast-phase while fully conscious. Distance and duration grow distorted. You found him at a bad time—while under sedation and subject to continuum-impact. Perhaps tomorrow will be better . . .

"I hope so."

"Yes, tomorrow"—Sandor.

"Tomorrow . . . Yes."

"There *was* one other thing," he added, "a thing in his mind . . . There was a sun where there was no sun before."

"A burn-job?"—Lynx.

"Yes."

"A memory?"—Sandor.

"No. He is on his way to do it."

The Lynx stood.

"I will phase-wave ICI and advise them. They can check which worlds are presently being mined. Have you any ideas how soon?"

"No, I cannot tell that."

"What did the globe look like? What continental configurations?"—Sandor.

"None. The thought was not that specific. His mind was drifting—mainly filled with hate."

"I'll call in now—and we'll try again. . . ?"

"Tomorrow. I'm tired now."

"Go to bed then. Rest."

"Yes, I can do that . . ."

"Good night, Mister Benedict."

"Good night . . ."

"Sleep in the heart of the Great Flame."

"I hope not. . . ."

Mala whimpered and moved nearer her Corgo, for she was dreaming an evil dream: They were back on the great snowfield of Brild, and she was trying to help him—to walk, to move forward. He kept slipping though, and lying there longer each time, and rising more slowly each time and moving ahead at an even slower pace, each time. He tried to kindle a fire, but the snow-devils spun and toppled like icicles falling from the seven moons, and the dancing green flames died as soon as they were born from between his hands.

Finally, on the top of a mountain of ice she saw them. There were three . . .

They were clothed from head to toe in flame; their burning heads turned and turned and turned; and then one bent and sniffed at the ground, rose, and indicated their direction. Then they were racing down the hillside, trailing flames, melting a pathway as they came, springing over drifts and ridges of ice, their arms extended before them.

Silent they came, pausing only as the one sniffed the air, the ground . . .

She could hear their breathing now, feel their heat. . . .

In a matter of moments they would arrive. Mala whimpered and moved nearer her Corgo.

For three days Benedick tried, clutching Corgo's heart like a Gypsy's crystal, watering it with his tears, squeezing almost to life again. His head ached for hours after, each time that he met the continuum-impact. He wept long, moist tears for hours beyond contact, which was unusual. He had always withdrawn from immediate pain before; remembered distress was his forte, and a different matter altogether.

He hurt each time that he touched Corgo, and his mind was sucked down through that subway in the sly; and he touched Corgo eleven times during those three days, and then his power went away, really.

Seated, like a lump of dark metal on the hull of the *Wallaby*, he stared across six hundred miles at the blazing hearth which he had stoked to steel-tempering heights; and he *felt* like a piece of metal, resting there upon an anvil, waiting for the hammer to fall again, as it always did, waiting for it to strike him again and again, and to beat him to a new toughness, to smash away more and more of that within him which was base, of that which knew pity, remorse, and guilt, again and again and again, and to leave only that hard, hard form of hate, like an iron boot, which lived at the core of the lump, himself, and required constant hammering and heat.

Sweating as he watched, smiling, Corgo took pictures.

When one of the nineteen known paranorms in the one hundred forty-nine inhabited worlds in the galaxy suddenly loses his powers, and loses them at a crucial moment, it is like unto the old tales wherein a princess is stricken one day with an unknown malady and the King, her father, summons all his wise men and calls for the best physicians in the realm.

Big Daddy ICI (*Rex ex machina-like*) did, in similar manner, summon wise men and counselors from various Thinkomats and think-repairshops about the galaxy, including Interstel University, on Earth itself. But alas! While all had a diagnosis none had on hand any suggestions which were immediately acceptable to all parties concerned:

"Bombard his thalamus with Beta particles."

"Hypno-regression to the womb, and restoration at a pre-traumatic point in his life."

"More continuum-impact."

"Six weeks on a pleasure satellite, and two aspirins every four hours."

"There is an old operation called a lobotomy."

"Lots of liquids and green leafy vegetables."

"Hire another paranorm."

For one reason or another, the principal balked at all of these courses of action, and the final one was impossible at the moment. In the end, the matter was settled neatly by Sandor's nurse Miss Barbara, who happened onto the veranda one afternoon as Benedick sat there fanning himself and drinking *xmili*.

"Why Mister Benedict!" she announced, plopping her matronly self into the chair opposite him and spiking her *redlonade* with three fingers of *xmili*. "Fancy meeting you out here! I thought you were in the library with the boys, working on that top secret hush-hush critical project called *Wallaby* Stew, or something."

"As you can see, I am not," he said, staring at his knees.

"Well, it's nice just to pass the time of day sometimes, too. To sit. To relax. To rest from the hunting of Victor Corgo . . ."

"Please, you're not supposed to know about the project. It's top secret and critical—"

"And hush-hush too, I know. Dear Sandor talks in his sleep every night—so much. You see, I tuck him in each evening and sit there until he drifts away to dreamland, poor child."

"Mm, yes. Please don't talk about the project, though."

"Why? Isn't it going well?"

"No!"

"Why not?"

"Because of *me*, if you must know! I've got a block of some kind. The power doesn't come when I call it."

"Oh, how distressing! You mean you can't peep into other persons' minds any more?"

"Exactly."

"Dear me. Well, let's talk about something else then. Did I ever tell you about the days when I was the highest-paid courtesan on Sordido V?"

Benedick's head turned slowly in her direction.

"Nooo . . ." he said. "You mean *the* Sordido?"

"Oh yes. Bright Bad Barby, the Bouncing Baby, they used to call me. They still sing ballads, you know."

"Yes, I've heard them. Many verses . . ."

"Have another drink. I once had a coin struck in my image, you know. It's a collectors' item now, of course. Full-length pose, flesh-colored. Here, I wear it on this chain around my neck—Lean closer, it's a short chain?"

"Very—interesting. Uh, how did all this come about?"

"Well—it all began with old Pruria Van Teste, the banker, of the export-import Testes. You see, he had this thing going for synthofemmes for a long while, but when he started getting up there in years he felt there was something he'd been missing. So, one fine day, he sent me ten dozen Hravian orchids and a diamond garter, along with an invitation to have dinner with him . . ."

"You accepted, of course?"

"Naturally not. Not the first time, anyway. I could see that he was pretty damn eager."

"Well, what happened?"

"Wait till I fix another *redlonade*."

Later that afternoon, the Lynx wandered out into the veranda during the course of his meditations. He saw there Miss Barbara, with Benedick seated beside her, weeping.

"What troubles thy tranquility, my brother?" he inquired.

"Nothing! Nothing at all! It is wonderful and beautiful, everything! My power has come back—I can feel it!" He wiped his eyes on his sleeve.

"Bless thee, little lady!" said the Lynx, seizing Miss Barbara's hand. "Thy simple counsels have done more to heal my brother than have all these highly-paid medical practitioners brought here at great expense. Virtue lies in thy homely words, and thou art most beloved of the Flame."

"Thank you, I'm sure."

"Come brother, let us away to our task again!"

"Yes, let us!—Oh thank you, Bright Barby!"

"Don't mention it."

Benedick's eyes clouded immediately, as he took the tattered blood-pump into his hands. He leaned back, stroking it, and moist spots formed on either side of his nose, grew like well-fed amoebas, underwent mitosis, and dashed off to explore in the vicinity of his shelf-like upper lip.

He sighed once, deeply.

"Yes, I am there."

He blinked, licked his lips.

". . . It is night. Late. It is a primitive dwelling. Mudlike stucco, bits of straw in it . . . All lights out, but for the one from the machine, and its spillage—"

"Machine?"—Lynx.

"What machine?"—Sandor.

". . . Projector. Pictures on wall . . . World—big, filling whole picture-field—patches of fire on the world, Up near the top—Three places—"

"Bhave VII!"—Lynx. "Six days ago!"

"Shoreline to the right goes like this And to the left, like this . . ."

His right index finger traced patterns in the air.

"Bhave VII"—Sandor.

"Happy and not happy at the same, time—hard to separate the two.

Guilt, though, is there—but pleasure with it. Revenge . . . Hate people, humans . . . We adjust the projector now, stop it at a flare-up—Bright! How good!—Oh good! That will teach them!—Teach them to grab away what belongs to others . . . To murder a race!—The generator is humming. It is ancient, and it smells bad . . . the dog is lying on our foot. The foot is asleep, but we do not want to disturb the dog, for it is Mala's favorite thing—her only toy, companion, living doll, four-footed . . . She is scratching behind its ear with her forelimb, and it loves her. Light leaks down upon them . . . Clear they are. The breeze is warm, very, which is why we are unshirted. It stirs the tasseled hanging . . . No force-field or windowpane . . . Insects buzz by the projector-pterodactyl silhouettes on the burning world—"

"What kind of insects?"—Lynx.

"Can you see what is beyond the window?"—Sandor.

". . . Outside are trees—short ones—just outlines, squat. Can't tell where trunks begin . . . Foliage too thick, too close. Too dark out.—Off in the distance a tiny moon . . . Something like *this* on a hill . . ." His hands shaped a turnip impaled on an obelisk. "Not sure how far off, how large, what color, or what made of . . ."

"Is the name of the place in Corgo's mind?"—Lynx.

"If I could touch him, with my hand, I would know it, know everything. Only receive impressions *this* way, though—surface thoughts. He is not thinking of where he is now . . . The dog rolls onto its back and off of our foot—at last! She scratches its tummy, my love dark . . . It kicks with its hind leg as if scratching after a flea—wags its tail. Dilk is puppy's name. She gave it that name, loves it . . . It is like one of hers. Which was murdered. Hate people—humans. *She* is people. Better than . . . Doesn't butcher that which breathes for selfish gain, for Interstel. Better than people, my pony-friends, better . . . An insect lights on Dilk's nose. She brushes it away. Segmented, two sets of wings, about five millimeters in length, pink globe on front end, bulbous, and buzzes as it goes, the insect—you asked . . ."

"How many entrances are there to the place?"—Lynx.

"Two. One doorway at each end of the hut."

"How many windows?"

"Two. On opposing walls—the ones without doors. I can't see anything through the other window—too dark on that side."

"Anything else?"

"On the wall a sword—long hilt, very long, two-handed—even longer maybe—three? four?—short blades, though, two of them—hilt is in the middle—and each blade is straight, double-edged, forearmlength . . . Beside it, a mask of—flowers? Too dark to tell. The blades shine; the mask is dull. Looks like flowers, though. Many little ones . . . Four sides to the mask, shaped like a kite, big end down. Can't make out features. It projects fairly far out from the wall, though. Mala is restless. Probably doesn't like the pictures—or maybe doesn't see them and is bored. Her eyes are different. She nuzzles our shoulder now. We pour her a drink in her bowl. Take another one ourself. She doesn't drink hers. We stare at her. She drops her head and drinks.—Dirt floor under our sandals, hard-packed. Many tiny white—pebbles?—in it, powdery-like. The table is wood, natural . . . The generator sputters. The picture fades, comes back. We rub our chin. Need a shave . . . The hell with it! We're not standing any inspections! Drink—one, two—all gone! Another!"

Sandor had threaded a tape into his viewer, and he was spinning it and stopping it, spinning it and stopping it, spinning it and stopping it. He checked his worlds chronometer.

"Outside," he asked, "does the moon seem to be moving up, or down, or across the sky?"

"Across."

"Right to left, or left to right?"

"Right to left. It seems about a quarter past zenith."

"Any coloration to it?"

"Orange, with three black lines. One starts at about eleven o'clock, crosses a quarter of its surface, drops straight down, cuts back at seven. The other starts at two, drops to six. They don't meet. The third is a small upside-down letter 'c'—lower right quarter . . . Not big, the moon, but clear, very. No clouds."

"Any constellations you can make out?"—Lynx.

". . . Head isn't turned that way now, wasn't turned toward the window long enough. Now there is a noise, far off . . . A high-pitched chattering, almost metallic. Animal. He pictures a six-legged tree creature, half the size of a man, reddish-brown hair, sparse . . . It can go on two, four, or six legs on the ground. Doesn't go down on the ground much, though. Nests high. An egg-layer. Many teeth. Eats flesh. Small eyes, and black—two. Great nose-holes. Pesty, but not dangerous to men—easily frightened."

"He is on Disten, the fifth world of Blake's System," said Sandor. "Night-side means he is on the continent Didenlan. The moon Babry, well past zenith now, means he is to the east. A Mella-mosque indicates a Mella-Muslim settlement. The blade and the mask seem Hortanian. I am sure they were brought from further inland. The chalky deposits would set him in the vicinity of Landear, which *is* Mella-Muslim. It is on the Dista River, north bank. There is much jungle about. Even those people who wish seclusion seldom go further than eight miles from the center of town—population 153,000—and it is least settled to the northwest, because of the hills, the rocks, and—"

"Fine! That's where he is then!"—Lynx. "Now here is how we'll do it. He has, of course, been sentenced to death. I believe—yes, I know!—there is an ICI Field Office on the second world—whatever its name—of that System."

"Nirer"—Sandor.

"Yes. Hmm, let's see . . . Two agents will be empowered as executioners. They will land their ship to the northwest of Landear, enter the city, and find where the man with the strange four-legged pet settled, the one who arrived within the past six days. Then one agent will enter the hut and ascertain whether Corgo is within. He will retreat immediately if Corgo is present, signaling to the other who will be hidden behind those trees or whatever. The second man will then fire a round of fragmentation plaster through the unguarded window. One agent will then position himself at a safe distance beyond the northeast corner of the edifice, so as to cover a door and a window. The other will move to the southwest, to do the same. Each will carry a two-hundred channel laser sub-gun with vibrating head. —Good! I'll phase-wave it to Central now. We've got him!"

He hurried from the room.

Benedick, still holding the thing, continued:

"Fear not, my lady dark. He is but a puppy, and he howls at the moon . . ."

It was thirty-one hours and twenty minutes later when the Lynx received and decoded the two terse statements:

## EXECUTIONERS THE WAY OF ALL FLESH.
## THE WALLABY HAS JUMPED AGAIN.

He licked his lips. His comrades were waiting for the report, and *they* had succeeded—they had done their part, had performed efficiently and well. It was the Lynx who had missed his kill.

He made the sign of the Flame and entered the library.

Benedick knew—*he* could tell. The little paranorm's hands were on his walking stick, and that was enough—just that.

The Lynx bowed his head.

"We begin again," he told them.

Benedick's powers—if anything, stronger than ever—survived continuum-impact seven more times. Then he described a new world: Big it was, and many-peopled—bright—dazzling, under a blue-white sun; yellow brick everywhere, neo-Denebian architecture, greenglass windows, a purple sea nearby.

No trick at all for Sandor:

"Phillip's World," he named it, then told them the city: "Delles."

"This time *we* burn *him*," said the Lynx, and he was gone from the room.

"Christian-Zoroastrians," sighed Benedick after he had left. "I think this one has a Flame-complex."

Sandor spun the globe with his left hand and watched it turn.

"I'm not preconning," said Benedick, "but I'll give you odds, like three to one—on Corgo's escaping again.

"Why?"

"When he abandoned humanity he became something less, and more. He is not ready to die."

"What do you mean?"

"I hold his heart. He gave it up, in all ways. He is invincible now. But he will reclaim it one day. Then he will die."

"How do you know?"

". . . A feeling. There are many types of doctors, among them pathologists. No less than others, they, but masters only of blackness. I know *people*, have known many. I do not pretend to know all about them. But weaknesses—yes, those I know."

Sandor turned his globe and did not say anything.

But they *did* burn the *Wallaby*, badly.

He lived, though.

He lived, cursing.

As he lay there in the gutter, the world burning, exploding, falling down around him, he cursed *that* world and every other, and everything in them.

Then there was another burst.

Blackness followed.


The double-bladed Hortanian sword, spinning in the hands of Corgo, had halved the first ICI executioner as he stood in the doorway. Mala had detected their approach across the breezes, through the open window.

The second had fallen before the fragmentation plaster could be launched. Corgo had a laser sub-gun himself, Guard issue, and he cut the man down, firing through the wall and two trees in the direction Mala indicated.

Then the *Wallaby* left Disten.

But he was troubled. How had they found him so quickly? He had had close brushes with them before—many of them, over the years. But he was cautious, and he could not see where he had failed this time, could not understand how Interstel had located him. Even his last employer did not know his whereabouts.

He shook his head and phased for Phillip's world.

To die is to sleep and not to dream, and Corgo did not want this. He took elaborate pains, inphasing and outphasing in random directions; he gave Mala a golden collar with a two-way radio in its clasp, wore its mate within his death-ring; he converted much currency, left the *Wallaby* in the care of a reputable smuggler in Unassociated Territory and crossed Phillip's World to Delles-by-the-Sea. He was fond of sailing, and he liked the purple waters of this planet. He rented a large villa near the Delles Dives—slums to the one side, Riviera to the other. This pleased him. He still had dreams; he was not dead yet.

Sleeping, perhaps, he had heard a sound. Then he was suddenly seated on the side of his bed, a handful of death in his hand.

"Mala?"

She was gone. The sound he'd heard had been the closing of a door.

He activated the radio.

"What is it?" he demanded.

"I have the feeling we are watched again," she replied, through his ring. ". . . Only a feeling, though."

Her voice was distant, tiny.

"Why did you not tell *me*? Come back—now."

"No. I match the night and can move without sound. I will investigate. There *is* something, if I have fear . . . Arm yourself!"

He did that, and as he moved toward the front of the house they struck. He ran. As he passed through the front door they struck again, and again. There was an inferno at his back, and a steady rain of plaster, metal, wood and glass was falling. Then there was an inferno around him.

They were above him. This time they had been cautioned not to close with him, but to strike from a distance. This time they hovered high in a shielded globe and poured down hot rivers of destruction.

Something struck him in the head and the shoulder. He fell, turning. He was struck in the chest, the stomach. He covered his face and rolled, tried to rise, failed. He was lost in a forest of flames. He got into a crouch, ran, fell again, rose once more, ran, fell again, crawled, fell again.

As he lay there in the gutter, the world burning, exploding, falling down around him he cursed *that* world and every other, and everyone in them.

Then there was another burst.

Blackness followed.

They thought they had succeeded, and their joy was great.

"Nothing," Benedick had said, smiling through his tears.

So that day they celebrated, and the next.

But Corgo's body had not been recovered.

Almost half a block had been hurled down, though, and eleven other residents could not be located either, so it seemed safe to assume that the execution had succeeded. ICI, however, requested that the trio remain together on Dombeck for another ten days, while further investigations were carried out.

Benedick laughed.

"Nothing," he repeated. "Nothing."

But there is a funny thing about a man without a heart: His body does not live by the same rules as those of others: No. The egg in his chest is smarter than a mere heart, and it is the center of a wonderful communications system. Dead itself, it is omniscient in terms of that which lives around it; it is not omnipotent, but it has resources which a living heart does not command.

As the burns and lacerations were flashed upon the screen of the body, it sat in instant criticism. It moved itself to an emergency level of function; it became a flag vibrating within a hurricane; the glands responded and poured forth their juices of power; muscles were activated as if by electricity.

Corgo was only half-aware of the inhuman speed with which he moved through the storm of heat and the hail of building materials. It tore at him, but this pain was canceled. His massive output jammed nonessential neural input. He made it as far as the street and collapsed in the shelter of the curb.

The egg took stock of the cost of the action, decided the price had been excessively high, and employed immediate measures to insure the investment.

Down, down did it send him. Into the depths of subcoma. Standard-model humans cannot decide one day that they wish to hibernate, lie down, do it. The physicians can induce *dauerschlaff* with combinations of drugs and elaborate machineries. But Corgo did not need these things. He had a built-in survival kit with a mind of its own; and it decided that he must go deeper than the mere coma-level that a heart would have permitted. So it did the things a heart cannot do, while maintaining its own functions.

It hurled him into the blackness of sleep without dreams, of total unawareness. For only at the border of death itself could his life be retained, be strengthened, grow again. To approach this near the realm of death, its semblance was necessary.

Therefore, Corgo lay dead in the gutter.

People, of course, flock to the scene of any disaster.

Those from the Riviera pause to dress in their best catastrophe clothing. Those from the slums do not, because their wardrobes are not as extensive.

One, though, was dressed already and was passing nearby. "Zim" was what he was called, for obvious reasons. He had had another name once, but he had all but forgotten it.

He was staggering home from the *zimlak* parlor where he had cashed his Guard pension check for that month-cycle.

There was an explosion, but it was seconds before he realized it.

Muttering, he stopped and turned very slowly in the direction of the noise. Then he saw the flames. He looked up, saw the hoverglobe. A memory appeared within his mind and he winced and continued to watch.

After a time he saw the man, moving at a fantastic pace across the landscape of Hell. The man fell in the street. There was more burning, and then the globe departed.

The impressions finally registered, and his disaster-reflex made him approach.

Indelible synapses, burnt into his brain long ago, summoned up page after page of The Complete Guard Field Manual of Immediate Medical Actions. He knelt beside the body, red with burn, blood and firelight.

". . . Captain," he said, as he stared into the angular face with the closed dark eyes. "Captain . . ."

He covered his own face with his hands and they came away wet.

"Neighbors. Here. Us. Didn't—know." He listened for a heartbeat, but there was nothing that he could detect. "Fallen . . . On the deck my Captain lies . . . Fallen . . .cold . . . dead. Us. Neighbors, even . . ." His sob was a jagged thing, until he was seized with a spell of hiccups. Then he steadied his hands and raised an eyelid.

Corgo's head jerked two inches to his left, away from the brightness of the flames.

The man laughed in relief.

"You're alive, Cap! You're still alive!"

The thing that was Corgo did not reply.

Bending, straining, he raised the body.

"'Do not move the victim'—that's what it says in the Manual. But you're coming with me, Cap. I remember now. . . . It was after I left. But I remember . . . All. Now I remember; I do . . . Yes. They'll kill you another time—if you do live. . . . They will; I know. So I'll have to move the victim. Have to . . .—Wish I wasn't so fogged . . . I'm sorry, Cap. You were always good, to the men, good to me. Ran a tight ship, but you were good . . . Old *Wallaby,* happy . . . Yes. We'll go now, killer. Fast as we can. Before the Morbs come. Yes. I remember . . . you. Good man, Cap. Yes."

So, the *Wallaby* had made its last jump, according to the ICI investigation which followed. But Corgo still dwelled on the dreamless border, and the seeds and the egg held his life.

After the ten days had passed, the Lynx and Benedick still remained with Sandor. Sandor was not anxious for them to go. He had never been employed before; he liked the feeling of having coworkers about, persons who shared memories of things done. Benedick was loath to leave Miss Barbara, one of the few persons he could talk to and have answer him, willingly. The Lynx liked the food and the climate, decided his wives and grandchildren could use a vacation.

So they stayed on.

Returning from death is a deadly slow business. Reality does the dance of the veils, and it is a long while before you know what lies beneath them all (if you ever really do).

When Corgo had formed a rough idea, he cried out:

"Mala!"

. . . The darkness.

Then he saw a face out of times gone by.

"Sergeant Emil . . . ?"

"Yes, sir. Right here, Captain."

"Where am I?"

"My hutch, sir. Yours got burnt out."

"How?"

"A hoverglobe did it, with a sear-beam."

"What of my—pet? A Drillen . . ."

"There was only you I found, sir—no one, nothing, else. Uh, it was almost a month-cycle ago that it happened."

Corgo tried to sit up, failed, tried again, half-succeeded. He sat propped on his elbows.

"What's the matter with me?"

"You had some fractures, burns, lacerations, internal injuries—but you're going to be all right, now."

"I wonder how they found me, so fast—again . . . ?"

"I don't know, sir. Would you like to try some broth now?"

"Later."

"It's all warm and ready."

"Okay, Emil. Sure, bring it on."

He lay back and wondered.

There was her voice. He had been dozing all day and he was part of a dream.

"Corgo, are you there? Are you there, Corgo? Are you . . ."

His hand! The ring!

"Yes! Me! Corgo!" He activated it. "Mala! Where are you?"

"In a cave, by the sea. Everyday I have called to you. Are you alive, or do you answer me from Elsewhere?"

"I am alive. There is no magic to your collar. How have you kept yourself?"

"I go out at night. Steal food from the large dwellings with the green windows like doors—for Dilk and myself."

"The puppy? Alive, too?"

"Yes. He was penned in the yard on that night . . . Where are you?"

"I do not know, precisely. . . . Near where our place was. A few blocks away—I'm with an old friend."

"I must come."

"Wait until dark, I'll get you directions.—No. I'll send him after you, my friend. . . . Where is your cave?"

"Up the beach, past the red house you said was ugly. There are three rocks, pointed on top. Past them is a narrow path—the water comes up to it, sometimes covers it—and around a corner then, thirty-one of my steps, and the rock hangs overhead, too. It goes far back then, and there is a crack in the wall—small enough to squeeze through, but it widens. We are here."

"My friend will come for you after dark."

"You are hurt?"

"I was. But I am better now. I'll see you later, talk more then."

"Yes—"

In the days that followed, his strength returned to him. He played chess with Emil and talked with him of their days together in the Guard. He laughed, for the first time in many years, at the tale of the Commander's wig, at the Big Brawl on Sordido III, some thirty-odd years before. . . .

Mala kept to herself, and to Dilk. Occasionally, Corgo would feel her eyes upon him. But whenever he turned, she was always looking in another direction. He realized that she had never seen him being friendly with anyone before. She seemed puzzled.

He drank *zimlak* with Emil, they ventured off-key ballads together. . . .

Then one day it struck him.

"Emil, what are you using for money these days?"

"Guard pension, Cap.

"Flames! We've been eating you out of business! Food, and the medical supplies and all . . ."

"I had a little put away for foul weather days, Cap."

"Good. But you shouldn't have been using it. There's quite a bit of money zipped up in my boots.—Here, just a second . . . There! Take these!"

"I can't, Cap. . . ."

"The hell you say! Take them, that's an order!"

"All right, sir, but you don't have to. . . ."

"Emil, there is a price on my head—you know?"

"I know."

"A pretty large reward."

"Yes."

"It's yours, by right."

"I couldn't turn you in, sir."

"Nevertheless, the reward is yours. Twice over. I'll send you that amount—a few weeks after I leave here."

"I couldn't take it, sir."

"Nonsense; you will."

"No, sir. I won't."

"What do you mean?"

"I just mean I couldn't take that money."

"Why not? What's wrong with it?"

"Nothing, exactly. . . . I just don't want any of it. I'll take this you gave me for the food and stuff. But no more, that's all."

"Oh . . . All right, Emil. Any way you like it. I wasn't trying to force . . ."

"I know, Cap."

"Another game now? I'll spot you a bishop and three pawns this time."

"Very good, sir."

"We had some good time together, eh?"

"You bet, Cap. Tau Ceti—three months' leave. Remember the Red River Valley—and the family native life-forms?"

"Hah! And Cygnus VII—the purple world with the Rainbow Women?"

"Took me three weeks to get that dye off me. Thought at first it was a new disease. Flames! I'd love to ship out again!"

Corgo paused in mid-move.

"Hmm . . . You know, Emil . . . It might be that you could."

"What do you mean?"

Corgo finished his move.

"Aboard the *Wallaby*. It's here, in Unassociated Territory, waiting for me. I'm Captain, and crew—and everything—all by myself, right now. Mala helps some, but—you know, I could use a First Mate. Be like old times."

Emil replaced the knight he had raised, looked up, looked back down.

"I—I don't know what to say, Cap. I never thought you'd offer me a berth. . . ."

"Why not? I could use a good man. Lots of action, like the old days. Plenty cash. No cares. We want three months' leave on Tau Ceti and we write our own bloody orders. We take it!"

"I—I do want to space again, Cap—bad. But—no, I couldn't."

"Why not, Emil? Why not? It'd be just like before."

"I don't know how to say it, Cap . . . But when we—burnt places, before—well, it was criminals—pirates, Codebreakers—you know. Now . . . Well, now I hear you—burn—just people. Uh, non-Codebreakers. Like, just plain civilians. Well—I could not."

Corgo did not answer. Emil moved his knight.

"I hate them, Emil," he said, after a time. "Every lovin' one of them, I hate them. Do you know what they did on Brild? To the Drillen?"

"Yessir. But it wasn't civilians, and not the miners. It was not everybody. It wasn't every lovin' one of them, sir.—I just couldn't. Don't be mad."

"I'm not mad, Emil."

"I mean, sir, there are some as I wouldn't mind burnin', Code or no Code. But not the way you do it, sir. And I'd do it for free to those as have it coming."

"Huh!"

Corgo moved his one bishop.

"That's why my money is no good with you?"

"No, sir. That's not it, sir. Well maybe part . . . But only part. I just couldn't take pay for helping someone I respected, admired."

"You use the past tense."

"Yessir. But I still think you got a raw deal, and what they did to the Drillen was wrong and bad and—evil—but you can't hate everybody for that, sir, because everybody didn't do it."

"They countenanced it, Emil—which is just as bad. I am able to hate them all for that alone. And people are all alike, all the same. I burn without discrimination these days, because it doesn't really matter *who*. The guilt is equally distributed. Mankind is commonly culpable."

"No, sir, begging your pardon, sir, but in a system as big as Interstel not everybody knows what everybody else is up to. There are those feeling the same way you do, and there are those as don't give a damn, and those who just don't know a lot of what's going on, but who would do something about it if they knew, soon enough."

"It's your move, Emil."

"Yessir."

"You know, I wish you'd accepted a commission, Emil. You had the chance. You'd have been a good officer."

"No, sir. I'd not have been a good officer. I'm too easygoing. The men would've walked all over me."

"It's a pity. But it's always that way. You know? The good ones are too weak, too easy-going. Why is that?"

"Dunno, sir."

After a couple of moves:

"You know, if I were to give it up—the burning, I mean—and just do some ordinary, decent smuggling with the *Wallaby*, it would be okay. With me. Now. I'm tired. I'm so damned tired I'd just like to sleep—oh, four, five, six years, I think. Supposing I stopped the burning and just shipped stuff here and there—would you sign on with me then?"

"I'd have to think about it, Cap."

"Do that, then. Please. I'd like to have you along."

"Yessir. Your move, sir."

★　　★　　★

It would not have happened that he'd have been found by his actions, because he *did* stop the burning; it would not have happened—because he was dead on ICI's books—that anyone would have been looking for him. It happened, though—because of a surfeit of *xmili* and good will on the part of the hunters.

On the eve of the breaking of the fellowship, nostalgia followed high spirits.

Benedick had never had a friend before, you must remember. Now he had three, and he was leaving them.

The Lynx had ingested much good food and drink, and the good company of simple, maimed people, whose neuroses were unvitiated with normal sophistication—and he had enjoyed this.

Sandor's sphere of human relations had been expanded by approximately a third, and he had slowly come to consider himself at least an honorary member of the vast flux which he had only known before as humanity, or Others.

So, in the library, drinking, and eating and talking, they returned to the hunt. Dead tigers are always the best kind.

Of course, it wasn't long before Benedick picked up the heart, and held it as a connoisseur would an art object—gently, and with a certain mingling of awe and affection.

As they sat there, an odd sensation crept into the pudgy paranorm's stomach and rose slowly, like gas, until his eyes burned.

"I—I'm reading," he said.

"Of course"—the Lynx.

"Yes"—Sandor.

"Really!"

"Naturally"—the Lynx. "He is on Disten, fifth world of Blake's System, in a native hut outside Landear—"

"No"—Sandor. "He is on Phillip's World, in Delles-by the-Sea."

They laughed, the Lynx a deep rumble, Sandor gasping chuckle.

"No," said Benedick. "He is in transit, aboard the *Wallaby*. He had just phased and his mind is still mainly awake. He is running a cargo of ambergris to the Tau Ceti system, fifth planet—Tholmen. After that he plans on vacationing in the Red River Valley of the third planet—Cardiff. Along with the Drillen and the puppy, he has a crewman with him this time. I can't read anything but that it's a retired Guardsman."

"By the holy Light of the Great and Glorious Flame!"

"We know they never did find his ship . . ."

". . . And his body was not recovered.—Could you be mistaken, Benedick? Reading something, someone else . . . ?"

"No."

"What should we do, Lynx?"—Sandor.

"An unethical person might be inclined to forget it. It is a closed case. We have been paid and dismissed."

"True."

"But think of when he strikes again. . . ."

". . . It would be because of us, our failure."

"Yes."

". . . And many would die."

". . . And much machinery destroyed, and an insurance association defrauded."

"Yes."

". . . Because of us."

"Yes."

"So we should report it"—Lynx.

"Yes."

"It is unfortunate."

"Yes."

". . . But it will be good to have worked together this final time."

"Yes. It will. Very."

"Tholmen, in Tau Ceti, and he just phased?"—Lynx.

"Yes."

"I'll call, and they'll be waiting for him in T.C."

". . . I told you," said the weeping paranorm. "He wasn't ready to die."

Sandor smiled and raised his glass with his flesh-colored hand.

There was still some work to be done.

When the *Wallaby* hit Tau Ceti all hell broke loose.

Three fully-manned Guardships, like unto the Wallaby herself, were waiting.

ICI had quarantined the entire system for three days. There could be no mistaking the ebony toadstool when it appeared on the screen. No identification was solicited.

The tractor beams missed it the first time, however, and the *Wallaby*'s new First Mate fired every weapon aboard the ship simultaneously, in all directions, as soon as the alarm sounded. This had been one of Corgo's small alterations in fire-control, because of the size of his operations: no safety circuits; and it was a suicide-ship, if necessary: it was a lone wolf with no regard for *any* pack: one central control—touch it, and the *Wallaby* became a porcupine with laser-quills, stabbing into anything in every direction.

Corgo prepared to phase again, but it took him forty-three seconds to do so.

During that time be was struck twice by the surviving Guardship.

Then he was gone.

Time and Chance, which govern all things, and some times like to pass themselves off as Destiny, then seized upon the *Wallaby*, the puppy, the Drillen, First Mate Emil, and the man without a heart.

Corgo had set no course when he had in-phased. There had been no time.

The two blasts from the Guardship had radically altered the *Wallaby*'s course, and had burnt out twenty-three fast-phase projectors.

The *Wallaby* jumped blind, and with a broken leg.

Continuum-impact racked the crew. The hull repaired rents in its skin.

They continued for thirty-nine hours and twenty-three minutes, taking turns at sedation, watching for the first warning on the panel.

The *Wallaby* held together, though.

But where they had gotten to no one knew, least of all a weeping paranorm who had monitored the battle and all of Corgo's watches, despite the continuum-impact and a hangover.

But suddenly Benedick knew fear:

"He's about to phase-out. I'm going to have to drop him now."

"Why?"—the Lynx.

"Do you know where he is?"

"No, of course not!"

"Well, neither does he. Supposing he pops out in the middle of a sun, or in some atmosphere—moving at that speed?"

"Well, supposing he does? He dies."

"Exactly. Continuum-impact is bad enough. I've never been in a man's mind when he died—and I don't think I could take it. Sorry. I just won't do it. I think I might die myself if it happened—I'm so tired now. . . . I'll just have to check him out later."

With that he collapsed and could not be roused.

So, Corgo's heart went back into its jar, and the jar went back into the lower right-hand drawer of Sandor's desk, and none of the hunters heard the words of Corgo's answer to his First Mate after the phasing-out:

"Where. are we?—The Comp says the nearest thing is a little ping-pong ball of a world called Dombeck, not noted for anything. We'll have to put down there for repairs, somewhere off the beaten track. We need projectors."

So they landed the *Wallaby* and banged on its hull as the hunters slept, some five hundred forty-two miles away.

They were grinding out the projector sockets shortly after Sandor had been tucked into his bed.

They reinforced the hull in three places while the Lynx ate half a ham, three biscuits, two apples and a pear, and drank half a liter of Dombeck's best Mosel.

They rewired shorted circuits as Benedick smiled and dreamt of Bright Bad Barby the Bouncing Baby, in the days of her youth.

And Corgo took the light-boat and headed for a town three hundred miles away, just as the pale sun of Dombeck began to rise.

"He's here!" cried Benedick, flinging wide the door to the Lynx's room and rushing up to the bedside. "He's—"

Then he was unconscious, for the Lynx may not be approached suddenly as he sleeps.

When he awakened five minutes later, he was lying on the bed and the entire household stood about him. There was a cold cloth on his forehead and his throat felt crushed.

"My brother," said the Lynx, "you should never approach a sleeping man in such a manner."

"B-but he's here," said Benedick, gagging. "Here on Dombeck! I don't even need Sandor—to tell!"

"Art sure thou hast not imbibed too much?"

"No, I tell you he's here." He sat up, flung away the cloth. "That little city, Coldstream—" He pointed through the wall. "—I was there just a week ago. I *know* the place!"

"You have had a dream—"

"Wet your Flame! But I've not! I held his heart in these hands and saw it!"

The Lynx winced at the profanity, but considered the possibility.

"Then come with us to the library and see if you can read it again."

"You better believe I can!"

At that moment Corgo was drinking a cup of coffee and waiting for the town to wake up. He was considering his First Mate's resignation:

"I never wanted to burn anyone, Cap. Least of all, the Guard. I'm sorry, but that's it. No more for me. Leave me here and give me passage home to Phillip's—that's all I want. I know you didn't want it the way it happened, but if I keep shipping with you it might happen again some day. Probably will. They got your number somehow, and I couldn't *ever* do—again. I'll help you fix the *Wallaby*, then I'm out. Sorry."

Corgo sighed and ordered a second coffee. He glanced at the clock on the diner wall. Soon, soon . . .

"That clock, that wall, that window! It's the diner where I had lunch last week, in Coldstream!" said Benedick blinking moistly.

"Do you think all that continuum-impact . . . ?"—the Lynx.

"I don't know."—Sandor.

"How can we check?"

"Call the flamin' diner and ask them to describe their only customer!"
—Benedick.

"That is a very good idea"—the Lynx.

The Lynx moved to the phone-unit on Sandor's desk.

Sudden, as everything concerning the case had been, was the Lynx's final decision:

"Your flyer, brother Sandor. May I borrow it?"

"Why, yes. Surely. . ."

"I will now call the local ICI office and requisition a laser-cannon. They have been ordered to cooperate with us without question, and the orders are still in effect. My executioner's rating has never been suspended. It appears that if we ever want to see this job completed we must do it ourselves. It won't take long to mount the gun on your flyer.—Benedick, stay with him every minute now. He still has to buy the equipment, take it back and install it. Therefore, we should have sufficient time. Just stay with him and advise me as to his movements."

"Check."

"Are you sure it's the right way to go about it?"—Sandor.

"I'm sure. . . ."

As the cannon was being delivered, Corgo made his purchases. As it was being installed, he loaded the light-boat and departed. As it was tested, on a tree stump Aunt Faye had wanted removed for a long while, he was aloft and heading toward the desert.

As he crossed the desert, Benedick watched the rolling dunes, scrub-shrubs and darting rabbophers through his eyes.

He also watched the instrument-panel.

As the Lynx began his journey, Mala and Dilk were walking about the hull of the *Wallaby*. Mala wondered if the killing was over. She was not sure she liked the new Corgo so much as she did the avenger. She wondered whether the change would be permanent. She hoped not.

The Lynx maintained radio contact with Benedick.

Sandor drank *xmili* and smiled.

After a time, Corgo landed.

The Lynx was racing across the sands from the opposite direction.

They began unloading the light-boat.

The Lynx sped on.

"I am near it now. Five minutes," he radioed back.

"Then I'm out?"—Benedick.

"Not yet"—the reply.

"Sorry, but you know what I said. I won't be there when he dies."

"All right, I can take it from here"—the Lynx.

Which is how, when the Lynx came upon the scene, he saw a dog and a man and an ugly but intelligent quadraped beside the *Wallaby*.

His first blast hit the ship. The man fell.

The quadraped ran, and he burnt it.

The dog thrashed through the port into the ship.

The Lynx brought the flyer about for another pass.

There was another man, circling around from the other side of the ship, where he had been working.

The man raised his hand and there was a flash of light.

Corgo's death-ring discharged its single laser beam.

It crossed the distance between them, penetrated the hull of the flyer, passed through the Lynx's left arm above the elbow, and continued on through the roof of the vehicle.

The Lynx cried, out fought the controls, as Corgo dashed into the *Wallaby*.

Then he triggered the cannon, and again, and again and again, circling, until the *Wallaby* was a smoldering ruin in the middle of a sea of fused sand.

Still did he burn that ruin, finally calling back to Benedick Benedict and asking his one question.

"Nothing"—the reply.

Then he turned and headed back, setting the autopilot and opening the first-aid kit.

"... Then he went in to hit the *Wallaby*'s guns, but I hit him first"—Lynx.

"No"—Benedick.

"What meanest thou 'no'? I was there."

"So was I, for awhile. I *had* to see how he felt."

"And?"

"He went in for the puppy, Dilk, held it in his arms, and said to it, 'I am sorry.'"

"Whatever, he is dead now and we have finished. It is over"—Sandor.

"Yes."

"Yes."

"Let us then drink to a job well done, before we part for good."

"Yes."

"Yes."

And they did.

While there wasn't much left of the *Wallaby* or its Captain, ICI positively identified a synthetic heart found still beating, erratically, amidst the hot wreckage.

Corgo was dead, and that was it.

He should have known what he was up against, and turned himself in to the proper authorities. How can you hope to beat a man who can pick the lock to your mind, a man who dispatched forty-eight men and seventeen malicious alien life-forms, and a man who knows every damn street in the galaxy.

He should have known better than to go up against Sandor Sandor,

Benedick Benedict and Lynx Links. He should, he should have known.

For their real names, of course, are Tisiphone, Alecto and Maegaera. They are the Furies. They arise from chaos and deliver revenge; they convey confusion and disaster to those who abandon the law and forsake the way, who offend against the light and violate the life, who take the power of flame, like a lightning-rod in their two too mortal hands.

# THE DEADLIEST GAME

Uncle Dudley sat in his study, gaze fixed on the blank screen of the set which hung on the wall before him. A rack of rifles hung to his right, flanked by the heads of Cape Buffalo and lion.

"Which was the deadliest of all?" I asked him.

He nodded directly ahead.

I studied the machine closely, saw the silvery ears laid flat along its brow as if it had been attacking when it took the hit. 30.06, I judged.

"Extinct now, aren't they?" I asked.

He fingered the scar on his cheek and nodded.

"Good thing, too," he said.

# KALIFRIKI OF THE THREAD

*Tops of different sorts, and jointed dolls,*
*and fair, golden apples from the clear-voiced Hesperides. . . .*
ORPHEUS THE THRACIAN

This is the story of Kalifriki of the Thread, the Kife, and the toymaker's daughter—in the days of the shifter's flight from the Assassin's Garden, wherefrom it bore a treasure almost without price. But even a Kife can be followed by a Master of the Thread. For the Thread may wander anywhere and need not have an end; the Thread has more sides than a sword; the Thread is subtle in its turnings, perhaps infinite in the variations it may play in the labyrinths of doom, destiny, desire. No one, however, can regard every turning of fate from the Valley of Frozen Time. Attempts to do so tend to terminate in madness.

When the man tracked the Kife to the ice-feik and slew it there, the Kife knew it was in trouble, for it was the third time the man had reached it, the third world upon which he had found it, and the third time that he had slain it, a feat none had ever accomplished before.

Now, five times in a year is the charm for destruction of a Kife, and it seemed that this one suspected as much, for he had managed the pursuit as none had ever done before. The Kife did not understand how the man had located it and reached it, and it realized it was important that it learn as much as possible before the lights went out.

So it stared at the hunter—hammer jawed, high of cheek, dark eyed beneath an oddly sensitive brow, dark hair tied back with a strip of blue cloth. The man still held the trident which had emitted the vibrations that had shattered several of the Kife's major organs, one of the few portable weapons capable of dispatching it from the high dragon form with such ease. The man wore mittens, boots, and a heavy white garment of fur, the hood thrown back now. The midnight sun stood behind his head, and stars glittered like ice moths beside his shoulders.

"And again it is you," the Kife hissed.

The other nodded. The Kife noted a slight irregularity to the man's lower teeth, a small scar beside his right eye, a piece of red thread wrapped about his left wrist.

"What is your name?" the Kife asked him.

"I am called Kalifriki," said the man.

"How do you do what you do?"

For the first time, the man smiled.

"I might ask the same of you," he replied.

"Shifter's secret," the Kife answered.

"To all tricks their trades," said the man.

"And why you?" the Kife asked.

Kalifriki continued to smile. If he replied, the Kife did not hear it. It felt the death seize and squeeze, and as the world went away it saw the man reach to touch the Thread.

Kalifriki watched as the body collapsed, fuming, leaving him with only the green and silver-scaled hide. As the essence emerged, he reached forward and trailed the Thread through it. At that moment, it was difficult to see precisely where the strand began or ended. The man's gaze followed it into the smoky distance, and then he moved.

There is a timeless instant where the world hangs frozen before you. It is map, sculpture, painting; it is not music, words, or wind. You may survey the course of your Thread through its time and space, attempt a rapid adjustment. Then the ice of Time is broken, the flow tugs at the strand of your existence, and you are drawn into the game.

The Kife came to consciousness without breaking the rhythm of its six arms as they chipped delicately at the mineral encrustations. The sky was black above its burnished head, gem-quality stars strewn wherever it looked. Frost came and went upon its body surfaces, dialogue of thermostat and environment.

It had not had time to choose well because of the conversation preceding its departure from the other world. This shifting had almost been a shot in the dark. Almost.

But not quite. Here, there was a little mental trick, a tuning. . . .

Yes.

It could reach back into the larger brain, shielded within a distant cave, which oversaw the operation of the entire robot prospecting team. The brain operated at perhaps 10 percent of capacity. It drowsed. It almost sleepwalked its charges through their chores. But this was sufficient. The job was, in this fashion, adequately performed. If more brain work were needed, it would rise to the occasion. Only—

It infiltrated several circuits, then paused. There was no resistance. Like a rising tide, it flowed farther, ebbed, flowed, ebbed. The processor in the cave drowsed on. The Kife saw that it had long ago set alarms. So long as nothing interfered with the robot team's collection of minerals, it was content to contemplate a randomized hypothesis program it had designed, called "dreaming." Perceiving this, the Kife extended the rest of itself into the thinking space it required.

Now, now there were places beyond the routines, room to manipulate memories and ideas, to reason, to imagine at levels none of the other robots could achieve.

The Kife recalled the man who had slain it a world away. It remembered how the telepathic hunting pack, the Necrolotti, had fled from the man, having sensed a predator more dangerous than themselves. The man Kalifriki was a hunter, a killer, with the ability to traverse the side-by-side lands. It struck the Kife then that the two of them had much in common. But it did not believe that the man was of its own kind. That is, he shifted, but the means he employed bore no resemblance to the Kife's own methods.

It pondered the hunter's motives. Vengeance? For any of the numerous acts which might have gained it the hatred of someone it had underestimated? It thought then of their duel on the world before the ice-feik. No, there was no passion there. If someone wanted vengeance, it had to be some other, which, of course, would make the man a professional at the business.

Recovery? The man might be after it to obtain a thing it had taken. The Kife sought, in its hip compartment, after the item it had transformed considerable dragon-mass to energy in order to transport. Yes, it was intact. It occurred to it then that a mission of both vengeance and recovery was not out of the question. The one certainly did not preclude the other. . . .

But might it be made to? It toyed with the thought. It had died twice now because it had been surprised, and once because it had underestimated its adversary. And it had been surprised and had underestimated because so few creatures were truly a threat to Kife-kind. The Kife were rare in the side-by-side lands because of their ferocity. Each required a large range, and they kept their numbers low by means of quick, lethal, territorial disputes with each other. But beyond another Kife, there wasn't much that a Kife feared. Realistically, the Kife now added Kalifriki to the list. The man was particularly dangerous because the Kife was uncertain as to his motives or the full range of his abilities. Best to devote thought to ensuring against another surprise. But perhaps, just possibly, it should consider the terms of a bargain.

The days passed, barely distinguishable from the nights, and the Kife fell into the rock-harvesting routine. It conveyed the minerals to a truck, troubled only by the occasional seizing up of a limb. Twice, the truck's storage compartment was filled and the Kife drove it to the warehousing area where other robots unloaded it. The second time this was being done a servicing unit approached, fastened leads to sockets beneath its backplates, and performed a series of tests.

"You are due for a major overhaul," it broadcast. "We will send another to tend to your diggings and perform this servicing now."

"I am functioning fine, and I am in the midst of a complicated excavation," the Kife replied. "Do it next time."

"There is some leeway," the servicing unit admitted. "We will do it next time, as you say."

As the Kife headed back to its diggings it pondered a fresh dilemma. It could not permit itself to undergo a major servicing, for the special item it carried would be discovered and perhaps damaged during the course of it.

Nor was the item the sort of thing it could merely hide for a long period of time.

The low temperatures which prevailed in this place would doubtless damage it.

Perhaps it were better simply to flee to another place. Only—

Only *this* might represent a problem. It had heard stories of shifters who could wait in the Valley of Frozen Time, watching another, waiting until that other moved to shift, and then pouncing. The Kife could not perform this feat, though it had often tried. The tale could well be apocryphal, for it had also heard that that way lay madness. Still, it were better not to underestimate the one called Kalifriki.

Therefore, it was better to remain at work. To remain, and to figure a means whereby it might manage the overhaul.

And so it slowed its pace, collecting minerals at half the rate it had earlier, saving wear and tear on its body and postponing another confrontation with a servicing unit. Still, the call took it by surprise.

"Prospector unit, are you damaged?" came the broadcast message.

"I am not," it replied.

"You have been in the field much longer than usual. Is there a problem?"

"The work goes slowly."

"Perhaps the vein has been played out and you should be relocated."

"I think not. I have just uncovered a fresh deposit."

"It has been a long while since you have been overhauled."

"I know."

"Therefore, we are sending a mobile unit to your diggings, to service you in the field."

"That will not be necessary. I will be coming in before long."

"You are beyond the safety limit. We will dispatch a mechanic unit."

The transmission ended. The Kife made a decision. It was difficult to estimate when the service unit would arrive. But it was determined to undergo the servicing rather than flee. This required that it secrete the item. At least, it had discovered a means for preserving it outside its own body for a brief while, with the recent discovery of a cave subjected to geothermal heating by way of a deep pit in its floor.

It departed the work area, traveling to the opening in the side of a fractured ridge. Wisps of steam moved about it, and when the ground rumbled lightly these puffed more forcefully toward the heavens. It flicked on its dome light as it worked its way into the opening and entered the chamber where the pit glowed red-orange and gravel occasionally rattled across the floor. It halted at the rim, staring downward. The level of the bubbling magma seemed somewhat higher, but not so much so as to represent a danger to anything left in the chamber. Nor, according to its sensors, was there an increase in seismic activity since the time it had discovered this opening. Yes, this would be an ideal place to store it for a few hours while—

There came a flash of light from the entranceway, and its sensors read heat overload as one of its forelimbs was fused. Turning, it beheld a humanoid figure in a pressurized suit, light in one hand, pistol in the other. It also noted the strand of red wrapped around the figure's forearm.

"Kalifriki!" It broadcast on the wavelength used for general communication in this place. "Hold your fire or you may defeat your own purposes."

"Oh?" The man answered at the same frequency. "When did you become aware of my purposes?"

"You were not hired simply to destroy me, but to recover something I took, were you not?"

"Actually, I was hired to do both," Kalifriki replied.

"Then it was the Old Man of Alamut who retained you?"

"Indeed. When the Assassins need to hire an assassin they come to Kalifriki."

"Would you consider making a deal?"

"Your life for the vial? No, I'd rather collect the entire fee."

"I was not really offering. I was merely curious," said the Kife, "whether you would accept."

Kalifriki's weapon flared as the Kife charged him.

Two more of its six forearms were melted by the bright discharge, and a large block of sensors was destroyed. This meant very little to the Kife, however, for it felt it could spare considerable function and still remain superior to a human. In fact—

"It was foolish of you to follow me here," it said, as it swung a blow that missed Kalifriki but pulverized a section of the cave wall. "Another robot is even now on the way."

"No," the man replied. "I faked that call to get you to come here."

"You *chose* this place? Why?"

"I was hoping you'd have produced the vial by the time I arrived," he replied, diving to his right to avoid another charge. "Unfortunately, my entry was a trifle premature. Pity."

He fired again, taking out several more sensors and a square foot of insulation. The Kife turned with incredible speed, however, knocking the pistol upward and lunging. Kalifriki triggered the weapon in that position, threw himself to the rear and rolled, dropping his light as he did so. A section of the cave's roof collapsed, half burying the Kife, blocking the entranceway.

Kalifriki rose to his feet.

"I can take a terrific beating in this body," the Kife stated, beginning to dig itself out, "and still destroy you. Whereas the slightest damage to that suit means your end."

"True," said the man, raising the weapon and pointing it once again. "Fortunately for me, that problem is already solved."

He pulled the trigger and the weapon crackled feebly and grew still.

"Oh," said the Kife, wishing his robot features capable of a smile.

Kalifriki holstered the weapon, raised a boulder, and hurled it. It smashed against the Kife's head and rolled off to the side where it fell into the pit. The Kife increased its efforts to uncover itself, working with only two appendages, as the fourth of its arms had been damaged in the rockfall.

Kalifriki continued to hurl rubble as the Kife dug itself out. Charging the man then, the Kife reached for his throat. Its left arm slowed, emitted a grating noise, and grew still. The right arm continued toward Kalifriki, who seized it with both hands and ducked beneath it, springing to the robot's side, then again to its rear. The Kife's treads left the ground in the light gravity of the moonlet. As it was turned and tipped, it felt a push. Then it was falling, the glow rushing up toward it. Before it struck the magma it realized that it had underestimated Kalifriki again.

*       *       *

The Kife regarded the Valley of Frozen Time. As always, it tried to stretch the timeless moment wherein it could consider the physical prospects and some of the sequences available to it. For reasons it did not understand, the hovering process continued. It rejoiced, in that this time it saw the means whereby it might plot and manipulate events to an extent it had never achieved before. This time, not only would it be able to lay a trap for Kalifriki, but it would create one of subtlety and refinement, by a shifter, for a shifter, worthy of a shifter in all respects.

It was able to hold back the flow until almost everything was in place.

As Kalifriki followed the Thread through the placeless time into the timeless place, he was puzzled by its course thereafter, into the world to which he was about to follow the Kife for their final confrontation. It ran through the most unusual pattern he had ever beheld. It was too complicated a thing for him to analyze in detail before its force drew him to the level of events. Therefore, he would have to trust the instincts which had served him so well in the past, regarding the array only in gross, seeking the nexus of greatest menace and providing a lifeline of some sort. Here, he would have chuckled—though laughter, like wind or music, could not manifest in this place. He twisted the strand and whipped it, the hot, red loop following his will, racing away from him among canyons and boulevards of his latest world-to-be. He followed . . .

. . . Setting foot upon the rocky trail which gave way immediately beneath him. He reached for the passing ledge and caught hold, only to have it, too, yield as his weight came upon it. Then, through risen dust, he beheld the long, steep slope below, with several rocky prominences near which he soon must pass. He raised his left arm to protect his face, let his body go limp, and attempted to steer the course of descent with his heels as he reflected upon the prudence of dealing with a great and distant menace while neglecting a smaller but nasty one so close at hand.

When he woke he found himself in a large, canopied bed, his head aching, his mouth dry. The room was dark, but daylight leaked about the edges of shutters on the far wall. He attempted to rise so as to visit the window, but the pain in his right leg told him that a bone could be broken. He cursed in Norman French, Arabic, Italian, and Greek, wiped his brow, fell to musing, and passed back to sleep.

When next he woke it was to the singing of birds and the soft sounds of another's presence in the room. Through slitted eyelids, he beheld a human-sized form advancing upon him, areas of brightness moving at its back. It halted beside the bed, and he felt a cold hand upon his brow, fingertips at the pulse in his wrist. He opened his eyes.

She was blonde and dark eyed with a small chin, her face entirely unlined, expressionless in her attention. It was difficult for him to estimate whether she was tall, short, or somewhere between, in that he was uncertain as to the height of the bed. Behind her stood a gleaming simulacrum of an ape, an upright, bronze-plated chimpanzee, perfectly formed in every detail, bearing a large, dark case in its right hand. On the floor beside it stood a huge, silver tortoise, a covered tray on its back, its head turning slowly from side to side.

Only for an instant did the metallic bodies cause a rush of apprehension, as he recalled his battle with the Kife in its robot form.

Then, "Do not be distressed," he heard her say, in a language close to one of the many he spoke. "We wish only to help you."

"It was a memory come to trouble me," he explained. "Is my leg broken?"

"Yes," she replied, uncovering it. He beheld an ornate swirl of black-and-yellow metal about his lower right leg. It seemed a work of art, such as might be displayed at the Byzantine Court. "Dr. Shong set it," she added, indicating the metal ape, who bowed.

"How long ago was this?" Kalifriki asked.

She glanced at Dr. Shong, who said, "Three days—no, three and a half," in a voice like a brassy musical instrument played low and slow.

"Thank you. How did I come to this place?"

"We found you on one of our walks," Dr. Shong said, "mixed in with the remains of a rock slide, beneath a broken trail. We brought you back here and repaired you."

"What is this place?" he asked.

"This is the home of the toymaker, Jerobee Clockman, my father," the lady told him. "I am Yolara."

The question in her eyes and voice was clear.

"I am called Kalifriki," he said.

"Are you hungry—Kalifriki?" she asked.

He nodded, licking his lips. The smell of the food had become almost unbearable. "Indeed," he replied.

Dr. Shong raised him into a seated position and propped him with pillows while Yolara uncovered the tray and brought it to the bedside. She seated herself on an adjacent chair and offered him the food.

"Still warm," he observed, tasting it.

"Thank Odas," she said, gesturing toward the tortoise. "He bears a heating element in his back."

Odas met his gaze and nodded, acknowledging his thanks with, "My pleasure," rendered in a high, reedy voice, and, "Come Doctor," he continued, "let us leave them to organic converse unless we may be of some further service."

Yolara shook her head slightly and the pair departed.

When he finally paused between mouthfuls, Kalifriki nodded in the direction the pair had taken. "Your father's work?" he inquired.

"Yes," she answered.

"Ingenious, and lovely. Are there more such about?"

"Yes," she answered, staring at him so steadily as to make him uncomfortable. "You will meet more of them, by and by."

"And your father?"

"He is, at the moment, ill. Else he would have overseen your awakening and welcomed you in person."

"Nothing serious, I hope."

She looked away replying, "It is difficult to know. He is a reticent man."

"What of your mother?"

"I never knew her. Father says that she ran away with a Gypsy musician when I was quite young."

"Have you brothers or sisters?"

"None."

Kalifriki continued eating.

"What were you doing in these parts?" she asked after a time. "We are fairly remote from the avenues of commerce."

"Hunting," he said.

"What sort of beast?"

"It is rare. It comes from a place very far from here."

"What does it look like?"

"Anything."

"Dangerous?"

"Very."

"How is it called?"

"Kife."

She shook her head.

"I have never heard of such a creature."

"Just as well. When do you think I might get up?"

"Whenever you possess the strength. Dr. Shong says that the device you wear should protect your leg fully—though you might want a stick, for balance."

He lowered his fork.

"Yes, I would like to try . . . soon," he said.

Shortly, she removed the tray and drew the cover higher, for he had fallen asleep.

When he woke that afternoon, however, he attempted to get up after eating. Dr. Shong rushed to assist him. While Yolara fetched a stick, the ape helped him to dress, performing neurological tests and checking his muscle tone during their frequent pauses. Dr. Shong picked away the Thread that clung to Kalifriki's wrist and tossed it aside. He did not see it drift back several moments later, settling upon his own shoulder, depending toward his hip.

They were halfway across the room when Yolara returned with the stick. Both accompanied him outside then and along the corridor to a balcony, whence he looked down upon a courtyard containing six sheep, two goats, four cows, a bull, and a flock of chickens, all fashioned of metals both dull and gleaming, all seeming to browse and forage, all producing peculiar approximations of the sounds made by their flesh-and-blood models.

"Amazing," Kalifriki stated.

"They are merely decorative machines, not possessed of true intellect," Dr. Shong observed. "They are but child's play for the Master."

"Amazing, nevertheless," said Kalifriki.

Yolara took his arm to steady him as he turned away, heading back inside.

"We'll return you to your room now," she said.

"No," he replied, turning toward a stairwell they had passed on their way up the hall. "I must go farther."

"Not stairs. Not yet," said Dr. Shong.

"Please do as he says," she asked. "Perhaps tomorrow."

"Only if we may walk to the far end of the hallway and back."

She glanced at the metal simian, who nodded.

"Very well. But let us go slowly. Why must you push yourself so hard?"

"I must be ready to face the Kife, anywhere, anytime."

"I doubt you will find it lurking hereabouts."

"Who knows?" he replied.

That evening, Kalifriki was awakened by strains of a wild music, faint in the distance. After a time, he struggled to his feet and out into the corridor. The sounds were coming up from the stairwell. Leaning against the wall, he listened for a long while, then limped back to bed.

The following day, after breakfast, he expressed his desire for a longer walk, and Yolara dismissed Dr. Shong and led Kalifriki down the stairs. Only gradually did he come to understand the enormous size of the building through which they moved.

"Yes," she commented when he remarked upon this. "It is built upon the ruins of an ancient abbey, and over the years it has served as fortress as well as residence."

"Fascinating," he said. "Tell me, I thought that I heard music last night. Was there some sort of celebration?"

"You might call it that," she answered. "My father left his rooms for the first time in a long while, and he summoned his musicians to play for him."

"I am glad that he is feeling better," Kalifriki said. "It was an eerie and beautiful music. I would like to hear it again one day—and perhaps even be present when the musicians perform it."

"They are returned to their crypts, somewhere beneath the floor," she said. "But who knows?"

"They, too, are creations of your father?"

"I think so," she answered. "But I've never really seen them, so it is difficult to say."

They passed an aviary of bronze birds, peculiar blue patina upon their wings, warbling, trilling, crying kerrew and fanning their feathers like turquoise screens. Some of them sat upon iron perches, some on nests of copper. A few of the nests contained silver eggs, while some held tiny birds, unfledged, beaks open to receive flies of foil, worms of tin. The air blurred and flashed about the singers when they moved.

In a garden in a southern courtyard she showed him a silver tree, bearing gleaming replicas of every sort of fruit he had ever seen and many he had not.

Passing up a corridor, Yolara halted before what Kalifriki at first took to be a portrait of herself, wearing a low-cut gown of black satin, a large emerald pendant in the shape of a ship riding the swells of her breasts. But upon closer regard the woman seemed more mature.

"My mother," Yolara said.

"Lovely," Kalifriki replied, "also."

At the end of the corridor was a red metal top as large as himself, spinning with a sad note, balanced upon the point of a dagger. Yolara told him that the top would rotate for ninety-nine years undisturbed.

She stated this so seriously that Kalifriki chuckled.

"I have not heard you laugh nor seen you smile," he said, "the entire time I've been here."

"These things are not fresh to me as they are to you," she replied. "I see them every day."

He nodded.

"Of course," he said.

Then she smiled. She squeezed his hand with a surprisingly firm grip.

The following day they went riding great horned horses of metal—he, mounted upon a purple stallion; she, a green mare. They sat for a long while on a hilltop, regarding the valley, the mountains, and the fortress of Jerobee Clockman. He told her somewhat of himself and her fascination seemed genuine, well beyond the point of courtesy. She seemed awkward when he finally kissed her, and it was not until the slow ride back that she told him she knew no humans other than her father, having met only an occasional merchant, minstrel, or messenger for brief spans of time.

"That seems a very odd way to live," he commented.

"Really?" she replied, "I was beginning to suspect this from reading books in the library. But since they are fiction to begin with, I could never be certain what parts were real."

"Your father seems like a peculiar man," aid Kalifriki. "I would like to meet him."

"I am not sure he is entirely recovered,"she said. "He has been avoiding me somewhat." Riding farther, she added, "I *would* like to see more of the world than this place."

That night when Kalifriki heard the music again he made his way slowly and quietly down the stairs. He paused just outside the hall from which the skirls and wailings flowed. Carefully, then, he lowered himself to his belly and inched forward, so that he could peer around the corner of the entranceway, his eyes but a few centimeters above the floor.

He beheld a metallic quartet with the blasted forms and visages of fallen angels. They were all of them crippled, their gray, gold, and silver bodies scorched, faces pocked, brows antlered or simply horned. Broken bat wings hung like black gossamer from their shoulders. There were two fiddlers, one piper, and one who performed on a rack of crystal bells. The music was stirring, chaotic, mesmerizing, yet somehow cold as a north wind on a winter's night. It was hardly human music, and Kalifriki found himself wondering whether the metal demons composed their own tunes. Behind them, in the floor, were five grave-sized openings, the four surrounding the fifth. Seated before them in a large, dark leather chair was a white-haired fat man whose features Kalifriki could not see, for the man had steepled his fingers and held them before his face. This did, however, draw his attention to a large sapphire ring upon the man's right hand.

When the piece was ended the creatures grew still. The man rose to his feet and took hold of a slim, red lance leaning against the nearest wall. Taking several steps forward, he struck its butt upon a crescent-shaped flagstone. Immediately, the musicians swivelled in place, approached their crypts, and descended into them. When they were below the level of the floor, stone covers slid into place, concealing all traces of their existence.

The man placed the lance upon a pair of pegs on the wall to his left, then crossed the room and went out of a door at its far end. Cautiously, Kalifriki rose, entered, and moved through. At the far door, he saw the form of the man reach the end of a hallway and begin mounting a stair, which he knew from an earlier walk to lead to the building's highest tower. He waited for a long while before taking down the lance. When he struck its butt against the curved stone, the floor opened and he stared down into the crypts.

The demon musicians emerged and stood, raising their instruments, preparing to play. But Kalifriki had already seen all that he cared to. He struck the stone once more and the quartet retired again. He restored the lance to its pegs and departed the hall.

For a long time he wandered the dim corridors, lost in thought. When, at length, he passed a lighted room and saw it to be a library with Dr. Shong seated within, reading, he paused.

"Kalifriki," said the doctor, "what is the matter?"

"I think better when I pace."

"You are still recovering and sleep will serve you more than thought."

"That is not how I am built. When I am troubled I pace and think."

"I was not aware of this engineering peculiarity. Tell me your trouble and perhaps I can help you."

"I have not met my host. Is Jerobee Clockman aware of my presence here?"

"Yes. I report to him every day."

"Oh. Has he any special orders concerning me?"

"To treat your injury, to feed you, and to see that you are extended every courtesy."

"Has he no desire to meet me in person?"

The doctor nodded.

"Yes, but I must remind you that he has not been well himself of late. He is sufficiently improved now, however, that he will be inviting you to dine with him tomorrow."

"Is it true that Yolara's mother ran off with a musician?" Kalifriki asked.

"So I have heard. I was not present in those days. I was created after Yolanda was grown."

"Thank you, Doctor," Kalifriki said, "and good night."

He limped on up to the hallway. When he turned the corner the limp vanished. Farther along the corridor he seated himself upon a bench, rolled up his trouser leg, and removed the elaborate brace he wore. Slowly, he rose to his feet. Then he shifted his weight. Then he smiled.

Later that evening Yolara heard a scratching upon her door.

"Who is it?" she asked.

"Kalifriki. I want to talk to you."

"A moment," she said.

She opened the door. He noted she was still fully clothed in the garments she had worn that day.

"How did you know which door was mine?" she asked him.

"I stepped outside and looked up," he replied. "This was the only room with a light on—apart from mine and the library, where I left Dr. Shong. And I know your father's rooms are in the North Tower."

She granted him her second smile.

"Ingenious," she stated. "What is it you wish to talk about?"

"First, a question—if I may."

"Surely." She stepped aside and held the door wide. "Please come in."

"Thank you."

He took the chair she offered him, then said, "When I awoke several days ago, Dr. Shong told me that I had been found at the scene of my accident three and a half days earlier."

She nodded.

"Were you present when I was discovered?"

"No," she answered. "I heard of you later."

"He used the pronoun 'we,' so I assumed that you were included. Do you know who else was with him?"

She shook her head.

"One of the other simulacra, most likely," she said. "But it might also have been my father. I think not, though, because of his illness."

"Yolara," he said, "something is wrong in this place. I feel that we are both in great danger. You have said that you would like to leave. Very well. Get some things together and I'll take you away, right now, tonight."

Her eyes widened.

"This is so abrupt! I would have to tell my father! I—"

"No!" he said. "He is the one I fear. I believe he is mad, Yolara—and very dangerous."

"He would never harm me," she said.

"I would not be too certain. You resemble your mother strongly, if that portrait be true. In his madness he may one day confuse you with her memory. Then you would be in danger."

Her eyes narrowed.

"You must tell me why you say this."

"I believe that he found your mother after her affair with the Gypsy, and that he killed her."

"How can you say that?"

"I've been to the hall where he keeps his demon quartet. I have opened their crypts—and a fifth one about which they assemble to play. In that fifth one is a skeleton. About its neck is the chain bearing the emerald ship which she is wearing in the painting."

"No! I do not believe it!"

"I am sorry."

"I must see this for myself."

"I would rather you did not."

"To make a charge like that and ask me to accept it on faith is too much," she stated. "Come! It would not be as bad as you may think, for my mother is a stranger to me. I would see this crypt."

"Very well."

He rose to his feet and they passed outside. Reaching into a shadowy alcove, he produced a length of bright steel, which he kept in his right hand as he led the way to the stairs.

"Where did you get the sword?" she asked.

"Borrowed it from a suit of armor downstairs."

"My father is a sick old man. It is hardly necessary to arm yourself against him."

"Then no harm is done," he replied.

"There is even more to this," she said, "isn't there?"

"We shall see," he answered.

When they came to the hall he had visited earlier, Kalifriki took the red lance down from the wall.

"Stand here," he directed, leading her to a place near to the middle crypt, and he stepped back and smote the crescent stone with the lance's butt.

The stones slid back and he hurried to her side. Her scream was not caused by the demons which rose to surround them, however. Looking down into the crypt, Kalifriki beheld the body of a fat, white-haired man whose head had been twisted around so that it faced completely to the rear. The body lay in the embrace of the ancient skeleton from whose neck the emerald ship depended.

"Who did this?" she asked.

"I don't know," Kalifriki said. "He was not there earlier. I don't understand. I—"

He knelt suddenly and reached down into the crypt. He raised the man's right hand.

"What is it?" she asked.

"A ring with a blue stone in it," he said. "He was wearing it earlier this evening. Now he is not."

"His signet," she said. "His seal as Master Toymaker. He would never part with it willingly."

Just then the demon quartet began to play and words became impossible. Lowering the toymaker's hand, Kalifriki picked up the red lance, which he had laid aside. He rose to his feet.

He passed between the crippled demons, and when he came to the crescent stone he struck it with the lance. Immediately, the music died. The performers retired to their crypts. The crypts began to close.

"Now do you at least believe that there is danger?" he said.

"Yes," she replied. "But—"

"Indeed there is," said the fat, white-haired man who entered through the far doorway, a flash of blue upon his right hand. "I heard your scream."

"Father's simulacrum," she said. "He'd often considered making one. I didn't know that he had. It's killed him and taken his place!"

The fat man smiled and advanced.

"Excellent," he said. "Hard to put one over on you, isn't it?"

"Where's its weakest spot?" Kalifriki asked her, raising the blade.

"Slightly below the navel," she answered, and he lowered the point of the weapon.

"Really," the simulacrum said, "beneath this guise of flesh you will find that you face metal against metal. It would take a good arm and a good blade to puncture me."

Kalifriki smiled.

"Shall we find out?" he asked.

The simulacrum halted.

"No, let's not," it replied. "It seems an awful waste of talent."

Its gaze moved past them then. Kalifriki turned his head, to see Dr. Shong enter through the other door.

"Doctor!" Yolara cried. "He's killed Father and taken his place!"

"I know," the ape replied, and she stared as he grinned. "He had an offer he couldn't refuse."

"My leg," Kalifriki said, "is not broken. I believe that it was, but it is healed now. That would have taken considerably longer than the few days you said it had been. I think I've been here for several weeks, that you've kept me drugged—"

"Very astute," Dr. Shong observed. "Also, correct. We had a special request of the late Jerobee Clockman. He did not finish the final adjustments until only a little while ago."

"And then you killed him!" Yolara cried.

"Just so," said the simian, nodding, "though his simulacrum did the actual physical business. But it is lèse majesté to call us killers in the presence of assassin royalty such as your guest. Isn't that right, Kalifriki?"

"Come closer, ape," he said.

"No. You seem to have figured out everything but why. So take the final step and tell me: What was Clockman's last creation—the thing he assembled that long while you slept?"

"I . . . I don't know," Kalifriki said.

"Come in!" Dr. Shong called out.

Kalifriki watched as his own double entered the room, a sword in its hand.

"Built according to your specifications," the ape stated. "Considerably stronger, though."

"I thought the Kife had fled."

His doppelganger bowed.

"You were incorrect," it told him.

Kalifriki slammed the butt of the lance against the crescent stone, Yolara cried, "Killer!" and rushed toward the portly simulacrum, while the doppelganger advanced upon Kalifriki, the point of its blade describing a small circle in the air.

"By all means, let us dance," said his double, smiling, as the musicians took up their instruments and tuned them. The ape laughed, and Yolara cried out as she was thrown across the room to strike her head upon the hearthstone.

Snarling, Kalifriki turned away from his advancing double and, with a quick leap and an even quicker lunge, drove his blade into the simulacrum of Jerobee Clockman with such force that its point passed through its abdomen and protruded from its lower back. The weapon was wrenched from Kalifriki's grip as the figure suddenly raised both arms to shoulder height, extending them out to the sides, twisted its head into a bizarre position, and began the execution of a series of dance steps. With this, a small ratcheting noise commenced in the vicinity of its midsection.

Turning then, swinging the red lance in a circle, Kalifriki succeeded in parrying his double's attack. Retreating, the music swirling wildly about him, he ventured a glance at Yolara, discovering that she still had not moved. The glance almost cost him an ear, but he parried the thrust and riposted with a double-handed blow of the lance, which would have cracked a human's ribs but only slowed the simulacrum for a moment. During that movement, however, he struck it between the eyes with the butt of the weapon and, reversing it with a spin, jabbed for the abdomen with the lance's point. The attack was parried, though; and seeming to shake off all its effects, his doppelganger pressed him again. In the distance, he heard Dr. Shong chuckle.

Then he began to retreat once again, turning, passing behind the simulacrum of Jerobee Clockman—which was now dancing in extreme slow motion and emitting periodic clanging sounds. As it shifted its weight from left foot to right, he kicked it hard and it toppled in that direction, falling directly in the path of the double. Laughing, the doppelganger leaped over the twitching figure to continue its attack.

Kalifriki passed among the musicians then, dodging the fiddlers' bows, sidestepping to avoid collision with the bell rack. And his double came on, stamping, thrusting, parrying, and riposting. When he reached the position toward which he had been headed, Kalifriki pretended to stumble.

Predictably, the other attacked. Continuing his drop onto one knee and turning his body, Kalifriki executed a downward, rowing stroke with the lance, which caught the simulacrum behind the knees, sweeping it off balance. Springing to his feet then, Kalifriki struck it between the shoulder blades and rushed away as it toppled into the opened crypt.

Slamming the butt of the lance against the crescent stone silenced the musicians immediately, and they tucked away their instruments, retreating toward their own crypts. Rushing among them, Kalifriki raised the lance once more to club down his doppeganger, should it try to emerge before the crypt sealed itself. It looked up and met his gaze.

"Fool!" it cried. "You guard me while the Kife flees!"

"Dr. Shong?" Kalifriki exclaimed, suddenly knowing it to be true.

Whirling, he hurled the lance at the running ape form, just as the crypt's lid slid shut above the simulacrum. The red shaft struck the hurrying figure's left shoulder with a terrific clang as it was about to cross the threshold of the nearer door. The impact turned it completely around. Miraculously, the ape did not fall, but teetered a moment, regained its balance, then rushed across the room toward the fireplace, left arm hanging useless.

Arriving before Kalifriki could take more than three paces, Dr. Shong knelt and reached, right hand fastening about Yolara's throat.

"Stop!" cried the ape. "I can decapitate her with a single movement! And I will if you come any nearer!"

Kalifriki halted, regarding the smear of blood on her temple.

"There was a time when I thought she might be a simulacrum," he said.

"I had toyed with the notion," said the other, "of replacing her with a version designed to kill you after you'd fallen in love with it. But I lack sufficient knowledge of human emotions. I was afraid it might take too long, or that it might not happen. Still, it would have been a delightful way of managing it."

Kalifriki nodded.

"What now?" he asked. "We seem stalemated here. Except that she does not appear to be breathing. If this is true, your threat is meaningless."

He began to take another step.

"Stop!" The Kife rose slowly, clasping her to its breast with forearm and elbow, its hand still at her throat. "I say she still lives. If you wish to gamble with her life, come ahead."

Kalifriki paused, his eyes narrowing. In the dim light, he saw the Thread upon the shoulder and waist of the simulacrum. Slowly, he raised his left arm. The Thread was also wrapped about his wrist. It extended back over his left shoulder. It extended forward. It joined with that segment of itself which hung upon the metal ape. It passed beyond, out of the door of the room. As Kalifriki flexed his fingers, it grew taut. As he continued the movement, the Kife turned its head, bewildered, as if looking for something in several directions. When Kalifriki closed his hand into a fist, the segments of Thread which had been looped about the Kife vanished from sight, slicing their ways into the metal body.

Moments later, the simulacrum collapsed, falling to the floor in three pieces. It had been decapitated and the torso separated from the legs at the waist. Yolara lay sprawled across its midsection, and its head rolled toward Kalifriki.

As Kalifriki stepped past it, it addressed him: "I lied. She is not breathing."

Kalifriki halted, picked up the head, and drew back his arm to hurl it against the nearest wall.

"But she may breathe again," it said, lips twisting into a smile, "if you but use your head."

"What do you mean?" Kalifriki asked. "Talk!"

"That which I stole from the Old Man of the Mountain—the Elixir of Life—it would revive her."

"Where is it?"

"I will tell you, in return for your promise that you will not destroy me."

Kalifriki turned the face away from his so that the Kife would not see him smile.

"Very well," he answered. "You have my word. Where is it?"

"Hidden among the gold and silver fruit in the bowl on the table beside the far door."

Kalifriki crossed the room, searched the bowl.

"Yes," he said at last, removing the small vial.

He unstoppered it and sniffed it. He placed his finger over the bottle's mouth, inverted it, returned it to an upright position. He placed upon his tongue the single droplet which clung to his fingertip.

"It is odorless and tasteless," he observed, "and I feel nothing. Are you certain this is not some trick?"

"Do not waste it, fool! It takes only a drop!"

"Very well. You had better be telling the truth."

He returned to Yolara's side and drew downward upon her chin to open her mouth. Then he removed another drop from the vial and placed it upon her tongue.

Moments later she drew a deep breath and sighed. Shortly thereafter, her eyelids fluttered and opened.

"What," she asked him, "has happened?"

"It is over," he said, raising her and holding her. "We live, and my job is finished."

"What was your job?" she inquired.

"To recover this vial," he explained, "and to bring back the head of its thief."

The brazen ape-head began to wail.

"You have tricked me!" it cried.

"You have tricked yourself," he replied, stoppering the bottle and pocketing it, helping Yolara to her feet.

"You are in charge here now," he told her. "If the memories are too bad for you, come with me and I will try to give you some better ones."

Now, as he led her through the Valley of Frozen Time, Kalifriki halted in a place that was sculpture, painting, map. He squeezed Yolara's arm and gestured at the incredible prospect which lay before them.

She smiled and nodded, just as the head of the Kife, which Kalifriki bore in his left hand, opened its mouth and bit him. He would have cursed, save that this was not a place of words (nor music, nor wind). He dropped the head, which rolled away, and he raised his hand to his mouth. The Kife's head fell into a crevice, where it rolled a considerable distance before coming to rest in precarious balance at the top of another incline, its position masked in darkest shadow. Search though he did, Kalifriki never found it, and had to settle for only half his pay, for the Old Man of Alamut is a harsh taskmaster. Still, this was not an inconsiderable amount, and with it he took Yolara on an amazing odyssey, to Byzantium, Venice, Cathay—but that is another story. The while, the Kife went mad of contemplating the turnings of fate; its brazen head fell from the ledge where it opened its jaw to scream, though this was not a place of screaming (nor music, nor wind); and it rolled the side-beside slopes down to a lane near Oxford, where a Franciscan named Roger Bacon found it. That, too, is another story. The Thread is always arriving and departing. It may wander anywhere and need not have an end.

# COME BACK TO
# THE KILLING GROUND,
# ALICE, MY LOVE

## 1

All the death-traps in the galaxy, and she has to walk into mine. At first I didn't recognize her. And when I did I knew it still couldn't be right, her, there, with her blindfolded companion in the sandals and dark kimono. She was dead, the octad broken. There couldn't be another. Certain misgivings arose concerning this one. But I had no choice. Does one ever? There are things to do. Soon she will move. I will taste their spirits.

Play it again, Alices. . . .

## 2

She came to him at his villa in Constantinople, where, in loose-fitting garments, trowel in hand, spatulate knife at belt, he was kneeling amid flowers, tending one of his gardens. A servant announced her arrival.

"Master, there is a lady at the gate," the old man told him, in Arabic.

"And who could that be?" the gardener mused, in the same tongue.

"She gave her name as Alyss," the servant replied, and added, "She speaks Greek with a foreign accent."

"Did you recognize the accent?"

"No. But she asked for you by name."

"I should hope so. One seldom calls on strangers for any good purpose."

"Not the Stassinopoulos name. She asked for Kalifriki."

"Oh, my. Business," he said, rising and passing the trowel to the man, dusting himself off. "It's been a long time."

"I suppose it has, Sir."

"Take her to the lesser courtyard, seat her in the shade, bring her tea, sherbet, melons—anything else she may desire. Tell her I'll be with her shortly."

"Yes, Sir."

Repairing within, the gardener removed his shirt and bathed quickly, closing his dark eyes as he splashed water over his high cheekbones, then his chest, his arms. After drying, he bound his dark hair with a strip of golden cloth, located an embroidered white shirt with full sleeves within his wardrobe, donned it.

In the courtyard at a table beside the fountain, where a mosaic of dolphins sported beneath waters which trickled in small rivers from a man-sized Mt. Olympus, he bowed to the expressionless lady who had studied his approach. She rose slowly to her feet. Not tall, he observed, a full head shorter than himself, dark hair streaked with white, eyes very blue. A pale scar crossed her left cheek, vanished into the hair above her ear.

"Alyss, I believe?" he inquired, as she took his hand and raised it to her lips.

"Yes," she replied, lowering it. "Alice." She gave it a slightly different accenting than his man had done.

"That's all?"

"It is sufficient for my purposes, sir." He did not recognize her accent either, which annoyed him considerably.

He smiled and took the chair across from her as she reseated herself. He saw that her gaze was fixed upon the small star-shaped scar beside his right eye.

"Verifying a description?" he inquired as he poured himself a cup of tea.

"Would you be so kind as to let me see your left wrist?" she asked.

He shook back the sleeve. Her gaze fell almost greedily upon the red thread that was wrapped about it.

"You are the one," she said solemnly.

"Perhaps," he replied, sipping the tea. "You are younger than you would have your appearance indicate."

She nodded. "Older, also," she said.

"Have some of the sherbet," he invited, spooning two dishfuls from the bowl. "It's quite good."

## 3

I steady the dot. I touch the siphon and the bone. There, beyond the polished brass mirror, sipping something cool, her remarking in Greek that the day is warm, that it was good to find a shaded pausing place such as this caravanserai, my doorstep, in which to refresh themselves—this does not deceive me in its calculated nonchalance. When they have finished and risen, they will not head back to the street with its camels, dust, horses, cries of the vendors, I know that. They will turn, as if inadvertently, in the direction of this mirror. Her and the monk. Dead ladies, bear witness. . . .

## 4

"I can afford you," she told him, reaching for a soft leather bag on the flagging beside her chair.

"You precede yourself," he responded. "First I must understand what it is that you want of me."

She fixed him with her blue gaze and he felt the familiar chill of the nearness of death.

"You kill," she said simply, "Anything, if the price is right. That is what I was told."

He finished his tea, refilled their cups.

"I choose the jobs I will accept," he said. "I do not take on everything that is thrust at me."

"What considerations govern your choices?" she asked.

"I seldom slay the innocent," he replied, "by my definitions of innocence. Certain political situations might repel me—"

"An assassin with a conscience," she remarked.

"In a broad sense, yes."

"Anything else?"

"Madam, I am something of a last resort," he responded, "which is why my services are dear. Any simple cutthroat will suffice for much of what people want done in this area. I can recommend several competent individuals."

"In other words, you prefer the complicated ones, those offering a challenge to your skills?"

"'Prefer' is perhaps the wrong word. I am not certain what is the right one—at least in the Greek language. I do tend to find myself in such situations, though, as the higher-priced jobs seem to fall into that category, and those are normally the only ones I accept."

She smiled for the first time that morning, a small, bleak thing.

"It falls into that category," she said, "in that no one ever succeeded in such an undertaking as I require. As for innocence you will find none here. And the politics need be of no concern, for they are not of this world."

She nibbled a piece of melon.

"You have interested me," he said.

## 5

At last, they rise. The monk adjusts the small bow he bears and places his hand upon her shoulder. They cross the refreshment area. They are leaving! No! Could I have been wrong? I realize suddenly that I had wanted it to be her. That part of me I had thought fully absorbed and transformed is suddenly risen, seeks to command. I desire to cry out. Whether it be "Come!" or "Run!" I do not know. Yet neither matters. Not when it is not a part of her. Not when they are departing.

But.

At the threshold, she halts, saying something to her companion. I hear only the word "hair."

When she turns back there is a comb in her hand. She moves suddenly toward the dot manifestation which hangs brightly upon the wall to her right. As she drops her veil and adjusts her red tresses I become aware that the color is unnatural.

## 6

"Not of this world," he repeated. "Whence, then, may I inquire?"

"Another planet, far across the galaxy from here," she replied. "Do these terms mean anything to you?"

"Yes," he answered. "Quite a bit. Why have you come?"

"Pursuit," she said.

"Of the one you would have me slay?"

"At first it was not destruction but rescue that we sought."

"'We'?"

"It took eight of me to power the devices which brought us here, an original and seven copies. Clones."

"I understand."

"Really? Are you, yourself, alien to this place?"

"Your story is the important one just now. You say there are eight of you about?"

She shook her head.

"I am the last," she stated. "The other seven perished in attempting the task I must complete."

"Which are you, the original or a clone?"

She laughed. Then, abruptly, her eyes were moist, and she turned away.

"I am a copy," she said, at length.

"And you still live," he remarked.

"It is not that I did not try, I went in after all of the others failed. I failed, too. I was badly injured. But I managed to escape—barely."

"How long ago was this?"

"Almost five years."

"A long time for a copy to stay alive."

"You know?"

"I know that many Cultures which employ clones for a particular job tend to build in some measure against their continued existence once the job is done, a kind of insurance against the . . . embarrassment . . . of the original."

"Or the replacement, yes. A small poison sac at the base of the skull in my case. I believe my head injury did something to nullify its operation."

She turned her head and raised her hair. There were more scars upon her neck.

"He thinks I am dead," she went on. "I am certain. Either from the encounter or from the passage of time. But I know the way in, and I learned something of the place's rules."

"I think you had better tell me about this person and this place," Kalifriki said.

## 7

The Alices are singing their wordless plaint. Now and forever. I build another wall, rings set within it, chains threaded through them. For all of them. Come back, come back, Alice, my last. It *is* you. It must be. Make the movement that will commit you, that will transport you. Else must I reach forth the siphon, as I have so many times. Even if it be not you, I must now. You resurrect an older self.

"Good," she says, putting away her comb, turning toward the door.

No!

Then she turns back, lips set in a tight line, raising her hand, touching the reflecting surface. A moment, as she locates the pulses, passes her hand through the activation sequence.

As her fingers penetrate the interface the bowman is suddenly behind her, laying his hand upon her shoulder. No matter. He may bear an interesting story within him.

## 8

"Aidon," she said. "He is Aidon."

"The one you seek?" Kalifriki asked. "The one you would have me kill?"

"Yes," she said. Then, "No. We must go to a special place," she finished.

"I don't understand," he said. "What place?"

"Aidon."

"Is Aidon the name of a man or the name of a place?"

"Both," she said. "Neither."

"I have studied with Zen masters and with Sufi sages," he said, "but I can make no sense of what you are saying. What is Aidon?"

"Aidon is an intelligent being. Aidon is also a place. Aidon is not entirely a man. Aidon is not such a place as places are in this world."

"Ah," he said. "Aidon is an artificial intelligence, a construct."

"Yes," she said. "No."

"I will stop asking questions," he stated, "for now. Just tell me about Aidon."

She nodded once, sharply.

"When we came to this system looking for Nelsor," she began, "the ship's instruments showed that something on this planet had gained control of a cosmic string, circumnavigating the universe, present since its creation. We dismissed this at the time, for it was actually one of the tiny holes of blackness—an object supercollapsed to an unworldly point, also present since the creation—that we were seeking. For this would lead us to Nelsor's vessel, from which a damage-pulse had come to us. We use the black objects to power our way through other spaces. Do you understand?"

"That part, yes," he said. "I don't understand who or what Nelsor is, let alone Aidon."

"They are the same," she said, "now. Nelsor was her—the original Alice's—lover, mate, consort, husband-relation. He piloted the vessel which had the trouble, and they came down in this general area of your planet. I believe that Aidon took control of the vessel—and of Nelsor as well—and caused the landing here, and that this is what triggered the damage-pulse."

She glanced at him.

"Aidon," she said, "is difficult to explain. Aidon began as one of those small, black, collapsed objects which make a hole in space. We use them as specialized devices. Bypassing space for distant travel is one of the ends for which they are employed. They are set up for most of their jobs—travel included—by swirling a field of particles about them at high velocity. These fields are impressed with considerable data for the jobs they are to perform. The field is refreshed at its outer perimeter, and the data is replicated and transferred outward in waves as the inner perimeter is absorbed. So there is a matching informed particle-feed to equal the interior information loss. The device draws on the radiation from the collapsed object for power and is programmed to be self-regulating in this regard."

"I understand what you are saying," Katifriki replied, "and possibly even where this is going now. Such a thing becomes intelligent—sentient?"

"Generally. And normally their input is well controlled," she answered.

"But not always?"

She smiled, momentarily. Kalifriki poured more tea.

"Of all categories of employment, there is less control over the input of those used in space travel," she responded, "and I suppose that the very act of traversing the peculiar domains they must has its odd results. The experts are not in agreement on this. One thing which definitely affects such a construct, however, is that for certain areas of space passage the pilot must maintain constant direct communication with it. This requires a special sort of person for pilot, one possessing the ability to reach it mentally—a telepathic individual with special training for working with constructed intelligences. Such a relationship will infect the construct to some extent with the operator's personality."

She paused for a drink of tea.

Then, "Sometimes such constructs become disordered, perhaps from staring too long into the heart of darkness between the stars. In a human we would call it madness. The vessels often simply vanish when this happens. Other times, if it occurs in known space there may be a signature pulse indicating the vehicle's destruction. As with Aidon, they may digest their operators' minds first—an overlay that could enhance the madness to a kind of schizophrenia."

"So Aidon ate Nelsor," said Kalifriki, raising his cup, "and brought the vessel to Earth."

She nodded.

"Whatever had grown twisted within him twists whatever it acquires. It twisted Nelsor's feelings for Alice. He destroyed the four Alices one by one, so that he might know them in their pain. For this is how he learned love, as a kind of pain, from the twistings of darkness that damaged him, to the pain of Nelsor's passing. Not totally alien, perhaps, for there are people who love through pain, also."

Kalifriki nodded.

"But how do you know that this is the case with Aidon?" he asked.

"Alice was also a pilot," she said, "and as such, a sensitive. She had a strong bond of this sort with Nelsor. All of her clones shared her ability. When she brought the final three of us and came seeking him—for he seemed still alive, but somehow changed—this was the means by which we located the entrance to the blister universe he had created."

"He has his own world?"

"Yes. He formed it and retreated to it quickly after coming to this place. And there he dwells, like a trapdoor spider. Alice entered and was destroyed by him. We all felt it happen. Then, one by one, the three of us who remained essayed the passage—each succeeding in penetrating a little farther into the place because of her predecessor's experience. But each of the others was destroyed in the process. I was the last, so I knew the most of how his world operated. It is a kind of slow killing machine, a torture device. I was injured but was able to escape."

She brushed at her scar.

"What could you have hoped to accomplish?" he asked. "Why did you keep going in when you saw what he was up to?"

"We hoped to reach a point where we could communicate with that part of him which is still Nelsor. Then, by linking minds, we had thought to be able to strengthen him to overcome Aidon. We hoped that we could save him."

"I thought he was dead—physically, that is."

"Yes, but in that place, with that power, he would have been godlike, if he could have been freed even briefly and gained control of Aidon again. He might have been able to reconstitute his body and come away in it."

"But . . ." Kalifriki said.

"Yes. Aidon proved so much stronger than what remained of Nelsor that I saw it could never be. There is no choice now but to destroy Aidon."

"Why not just let him be if he's retreated to his own universe?"

"I can hear their cries—Nelsor's, and those of the ravished souls of my sisters. There must be some release for what remains of them all. And there are others now. The entrance to his underworld lies hidden in a public house on a trade route. When a sufficiently sensitive individual enters there, Aidon becomes aware of it, and he takes that person to him. He has developed a taste for life stories along with his pain He extracts them both, in a kind of slow feasting. But there is more. You are aware of the nature of such objects. You must realize that one day he will destroy this world. He leeches off it. Eventually, he will absorb it all. It will hover forever in a jumble of images on his event horizon, but it will be gone."

"You would hire me to destroy a black hole?"

"I would hire you to destroy Aidon."

Kalifriki rose and paced through several turns.

"There are many problems," he said at last.

"Yes," she replied, drinking her tea.

## 9

... Passing through the mirror into my world, hand emerging from a lake, slim white arm upthrust as if holding the sword in that story the Frenchman had. And hesitation. Coy, her return, as if waiting for me to reach out, to hand her through. Perhaps I shall. There is amusement to be had in this. Come, siphon . . . .

Fading, faded, gone. The arm. She wavered and went out, like a flame in a sudden draft. Gone from beneath the lake, behind the mirror. Along with the blind monk. To what realm transported? Gone from the inn, from my world, also.

But wait. . . .

## 10

"You are asking me to pit my thread, in some way, against a singularity," he said.

"How is it that your string resembles a piece of red thread?" she asked.

"I require a visible appearance for it locally," he said, "to have something to work with. I do not like your idea."

"As I understand these things, your thread goes all the way around the universe. It was this that we detected on our approach. There are fundamental physical reasons why it can never have an end. A singularity could not bite a piece out of it. The antigravity of its pressure would exactly cancel the gravity of the energy. So there would be no net change in the gravity of the black hole which tried to take it in. The hole would not grow in size, and the situation would remain static in that regard. But you would have Aidon hooked with the string passing through him. Could you then transfer him to another universe?"

Kalifriki shook his head.

"No matter what I might do with him that way, the hole would remain permanently attached to the thread, and that is unacceptable. It might cause unusual loopings. No. I will not match two such fundamental objects directly against each other. If I am to be retained to destroy Aidon I will do it my way, Alice. Aidon, as I understand it, is not really the black hole itself, but a self sustaining, programmed accretion disc which has suffered irreparable damage to its information field. That could be the point of my attack."

"I don't see how you would proceed with it."

"I see only one way, but it would mean that you would not be able to return to your home world."

She laughed.

"I came here prepared to die in this enterprise," she said. "But, since the black hole cannot be destroyed and you will not attempt shifting it to another universe, I need to know what your attack will involve—as further disruption of the information will involve Nelsor as well as Aidon."

"Oh? You said you'd given up on Nelsor, that what was left of him was ruined and merged with Aidon, that that only course remaining was to destroy the entire construct."

"Yes, but your talk of my not returning home implied that you wanted my ship or something from it. That could only be its singularity drive."

"You're right."

"So you intend somehow to use one black hole against the other. And it could work. Such a sudden increase in mass without a compensating acceleration of the field could result in its absorbing the field faster than the field could replicate itself. You would make the hole eat Aidon and Nelsor both."

"Correct."

"I don't see how you could get close enough to do it. But that is, as you say, your problem. I might be able to penetrate Aidon's world to a point where I could communicate with Nelsor mentally and make a final effort to save him, to complete my mission. I want you to hold off on doing what you contemplate until I've tried."

"That would narrow our safety margin considerably. Why this sudden change of heart?"

"It was because I saw the possibility when I began to understand your plan. Bringing another singularity into that place might perturb Aidon to the point where he may lose some control over what he holds of Nelsor. If there is any chance he might still be freed . . . I must try, though I be but an image of his lady. Also, my telepathic bond with him may be stronger than that of any of the other six."

"Why is that?" Kalifriki asked.

She reddened and looked away. She raised her cup and lowered it again without drinking.

"Nelsor took no sexual pleasure with the clones," she said, "only with the original Alice. One time, however, I was in her quarters seeking some navigational notes we had discussed while she was occupied in another part of the vessel. He came seeking her and mistook me for his lady. He had been working hard and I felt sorry for him in his need for release. So I assumed her role and let him use me as he would her, giving him what pleasure I could. We enjoyed each other, and he whispered endearments and later he went away to work again. It was never discovered, and I've never spoken of it till now. But I have heard that such things can strengthen the bond."

"So you care for him in a somewhat different way than the others," Kalifriki said, "as he did for you, whatever the circumstances."

"Yes," she replied, "for I am her equal in all ways, not just genetically, having known him as the other six did not."

"So you would undertake an even greater risk for him?"

"I would."

"And if you fail?"

"I'd still want you to destroy him, for mercy's sake."

"And if you succeed, and the world is coming apart about us? It may be harder to escape under those circumstances. I don't really know."

She reached for her bag.

"I brought all the gold bars I could carry comfortably. There are a great many more aboard my vessel. "I'll give them all to you—"

"Where is your vessel?"

"Beneath the Sea of Marmara. I could summon it, but it were better to go out in a boat and simply raise it for a time."

"Let me see how much gold you have in the sack."

She hefted it and passed it to him.

"You're stronger than you look," he said as he accepted it. He opened it then and examined its contents. "Good," he said. "But we will need more than this."

"I told you you can have it all. We can go and get it now."

"It would not be for me, but for the purchase of equipment," he told her. "This bag and another like it should suffice for that, if I take the job."

"There will still be ample metal left for your fee," she said. "Much more than this. You *will* take the job, won't you?"

"Yes, I will."

She was on her feet.

"I will get you the gold now. When can we leave for Ubar?"

"Ubar? That is where Aidon has opened his office?"

"Yes. It lies near an Arabian trade route."

"I know the place. We cannot go there immediately, however. First, there are preparations to be made."

"Who are you really?" she asked him. "You know too much. More than the culture of this world contains."

"My story is not part of the bargain," he said. "You may rest now. My servant will show you to a suite. Dine with me this evening. There are more details that I wish to know concerning Aidon's world. Tomorrow I would inspect your vessel and obtain the additional gold we will need for a trip we must take."

"Not to Ubar?"

"To India, where I would obtain a certain diamond of which I have heard, of a certain perfection and a certain shape."

"That will be a long journey."

"Not really. Not as I shall conduct it."

"By some employment of the string? You can do that?" He nodded. "How did you gain such control over a thing like that?"

"As you said, Alice, I know too much."

## 11

. . . But wait. Now they are back. Her arm still extends above the waters of my lake. Likely but some trick of the interface, some roving particle's hit within the nanocircuitry, that fogged the transfer. They come now into my world, wet white garment clinging to the well-remembered contours of her form—nipples above their orbs, curves of hip and back and buttocks, shoulders, thighs—ripe for the delicate raking of claws. And the man, he is more muscular than first I thought. A lover, then, perhaps. Then to see those muscles flex when the skin has been removed to the waist . . . there is that to fill the air with the music of outcry and weeping. Dead Alices, give them a song as they come ashore, of welcome to their new home, through crystal forest beneath a sky of perfect blue. How long from that then to this now? Centuries. As entropy here rockets to the sharp curves of my architecture, the contours of its form rake of my desire. The arrow of time passes and returns down sharp geodesics, pierces memory to the rage, impales rage that the love may flow. Why did you come back, form of hatred and its opposite? You will tell me, upon the ground I have prepared for you, tell, to the chorus of your sisters beneath a bleeding sky. But we must not rush these things, Alice, my last. For when you are done the ages will be long, the glory of your exposed architecture a piece of frozen time, distributed in monument about the crying landscape. Come back to the Killing Ground, Alice, my love. I've many a present to gift you there, the entire universe our angel of record against the long dark time. Set foot upon the shore and find your way. The ladies sing your nuptials in the Place of Facing Skulls.

## 12

Kalifriki dropped the anchor and struck the sails of their boat, as Alice moved to the bow and began singing in a lilting language he did not understand. The beginning morning's light touched the waves with flecks of gold and a cool breeze stirred her zebra hair upon her shoulder. He leaned against the gunwale and watched her as he listened. After a time the boat rose with a long, slow swell, subsiding only gradually. Her voice went out across the water, vibrated within it, and suddenly her eyes widened, reminding him of one of the Acropolis Maidens, as the water roiled to starboard and a curving, burnished form surfaced there like the back of some great, mysterious sea creature rising to meet the day.

He stirred himself, fetching a pole with a hook affixed to its end to grapple them closer to the bronzed surfaces. He glanced back at her before he used it, and she nodded. Reaching then, he caught it within one of the stair-like projections which had rippled into being upon its side, leading up to a hatch. He drew them nearer until he felt the scraping of their hull upon metal.

"Grown, not fabricated," he remarked.

"Yes," she replied, moving forward.

He held the grapple until she had crossed over to the alien vessel's companionway. Then he set it aside and followed.

By the time he came up behind her she had the hatch open. She entered and he looked down into a lighted interior, down to a soft green deck which might be covered with tailored grasses, furniture built into niches in contoured walls without corners.

Entering, he descended. Barely visible scenes flashed across surfaces he passed. A small vibration communicated itself to him, through the floor, through the air. They passed rooms both bright and muted, traversing corridors with windows that seemed to open upon alien landscapes—one, where red, treelike forms scrambled across an ebony landscape beneath a double sun causing him to pause and stare, as if remembering.

At length, she halted before a tan bulkhead, manipulated a hatch set within it, flung it open. Stack upon stack of small golden bars lay within the revealed compartment, gleaming as through a hint of green haze.

"Take all you want," she said.

"I want another bag such as the first, for the transaction of which I spoke," he told her, "and another after that for the first half of my fee. I will claim the final payment when the job is done. But we can collect these on the way out. I wish to view the source of the ship's power now."

"Come this way."

He followed her farther into the vessel's interior, coming at last to a circular chamber where watery visions appeared around the walls, including one of the underside of his boat, off to his right.

"This is the place," Alice said.

Kalifriki did not see what she did, but suddenly the floor became transparent and far beneath his feet it seemed that something pulsed darkly. There came a dizziness and he felt drawn toward the center of the room.

"Open it," he said.

"Move back two paces, first."

He obeyed. Then the floor opened before him, the section where he had been standing dropping to become three steps leading down to a narrow well. Its forward wall housed a clear compartment within which he seemed to feel the presence of something drawing him. He descended the steps.

"What are the dangers? What are the safeguards?" he asked.

"You are safe where you are," she answered. "I can open the panel and give you a closer look."

"Go ahead."

It slid back and he stared for a moment.

"How would you manipulate it?" he asked.

"Forcefield pressures against its container," she replied.

He shook out a strand of the thread from his wrist, snaked it about the opening several times, withdrawing it slowly on each occasion.

"All right, I can work with this," he said a little later. "Seal it in again."

The compartment closed before him.

". . . Pure carbon crystal lattice, antigrav field webbed throughout," he said as to himself. "Yes. I saw something like this managed once, a long time ago." He turned and mounted the stair. "Let's go in and get the gold. Then we can head back."

They withdrew the way they had come in, returning to the boat with two heavy sacks. The vessel's hatch secured, she sang it back beneath the waves. The sun stood now fully risen, and birds dipped toward the waters about them as he weighed the anchor and set the sails.

"Now?" she said.

"Breakfast," he replied.

"Then?" she asked.

"India," he said.

## 13

Now the monk has fully entered my world, following her. Suddenly, things are no longer as they have been. Things are no longer right. Things seem to collapse like strange wave functions about him as he passes. Yet nothing seems really changed. What has he brought with him into my world, that I feel uneasy at his presence here? Is it a kind of turbulence? Is it that I am running faster? It would be hard to tell if my spin state were affected. Where did she find him? Why did she bring him? An aged tree reaches the end of its growth and shatters as he goes by it. I do not believe I like this man, shuffling unseeing through my gardens of crystal and stone. Yet perhaps I shall like him a great deal when the time comes. Such feelings are often close akin. In the meantime, it is always amusing to observe when a new thing comes to this place. My *arbor decapitant* awaits, but fifty paces ahead. She knows of it, of course. All of the Alices learned of it, the first the hard way. Yet it is good sport to see such things do their business. Yes, he will be all right. New blood must be brought to the game from time to time, else there is no bite to it. I will let them play through, to the end of her knowledge. . . .

## 14

In Maharajah Alamkara's palace of white marble they were feasted and entertained with music and dance, for Kalifriki had once done some work for that ruler involving a phantom tiger and some missing members of the royal family. Late into the evening a storyteller regaled them with an almost unrecognizable version of the event.

The following day, as Kalifriki and Alice walked amid walls of roses in the royal gardens, the chamberlain, Rasa, sent for them to discuss the business to which Kalifriki had alluded the previous evening.

Seated across the counting table from the heavy dark man of the curled and shiny mustaches, they beheld the stone known as the Dagger of Rama, displayed on a folded black cloth before them. Almost four inches in length, it was broad at the base, tapering upward to a sharp apex; its outline would be that of a somewhat elongated isosceles triangle, save that the lower corners were missing. It was perfectly clear, without a hint of color to it. Kalifriki raised it, breathed upon it. The condensation of his breath vanished immediately. He scrutinized it then through a glass.

"A perfect stone," Rasa said. "You will find no flaws."

Kalifriki continued his examination.

"It may hold up long enough," he said to Alice in Greek, "if I frame it appropriately, using certain properties of the thread to control external considerations."

"A most lovely stone for your lady to wear between her breasts," Rasa continued. "It is sure to influence the *chakra* of the heart." He smiled then.

Kalifriki placed a bag of gold upon the table, opened it, poured forth its contents.

Rasa picked up one of the small bars and studied it. He scratched it with his dagger's point and measured it, turban bobbing above the gauge. Then he placed it upon a scale he had set up to his left and took its weight.

"Of great purity," he remarked, tossing it back upon the table. Then he raised several of the bars from the pile and let them fall from his hand. "Still, it is not enough for so remarkable a stone. It may well have accompanied Rama on his journey to confront Ravan in the matter of Sita's abduction."

"I am not interested in its history," Kalifriki replied, and he brought up the second bag of gold and added its bars to the heap. "I've heard report that the tax collectors have had a lean time these past several years."

"Lies!" Rasa stated, opening a nearby chest and dipping his hand into it. He withdrew and cast forth a fistful of semiprecious stones upon the tabletop. Among them lay a small carved mountain of pale green jade, a pathway winding about it in a clockwise direction from base to summit. His gaze falling upon this piece, he reached out and tapped it with a thick forefinger. "Sooner would this spiral change direction," lie said, "than would I undersell a treasure simply to raise funds."

Kalifriki raised his wrist. The thread touched upon the piece of jade, seemed to pass within it. The stone moved slightly. The spiral now wound in the opposite direction.

Rasa's eyes widened.

"I had forgotten," he said softly, "that you are the magician who slew the phantom tiger."

"I didn't really kill him," Kalifriki said. "He's still out there somewhere. I just came to terms with him. Storytellers don't know everything."

The man sighed and touched his middle.

"This job is sometimes very trying," he said, "and sometimes seems to give me pains in my stomach. Excuse me."

He removed a small vial from a pouch at his sash, as Kalifriki moved his wrist again. As he unstoppered the container and raised it to his lips, Kalifriki said, "Wait."

Rasa lowered the vial.

"Yes?" he asked.

"If I heal your ulcer," Kalifriki said, "you may well bring it back with too much worry and aggravate it with too many spices. Do you understand?"

"Heal it," he said. "It is hard to cultivate philosophy in the face of necessity, and I do like my foods well seasoned. But I will try."

Kalifriki moved his wrist again and Rasa smiled. He stoppered the vial and replaced it in the pouch.

"All right, magician," he said. "Leave the gold. Take the stone. And if you see the white tiger again, let it know that you pass this way occasionally and that bargains are to be kept."

Later, in the garden at twilight, Alice asked him, "How did you do that reversal on the stone?"

"The full circumference of the thread is less than 360 degrees," Kalifriki replied. "The negative pressure of antigravity affects the geometry of space about it. Its missing angle is my key to other spaces. I simply rotated the stone through a higher space."

She nodded.

"I seem to recall something of this property from my training," she said. "But how did you heal the ulcer?"

"I speeded up time in its vicinity, letting the natural processes of his body heal it. I hope that he takes my advice and learns some detachment, from his work and his food."

They took a further turn, into an area of the garden they had not yet explored. The Bowers seemed to grow flat upon a flattening prospect along the twisting trail they followed. Then they were gone and it was the dead of night with great winnowings of stars blazing above them as they entered the lesser courtyard of Kalifriki's villa at Constantinople.

"You still smell of roses," she said.

"So do you," he replied, "and good night."

## 15

. . . Walking through my forest, ridiculous archaic weapon upon his back, his hand upon her shoulder, the monk follows the Alice. This one, I note, is scarred. My last Alice, then. She did escape, of course. And gone all this time. Planning, surely. What might she have in mind for the final foray, the last gasp of the octad? Its aim, certainly, is to free Nelsor. Nelsor . . . Even now, I feel her reaching out toward him. Disturbing. She is the strongest in this regard. Yet soon she will be distracted. They approach my favorite tree. Soon now . . . It spins in its socket, each limb a saber of glass. But she drops to the ground at precisely the right moment, and her monk moves with her in instant response. They inch their way forward now, the limbs flashing harmlessly, cold fire above them. Yet Endway's Shoot is next, where I took my second Alice, and the Passage of Moons may take them yet, even aware of the peril. And already she calls again. Nelsor . . . ?

## 16

Kalifriki sat all the next day in meditation, his bow before him upon the ground. When he had finished he walked on the shore for a long while, watching the waves come in.

Alice met him on his return and they took a late supper together.

"When do you plan to embark for Ubar?" she asked him, after a long silent time.

"Soon," he said, "if all goes well."

"We will visit my vessel in the morning?"

"Yes."

"And then?"

"It depends partly on how long the work there takes."

"Partly?"

"I think that I will want to meditate some more afterwards. I do not know how long that will take."

"Whenever . . ." she answered.

"I know that you are eager," he said later. "But this part must not be rushed."

"I understand."

He walked with her then into the town, passing lighted residences, some shops, government buildings. Many of the sounds of the city had grown still with the darkness, but there was music from some establishments, shouts, laughter, the creaking of a few passing carts, the stamping of horses' feet; they smelled spices in some neighborhoods, perfumes in others, incense from a church.

"What did you do," he asked her, from across a table where they sat sipping a sharp yellow wine, "in the five years between your escape from Aidon and your coming to see me?"

"I traveled," she replied, "seeking you—or someone like you—and trying to find the surface locus of that string. It had seemed bound to this world, as if it were somehow being employed. I supposed that one who had mastered it could be the one I needed to help me in this. I traveled with many servants—with some large male always in charge—as if I were part of a great man's retinue rather than owner of the lot. It is difficult being a woman on this world. I visited Egypt, Athens, Rome, many places. Finally, I heard stories of a man called Kalifriki, who had been employed by Popes, Emperors, Sultans. I traced the stories down. It took a long time, but I could afford to pay for every scrap of information. They led me here."

"Who told you the stories?"

"A poet. He called himself Omar, tentmaker."

"Ah, yes. A good man. Drank too much, though," said Kalifriki, sipping his wine. "And locally?"

"A priest named Basileos."

"Yes. One of my agents. I am surprised he did not warn me."

"I came immediately. I hurried. There was no opportunity for him to beat my arrival with a message. He told me to make further inquiry of Stassinopoulos, but I decided to ask for you here by name instead. I suspected by then that you had a second identity, and I was certain that a man such as yourself would be too curious not to give me audience under the circumstances. I was in a hurry. Five years of hearing their cries has been too long."

"You still hear them, right now?"

"No. Tonight they are silent," she said.

The moon fell down the sky, was caught in the Golden Horn.

## 17

Now, Nelsor, they have reached the Shoot, a mountain hurtling by them, but feet above the ground. They must crawl upon their bellies here, and even then, if one of my small satellites whose long ellipse brings it by here has so rotated that some downward projection rakes the land—*quish*! A pair of stepped-on cockroaches. Too fast? True. But this is but the foreplay, dear companion, my mentor. She calls to you again. Do you hear her? Do you wish to answer her? Can you? Ah! another rock and a jagged beauty it is!—races its purple shadow above the blood-red way. By them. And still they crawl. No matter. There will be more.

### 18

They completed the transfer on the Sea of Marmara that morning and afternoon. Then Kalifriki, clad in brown kimono and sandals, meditated for a brief time. At some point his hand went forward to take hold of the bow. Bearing it with him, he walked away from his villa down toward the sea. Alice, glimpsing his passage from her window, followed him at a distance. She saw him walk upon the shore, then halt, take forth a cloth and bind his eyes with it. He braced the bow, removed an arrow from its case, set it against the string. Then he stood holding them, unmoving.

Minutes passed on toward the end of day and he did not stir. A gull flew near, screaming. The better part of an hour went by. Then another gull passed. Katifriki raised the bow almost casually, drew it, released the arrow into the air. It passed beside the bird and a single feather came loose, drifted downward.

He removed the cloth from his eyes and watched the feather rock its way to the water. She wanted to sing, but she only smiled.

Kalifriki turned then and waved to her.

"We leave for Ubar in the morning," he called out.

"Did you want the bird or the feather?" she asked, as they walked toward each other.

"To eat the bird is not to digest its flight," he replied.

### 19

They have passed Endway's Shoot, where my moons flow like a string of bright beads. Leaving the passage like a trail of blood behind them, they rise, turning sharply to the left, climbing to the yellow ridge that will take them down into the valley where they must pass through my Garden of Frozen Beings, the place where I collected my third Alice. . . . What is that? A question? A chuckle?

Nelsor? Do you stir? Would you enjoy a ticket to this final festival? Why, then you shall have one, if you be able to use it. I have not felt such enthusiasm from you in ages. Come then to me if you can. I touch the bone, your skull. I summon you, lord, my mentor, to this place and time, Nelsor, for you were always my master in the matter of killing Alices. It is fitting that you be present when the collection is made complete. Come to me now, Nelsor, out of darkness. This spectacle is yours. By hone, siphon, and clot, I summon you! Come!

### 20

They came to Ubar, city of Shaddad ibn Ad, to be called Iram in the Koran, oasis town of lofty pillars, "the like of which were not produced in the land." Alice's hair was red now, and she wore a white garment and a light veil upon her face; Kalifriki had on his kimono and sandals, a cloth about his eyes, his bow upon his back, lacquered case beside it containing a single arrow.

Passing amid a sea of tents, they made their way down avenues lined with merchants, traders, beggars, to the sound of camel bells, gusts of wind, and the rattle of palm fronds. Conversation, song, and invective sounded about them in a double-dozen tongues. They came at last to the great gated pillars through which they passed, entering into the town proper, where the splashing sounds of fountains came to them from within adobe walled gardens; and white-stuccoed buildings gleamed in the morning sun, bands of blue, green, red, and yellow tiles adorning their palace-high walls.

"I seem to recall the dining area of the inn as being located in a kind of grotto," Kalifriki said, "within a rocky hillside, with the rest of the establishment constructed right, left, and forward of it, using the face of the hillside as a rear wall."

"That is correct," she said. "The cavern keeps the place cool by day. The cooking fires are well vented to the rear. You descend four or five stone steps on entering, bearing to the right—"

"Where is the mirror located?"

"On the wall to the left as you go in, below the steps."

"Metal, isn't it?"

"Brass or bronze—I forget."

"Then let us go in, be seated, have a cooling drink, and make certain that everything is still this way. On the way out, pause and investigate the mirror as you pretend to study your appearance. Lower the veil as you do so. If it attempts to draw you through, I will be near enough for you to take my hand. If it does not, turn away as if you are about to depart. Then return, as in afterthought, and employ that transport sequence you learned from your predecessors."

"Yes. There is the place up ahead now," she said.

He followed, and she took him in.

## 21

See, Nelsor? They are at the Garden of Frozen Beings now, place of your own design, if you recall—though in your original plan it was only for display. I came across it in an odd memory cache. See how cunningly it is wrought? It holds your studies of living things from a dozen worlds, in all sizes and colors, set upon many levels, in many interesting poses. Impossible not to pass it on several at any given time. I added the Series Perilous.

I took an Alice here, crushed by the blue spiral, eighth from the left— where she lay long in two pieces, gasping—for not calculating the death sequence correctly; and one back at Endway's Shoot, smeared to a long streak, though barely noticeable upon the red-stone, and another well flayed and diced in the crystal forest, by my *arbor decapitant*.

The first three, which you managed yourself—before your second disorientation—were so much more elegantly done. . . .

## 22

Finishing their drinks, Kalifriki and Alice rose and crossed the refreshment area. They passed the metal mirror and mounted the steps. At the threshold, she paused.

"A moment," she said. "I want to check my hair in that mirror we passed."

Returning down the stair, she produced a comb. At the mirror, she made a quick adjustment of several stray tresses, letting her veil fall as she did so.

Kalifriki stood behind her. "We must be at least partway entered before I shift," he whispered, "if I am to lay the thread in that universe so as to benefit our course through it. Remember what I said of the phenomenon. Whenever you are ready . . ."

"Good," she said, putting away her comb, turning toward the door.

Three beats later she turned back, lips set in a tight line, raising her hand, touching upon the reflecting surface. After a moment she located the pulses, passed her hand through the activation sequence.

As her fingers penetrated the interface, Kalifriki, behind her, placed his hand upon her shoulder, following a small squeeze from her free hand.

Her entire arm passed through the interface, and Kalifriki took them to the Valley of Frozen Time, where he removed his blindfold. He regarded the thread's passage through the placeless time into the timeless place, its twistings were complicated, the nexuses of menace manifold. Alice tried to speak to him, not knowing that words, like wind or music, could not manifest in this place of sculpture, painting, map. Twisting the thread, he flicked it three times, to see it settle at last into the most appropriate bessel functions he could manage under the circumstances, racing ahead to meet himself down thoroughfares of worlds-yet-to-be, and even as it plied its bright way he felt the tug of Time Thawing, replaced his blindfold, and set his hand again upon Alice's shoulder, to feel them drawn back to the waters of a small lake in the toy universe of the collector of Alices, piecemeal, who must even now be wondering at their interrupted passage.

## 23

Good of you to have summoned me back to my world, Aidon. What have you done to it? What are these silly games you have been about? Aidon, Aidon . . . Is this how you read my intention? Did you really think the bitches worth the concerted efforts of an entire universe, to crush them in manners you found esthetically gratifying? Did you think I wanted to construct a theme amusement park? You profane the memory of the woman I love. You should have taken instruction from my disposition of the first three. There was a point to those—a very important point. One which you have been neglecting.

*Lord, Nelsor, master, my mentor. I am sorry if the program is faulty. I had it that the killing of Alices was the highest value in the universe, as taken from your own example. See! See how this one must scramble, to avoid the hanging* twar? *She has generalized the experience of two of her sisters, to learn it is not the* twar *nor the* twar's *physical position that matters, but rather that position in the sequence of encounters. She had to abstract the series from the previous deaths. See how she must scramble—and her companion after her—to dodge the falling* frogbart, *leap high above the lower limb of the* gride? *When the* bropples *rolled around them she knew just how to dive—and to stand perfectly still till the* wonjit *exhausted its energies. See where the* jankel *has cut her arm? And even now she must pass the way of the* vum. *There is fine sport in her gasping, her bleeding, the tearing of her garments in seeing the sweat pour from her. And the* slyth *yet remains, and the* fangrace-pair. *Tell me how this differs from the doomed races where you ran the earlier Alices. How have I mistaken your intent? When you ceased being able to function, I was proud to take on your role. I am sorry if—*

Aidon, it broke me to do as I did with the first three. I retreated into my second madness over my actions, still unsatisfied, worse than unsatisfied, actually. I hated them, true, and it made it easier to do what I had to, to learn certain things. Still, it hurt me, also, especially in that I did not learn what I wished, though it narrowed the field. You should have summoned me for the fourth, the fifth, the sixth. There was data that I required there—lost to me now!

*Not so, lord! For I recorded them! You can summon them! Have them back! Deal with them further! I have done it many times—for practice. I even bring in outsiders for fresh rites. I have performed the ritual of the dying Alices over and over in your name—hoping to effect your repair in the reenactment. I have been faithful to your procedure—What? You have not employed that command mode since ship-time. . . . You would retire me? Do not! There is an important thing I have yet to tell you! I—*

Go away, Aidon. Go away. I would rid myself of your bumbling presence, for you have offended me. Let us say that it was an honest mistake. Still, I no longer wish to have you about, chortling over my undertakings, misreading all my actions, distracting me with your apologies. Before you fade entirely, see how I dismantle your remaining stations of blood. It is not games that *I* desire of the scarred lady I hate. But you are right in one thing. I will have the others back, as you recorded them, messy though the prospect be. She will follow the thread of a new course to the Place of Facing Skulls. By dot, bone, and siphon, this one will give me what

I want. Go away, Aidon. Go away.

Come back to the Killing Ground, Alice, my last. The rules you've learned no longer apply. Keep calling to me. You shall have my answer, a piece at a time.

## 24

Provoking the *fangrace-pair* to attack simultaneously, Alice left them tangled in each other's many limbs. Passing behind the nearer then, she led Kalifriki to a narrow bridge which took them above a canyon whose bottom was lost in blackness. Achieving its farther side, she took him down a twisting way beneath an evening sky of dark blue wherein lights that were not stars burned unblinking at near distances. Vivid, against the darkness, an incandescent rainbow took form.

"Strange," she muttered.

"What?" Kalifriki asked.

"There was never a rainbow here before."

"And it is night, is it not?" Kalifriki asked.

"Yes. It began darkening as we entered that last place."

"In some traditions on Earth a rainbow is the sign of a new covenant," Kalifriki said.

"If that is the message, it is more cryptic than communicative," she said.

Suddenly, the faint sounds of female voices which had been with them constantly since their arrival rose in volume. From sighs to wailings, they had been shaped somehow into a slow, eerie tune which rose and fell as if working toward an ominous crescendo it never quite reached, returning constantly to begin again, yet another variation on plaints of pain, punctuated with staccato bursts of hysterical laughter.

A cool wind came by, gusting among the high rocks amid which they moved. On several occasions, the ground shook beneath their feet.

Reaching the end of their downward way and turning to the left, Alice beheld a deep crater in which a lake of orange lava boiled, flames darting above it, casting its light upon the high, piped walls which surrounded it. Their trail split here, an arm of it going in either direction about the lake's oval perimeter, cinder-strewn between its jagged shores and the rise of the organpipe walls.

Alice halted.

"What is the matter?" Kalifriki asked.

"A burning lake," she said. "It wasn't here before."

"What was?"

"A maze, full of pits and deadfalls, flooded periodically with rushing torrents."

"What now?"

"I suppose we must choose a way and go on, to find the place of which I told you that first night over dinner—the place we have glimpsed but never quite reached. There are bones there, and an open wall. I think it is the place of the singularity. Which way should I go?"

"Let us trust to the falling of the thread. Find a random way to choose."

She stooped and picked up a pebble. Turning, she cast it, hard, back in the direction from which they had come. It struck against the rock wall and bounded back. It rolled past them to the right.

"Right," she said, and they turned and took up their way again, in that direction.

The trail was perhaps six feet in width, light from the blazing cauldron to their left casting their shadows grotesquely upon the fluted wall. The way curved in and out as they went; and they felt the heat—painfully, after a time—upon their left sides. Dark fumes obscured the starlike lights in the sky, though the rainbow still glowed brightly. The chorus of pained voices was partly muted by the popping and crackling from below, by the faint roaring that came in undertone.

As they rounded a bend they heard a moaning.

"Alice . . ." came a soft call from the right.

She halted.

Bleeding from countless cuts, one leg missing from below the knee, the other from above it, left arm dangling by a thread of flesh, a woman who resembled her lay upon a low ledge to the right, face twisted in the orange glow, her remaining eye focused upon them.

"Alice—don't—go—on," she gasped. "It—is—awful. Kill me—quickly—please. . . ."

"What happened? What did this to you?" Alice asked.

"The tree—tree of glass—by the lake."

"But that is far. How did you get here?"

"Don't know," came the reply. "Why is it—so? What have we done?"

"I don't know."

"Kill me."

"I cannot."

"Please. . . ."

Kalifriki moved forward. Alice did not see what he did. But she knew, and the broken lady did not call to them again.

They passed on in silence then, the lake growing more turbulent as they moved, now shooting great fountains of fire and molten material high into the air. The heat and fumes grew more oppressive. Periodically, niches glowed again in the wall to their right, wherein bleeding Alices stood, eyes staring, unseeing, straight ahead, lips twisting in their song which rose in intensity now, overcoming the lake's roaring. Whenever they approached these figures, however, they faded, though the song remained.

Then, in the flaring light, as they neared the far end of the trail, Alice beheld a rough area amid the cinders and congealed slag. She slowed, as she realized that the mangled remains of a human body were smeared before her, still somehow stirring. She halted when she saw the half-crushed head beside the way.

Its lips moved, and a wavery voice said, "Give him what he wants, that I may know peace."

"What—What is it that he wants?" she asked.

"You know," it gasped. "You know. Tell him!"

Then the lake bubbled and roared more loudly. A great strand of flame and lava leaped above it and fell toward them. Alice retreated quickly, pushing Kalifriki backward behind her. The fiery mass fell across the trail, obliterating the remains, draining, fuming, back into the lake. When it was gone, the ground smoking before them, the remains of the dead Alice had vanished, also.

They halted, waiting for the way to cool, and Kalifriki asked, "What is this knowledge of which she spoke?"

"I—I'm not certain," Alice replied.

"I've a feeling," Kalifriki said, "the question will be repeated in more specific and equally colorful terms at some point."

"I'd guess you're right," she told him.

Shortly, they walked on, treading quickly across the ravaged area, beneath the rainbow, the song suddenly reaching a higher pitch of wailing as they went.

As they neared the farther end of the lake, another molten spume reached near at hand. Alice halted, waiting to see in which direction the flashing tower might topple. But it stood, swaying, for a long while, almost as if trying to decide the matter itself. It took on a spiraling twist for a while before abruptly falling toward the wall perhaps twenty paces ahead of them.

They retreated even farther as this occurred. The spume fell in slow motion above the trail, its tip touching the wall, whence it flowed downward to the right hand trail's edge. Its upper portion remained in place, ten or twelve feet overhead, spirals working through it in two directions, braiding themselves now into a sputtering yellow-orange fretwork of light and molten material. The archway thus formed ceased its swaying and stood pulsing before them.

"We suddenly have a burning gate ahead of us," Alice stated.

"Is there any other way to proceed?" Kalifriki asked.

"No," she said.

"Then it would seem we have little choice."

"True. I just wanted you to know the nature of this encounter."

"Thank you. I am ready."

They moved ahead, and the archway maintained its position as they approached. Passing beneath it, the air was filled with crackling sounds and the prospect wavered. Alice's next step took her onto a rough silvery way with nothing about her but the starlike lights. Another pace, and Kalifriki had passed through also, the gateway vanishing behind him.

It was not a continuous surface upon which they stood, but rather a forty-foot span of about the same width as the trail they had quitted. It ended abruptly in all directions. Looking downward over its edge, she saw, at a distance impossible to estimate, the twisted surface of the land they had been traversing, cracked, pierced, brightly pied, monoliths darting about its surface, the rainbow still arched above it; and even as she watched, it seemed to change shape, lakes flowing into valleys, flames leaping up out of shadows and crests, new jigsaw pieces of color replacing old ones with less than perfect fit. And about them, still, rang the plaints of the dead Alices. She moved ahead, toward the farther end of the silver way.

"We're high above the land," she said, "walking on the surface of a narrow asteroid. It is like a broken-out piece of a bridge. I'm heading toward its farther end."

"Alice," Kalifriki said as they began to move again, "I have a question."

"What is it?"

"Did you come to Earth on the first vessel or the second?"

"Why do you ask that?"

"You said that Nelsor and four clones came here and had their trouble. Then later, his Alice, learning of this, made the voyage with the three remaining clones, yourself among them."

"Did I? I don't recall exactly how I phrased it."

"Then, when you told me of your bedroom encounter with Nelsor, it sounded as if you, he, and the original Alice all made a single journey together."

"Oh. That happened on a different voyage, elsewhere."

"I see," Kalifriki said, matching her pace.

Tenuous wisps of fog swept by them as they walked, followed by larger puffs. Something massive drifted downward from overhead, possibly on a collision course, possibly about to miss them. It was of about the same shape and albedo as the thing on which they moved.

"Another asteroid headed this way," she reported. "A bit of fog's come by, too."

"Let's keep going to the end."

"Yes."

Just as they reached the extremity of their way, the second piece of spanning slid into place before them and remained there, as if joined with their own. This one curved to the left.

"We've acquired an extension," she said. "I'm going to continue along it."

"Do so."

Several additional pieces moved by as they walked—one of them the section they had quitted, removing itself from the rear and drifting forward to join them again ahead.

"It's extending itself down toward a cloud bank," she told him, as she peered in the new direction it was taking. Then, too, they seemed to be moving, relative to the overall form of the shifting panorama below.

She crossed to another section. The clouds came on quickly, they were of soft pink, pale blue, light lime, streaked through each other in delicate abstract waves.

Several hundred paces later she heard a scream. Halting, and looking to the right, whence it seemed to have come, she beheld nothing but clouds. She began to gnaw at her lower lip as the cry was repeated.

"What is it?" Kalifriki asked.

"I don't know."

Then the clouds parted, and she saw a pair of drifting boulders but a few feet distant. The upper torso, head, and shoulders of a woman resembling herself lay sprawled upon the left-hand stone. Severed from these and occupying the slightly lower right-hand one lay the rest of her, twitching.

"Alice!" the figure cried. "He would know which of us was responsible. None of us could tell him. That leaves only you. Tell him what happened, for mercy's sake!"

Then the two rocks flew off in opposite directions and the clouds closed in again. Kalifriki could feel Alice shaking.

"If you know whatever it is he wants," he said, "perhaps you should tell him. It may make life a lot easier."

"Perhaps I do and perhaps I don't," she said. "I suppose I'll learn when I'm asked a direct question. Oh!"

"What? What is it?"

"Nelsor. I reached him for a moment. Or he reached me. He is gone now."

"Could you tell anything about his condition?"

"He seemed a mix of emotions. Happy that I was coming—in some other way disturbed. I don't know."

They walked again. The singing went on, and periodically they could feel the vibrations as new pieces of their twisted passageway through the sky assembled themselves. The colored fogs parted and came together again, flirting with her vision, providing tantalizing glimpses of some vantage that lay far ahead.

Their way seemed telescoped from break to break in their passage through the fog. Suddenly, Alice halted, stiffening, saying "Stop!" sharply.

"What is it?" Kalifriki asked.

"End of the trail, for the moment," she replied. "It just stops here. We are at the edge, and I am looking down again, through a thinning fog, at the distant land. The fog at our sides is dissipating now, too. That which is ahead of us is still thick. A redness flows through it."

They waited, and the red mist passed by degrees, revealing, first, an almost sculpted-seeming rocky prominence, pointed centrally, descending symmetrically at either hand and curving forward into a pair of gray-blue stony shoulders, and before them a flat yellow oval of sandy stone, raised above lesser steplike formations, irregular, more blue than gray, descending into mist. To the rear, set within the bulk of the prominence, a shelf-like niche was recessed at shoulder height; and at the oval's approximate center lay a well, a low wall of red stone blocks about its mouth. Another structured wall—this one of black stone—stood to the far left and downward of the oval, perhaps twenty feet in length, eight in height. Chains hung upon it. And this entire vision seemed to be quivering, as through a heat-haze.

More of the mist blew away, and the lines of the lower slopes came into view. Watching, as the last of it fled, Alice saw that the base of the entire prominence was an abruptly terminated thing, at about twice the height's distance below the oval, jagged blue icicles hanging beneath, as if a frozen mountaintop had been torn loose and hurled into space to hover against the blackness and the unblinking points of light; and now she could see that the rainbow's end lay within the oval.

Despite this clearing, the entire monumental affair still seemed to be vibrating.

"What is it?" Kalifriki asked at last.

Slowly, she began describing it to him.

## 25

Nelsor, I had only one thing to tell you before, but now I have two. Please acknowledge. There is perturbation within the well of the dot because another singularity is approaching—also a second peculiar item, of energy and negative field pressure trapped within a tube. Please acknowledge. This is a serious matter. I understand now what it was about the monk which first troubled me. Here at the center of things I can feel it clearly. He is very dangerous and should be removed from our universe at once. Release me and I will deal with him immediately. Acknowledge, Nelsor! Acknowledge! There is danger here!

Oh. The other thing I wanted to tell you concerns the first Alice. I had located some small memory caches for her. They were inadvertently recorded because of a peculiar conflict situation. Nelsor, I am going to begin pushing against this retirement program if you do not answer me. . . .

## 26

Alice stared at the vibrating landscape in the sky. A final span of bridge came drifting in slowly from her right, streaming colors as it passed through the rainbow. The voices of her dead sisters ceased, and only the wind that blows between the worlds could be heard in its chill passage.

"It is called the Killing Ground," she said then. "It has been transferred here from another location since my last visit. It is the final place."

"You never referred to it so before," Kalifriki said.

"I only just learned the name. I have reached Nelsor again. Or he has reached me. He bids me cross over. He says, 'Come back to the Killing Ground, Alice, my last.'"

"I thought you had never been to the final place."

"I told you I had glimpsed it."

As the last piece of bridge slid into place, connecting their span with the lowest step beneath the oval, she saw the vibrations shake loose a small white object from the niche. With a sudden clarity of vision, she discerned it to be a skull. It bounced, then rolled, coming to rest in the sand near a spreading red stain.

"Kalifriki," she said, "I am afraid. He is changed. Everything is changed. I don't want to cross over to that place."

"I don't believe I can get us out at this point," Kalifriki said. "I feel we are bound too tightly to my initial disposition of the thread, back in the Valley of Frozen Time, to employ it otherwise here. We must pass through whatever lies ahead, or be stopped by it."

"Please make certain," she asked, licking her lips. "He is calling again. . . .

## 27

Alice, Alice, Alice. You must be the one. It could have been none of the other wasted ladies. Even if Aidon fumbled in his approach by not putting the questions, there should have been some lapse on their part, some betrayal of the truth, should there not? The guilty one would not even have come in. . . . Why, why are you here at all? And that stranger at your side. . . . What is your plan? If it is you, why are you here? I am troubled. I must put you the questions. Why did you come back, Alice my last? It must be you . . . mustn't it? And why do you hesitate now? Come back to the Killing Ground, where her blood stains the sand and our skills lie in constant testimony to the crime. Come back. No? Then I call upon the siphon to bear you to me, here in the last place, beside the well of the dot that is the center of the universe. Even now it snakes forth. You *will* come to me, Alice, here and now, on this most holy ground of truth. I reach for you. You cannot resist.

Not now, Aidon. Not now. Go back. Go back. I have retired you. Go back.

It comes for you, Alice.

## 28

"I am sorry," Kalifriki said. "It is as I told you."

Staring ahead, Alice saw a black line emerge from the well, lash about, grow still, then move again, rising, swaying in her direction, lengthening. . . .

"The siphon," she said. "A piece of ship's equipment. Very versatile. He is sending it for me."

"Is it better to wait for it or go on?"

"I would rather walk than be dragged. Perhaps he will not employ it if I come on my own."

She began moving again. The black hose, which had been approaching, snakelike, halted its advance as she came toward it down the final length of silver. When she came up in front of it, it retreated. Step by step then, it withdrew before her. She hesitated a moment when she came to the end of the span. It leaned slightly toward her. At this, she took another step. It backed off immediately.

"We're here," she said to Kalifriki. "There are several ledges now, like a rough stairway, to climb."

She began mounting them, and as soon as she reached the flat sandy area the siphon withdrew entirely, back into the well. She continued to advance, looking about. She came to the well, halted, and peered down into it.

"We are at the well," she said, and Kalifriki removed his hand from her shoulder and reached down to feel along its wall. "It goes all the way through this—asteroid," she continued. "The dot—the black hole—is down there at its center. The siphon is coiled about the inner perimeter, near to the lip. It shrinks, so that one circuit is sufficient to house it. Below, I can see the bright swirling of the disc. It is far down inside—perhaps midway."

"So this place is being eaten, down at its center," Kalifriki said. "I wonder if that is the cause of the vibration?"

She walked on, past the red stain and the skull, to regard the niche from which the skull had tumbled. Another skull rested there, far to the right, and a collection of pincers, tongs, drills, hammers, and chains lay in the middle area.

"Torture tools here," she observed.

Kalifriki, in the meantime, was pacing about the area, touching everything he encountered. Finally, he stopped beside the well. Looking back, Alice saw that the rainbow fell upon his shoulders.

Then, above the sighing of the wind, there came a voice.

"I am going to kill you, Alice," it said. "Very slowly and very terribly."

"Why?" she asked.

The voice seemed to be coming from the vicinity of the skull. It was, as she recalled it, the voice of Nelsor.

"All of the others are dead," he said. "Now it is your turn. Why did you come back?"

"I came here to help you," she said, "if I could."

"Why?" he asked, and the skull turned over so that the empty sockets faced her.

"Because I love you," she replied.

There came a dry chuckling sound.

"How kind of you," he said then. "Let us have a musical accompaniment to that tender sentiment. Alices, give us a song."

Immediately, the awful plaint began again, this time from near at hand. To her right, six nude duplicates of herself suddenly hung in chains upon the black wall. They were bruised but unmutilated. Their eyes did not focus upon any particular objects as they began to shriek and wail. At the end of their line hung a final set of chains.

"When I have done with you, you shall join my chorus," Nelsor's voice went on.

"Done?" she said, raising a pair of pliers from the ledge and replacing it. "Employing things such as this?"

"Of course," he replied.

"I love you, Nelsor."

"That should make it all the more interesting."

"You are mad."

"I don't deny it."

"Could you forget all this and let me help you?"

"Forget? Never. I am in control here. And it is not your love or your help that I seek."

She looked at Kalifriki, and he removed the bow from his shoulder and strung it. Then he opened the case and withdrew its arrow, the spectrum blazing upon its tip.

"If your friend wishes to punch a hole in my head, that is all right with me. It will not let out the evil spirits, though."

"Is it possible for you to reembody yourself and come away with me?" she asked.

Again, the laugh.

"I shall not leave this place, and neither shall you," he said.

Kalifriki set the arrow to the bowstring.

"Not now, Aidon!" Nelsor shouted. Then, "Or perhaps your friend would shoot an arrow down the well to destroy the dot?" he said. "if he can, by all means bid him do so. For destroying the universe is the only thing I know to protect you from my wrath."

"You heard him, Kalifriki," she said.

Kalifriki drew back upon the bowstring.

"You are a fool," Nelsor said, "to bring—of all things—an archer here to destroy me . . . one of the legendary ones, I gather, who need not even see the target . . . against a dead man and a black hole."

Kalifriki turned suddenly, leaning back, arrow pointed somewhere overhead.

". . . And a disoriented one, at that," he added.

Kalifriki held this position, his body vibrating in time with the ground.

"You are a doomed, perverse fool," Nelsor said, "and I will use your sisters in your questioning through pain, in testament against you. They will rend you, stretch you, dislocate you, crack your bones."

There came a sound of chains rattling against stone. The chorus was diminished by half as the restraints fell from three of the Alices and their singing ceased. At that moment, their eyes focused upon her, and they began to move forward.

"Let it begin," he said, "in this place of bloody truth."

Kalifriki released his arrow, upward. Bearing its dark burden, the Dagger of Rama sped high and vanished into the blackness.

## 29

Nelsor! She has brought with her a being capable of destroying our universe, and it is possible that he just has. I must perform some massive calculations to confirm my suspicion—but in the meantime our survival depends upon our acting as if it is correct. We cannot return to our alpha point and start again if I am destroyed. And if I am destroyed you are destroyed, along with this place and all of your Alices. We are facing the end of the world! I must confer with you immediately!

## 30

The three Alices advanced upon the first stair.

## 31

Aidon! Whatever it is, this is not the time for it! I am finally arrived at the moment for which I have waited all these years. I find your importunities distracting. Whatever it is, deal with it yourself, as you would. I will not be interrupted till I have done with this Alice. Stay away from me until then!

## 32

The three Alices mounted the first step. At their back, their sisters' song reached a new pitch, as if the crescendo might finally be attained.

## 33

Very well, Nelsor. I shall act. First Alice, I summon what remains of you. By bone, dot, and siphon, I call you to embodiment upon the Killing Ground! Perhaps you can reason with him.

## 34

Alice glanced at her three sisters, approaching now upon the farther stair. Kalifriki lowered his bow and unbraced it, slung it. He reached up then and removed the bandage from his eyes.

"Nelsor, listen to me," Alice said. "Aidon will be destroyed. So will the programs which maintain your own existence—unless you reembody and shift your entire consciousness back into human form. Do that and come away with me, for this place is doomed. No matter what our differences, we can resolve them and be happy again. I will take good care of you."

". . . 'Again'?" Nelsor said. "When were we ever subject to mutual happiness? I do not understand you, clone. What I do not understand most, however, is why one of you killed my wife. And I feel strongly that it was you, Alice my last. Would you care to comment on this?"

From somewhere, a bell began to ring.

"Who sounds the ship's alert?" he cried.

"Probably Aidon," she responded, "as it realizes the truth of what I have been saying."

"You have not yet answered my question," he said. "Did you kill my wife?"

The second skull fell from the niche, rolled to the bloody area near to the first. The bell continued to ring. The voices of the three chained Alices rose and rose.

She grimaced. The other Alices mounted another step.

"It was self-defense," she said. "She attacked me. I had no desire to harm her."

"Why would she attack you?"

"She was jealous—of us."

"What? How could that be? There was nothing between us."

"But there was," she said. "You once mistook me for her, and we had our pleasure of it."

"Why did you permit it?"

"For you," she said. "I wanted to comfort you in your need. I love you."

"Then it could have gone by and been forgotten. How did she learn of it?"

"I told her, when she singled me out for reprimand over something one of the others had done. She slapped me and I slapped her back. Soon we were fighting on the ground, here—when this place was elsewhere. She struck me about the head with a tool she had at her belt. This is why I wear these scars. I thought she would kill me. But there was a rock nearby. I raised it and swung it. I was not trying to kill her, only to save myself."

"So you are the one."

"We are the same. You know that. Down to the cellular level. Down to the genes. You cannot have her back. Have me instead, I am the same flesh. You could not tell the difference then. It will feel the same now. And I will be better to you than she ever was. She was rude, imperious, egotistical. Come back. Come away with me, Nelsor my love. I will care for you always."

He screamed, and the three Alices halted at the top of the stair.

Slowly, a haze formed about the skull which faced her.

"Go back, Alices. Go back," he said. "I will deal with her myself."

The skull fell backward—now somewhat more than a skull, as the outlines of features had occurred about it in the haze—and a wavering began beneath it, delineating the form of a body, pulsing it into greater definition. Beside it, however, a similar phenomenon began to invest the second skull. The three Alices at the edge of the oval turned away, began walking back down the stair just as their sisters hit and ran the crescendo, voices changing from wailing to pure song. The three never returned to the wall, however, but faded from sight before they reached the bottom stair. At that time, the chains rang against the wall, and Kalifriki saw that the others had vanished as well.

Shortly, the nude form of a dark-haired, short-bearded man of medium stature took shape, breathing slowly, upon the sand. Beside him, another Alice came into focus, grew more and more substantial.

"You did not tell me the full story," Kalifriki said as they watched.

"I told you everything essential to the job. Would more detail have changed anything?"

"Perhaps," he said. "You fled after the fight, and this is your first time back then, correct?"

"Yes," she said.

"So you were not party to the other six Alices' journeys to this place, save that you monitored them to learn what you could of it."

"That's right."

"You might have warned them that any of them would be suspect. And after the first of them died you knew Nelsor's state of mind. You let your sisters go to their deaths without trying to stop them."

She looked away.

"It would have done no good," she said. "They were determined to resolve the matter. And you must remember that they were monitoring, too. After the first death, they were as aware as I was of his state of mind, and of the danger."

"Why didn't you stop the first one?"

"I was . . . weak," she said. "I was afraid. It would have meant telling them my story. They might have restrained me, to send me home for trial."

"You wished to take the place of the first Alice."

"I can't deny it."

"I suppose that is her upon the ground now."

"Who else could it be?"

Nelsor and the new Alice opened their eyes at about the same time.

"Is it you?" Nelsor asked softly.

"Yes," she answered.

Nelsor raised himself onto his elbows, sat up.

"So long . . ." he said. "It has been so long."

She smiled and sat up. In a moment they were in each other's arms. When they parted and she spoke again, her words were slurred:

"Aidon—message for you—to me gave," she said.

He rose to his feet, helped her to hers.

"What is the matter?" he asked.

"'Portant, 'im, to talk to. World ending. Arrow."

"It is nothing," Nelsor said. "He shot it off in the wrong direction. What is wrong with you?"

"Cur-va-ture. Perfect vector," she said, "to cir-cum-navi-gate small our uni-verse. Back soon. Other way."

"It doesn't matter," he said. "It's just an arrow."

She shook her head.

"It bears—an-other—dot."

"What? It's carrying a singularity around the universe on a collision course with Aidon?"

She nodded.

He turned away from her, to face Kalifriki.

"This is true?" he asked.

"This is true," Kalifriki replied.

"I don't believe it."

"Wait awhile," he said.

"It still won't destroy Aidon."

"Perhaps not, but it will destroy the programmed accretion disc and probably wreck your world that it holds together."

"What did she pay you to do this?"

"A lot," he said. "I don't kill for nothing if I can help it."

"The conscience of a mercenary," Nelsor said.

"I never killed three women who were trying to help me—for nothing."

"You don't understand."

"No. Is that because we're all aliens? Or is it something else?"

Just then, the new-risen Alice screamed. Both men turned their heads. She had wandered to the niche where her skull had lain, and only then seemed to notice her scarred clone standing nearby.

"You!" she cried. "Hurt me!"

She snatched the hammer from the ledge and rushed toward the clone.

The Alice dodged her assault, reached for her wrist and missed, then pushed her away.

"She's damaged," Nelsor said, moving forward. "She's not responsible . . ."

The original Alice recovered and continued her attack as Nelsor rushed toward them. Again, the other dodged and pushed, struck, pushed again. The incomplete Alice staggered backward, recovered her footing, screamed, swung the hammer again as her double moved to close with her.

Nelsor was almost upon them, when a final push carried her backward to strike her calves against the lip of the well.

He was wellside in an instant, reaching, reaching, leaning, and catching hold of her wrist. He continued to lean, was bent forward, fell. He disappeared into the well with her, their cries echoing back for several seconds, then ceasing abruptly.

"Lost!" the remaining Alice cried. "She has taken him from me!"

Kalifriki moved to the edge of the well and looked downward.

"Another case of self-defense," he said, "against the woman you wished to replace."

"Woman?" she said, moving forward. "She was incomplete, barely human. And you saw her attack me."

He nodded.

"Was it Nelsor you really wanted?" he said. "Or this? To be the last, the only, the mistress—the original?"

Tears ran down her cheeks.

"No, I loved him," she said.

"The feeling, apparently, was not mutual."

"You're wrong!" she said. "He did care!"

"As a clone. Not as his woman. Give up the memory. You are your own person now. Come! We should be leaving. I don't know exactly when—"

"No!" she cried, and the ground shook and the chains rattled. "No! I am mistress here now, and I will reembody him without memory of her! I will summon the three recorded clones to serve us. The others were witless. We shall dwell here together and make of it a new world. We can bring in what we choose, create what we need—"

"It is too late for that," Kalifriki said. "You brought me here to destroy a universe and I did. Even if it could be saved, you cannot dwell on the Killing Ground forever. It is already destroying you. Come away now, find a new life—"

"No!" she answered. "I rule here! Even now, I take control of Aidon! I remember the command modes! I have reached him! I hold this universe in my hand! I can alter the very physical constants! I can warp space itself to turn your silly arrow away! Behold! I have digested its flight!"

The lights in the sky flickered for the first time and jumped to new positions.

"Change the topology and the geodesic will follow," Kalifriki said. "The Dagger of Rama will still find you. Come away!"

"You! You have hated me all along for what I am! As soon as I told you I was a clone you knew I was something less than the rest of you! But I can destroy you now, assassin! For I am mistress of the dot! I can wish you away in any manner I choose! There is no defense!"

"So it comes to that again," he said. "You would have me pit my thread against a singularity."

She laughed wildly.

"There is no contest there," she said. "You have already described the entanglement that would result. I believe I will burn you—"

Kalifriki moved his wrist, slowly, to a position above the well.

"What are you doing?" she said. "How can you interfere with my omniscience? My omnipotence? You can't touch me!"

"I told you that the circumference of the thread is less than a full circle," he stated. "I am cutting out a wedge from your disc."

"That close? You can't. If the warp extends to the hole you would violate thermodynamics. A black hole cannot shrink."

"No," he said. "The thread would probably be caused to deliver energy to replace it and increase the mass and the radius in compensation. But I am being careful not to let it stray so near, and not to have to test this hypothesis. My sense is extended along it."

"Then you will not die by fire," she said, slurring her words slightly. "By bone—dot—and siphon—I summon you! Sisters! Destroy this man!"

Kalifriki's head jerked to the left, the direction of her gaze.

The three Alices whose eyes focused were flickering into existence across the oval from him. Slowly, he withdrew his wrist beyond the well's wall.

"Kill him!" she said. "Before he kills us! Hurry!"

The three Alices moved, wraithlike, even before they were fully embodied, rainbow's light passing through them as they came on.

Solidifying before they arrived, they rushed past Kalifriki, to attack the one who had summoned them.

"Murderess!" one of them cried.

"Liar!" shrieked another.

"Cause of all our pain!" screamed the third.

The scarred Alice retreated, and Kalifriki shook out his thread so that it fell among them. A wall of flame rose up between the Alices and their victim.

"There is no time," he called out, "to stain this ground further! We must depart!"

He moved the thread to enclose the three Alices.

"I am taking them with me," he said. "You come, too! We must go!"

"No!" she answered, eyes flashing. "I will shunt your arrow. I will move this place itself! I will warp space even more!" The lights in the sky winked again, danced again. "I will avoid your doom, archer! I will—rebuild! I will—have—him—back! I—am—mistress—here—now! Begone! I—banish—the—lot—of—you!"

Kalifriki retreated with the three ladies, to the Valley of Frozen Time. There, in the place that is sculpture, painting, map, he laid his way home. He could not speak to explain this, for this was not a place for words (nor wind, music, cries, wailing), nor they to thank him, were that their wish. And while scarred Alice stood upon the Killing Ground and invoked the powers of dot, siphon, and bone against the rushing Dagger of Rama as it cut its way around the universe, Kalifriki transported the three Alices from the land behind the mirror in vanished Ubar, taking them with him to his villa near the sea, though he feared them, knowing that he could never favor one over the others. But that was a problem to be dealt with at another time, for the ways of the thread are full of arrivals and departures, and even its master cannot digest its flight fully.

## 35

Alice at the end of the rainbow stands upon the red stain and watches the sky. The siphon brings her nourishment as she plies powers against powers in her contest with the inexorable doom she has loosed. A darkhaired, short-bearded man of medium stature sits upon the edge of the well and seems to watch her. Occasionally, she takes her pleasure of him and he tells her whatever she wishes to hear. She returns, refreshed then, to her duel, though it sometimes feels as if the circle of her universe no longer possesses 360 degrees. . . .

# LADY OF STEEL

Uttering a curse in his well-practiced falsetto, Cora swung his blade and cut down the opposing swords-woman. His contoured breastplate emphasized features which were not truly present.

Simultaneous then, attacks came from the right and the left. Beginning his battle-song, he parried to the left, cut to the right, parried left again, cut through that warrior, parried right, and thrust. Both attackers fell.

"Well done, sister!" shouted Edwina, the aging axe-woman, from where she stood embattled ten feet away. High compliment from a veteran!

Smiling, Cora prepared for another onslaught, recalling when he had been Corak the cook but months before. He had had a dream then, and now he was living it.

He had thought of being a great warrior, laying about him in battle, famed in song and story for his prowess. How he had practiced with the blade! Until one day he realized he need also practice his walk and his speech—as well as shaving closely and clandestinely every day—if he were ever to realize that dream. So he did. And one day he disappeared, Cora appeared weeks later, and a legend was born. Several months into the campaign now, and he was not only accepted but celebrated—Cora, Lady of Steel.

But the enemy, too, had heard of him, and all seemed anxious to claim the glory of reaping his head. Perspiration broke out on his brow as five warriors moved to engage him. The first he took out quickly with a surprise rush. The others—more wary now—fought conservatively, seeking to wear him down. His arms ached by the time he had dealt with the second. His battle-song broke as he dispatched the third and took a cut deep in his right thigh from one of the others. He faltered.

"Courage, sister!" shouted Edwina, hacking her way toward him.

He could barely defend himself against the nearer warrior as Edwina took out the fourth . Finally, he stumbled, knowing he could not rise in time to save himself from the death-blow.

At the last moment, however, an axe flashed and his final assailant's head rolled away in the direction of her retreating sisters.

"Rest!" Edwina ordered, taking up a defensive position above him. "They flee! We have the field!"

He lay there, clutching his thigh and watching the retreat, fighting to retain consciousness. "Good," he said. This was the closest it had ever been. . . .

After a time, Edwina helped him to his feet. "Well-acquitted, Steel Lady," she said. "Lean on me. I'll help you back to camp."

Inside her tent, the fractured leg-armor removed, she bathed the wound. "This will not cripple you," she said. "We'll have you good as new shortly."

But the wound extended higher. Suddenly, she had drawn aside his loincloth to continue her ministrations. He heard her gasp.

"Yes," he said then. "You know my secret. It was the only way for me to distinguish myself—to show that I could do the work as well or better than a woman.

"I must say that you have," Edwina admitted. "I remember your prowess at Oloprat, Tanquay, and Pord. You are a most unusual man. I respect you for what you have done."

"You will help me keep my secret then?" he asked "Let me complete the campaign? Let me make a record to show the world a man can do this work, too?"

She studied him, then winked, pinched his fanny, and smiled.

"I'm sure we can work something out," she said.

# COME TO ME NOT IN WINTER'S WHITE

## by Harlan Ellison and Roger Zelazny

She was dying and he was the richest man in the world, but he couldn't buy her life. So he did the next best thing. He built a house. He built *the* house, different from any other house that had ever been. She was transported to it by ambulance, and their goods and furnishings followed in many vans.

They had been married little over a year; then she had been stricken. The specialists shook their heads and named a new disease after her. They gave her six-months-to-a-year; then they departed, leaving behind them prescriptions and the smell of antiseptics. But he was not defeated. Nothing as commonplace as death could defeat him.

For he was the greatest physicist ever employed by AT&T in the year of Our Lord and President Farrar, two-thousand and twenty-nine.

(When one is incalculably wealthy from birth, one feels a sense of one's own personal unworthiness; so having been denied the joys of grueling labor and abject poverty, he had labored over himself. He had made of himself one who was incalculably worthy—the greatest physicist the world had ever known. It was enough for him . . . until he had met her. Then he wanted much more.)

He didn't *have* to work for AT&T, but he enjoyed it. They allowed him the use of their immense research facilities to explore his favorite area— Time, and the waning thereof.

He knew more about the nature of Time than any other human being who had ever lived.

It might be said that Carl Manos was Chronos/Ops/Saturn/Father Time himself, for he fitted even the description, with his long, dark beard and his slashing, scythe-like walking stick. He knew Time as no other man had ever known it, and he had the power and the will and the love to exploit it.

How?

Well, there was the house. He'd designed it himself. Had it built in less than six weeks, settling a strike by himself to insure its completion on time.

What was so special about the house?

It had a room; a room like no other room that had ever existed, anywhere.

In this room, Time ignored the laws of Albert Einstein and obeyed those of Carl Manos.

What were those laws and what was this room?

To reverse the order of the questions, the room was the bedroom of his beloved Laura, who had had *Lora Manosism*, an affliction of the central nervous system, named after her. The disease was monstrously degenerative; four months after diagnosis, she would be a basket case. Five months—blind, incapable of speech. Six-months-to-a-year—dead. She dwelled in the bedroom that Time feared to enter. She *lived* there while he worked and fought for her. This was because, for every year that passed outside the room, only a week went by within. Carl had so ordained it, and it cost him eighty-five thousand dollars a week to maintain the equipment that made it so. He would see her live and be cured, no matter what the cost, though his beard changed its appearance with each week that passed for her. He hired specialists, endowed a foundation to work on her cure; and every day, he grew a trifle older. Although she had been ten years his junior, the gap was rapidly widened. Still he worked to slow her room even more.

"Mister Manos, your bill is now two hundred thousand dollars a week."

"I'll pay it," he told the power & light people, and did. It was now down to three days for every year.

And he would enter her room and speak with her.

"Today is July ninth," he said. "When I leave in the morning it will be around Christmas time. How do you feel?"

"Short of breath," she replied. "What do the doctors tell you?"

"Nothing, yet," he said. "They're working on your problem, but there's no answer in sight."

"I didn't think so. I don't think there ever will be."

"Don't be fatalistic, love. If there's a problem, there's an answer—and there's plenty of time. All the time in the world . . ."

"Did you bring me a newspaper?"

"Yes. This will keep you caught up. There's been a quick war in Africa, and a new presidential candidate has come on the scene."

"Please love me."

"I do."

"No, I know that. *Make* love to me."

They smiled at her fear of certain words, and then he undressed and made love to her.

Then, after, there came a moment of truth, and he said, "Laura, I have to tell you the way it is. We're nowhere yet, but I have the best neurological minds in the world working on your problem. There's been one other case like yours since I locked you away—that is, since you came to stay here—and he's dead already. But they have learned something from him and they will continue to learn. I've brought you a new medicine."

"Will we spend Christmas together?" she asked.

"If you wish."

"So be it."

And so it was.

He came to her at Christmastime, and together they decorated the tree and opened presents.

"Hell of a Christmas with no snow," she said.

"Such language—and from a lady!"

But he brought her snow and a Yule log and his love.

"I'm awful," she said. "I can't stand myself sometimes. You're doing everything you can and nothing happens, so I harass you. I'm sorry."

She was five feet seven inches in height and had black hair. Black? So black as to be almost blue, and her lips were a pink and very special pair of cold shell-coral things. Her eyes were a kind of dusk where there are no clouds and the day sets off the blue with its going. Her hands shook whenever she gestured, which was seldom.

"Laura," he told her, "even as we sit here, they work. The answer, the cure, will come to pass—in time."

"I know."

"You wonder, though, whether it will be time enough. It will. You're virtually standing still while everything outside races by. Don't worry. Rest easy. I'll bring you back."

"I know that," she said. "It's just that I sometimes—despair."

"Don't."

"I can't help it."

"I know more about Time than anybody else . . . You've got it: on your side."

He swung his stick like a saber, beheading roses that grew about the wall. "We can take a century," he said, quickly, as though loath to lose even a moment, "without your being harmed. We can wait on the answer that has to come. Sooner or later, there *will* be an answer. If I go away for a few months, it will be as a day to you. Don't worry. I'll see you cured and we'll be together again in a brighter day—for God sake don't worry! You know what they told you about psychosomatic conversions!"

"Yes, I shouldn't have one."

"Then don't. There are even other tricks I will be able to play with Time, as it goes on—such as freezing. You'll come out okay, believe me."

"Yes," she said, raising her glass of Irish Mist. "Merry Christmas."

"Merry Christmas!"

But even for a man who has been thought incalculably wealthy, lack of attention to compounding that wealth, monomaniacal ferocity in pursuing a goal, and a constant, heavy drain, inevitably the end comes in sight. Though the view to that end was a far horizon, though there were more years that could be put to use, even so it became obvious to everyone around him that Carl Manos had committed himself to a crusade that would end in his destruction. At least financially. And for them, that was the worst sort of destruction. For they had not lived in the thoughts of Manos, were unaware that there were other, far more exacting destructions.

He came to her in the early summer, and he brought a recording of zarzuela love duets by de la Cruz, Hidalgo Bréton. They sat beside each other, their hands touching, and they listened to the voices of others who were in love, all through July and August. He only sensed her restlessness as August drew to a close and the recording shusssed into silence.

"What?" he asked, softly.

"It's nothing. Nothing, really."

"Tell me."

She spoke, then, of loneliness.

And condemned herself with more words; for her ingratitude, her thoughtlessness, her lack of patience. He kissed her gently, and told her he would do something about it.

When he left the room, the first chill of September was in that corner of the world. But he set about finding a way to stave off her loneliness. He thought first of himself living in the room, of conducting his experiments in the room without Time. But that was unfeasible, for many reasons— most of them dealing with Time. And he needed a great deal of space to conduct the experiments: building additions to the room was impossible. He could see, himself, that there would not be sufficient funds to expand the experiment.

So he did the next best thing.

He had his Foundation scour the world for a suitable companion. After three months they submitted a list of potentials to him. There were two. Only two.

The first was a handsome young man named Thomas Grindell, a bright and witty man who spoke seven languages fluently, had written a perceptive history of mankind, had traveled widely, was outspoken and in every other possible way was the perfect companion.

The second was an unattractive woman named Yolande Loeb. She was equally as qualified as Grindell, had been married and divorced, wrote excellent poetry, and had dedicated her life to various social reforms.

Even Carl Manos was not so deeply immersed in his problem that he could not see the ramifications of possible choice. He discarded the name of Grindell.

To Yolande Loeb he offered the twin lures of extended life and financial compensation sufficient to carry her without worry through three lifetimes. The woman accepted.

Carl Manos took her to the room, and before the door was keyed open from the control console, be said, "I want her to be happy. To be kept occupied. No matter what she wants, she's to have it. That is all I ask of you."

"I'll do my best, Mr. Manos."

"She's a wonderful person, I'm sure you'll love her."

"I'm sure."

He opened the outer chamber, and they entered. When they had neutralized temporally, the inner chamber was opened, and he entered with the woman.

"Hello."

Laura's eyes widened when she saw her, but when Carl had told her Miss Loeb had come to keep her company, to be the friend Laura had needed, she smiled and kissed his hand.

"Laura and I will have so much time to get acquainted," Yolande Loeb said, "why don't you spend this time together?" And she took herself to the far corner of the room, to the bookshelf, and pulled down a Dickens to re-read.

Laura drew Carl Manos down to her and kissed him. "You are so very good to me."

"Because I love you. It's that simple. I wish *everything* was that simple."

"How is it coming?"

"Slowly. But coming."

She was concerned about him. "You look so tired, Carl."

"Weary, not tired. There's a big difference."

"You've grown older."

"I think the gray in my beard is very distinguished."

She laughed lightly at that, but he was glad he had brought Miss Loeb, and not Grindell. Thrown together in a room where Time nearly stood still, for endless months that would not be months to them, who knew what could happen? Laura was an extraordinarily beautiful woman. *Any* man would find himself falling in love with her. But with Miss Loeb as companion—well, it was safe now.

"I have to get back. We're trying some new catalysts today. Or rather, however many days ago it was when I came in here. Take care, darling. I'll be back as soon as I can."

Laura nodded understanding. "Now that I have a friend, it won't be so lonely till you return, dearest."

"Would you like me to bring anything special next time?"

"The sandalwood incense?"

"Of course."

"Now I won't be lonely," she repeated.

"No. I hope not. Thank you."

And he left them together.

"Do you know Neruda?" Miss Loeb asked.

"Pardon me?"

"The Chilean poet? *The Heights of Machu Picchu*? One of his greatest works?"

"No, I'm afraid that I don't."

"I have it with me. It is a piece of blazing power. There is a certain strength within it, which I thought you—"

". . . Might take heart from while contemplating death. No. Thank you, but no. It was bad enough, just thinking about all the things the few people I *have* read have said about life's ending. I am a coward, and I know that one day I will die, as everyone must. Only, in my condition, I have a schedule. *This* happens, then *this* happens, and then it is all over. The only thing between me and death is my husband."

"Mr. Manos is a fine man. He loves you very much."

"Thank you. Yes, I know. So if you wish to console me concerning this, then I am not especially interested."

But Yolande Loeb pursed her lips, touched Laura's shoulder, said, "No. Not consolation. Not at all."

"Courage or faith, perhaps," she said, "but not consolation or resignation," and, "'Irresistible death invited me many times: / It was like salt occulted in the waves / and what its invisible fragrance suggested / was fragments of wrecks and heights / or vast structures of wind and snowdrift.'"

"What is that?"

"The beginning of Section Four."

Laura dropped her eyes, then said, "Tell me the whole story."

"'From air to air, like an empty net,'" said Yolande, in her deep, impressive tones, and with a slight accent, "'dredging through streets and ambient atmosphere, I came / lavish, at autumn's coronation . . .'"

Laura listened, and some variety of truth seemed to be present there.

After a time she reached out and their fingertips touched, gently.

Yolande told her of her girlhood in a *kibbutz*, and of her broken marriage. She told her of her life after that thing, and of the suffering attendant thereto.

Laura cried, hearing of this misery.

She felt bad for days thereafter.

Yet these were not days to Carl Manos, who also had cause to feel bad. He met a girl whose company he enjoyed, until she said that she loved him. He dropped her like poison sumac and hot potatoes. After all, Time—their friend / their enemy—had a deal going with Laura and Carl. There was no room for intruders in this fated threesome.

He cursed, paid his bills, and figured ways to make Time even more amenable to his bidding.

But suddenly he was in pain. He knew nothing of Pablo Neruda, or this Pasternak, Lorca, Yevtushenko, Alan Dugan, Yeats, Brooke, Daniels— any of them—and Laura spoke of them constantly these days. As he had no replies for this sort of thing, he just nodded. He kept on nodding. Time after time . . .

"You're happy with the present arrangement?" he finally asked.

"Oh, yes! Of course," she replied. "Yolande is wonderful. I'm so glad that you invited her."

"Good. That's something, anyway."

"What do you mean—?"

"Yolande!" he called out, suddenly. "How are you?"

Yolande Loeb emerged from the screened-off section of the apartment to which she discreetly retired during his visits. She nodded to him and smiled faintly.

"I am quite well, Mr. Manos. Thank you. And yourself?" There was a brief catch in her voice as she moved toward him, and realizing that her eyes were fixed on his beard, he chuckled within it, saying, "I'm beginning to feel a trifle like a premature patriarch." She smiled, and his tone was light, but he felt pain, again.

"I've brought you some presents," he went on, placing sealtite packages on the table. "The latest art books and tapes, recordings, some excellent film beads, poems which have been judged by the critics to be exceptional."

Both women moved to the table and began running their fingertips down the sealstrips, opening the parcels, thanking him for each item as it was unwrapped, making little noises of pleasure and excitement. As he studied Yolande's swart face, with its upturned nose, numerous moles, small scar upon the brow, and as his eyes moved on to Laura's face, flushed now and smiling—as he stood there, both hands upon his walking-stick, reflecting that it was good to have chosen as he had— something twisted softly within him and he knew pain once more.

At first, he was unable to analyze the feelings. Always, however, they returned to him as accompaniment to his recollection of that tableau: the two of them moving about the package-laden table, leafing through the foilpages of the books, holding the recording cassettes at arm's length, the better to study their dimensional-covers, chatting about their new treasures, excluding him.

It was a feeling of separation, resulting in a small loneliness, as well as something else. The two women had a thing in common, a thing which did not exist between Laura and himself. They shared a love for the arts—an area of existence for which he could allow himself little time. And, too, they were together in a war zone—alone in the room with the opponent Time laying siege. It had brought them closer together, sharing the experience of defying death and age. They had this meeting place where he was now a stranger. It was . . .

Jealousy, he decided suddenly; and was quite surprised by the notion. He was jealous of that which they had come to share. He was shocked at the thought, confused. But then, impressed as he always had been with a sense of personal unworthiness, he recognized it as another evidence of this condition. He then sought to banish the feeling.

But then, there had never been another Laura, or another *ménage* such as this.

Was it guilt that came now in response?

He was not certain.

He coded a fresh cup of coffee, and when it arrived, smiled into the eyes—his own, perhaps—which regarded him through the steam and darkness of its surface. His knowledge of the ancients stopped short with their legends and theories of Time. Chronos, or Time, had been castrated by his son, Zeus. By this—it had been contended—the priests and oracles meant to convey the notion that Time is incapable of bringing forth any new thing, but must ever repeat himself and be satisfied with variations of that which has already been begotten. And that is why he smiled . . .

Was not Laura's disease a new thing come into the world? And was not his mastery of Time now to be the cause of another new thing—its remedy?

Guilt and jealousy alike forgotten, he sipped at his coffee, tapping his fingers all the while to the beat of an unheard tune as the particles and antiparticles danced before him in their chambers—and thus time was kept.

And when, later that evening, the viewer chimed, that evening as he sat there, white-smocked, before the Tachytron, archaic glasses pushed up onto his forehead, cold cup of coffee before him on the console, as he sat looking inside himself, he put aside remembered guilt for a premonition.

The viewer chimed again.

That would be one of the doctors . . . and it was . . .

The results of his latest experiments—rainbow journeys where no physicist had ever gone before—had been integrated with the work the doctors had been doing, and his premonition became a hallelujah reality.

He went to tell Laura they had won; went to the room outside which

Time lay siege with growing frustration; went to restore the full measure of his love. Where he found them.

Making love.

Alone, outside the room where Time now waited smugly, finally savoring the taste of victory, Carl Manos lived more lifetimes than *any* special room could hoard. There had been no scene, save in the tortured silences. There had been no words, save in the linear impressions of three who were surrounded by all that had happened in that room, locked invisibly in the walls.

They wanted to stay together, of course. He had not needed to ask that. Alone together in the timeless room where they had found love, the room Carl Manos could never again enter. He still loved her, that could never be changed. And so, he had only two choices.

He could work for the rest of his unworthy life, to pay for the power to keep the room functioning. Or he could turn it off. To turn it off he would have to wait. Wait for Time the Victor to turn his all-consuming love into a kind of hate that would compel him to stop the room's functions.

He did neither. Having only two choices, he took a third course, a choice he did not have, had never had.

He moved to the console and did what had to be done, to *speed up* Time in the room. Even Time would die in that room, now. Then, unworthy, he went away.

Yolande sat reading. Neruda, again. How she always came back to him!

On the bed, what had been Laura lay decomposing. Time, unaware that all, including himself, would be victims, had caught up, had won victory finally.

"'Come, diminutive life,'" she read, "'between the wings / of the earth, while you, cold, crystal in the hammered air, / thrusting embattled emeralds apart, / O savage waters, fall from the hems of snow.'"

> *Love, love, until the night collapses*
> *from the singing Andes flint*
> *down to the dawn's red knees,*
> *come out and contemplate the snow's blind son.*

She laid the book in her lap, then sat back in the chair, eyes closed. And for her, the years passed swiftly.

# THE NEW PLEASURE

Having successfully essayed most vices known to man, James Andrew Dinker III was understandably eager to try something new. Offhand, it would be difficult to detail his last two decades without becoming mightily repetitious. Repetition, in general, is soporific. Therefore, it is easier simply to describe the physical appearance of James Andrew Dinker III and throw in a couple attributes:

Five feet eight inches in height, perpetually in need of a shave, possessed of amazingly innocent blue eyes while wearing tinted glasses, and bloodshot, watery ones when going unglassed, he weighed one hundred fifty-six pounds and hated dogs, children, and his father, James Dinker II.

His father is worth several paragraphs of his own, but they may be skipped over, inasmuch as he only maintained the family fortune—whereas *his* father, James Dinker I, had single-handedly hewed the whole Dinker Empire from out of the kingdom of videoland.

James Dinker Number One did his thing by introducing a new standard of quality into mass-enterainments, so that everyone came to love and respect him. He pioneered in audience-participation broadcasts. That is to say, he peddled romances possessed of the added dimension of tactile sensations. So successful was he in promoting the present quality of the medium known as feel-o-vision, that he left an exceedingly fat fortune to his son—whose heir, our hero, could do little to further improve the industry's standards. The family imagination had been exhausted and was put out to pasture by the third James on the dynasty chart.

Be it noted that means and a lack of notable ideals often give rise to wantonness. Accordingly, as our story opens, Jas. Three is about to patronize (incognito, of course) a former competitor of his grandsire's:

"Madam," said he, addressing the tiny lady whose hair matched her faded eyes, "can you give me positive assurance that there is no danger involved in a Body Vacation?"

"Scarcely any danger at all," she observed, "which is why it was such a wicked, wicked thing for James Dinker, our old competitor, to use his political influence to have Body Vacations declared illegal and immoral."

"By Act of Congress," added J. D. 3 knowingly. "Still, prohibition makes things ever more intriguing. Is it true that when one's consciousness has been transferred to the body of an animal one then experiences all the sensations just as that creature would, and not as a human being?"

"That is true," she said, smiling, "all the delicate feelings of our furry and feathery friends can be known to a sensitive young man such as yourself—the moist morning as seen through the eyes of a fawn, the taste of crisp lettuce to a nibbling bunny, the patchwork earth fleeing north beneath the wings of the migrant mallard, new pleasures all—for only fifty thousand dollars, cash."

"Any animal?" he asked.

"Why yes," she stated, following his walletward reach. "If we don't have what you want here on the farm, we'll make arrangements to obtain it.—And tell me, where did you get that lovely ring with the picture-tube stone?"

"It was my dear old granddad's. Here's your money. I want to be a stallion for a day," he declared, "and turned loose in a herd of mares."

"Oh my!" She reddened.

"I suppose you lack the facilities," he jeered.

"No, that's not it. It's just that with those amazingly innocent blue eyes you did not impress me as . . ." Her voice trailed off as he removed his glasses. "Yes, I can see," she noted. "Well, as a matter of fact, we *are* prepared to make such an arrangement—here, today, if you wish."

"Fine and gamey, and like let the thing swing," he observed.

She pressed a button. After a short time a young man in a laboratory jacket entered the room.

"Conduct our client to a Transfer Chamber," she instructed him. "He is going to be a stallion on the north forty."

The young man smiled as she deposited the bills in a quaint and amazingly innocent handbag—for he knew that there was no north forty.

Dinker awakened, puzzled. He tried to remember where he was. In a flash, it all returned to him—the electric skullcap, the spinal leads, the injections. But where was he? It was so dark. . . .

". . . You are awake by now," he heard her saying.

He tried to answer, but he lacked the vocal facilities.

"I should have known you were a Dinker," she said, "without seeing my ex-fiancé's ring. Your grandfather was a very wicked man. That is why I jilted him. Then he bankrupted my father and drove him to suicide.

"And your father is a very, very wicked man," she continued. "He has tried to drive *me* out of business.

"And *you* take after both of them," she concluded, "in your own small way. Too bad."

The lights came on then, and he saw her far below him, and she was smiling.

She was black-and-white, as in an old newsreel. He had a hard time focusing his eyes on her.

He seemed to be astride a tightrope. Well, not exactly. It was more like some kind of a net.

It began to sway beneath his feet then.

*All* of his feet, he noted uncomfortably.

Suddenly he was no longer hung up there all by himself—

For she was jet black and she moved to the center of the web with delicate, dancing steps. She stopped and waited.

Spiders are unable to scream, or he would have.

He stared at her shiny, graceful form. He looked into her waiting eyes.

All of her waiting eyes . . .

Quickly then, most ideal of all audiences, he tested the web—for it had only taken but a moment for him to realize just how lovely she was.

# THE HOUSE OF THE HANGED MAN

As I walked through the House of the Hanged Man, there came to me a voice from behind in the darkness.

"Where are you going?" it asked.

But I did not answer. I walked on through the Red Room for an age and a half, and as I paused at the threshold of the great Orange Hallway the voice from the distant cellar-darkness came again.

"Where *are* you going?"

I moved up the Orange Hallway, and the walls receded and returned like the pulsebeat of Time, bringing with them loads of orange chairs and high paintings of great orange expanses. The orange-rust was upon the empty suits of clanking armor, and on the banisters that swirled with the stairways up and up and up.

After generations of orange furniture and tapestries, I saw ahead through the mist the entrance to the Yellow Vestibule. I quickened my pace, but the black voice appeared again behind me, just as I drew near.

"*Where* are you going?"

Hurrying, I entered the Yellow Vestibule, which was filled with cast yellow cloaks and yellow masks and great mirrors in which I saw nothing but yellow and my eyes. I pushed through the soft yellow hangings and brushed against the smooth padding of the lemon walls.

A yellow silk glove lay at my feet, and I stopped and picked it up. There came a soft laugh from behind a pillar, but when I looked there was no one.

I kept the glove and hurried through the yellow eras, for I was afraid.

The deep-dark, stark-dark voice followed me, timed to arrive just as I set foot beneath the archway to the Green Drawing Room.

"Where are *you* going?"

I rushed ahead, for I had to see Green, now that I had known Red and Orange and Yellow. I plunged through the million angles of the Green Drawing Room, for that was the color of grass, he had told me, that was the color of grass. Green wind, green boughs, ship on a green sea . . . That was the color. Horse on a green mountain . . . The color of . . .

Something.

Now it seemed as if there were footsteps behind me, or at least a steady clicking sound. I skidded across green centuries, wishing to linger, but fearing, wishing to stay awhile amid the color of grass, but fearing, to step behind hanging, to pass within a green place, to stay.

Then I came to the Blue Boudoir; and the voice, right at my back now, addressed me again.

"Where are you *going*?"

I sped ahead into the place of robin's egg, sky, morning glory, which he had told me would be there. I burst through blue-canopied bed-hangings, swerved by blue dressing-tables, couches, *petite* divans, tasselled hangings (like waterfalls, the Hanged Man had told me), through closets, around and over vanities, luggage, linens.

The clicking came nearer, and I burnt ages in a blue flame of passage, speeding.

Then I came to the foot of the Violet Stairway.

"WHERE ARE YOU GOING?" asked the voice of cellar-based, cellar-hearted blackness I had left.

"Out!" I cried. "Outside! Where there is grass, and trees, water, birds, wind, sun . . .

"In all colors—married!"

"There is no outside," said the soot-dark voice. "There is only the House of the Hanged Man, forever and ever and everywhere. There is *only* the house of the Hanged Man."

"You lie!" I said, setting foot upon the first violet stair.

"There is no outside," repeated the black, black voice.

"The ghost of the Hanged Man told me—as he hovered, batlike, from a rafter in the Black. *He* told me!"

"He lied, lied, lied. There is only the House. Come back now to the Dark."

"No!"

I ran, taking the steps two at a time, flashing by the violet statues, the people who had forgotten how to move, there in their violet niches along the Violet Stairway, where they stood, unseeing, having also forgotten how to look outside themselves.

Up and up, I raced, slipping on soft millennia of violet carpeting.

Then far up ahead of me I saw the Rainbow Door, reaching high beyond belief, standing slightly ajar, just as it must always have been, waiting for me to pass through it, forever.

"Outside!" I cried.

A hand fell on my shoulder.

I screamed all the way back, but the hand remained, guiding me through the violet, blue green, yellow, orange, red—back.

I cried as I passed through the Green Drawing Room and the Yellow Vestibule, but in the puff of an instant they were gone.

The hand would not let go, because I wanted to run away.

I will never get out again. Never, never, ever. They had trusted me near the fringes of the darkness, but they will never trust me there again.

I will remain in the cellar-dark forever, and if I ever meet the ghost of the Hanged Man, hovering inverted, bat-like, from a rafter in the Black again, I will either curse him or bless him. I do not know.

If *you* should ever meet him, pass by.

But if ever you should somehow leave here, and pass through the Rainbow Door, and go outside, and depart from the House of the Hanged Man . . .

Then come back, please. Try. Try to slip back. Return here and tell me of the marriage of the colors, of the ship on the ocean, the horse on the mountain. . . .

They tell me now that there are no colors: No. Nothing. Nothing ever was.

I was mistaken, they say, by a lightening of the Shadow. I saw wrongly, they say.

But they will never let me near the fringes again. No. Never.

But listen. Lean close, comrade, and listen. I have a thing to show you, a thing which they do not know I have.

It is a yellow silk glove. . . .

# EPITHALAMIUM

It rained that night and the old lady made tea, as was generally the case. Sipping it, there at the kitchen table, she looked back over her quiet life. Memories of childhood came to fascinate her, and she wondered again at the quietude that had followed. Though she'd inherited the house and received a small stipend from a trust fund and had traveled considerably she'd never found the right man; or vice versa. The game was about over for her now, though she'd never really been invited to play. There had been nothing of great interest or reminder save for a few visits with the man who hunted people, and the last of these had been years ago. Now . . . Now it was peaceful to drink her tea and listen to the rain, to reflect on the complexity of existence and one's own useless role in most of it. She had done a lot of volunteer work, read a lot of books, remembered the wars. She'd been a nurse in both of them, though the second time had involved luck, expediency, and a need that transcended age. Well, there had been one man, back in the first war, she recalled—a quiet British lieutenant named Colin. They might have been happy together, she mused, but the fields of Flanders had eaten him, along with so many others.

She moved to the other room and stoked the fire, adding a few sticks, as she meant to take a second cup of tea in the parlor.

Halfway through the cup and some old thoughts, the doorbell rang. She glanced at the clock. It was near midnight.

She rose and crossed the room, opening the door partway.

"'Evening, Miss Alice," he said. "Axel J. Beangern at your service. I was wondering whether we might use it tonight."

"Goodness! I don't know whether it's still working," she said, opening the door more widely. "Come in out of the rain."

Beangern, as always, was clad in brown leather. He wore a hunting knife on his belt, a pistol on his right hip, and he carried a shotgun in his hand.

"Why the shotgun?" she asked.

"It slows him down," Beangern said.

With that, he pushed in his prisoner—a tall, slim, dark-eyed, dark-haired fellow clad in black. He was handcuffed and he wore leg irons as well.

"Evening, Miss Alice," he said. "It's been a long time."

"Indeed it has, Lucer," she responded.

He smiled, raised his hands, and the right one incandesced.

"You cut that out, Lucer," Beangern said to him, and the fire died.

"Just an old flame for an old flame," Lucer said.

"You always were a flirt," she responded, returning his smile. "Will you gentlemen have some tea?"

"Of course," they both replied, "on a night like this. We'll stand, though, if you don't mind. Hate to soil your furniture."

"Nonsense. I insist you sit," she said.

"He is good at guarding people when they're chained and he's standing by them with a shotgun," Lucer said.

"That is not the reason," Beangern stated.

She shrugged and returned to the kitchen. Shortly, she came back with a tray bearing two cups of tea and some biscuits. Both men were now seated.

She served them, then seated herself.

"Same as usual?" she asked.

"Pretty much," Lucer replied. "I escaped prison, came over to here, got a job, and the bounty man came after me."

"Same as usual," Beangern said. "He escaped from prison, injuring a lot of people on his way out, came here and organized a secret society dedicated to revolution and commenced buying weapons and training the members in their use. I caught him just in time."

"So what happens to him now?" Alice asked.

"I take him back," said Beangern.

"You seem the only one able to bring him back when something like this happens," Alice said.

"True. He's quite dangerous, but then so am I," Beangern said.

"This is all a lie," Lucer said. "But I haven't yet seen the truth make any difference."

"I'd listen," Alice said.

"'I'm sorry," said Beangern, "but he hasn't the time to tell you all of his lies. We must be departing soon."

"He's like a samurai," Lucer said. "Terribly well-trained and true to his code—whatever it is. If you tried to detain him, he might do you harm."

"I would not," said Beangern. "Alice is an old friend."

"Very old," Alice said.

"Why do you keep escaping if it always comes to this?" she asked Lucer.

"It will not. This is the last time," Lucer replied.

"Oh, why is that?"

"Because the cycle is at an end."

"I don't understand," she said.

"Of course not. But I have eaten the Whitcomb Pie and know that it is so."

"Whatever you say," she said, pouring more tea for them all. "My part in your business ended long ago."

Lucer laughed.

"Callooh! Callooh!" he said. "The story never ends."

Beangern laughed, too.

"It will end very soon," he said.

"In a way, callay! In a way," the other said.

"So long as Beangern holds his fief, the world runs well," Beangern said.

"Well, it runs," Lucer acknowledged, "with the lunatics in charge, as you left them."

Beangern chuckled.

"I find this vastly amusing," he said. "And surely Alice remembers."

"How could I not?" she said. "There were times when it terrified me."

"And there were times when it showed you wonders such as few of your world have ever seen," Lucer added.

"I can't deny it. But they don't balance."

"What of it? It has changed considerably since your visit—and tonight it shall change again."

"From what to what?" she asked.

"It must be seen," Beangern replied.

"At my age it no longer matters."

"On the contrary. It means a great deal that you be present for the enactment and return. There was a reason you were tempted to visit us so long ago, Alice."

Lucer snorted and his chains rattled. Beangern sipped his tea.

"You were brought in to be viewed by your prospective husband," he said.

"Oh, and who might that have been?"

"The real ruler of the place."

"I'm a little old for that part now. If someone like that wanted me, he should have done something about it a long time ago."

"Events," said Beangern, "rose to spoil his plans."

"What events?"

"A small war."

She sipped her tea. "So you must accompany us on this special occasion."

"Sorry. The story is ended now," she said. "Over. Done with. You've come too late."

"It is never too late," Beangern said, "while I live. And I will not die."

He ate a biscuit. Lucer sipped his tea.

"Will I?" Beangern suddenly asked.

"Whom are you asking?" said Lucer.

"You."

"You fear this night," the other replied, "that it holds your death."

"Well, does it?"

"Even if I knew I wouldn't tell you."

Beangern began to raise his shotgun, glanced at Alice, and lowered it again. He ate another biscuit.

"Quite good," he remarked.

"There is still the enactment," Lucer stated.

"Hush now."

"Of course. It matters not."

"What is this enactment?" Alice asked.

"It is a ritual in which the fallen star Beangern must participate. Else will he be swept away."

"Nonsense!" Beangern roared, spilling tea on his jacket. "I perform the rite for old times' sake. Nothing more."

"What rite?" Alice inquired.

"The ritual of return to the heavens from which he came," said Lucer. "On Yuleki's Day. His place has been vacant too long."

"You make him sound like a god," Alice said.

"He is, like one of the god kings of old in your world."

"I thought that the Red King and Queen—or the White," Alice began.

"There were many lunatics in Wonderland," Lucer responded. "Beangern sent many of them into strong exile or imprisonment and rules now himself."

"Is that true?" Alice asked.

"The man exaggerates," Beangern replied. "The Red King and Queen still rule. I occasionally assist."

"And what is the part you would have me play in all this?" asked Alice.

"A small one," Beangern replied.

"He lies," said Lucer.

"What then?" asked Alice.

"Witness," Beangern replied.

"I am an old lady you have confused considerably," Alice said. "I'll have no more of this rabbitholing and mirroring. Let us finish our tea and I'll see you off."

"Of course," Beangern stated. "Come, Lucer. Drink up, and we'll be on our way."

The men finished their tea and Lucer took another biscuit. Both men rose then, and Beangern looked toward Alice. "Would you conduct us to the conveyance now?" he said.

"You mean the mirror?"

"Yes."

"Come this way," Alice said.

Rising, she led them to a flight of stairs and took them up it. Pushing back a hatch and throwing a light switch, she illuminated a low-wattage bulb, which revealed a dusty attic filled with the detritus of decades. At the room's far end hung a mirror, its reflective surface facing the wall.

Alice halted and suddenly asked, "Why do you need it? You obviously got here without it."

"The other way is strenuous," Beangern replied, "and subduing this fellow takes a lot out of one. The other reason is convenience."

"Convenience?" Alice said.

"Yes," Beangern replied. "On the night of Yuleki in the place where the kinyon grass grows, and the Ulb who ate a Jabberwock goes forbling forth to vie, with Kibling and Dars Dadisdada, 'tis soon enough to die, Ryanda! Step through, Lucer!"

He nudged the other man with the shotgun barrel. Lucer approached the mirror and vanished.

"I'm not going back to that place," Alice said.

Beangern laughed and stepped through the mirror. Shortly afterwards, Alice felt herself drawn toward it. She tried to resist but the effect was too strong. Step after resisting step, she was forced to advance until she stood before it and, after all these years, entered.

She stood for several moments within the reversed image of her attic. Then she turned, seeking the mirror, but could not find it. She knew then that she must depart the attic. Turning, she crossed the room, switched off the light, and descended the stair.

She made her way to the back door, opened it, and stepped outside.

It was no longer her garden. It had become a glade in the midst of sunset, two roads emerging from the trees to cross at its center. Beangern stood on the crossroad, shotgun still a-smoke. Lucer lay panting at his feet.

"Tried to escape," Beangern said. "I expected it."

"Is he going to be—all right?" Alice asked, moving to the man's side and kneeling, her nursing training returning in a great rush through her mind.

"Of course," Beangern replied. "He's healing already. Practically impervious. And stronger than an ox. Stronger than me, even. Lacks my combat training, though."

"How do you know these things about him?" she asked.

"He used to be my servant, my man-at-arms. We came here together."

"From where?" she said.

He pointed skyward. "Up there. I am of the fallen star they could not return."

"Why not?" she asked.

"Some metaphysical crime for which the others would never release him, should he come into their power," Lucer moaned.

"Nonsense. 'Twas a mere difference of opinion we had," Beangern stated.

Lucer rose slowly to his feet, hand pressed against his side. "That does smart," he remarked.

"Tell her that you lied," Beangern stated.

"I will not. 'Tis true."

"I'll blast you again."

"Go ahead. Waste our time. Callooh."

"Callay. She'll see for herself this day."

"This night, I say. Away. Let's away."

"By the bye, I say. A little rite to light our way."

With that, he commenced a series of arcane hand movements. The air seemed to brighten about him as he did. Finally, he stopped and indicated that the journey was to continue.

"What was that all about?" Alice asked.

"Dars Dadisdada and Rottery Khan will be riding out tonight," Beangern said.

". . . And the Choipery Girl will circle the world on wings like a bat," said Lucer. "The Challkers Rose will rise from the sea and bloom, and the foongli lights dance on bay and slope. A reminiscence of your Halloween, and a ritual protection against it."

"It would seem that things have changed," she said.

"Just the names," said Beangern.

"More than just the names," said Lucer.

"I would like to be returned to my home now," said Alice.

"I am afraid that that is impossible," said Beangern. "You are needed here."

"Why?"

"This will become apparent later."

"I may choose to withhold my cooperation."

"I think not," said Beangern, raising a small whistle which he wore on a chain about his neck. He put it to his lips and blew upon it.

A minute passed.

"I think I am going to go back," Alice said.

"Impossible," Beangern replied, and in the distance a low rumble rose up.

She listened for a moment, then asked, "What is that sound?"

"Motorcycles," he replied. "Members of the royal guard—the Twittikins—are on their way."

"That was an awfully quick response," she remarked as their shapes came into view on the road ahead.

"Actually, I whistled for them before I left. This one is a new request, for later. You must recall that one can run and get nowhere, or stay in place and make progress—or phone to speak with yourself yesterday."

"Well, somewhat."

"It has its fine points. That's all."

The bikers approached, drew near. When they halted before them,

Beangern approached their leader, a big-bellied man with arms like tree trunks. He wore blue jeans, a black leather vest, and hordes of tattoos. His scarred face broke into a smile.

"Someone you want done for?" he asked Beangern.

"Just guarded," Beangern said. "Miss Alice here."

"Why, she's just an old bag. Why's she need guardin'?"

"Watch your language, Nik. She's a friend of mine. But we can't let her go until tomorrow. So hang around and keep an eye on her. She's got an odd element of probability calls."

"What's that mean?"

"Funny things used to happen around her. They still could, in this place."

The Twittikins advanced to be near her. Above them, amid the branches of a nearby tree, she thought for a moment that she spied the form of a grinning cat.

"Let's be movin' along now," Beangern said.

"Where to?" asked Lucer.

"Why, the palace, of course. To get a fresh judgment pronounced against you."

"Yes, for they do get stale, I know," Lucer said, "like moldy bread."

Beangern laughed. "We'll find you some fresh words to chew over," he said, "in a fresh cell, where mold and oxidation enter not."

"No, for tonight is a very special night, demon star."

"Lucer, you wrong me."

They began walking.

"If that way be north today, we'll be to the palace shortly after sunset," Lucer remarked.

Alice moved nearer.

"There is something about him," she said, "that seems even more abnormal than usual."

"Oh, he's certifiable material, all right," Lucer said, "like most of us. But he's grown too dangerous to buck. And his powers are at a peak come Yuleki."

"And your own?" she asked. "You do seem to have a few of those yourself."

"True," he said. "One never knows how things will fall out in this place. Callooh!"

"Callay!" she responded, smiling. "Are we both crazy, Lucer?"

"Maybe a little," he replied.

"What about letting the prisoners talk?" Nik hollered.

"Let them," Beangern said. "It doesn't matter."

They trekked into the twilight, away from the setting sun.

"Things are a little different this time," Lucer told Alice. "I think they want everything legal and proper."

"What does that mean—in this place?" she asked.

"He'll get the King and Queen to say that it's okay to send me to the mines, that you must attend the rite of Yuleki, and that Beangern's fief remains secure."

"That makes him the real ruler here, doesn't it?"

"I'd say so."

"Does that mean that he was the one who'd summoned me and observed me years ago, looking for the bride he never married?"

"Yes. I was with him at the time. Hidden, he observed all your adventures."

"Why, for heaven's sake?"

"To see how you responded to such unusual stresses."

"Why that?"

"Should you come to reign here, it would be useful to know how you dealt with the environment."

"And I failed."

"No. There was a war here as well as in your world. It caused such things to be bypassed until too late."

"You're saying I should have been queen."

"Empress."

". . . To Beangern."

"Undoubtedly."

"In that case, I'm glad things fell out as they did."

"And I, also. I don't think you'd really have liked it."

"What now?"

"There seems to be no choice. We go through with it. I've a feeling I'll have a part in this one since it's the ending of a celestial cycle and the beginning of a new one, and spirits may mount or descend."

"I don't understand."

"Natural laws in this place. If we ever have an opportunity longer than this, I'll try to explain."

"Why not try it now?"

"Because that bulk up ahead is the castle, and we'll be there before very long. Suffice it to say that Beangern is a stellar spirit who fell to earth at the last major cycle. He saw that this place was a looney bin, and he took it over and set it right."

"Why, then, do you oppose him?"

"He went too far. Now it is a matter of his whim, rather than law or principle, that rules. Perhaps he has gone truly mad. He fears that the Feast of Yuleki, the Yark Angel, may be a time when he could be drawn back to his true realm, never to return."

"You'd think that would make him happy."

"Yes, but it doesn't. He likes it here. He has near fought Yuleki himself over this point."

"This is good?"

"For everyone here there was some good at first."

"Except me," she said.

"Don't say that. You are necessary."

"For what?"

"It must have seemed different to you when you were but a girl, but your adventures then can be viewed in two different ways."

"Oh. I stumbled into a magical kingdom and had some strange experiences. That's how I view it. You have an alternative?"

"Yes. How do you like this one? You were the magical being that entered here. You, as observer, precipitated all the strange experiences you had."

"That is certainly a novel way of regarding it."

"I think you had it, and that you still might."

"What does it mean if I do?"

"You might be able to help to expel him, this time of all times. Everything else will be poised for such a thrust."

"You sure such a thing will work?"

"No, but if we don't try it now it may be eons before another chance occurs. Not all of the royalists will be left. Perhaps not any."

"Let me think about it."

"Better think fast."

They continued their trek to the Castle of Hearts. Beangern told the first person he saw—a short, red-haired gardener—to announce his arrival. The man ran off screaming, "Beangern has come! Beangern has come!"

"I find their enthusiasm touching," Beangern remarked. "Come, let us enter. We shall hunt down their majesties."

Beangern drove the others ahead of him now, lest Lucer free himself and lead Alice astray. He left the Twittikins to guard the gate. He located the King and Queen dressed in rags and hiding beneath the bed in a fourth-floor bedroom.

"Why do we find them so?" Alice asked.

"Guards! Protect us! Off with his head! Beangern! Beangern! Dead! Dead! Dead!" cried the emaciated Queen of Hearts and her diminutive husband.

"They have conceived some ill fancy of me," Beangern replied, his eyes flashing fire, "and compounded it with their tendency to shirk their duties. Come now! Both of you! Out of there! There's a royal decree in need of issuing."

"Why us? Why us?"

"Because you're royal. The decretals need decreting, the world it needs its words, Lord Lucer to the mines again, Beangern to his fiefdom, Alice to her Judgment Chair. Write it down! Write it down! Sign it at the bottom! Circulate the ruddy 'crete to everything alive! And save a ruddy copy for the bloody archive!"

"Scrivener! Scrivener!" cried the Queen.

"Why call only two?" asked the King. "Make it more plural."

"'S, 's," added the Queen.

"Sounds like a tired serpent," said the King.

"Retired servants claim pensions," said the Queen. "What has this to do with them? And what has become of them? What? What?"

"The mines!" cried Lucer. "To save on pay. Release them, release them, release them, pray!"

"This cannot be," said the Queen. "Who would order such?"

Lucer turned and stared at Beangern.

"You liked them overmuch," said the man.

"Release them!"

"Not today."

"Where are our robes royal?"

"In the laundry."

"You sold them. You're disloyal," said the King.

"And the Jewels of the Crown?" asked the Queen.

"On exhibition in the town."

"Lies! Lies! You've robbed us. Bring them back! Bring them back!"

"I hear the scriveners in the hall," said Beangern. "Let us set them up, and tell them what I say."

"I think we do not need your help. We'll do it our own way."

"In that case friends and favorites will be the ones to pay," Beangern said, as he raised his whistle.

"Stop!" cried the King. "We'll do as you say."

"I thought you'd see the light. It must be done tonight. Now, as a matter of fact."

He opened the door and let them in. There were four.

"You lack tact. But you hold the winning cards," said the Queen.

". . . Lucer Starborn is hereby reassigned to the mines. All other political imprisonments are reconfirmed. Axel J. Beangern is reconfirmed in the possession of his fief—" Beangern said.

"That," Lucer said, "is contingent on your sitting through the Feast of Yuleki in the chapel on your property."

"I know that!"

"Very well. Write it down."

". . . And Alice finally present on this night of all nights of the year."

"I know no fear!" said Beangern.

"None spoke of fear but thee."

"This is not part of the decree!" Beangern shouted. "Add the salutatories and affirmations to what has gone before, and be damned with them!"

"Such language!" said Alice.

"He's not at all a gentleman," said Lucer.

"Execute the order! Return him to the pits!" cried Beangern.

"I claim my right to be present at the service," said Lucer.

"Bring him along, then. We'll send him from there when it's done."

Lucer raised his hand and squeezed one of Alice's. "I am to be myself this night," he said, "and likely he will not."

"This is good?" she asked.

"Rejoice and honest be," Lucer replied, "and we shall make it so, come St. George and Low Heaven."

"I fear that I do not understand."

"You will when the time's at hand."

"But Beangern always seemed the gentleman, and you the criminal—though a very polite one."

"He lies. You've seen how he deals. In fact, he also steals."

"I believe. He does deceive."

"Soon we will leave, for the service. Are you hungry? He would see that you are fed, if you are. Wants you strong."

"I'll come along without the bread. I don't know that I care to brave a meal in this place now."

"Why should that be bad?"

"Because everyone's half-mad."

"Yes, but they're half-sane, too."

"I'm on your side. Enough said. Callooh!"

"Callay!"

"Let's be away!" cried Beangern.

They left the castle and the day. They traveled through the hilly lands, to the realm of Whileaway.

"Sing for me, Alice," said Lucer, and she began "Auld Lang Syne."

The Twittikins roared on ahead and behind, the moon dripped butter and venom, and everywhere she looked, it seemed the cat's grin was upon her. A cool, near chill breeze swept them, and all the shadows became a blanket of black.

The moonlight sparkled on a massive block of ice to the right of the trail. They examined it as they passed, and Alice's voice wavered as she beheld within it—frozen in mid-gesture—a March Hare, a Dormouse, and a demented-looking Hatter.

As they crossed the next hill she heard a great, crystal-like shattering, though no one else seemed to.

"Sing more loudly here," Lucer said, and she did. A snuffling, chuffling, snorting followed, as of a laboring walrus climbing a slope.

Again, nobody else seemed to notice.

And at this glade you must sing with particular sweetness," he said.

She did, and the chortling roar that near shook the darkness from the night seemed heard by everyone, from the automatic weapon fire that followed from the Twittikins. The rearmost vanished and their weapons grew still as a dark cloud swept across the road, passing over them.

"Lucer," she whispered, seizing his biceps, "what is it you have me doing?"

"Sorry, naught but pure song, m'lady. Think, think back on all you remember from your earliest visits. If there was aught that you loved, sing to that. Remember, remember, Alice, this place as it was."

And Alice's old voice broke, many, many times, as she recalled and reworded old ballads and music hall songs.

"What is that caterwauling?" Beangern cried, his ears now long and silky, his mouth more full of teeth than before.

"Lady Alice would sing," Lucer replied, "as is her right."

Beangern growled and grew silent.

"He must allow it," Lucer said. "You must unscathed be."

"Why?" she asked.

"Your power is sacrosanct," said he. "You are she who came long ago."

"A lifetime wasn't that far back," she said.

"In this place time doth different flow."

"I'll never understand."

"I say you will. Pray, sing on."

And again she sang. This time, the night came alive with bird cries, cricket calls, and the rustling of leaves. Overhead, the stars shone more brightly than Alice had ever seen them glow, and the moon seemed to swell as it made its slow way zenithward.

"Confound!" Beangern cried, his trousers now split to free his jointed tail, eyes still flashing fire.

"Sing on," said Lucer, and she did.

At last, they reached the top of a high hill, overlooking a vale splashed with moonlight like buttermilk. At their back, Alice heard noises. Beangern called a halt and regarded the prospect for a moment. He raised his right arm and extended a claw. "This is the place where music comes to die," he said. "This is the fief of Beangern. My powers increase here."

". . . And your form seems to have shifted," Alice said.

"Tonight 'tis unavoidable," he said, "when the Powers descend and rise to walk the world."

"I thought that Beangern was a god or demigod. Your form seems more demonic."

"These terms are meaningless in this twisted place," said he, "and as for the rest, read your Nietzsche."

"I understand," said she.

"So I have won, you see. I made you wait till your powers waned and drained. A draft of damp air would blow you away."

"You've watched me all these years?"

"Indeed, through laughter and tears."

"Not too much laughter."

"Nor many tears. Sorry 'tis such a bland life you've led. But so it had to be."

"All for this night?"

"All for this night."

The crest on his backbone rose to a ridge on his head. His hoofs clattered against rocks as he shifted position.

He pointed again. "And there is the chapel, in yonder valley."

They saw the diminutive building, all alight.

"Come," he finally said. "Tonight is indeed the night."

They followed him down the hillside and through the twisting ways of the valley—Beangern, Alice, Lucer, the King and Queen of Hearts, the Twittikins, unassorted courtiers and nobles. The Twittikins were again diminished, in a firefight with something that had howled from behind a boulder. When they searched the area afterwards, nothing could be found.

Great numbers of dark birds passed overhead as they advanced upon the chapel, and there were rustlings within the high grasses all about them. The earth seemed to tremble on several occasions, and deadwood snapped as heavier footfalls occurred.

Lucer had hold of her arm now and she had a stick in her other hand. She leaned on both.

"Not too much farther to the chapel," Lucer remarked. You'll be able to rest once we've arrived."

"I'll make it," she said. "I must see the story through."

"I'm sure you will. Your presence is necessary, either way," said he. "You are she who came."

"Win or lose? Live or dead?"

"Exactly."

An owl dipped above them. "Who?" it asked.

"Me," she answered.

Beangern growled, and birds fell dead from the sky. The earth shook and the wind grew stronger. At last they reached the chapel and Beangern let them in. The place was filled with candlelight, there was a low altar against the forward wall, and a circular skylight poured starshine and the glow of the rising moon down upon the pentagram drawn on the floor beneath. Against the chapel's rear wall was a throne all of red stone, and to this Alice was led.

"Pray, rest yourself!" cried Beangern, and the ground shook as he increased in stature. He moved forward then, motioning the others to seat themselves in pews. Lucer and the King and Queen he allowed to remain near Alice. He moved then to the front of the chapel, and, looking upward, addressed some unseen presence beyond the skylight:

"You up there. This is Beangern," he said. "I know you can hear me, tonight. All right. Tonight is the night, but I want you to know that I hold everything in the palm of my hand. You waste your time if you think that you can do much about it. I know you've been waiting to nail me, Yuleki, but it's too damned late. I've been sucking power out of this land down the years. I'm too strong for you now. One touch more, and the world I have set up will endure forever."

"Alice," Lucer said softly, "I am going to break these chains now and fight him. We are of about equal strength but I will lose because his technique is better. When I appear to be going down for the third time, cry out for Yuleki to come to you. And use your name."

"Why are you as strong as that thing he has become?" she asked.

"I forget."

". . . And why is his technique better?"

"Not sure. No matter."

"Then why must you fight?"

"I must hold him till the moon is higher."

"Why?"

"I don't remember. But it will help us against him."

". . . Now, on this night of all nights of the year," Beangern intoned, "we are gathered together in the eyes of Yuleki and anyone else who cares to look, and we will join in matrimony the master and lady of this place."

"Lady?" Alice said. "Where is she?"

"That's you," Lucer answered, raising his hands and spreading them. He drew them taut and beads of perspiration broke out upon his brow. Then the chains snapped and he bent to draw upon those which held his ankles.

Beangern raised his shotgun. Alice moved to stand before Lucer.

"Damn it, lady! Get out of the way!" Beangern cried.

"No," Alice replied. "Something's wrong here and I want to see it right."

"You're going about it wrong!" he roared.

Lucer's chains broke and he rose to his full height. Beangern sighed. "All right. We must settle this yet again," he said.

Lucer advanced to the center of the chapel and Beangern set aside the shotgun and moved to meet him.

A flash of lightning crossed the sky as they met. Then the two were rolling about the pentagram.

The door to the chapel was opened and the figure of a White Rabbit entered. Alice thought that she heard him mutter, "Oh dear!" as he seated himself in a pew near the front. He watched the fray as the two combatants struck, their fists shattering brick, stone, or flagging when they missed each other.

Finally, she felt the rabbit's gaze upon her. He stared for a long while before his eyes widened in recognition. She nodded then.

The Rabbit rose and made his way slowly along the lefthand wall. When he came to the throne he said, "Alice."

"How's the Dormouse?" she asked.

"Still in the teapot. How are you?"

"Oh, time has taken its ticket for the show," she said. "And yourself?"

"You freed me earlier with your singing."

"What? How?"

"You're magic. You must know that by now. I was with the Jabberwock after you sang him loose. He's waiting outside to eat Beangern if he can."

The Rabbit's eyes turned toward the combatants. "Tough pair, those two. Hard to tell which is master or man."

"Not for me. Beangern has ceased to be a man."

"He will always be a mere man-at-arms among the skiey hosts."

"What are you saying? He is a fallen star—a higher being whose contact with this world may have corrupted him."

The Queen of Hearts shrieked as the combatants rolled near to her, Beangern's horns scoring the stone at her feet. Then the combatants rolled away again.

"Lord Lucer is the fallen star," replied the Rabbit, "who must be made this night to remember himself. Beangern was his servant, who usurped his place when the forgetfulness fell upon Lucer."

"What?" cried Alice. "Beangern an imposter?"

"Indeed. Now that you've freed me, I hope to see him pass one way or the other this night."

There came a crash as the two men struck the wall and the building shook.

"Why does Beangern outclass his boss?" Alice asked.

"A man-at-arms has special combat training, for service against the dark legions," replied the rabbit.

It seemed that Beangern and Lucer hammered upon each other forever, as the moon rose higher and higher. Then Beangern's blows began to appear more telling, and finally he knelt upon Lucer, and, catching hold of his head, began to bang it upon the stone floor. Seeing this, Alice cried out, "Yuleki, Yark Angel, help us now! This is Alice calling." Then she moved toward them.

With a flash, a ball of white light appeared above the pentagram. Beangern rose and faced it, leaving a panting, bleeding figure upon the floor.

"It is not fair that you should come for me now, Yuleki!" he cried. "I am tired and cannot face you properly!"

"All the better then," a musical voice rang out. "Transform! You lose no face by coming along with me without strife."

Beangern glanced at Lucer. "Do you remember?" he called out.

"Remember what?" Lucer responded.

Beangern looked back at Yuleki. "I maintain my battle mode and we fight," he said.

"Very well."

He plunged forward. When he made contact with the bright sphere, it raised him above the ground, spun him round like a whirlwind, then slammed him down upon the stone. It drifted into a position above his chest. He attempted to raise his arms and legs and could not.

"You should have made it last longer," he whispered, "for his sake. I have been trying to cure him for decades. I thought that this might do it. I wanted him whole, so that he could be returned."

"My plan was otherwise."

Beangern turned his head toward Lucer. "Master!" he cried. "Remember! Please!"

"I do, faithful servant," came the response; and Lucer took Alice's hand in his own. A faint glow suddenly surrounded her.

"Your job here is done," Yuleki said to Beangern. "But his is not, though he is whole again. He will repair this land, which you sacrificed in the cause of his healing."

"I could help him!"

"That would not be prudent. Their memories of you are bad."

There followed a crash of thunder and both Beangern and the light were gone.

Alice felt the years fall away as her odd aura strengthened.

"What is happening?" she asked.

Lucer drew her to her feet.

"I take you back along the years to your youth, old friend," he said. "By the way, there really should be a wedding tonight. Are you game?"

"Are you serious?"

"Indeed I am. I do want your help as well as your company. After all, you are the true goddess of this place."

"This is too much," she said, staring at the back of her hand as the wrinkles faded. "I'll never understand."

"Come with me."

He walked to the door of the chapel and flung it open. They were all there, Humpty and the grinning Cat, the Dormouse and the Hatter, the March Hare, the Walrus and the Jabberwock. The Choipery Girl passed overhead. A great cry rose up.

"Lucer and Alice! Lucer and Alice!"

"This seems as good a place as any," he said. "Will you have me, Alice?"

She looked out over the multitude of creatures, many still arriving. Then the Queen said, "Do it, Alice. I know we need you. Beangern's fief is yours now, of course. Do it."

Alice looked at Lucer, looked at the crowd, then back at Lucer.

"You're all mad," she said. "But so am I."

Music fell from the skies. Looking up, she saw a small star rising through the spheres to the empyrean.

# THE LAST INN ON THE ROAD

## by *Roger Zelazny and Danny Plachta*

Father Bob flicked a quick Sign of the Cross with the point of his switch-blade and dropped into a crouch. He stared up the alleyway, his leather jacket tight across his shoulders. There was a faint flash of metal not more than six feet away.

"Who is it?" he demanded.

A fleet of motorcycles crackled down the adjacent street. He waited for their lights to outline his adversary.

But the bikes belonged to the Red Holy Rollers from Saint Bob's, and they always rode blacked-out.

"Who is it?" he asked again, after the silence had returned.

"Sister Cameo. That *is* you, Father?"

"Blessed be the Holy Name of Jesus," he intoned, snapping his blade closed.

"Blessed be the Holy Name," she agreed, and another blade snicked shut within the darkness.

"Praise be that I got here when I did, Sister. That sounded like the Rollers going by."

"I'd say so, Father. Full strength."

She touched the priest's arm.

"But come. It isn't far."

"Just to be on the safe side, Sister, we'd better spread some broken glass. You get the far end of the alley and I'll get this one."

He moved toward the nearer street.

"It's in the centre of the block," she whispered, before they parted.

Father Bob spent five minutes smashing empty beer bottles on the rough pavement. All the street lights had been shot out. In fact, Father Bob had never seen a lighted one. Nevertheless, there was a certain amount of light tumbling from a large neon sign: BUY OUR JUNK, it urged. Below it, smaller letters spelled out the familiar slogan: ACID, HORSE, SEEDS, AND LI. TAKE TEA AND SEE.

He was about to return to the safety of the alley and its darkness when he noticed the dog. Its long dark tail rippled in the wind as it trotted toward him. Small, yet for some strange reason unafraid, it came up to him. Its tongue hung out over its side teeth as though it were laughing, and its ears were long and ragged. He patted its head and was vaguely pleased when it followed him back up the alley.

"This is it, Father," whispered the nun when they met again. "We're home."

Rusted hinges grated, and Father Bob felt her hand on his arm.

"Don't fall over anything, Bob. It's a mess in here."

He heard the dog patter in after them. The ancient door creaked again and clicked at their backs.

"It's an old garage," she told him. "The house in front is completely wrecked. I covered our only window with tar paper."

Then she rummaged for a dark moment and a match scratched, flashing yellow pain into his eyes. "Make yourself at home."

It was, he observed after a moment, a compact indoor junkyard, an attic and cellar that had somehow gotten together for money, not love.

"A wreck room," he muttered, and the girl giggled.

She lit a votive candle and the room was drenched in the bloodlight of its glass container. Twisted shadows from a hundred shipwrecked homes filled the walls, the floor, the ceiling.

"I think we'd best put it out as soon as we're settled," she suggested. Her black leather jacket and stretch pants became a reddish bronze in the candlelight, and he glanced furtively at his own clothing. The dog nipped at Sister Cameo's boots. "Here," she said, lifting it in her arms, "I think I can fix you up for the night." She found an empty beer case, removed the partitions, and placed the dog gently within it. ". . . but I won't have you sleeping on any of these dirty rags!"

There was a slight movement in the corner of the garage, and two cats glided forth to peer in at the dog. They leaned and watched without moving. "One happy family," smiled the priest, and the man and the woman knelt on the cold concrete, joining together in prayer.

Sister Cameo extinguished her candle, and they went to bed, the dog making faint noises, half-snore, half-growl, behind them.

*They looked like stars and they were among the stars. They moved with seeming slowness, yet somehow they passed quickly.*

*"We are near," said Amar.*

*"The star guides us well," replied Borin.*

*"Still, we shan't arrive in time," said Calat.*

*The three points of light arced across another hundred parsecs.*

*"Perhaps. Perhaps not. But it's our only chance to see," said Amar.*

*"Their star nears the apex," observed Borin.*

*"We cannot stay long," Calat noted.*

*The three points crossed another dark gap.*

Right there on Saint Bob's parking lot, in the middle, the Red Holy Rollers parked their bikes. They parked them and they slept there, resting their heads upon the polished chrome of the handlebars. None of them were really tired, having slept most of the day. But they were a legend around town. They slept on their bikes, it was told. So don't kill a good thing. They stayed in the lot until eleven o'clock, passed another ten minutes debating where to go. Finally, they roared off to the Junk Yard, three blocks away. . . .

The place was spinning when they hit it. They knew it would be, and it revved up when they moved into action. The in-drink that night was Old Krupnik on the rocks, for God's sake, and they uncorked it, learned to live with it.

Some old broad in a topless ski suit swivelled it over and asked would anyone care to move around the floor, so Tiny Tim the Big Man called her hand, took it, yanked her into service. They swung to the strings twisted and the skins thumping; the Molesters' "Old Rugged Cross Writhe" it was, and everybody did, making with the outstretched arms bit. But Tiny Tim, he got a thumb in the right eye and that was it for indoor exercise.

After the debacle that ensued, they were all of them about seven handlebars to the wind when it fell upon them like damn let's go Of-the-Cloth hunting. Real big this went, up and over like a pregnant pole-vaulter, and. . . .

They cut at 11:47. One more round of Old Krupdammitnik . . .

*Crawling in the deep shadows, darkness all about them, yet able to see, the three moved down the alien roadway.*
"*A strange world . . .*" said Amar.
"*Like no other,*" Borin agreed.
"*Perhaps it will be for the best*"—Calat.
*They skittered and churned, boffed and scaffonted, then paused.*
"*I am weary of my burden*"—Amar.
"*There is so little time. . . .*"—Borin.
"*The stars! I fear we must miss our chance to see!*"—Calat.
"*Yes! We must leave our prizes! Make haste!*"—Borin.
*They moved on, up, out, their tears falling upon the stones.*

Father Bob was awakened by a creaking noise. He listened, tense, motionless, to the sound of the dog's breathing. Could someone have entered the garage without awakening the animal? Regretting the sound, he snapped open his switchblade.

"Father. It's me."
"What're you doing, Sister?"
"I heard a noise outside. I waited awhile before checking."
"Someone prowling?"
"I don't really know, but when I went out I stumbled over . . . these."

She lit a match, spreading the flame to the candle.

He inspected the three items in the ruddy light.

"Very strange," he admitted. "Perhaps we overlooked them when we entered."

"Perhaps," she said.

The priest held one of the objects near the candle.

"It's a concave disk, with little projections all over. . . . Beautiful!" he decided, "whatever it is."

"Here's a metal box, covered with some kind of spongy stuff," said the man.

The last item was a wire band with an attached oval of what seemed a shiny plastic substance. Impulsively, she took the band and gently forced it over the head of the awakened puppy, who had been sniffing at it.

"Pretty doggie . . ." she said, fondling its ears.

"Let the little fellow sleep on the spongy thing," said the priest, and the girl lifted the dog as Father Bob placed the makeshift cushion in the beer case.

"I took a bottle of milk tonight, God forgive me," said the nun, her blush invisible in the red light. "We can put some in this odd dish for the dog and the cats and drink the rest ourselves. I was saving it for breakfast. What is that smell?"

The dog came out of the beer case again, to splash with his pink tongue at the milk as she poured it. The cats only sat and watched. Their tongues smoothed their whiskers, but they did not draw near.

As Sister Cameo was about to place the dog back in the box, both garage doors banged open. She reached for her switchblade and cried out.

Father Bob froze, his right hand at his belt, as an empty beer bottle struck against his forehead. He swayed for a moment, then fell back against an old washing machine. Slashing furiously, the nun went down with a length of chain around her thighs.

"I'm cut!" roared Tiny Tim. "Thirty-eight years a Roller and never a scratch! Now I get it from a broad!" His sobs were inaudible above the screams when they nailed the nun and the priest to the garage doors. "It was the glass at the end of the alley tipped us off!" he taunted them, feeling better for it.

The old men stayed to hear the screaming and whimpering for the minute or two that it lasted. Then they stamped out and returned to their bikes, parked up the block.

The dog looked at the unconscious figures on the doors. He licked his paws in the bloody candlelight. He sniffed at the overturned dish. The plastic and metal jangled together below his neck, and he paused to glance back into the mangled beer case. There was a strange smell about the place. . . .

A vague curtain of coloured light forming in the midnight sky shifted, was gone, before the dog entered the shadows of the alley. Briefly then, he paused, but only to aim a single, short howl at the moon before it vanished behind a cloud; and then he passed the darting neon, going up the street, off the street, by the street and into the night beyond, his gift a choking collar around his puppy throat.

# STOWAWAY

He disembarked in New York harbor in the dead of night. A light rain was falling, but it didn't disturb him especially. Not after all those weeks in the stifling cargo hold of the vessel. It had been rainy in Algeria, also.

He'd slipped from the rail and fallen into the water. Since he could not reboard the vessel, he swam to the wharf and climbed a piling.

He shook himself and moved toward a warehouse. He wasn't feeling well.

After perhaps ten minutes, he found entrance. Five more, and he'd located a meal.

They had broken into a storage bin and torn open a sack. He pushed his way through the throng. He was very hungry.

They pushed back, and he slashed at them, and their blood fell upon the floor. He ate.

He spent the next three days in the warehouse, and was wakened by a cry at approximately 5:30 P.M. as the watchman fell upon one of his companions with a club and was slashed in the course of the foray. When it was all over, the watchman washed his hand, daubed it with iodine, covered the wound with a Band-Aid, and continued his rounds.

He left the warehouse, the same way he had entered, and made his way up a narrow street lined with brick buildings, all of their windows dark.

The alley up which he turned was filled with bottles, broken and unbroken, and various items of rubbish which had been thrown from the upstairs apartments.

At one point, a dog barked at him, but the only other sounds within the chill morning were an occasional squeal of tires and the distant wail of a siren.

Moving farther and farther into the city, he turned a corner and looked upon a broad avenue, just as the black egg was touched in the east by morning, cracks of rose and vermilion widening within it. He rested on a stair leading down to a basement and watched the city come to life. The light at the intersection held two cars, then released them and the beams of their headlamps raked him as they went by. An airplane growled above the brightening smog, and he heard the curses of a drunk who had awakened in the alley. Four more cars passed. Then a small man in a gray sweater and beard began unlocking a newsstand on the corner. Beneath him came the rumble, clatter, screech of a subway car, and after a moment people began to emerge from the kiosk across the street. He could hear their voices as they passed. One of them stopped before a clothing store, unlocked it and entered. A light went on within. The subway train departed, and the smell of it rose through the grating in the sidewalk and drifted toward him. Two more stores were opened. The sun became a red dome, an orange bubble clinging to the horizon. Telephone lines slashed it. The streetlights went out. There came the smack of a bundle of papers as they struck the concrete beside the newsstand. Day had begun.

He descended the stairs and entered a deserted basement. After a time, he found a dark and quiet place and he slept once more, for he was feeling worse. When the watchmen left the warehouse, he had breakfast at a nearby diner, orange juice, toast, scrambled eggs, two cups of coffee. Then he went home and kissed his wife, who was on her way out the door, Wednesday being the day she cleaned house for the Simpsons. He drank a glass of water, undressed and went directly to bed, for day had begun.

Of course it moved like lightning. Think about the drippy season for a moment, and you'll see why.

Take twelve million people, confine them in five boroughs, require that they move around every day in order to earn their livelihood, shake hands, eating and drinking together, sitting in rooms full of desks or toilets, laughing, sneezing, coughing in each other's faces and, "Kiss you? I shouldn't be doing this!" to each other, and let one man with a cold decide against staying home that day and you've got a drippy season.

All right, take it from there. . . .

When he crawled out of the basement, on Saturday, there was no traffic for a long time, and then a black car passed. The store was closed, and the newsstand. He heard a bell ringing, over and over. He drank from a mud puddle, but it did not slake his thirst.

He lay on his side, panting, and after a time he closed his eyes. He gasped and lay still.

It comes in three varieties: bubonic, systemic, pneumonic. Depending on this, it may take two days or a couple of weeks. There is an anti-serum, but try getting enough to vaccinate twelve million people in a hurry.

The newspaper in the unopened bundle beside the stand warned of sick rats and rats found dead out in the open.

Later that year, the two million inhabitants of the five boroughs experienced another drippy season.

# ANGEL, DARK ANGEL

He entered the kiosk and escalated down to the deck that stood beside the rumbling strip. He was fifty-five years of age and he bore a briefcase in his right hand.

As he crossed toward the conveyor belt, a dozen heads turned in his direction because of the flash of light which occurred immediately before him.

For one bright instant, a dark figure stood in his path.

Then there came the *crack* of imploding air, as the figure vanished and the man fell to the deck. Later that day, the death record read, "Natural causes."

Which was true. Quite, quite true.

It slithered along the moist tunnel, heading toward the river.

It knew that its life had ended the moment that the blaze occurred; and the facets of its eyes held sixty-four images of the tall, leather-masked figure, garbed all in black, with its hard, dark hand upraised.

The hand extended toward it, offering that which it could not refuse.

The gift was thunder and pain, and the medical record prepared later that day said, "Natural causes."

Putting down his champagne glass, he unfastened her negligee and pushed it back over her shoulders. His hands molded her, described her sex, drew her down onto the bed. She sighed as he raised himself onto an elbow and touched her lips.

She felt him stiffen, in the glare that came from the corner of the suite. She screamed within the thunderclap that followed, having glimpsed the Angel of Death for a single, dark moment as she felt her lover stop his loving, forever.

This, too, was the result of natural causes.

The man called Stain was in his greenhouse, where he had spent some part of almost every day for the past two years, plucking dead leaves and taking cuttings.

He was slightly under six feet in height, and his eyes were iodine-dark within his sharp-cornered, sunbaked face beneath black hair salted lightly at the temples.

His left shoulder brushed against an earthenware pot on the shelf at his back, and he felt its movement and departure

Turning, he caught it at waist level and replaced it on the shelf.

He began repotting a geranium, and then the instrument strapped to his left wrist buzzed and he pressed a button on its side and said, "Yes?"

"Stain," said the voice, which could have been coming from the red flowers in his hand, "do you love the human races and all other living things within the universe?"

"Of course," he replied, recognizing the crackling sibilance that was the voice of Morgenguard.

"Then please prepare yourself for a journey of some duration and report to your old cubicle in Shadowhall."

"But I am retired, and there must be many others whose speed now exceeds my own."

"Your last medical report shows that your speed is undiminished. You are still one of the ten best. You were retired at the proper age because it is your right to enjoy the rest of your days as you see fit. You are not ordered to do the thing I now say. You are requested to do it. So you may refuse if you see fit. Should you accept, however, you will be compensated, and you will have served the things you profess to love."

"What would you have of me?"

"Come not in uniform, but in civil garb. Bring with you your gauntlets and your daily requirements in all things, save nourishment, for a period of approximately two weeks."

"Very well. I will attend directly."

The communication ended, and he finished potting the geranium and returned to his quarters.

To his knowledge, none such as himself had ever been recalled from retirement, nor was his knowledge inaccurate.

Her name is Galatea, and she has red hair and stands to slightly over five and a half feet in height. Her eyes are green and her complexion pale, and men call her lovely but generally avoid her company. She lives in a big, old house which she has remodeled, on the outskirts of Cyborg, an ancient city on Ankus in the Ceti System. She keeps to herself and runs up large bills with the Cyborg Power Co.

She lives alone, save for mechanical servants. She favors dark colors in her garb and her surroundings. She occasionally plays tennis or else fences at the local sports center. She always wins. She orders large quantities of chemicals from local wholesalers. Men who have dated her say that she is stupid, brilliant, oversexed, a prude, fascinated with her deathwish, full of *joie de vivre*, an alcoholic, a teetotaler and a wonderful dancer. She has had many dates/few friends/no suitors, and her lovers be unknown. It is suggested that she maintains a laboratory and perhaps engages in unknown researches.

"We do not know the answer," said Simule. "There is no defense against him, save here. I cannot remain here if I am to serve my function. Therefore, I must leave soon, and secretly."

"Wait," she said. "You are not yet ready to survive on your own. Another month, perhaps . . ."

"Too long, too long, we fear," Simule replied.

"Do you doubt my power to protect you?"

Simule paused, as if to consider, then, "No. You can save this body, but the question, 'Is it worth it?' comes forth. Is it worth it? Preserve yourself, lady. We love you. There remains yet more that you may do."

"We shall see," she said, "But for now, you remain."

She replaced him, upon the reading stand in her library, and she left him there with *Lear*.

His name was Stain, and he came to her door one day and announced himself, saying, "Stain, of Iceborg."

After a time, the door let him in.

She appeared and asked, "Yes?"

"My name is Stain," he replied, "and I have heard that you play tennis, and are very good. I am looking for a partner in the Cyborg Open Mixed Doubles. I am good. Will you play with me?"

"How good?" she asked him.

"They don't come much better."

"Catch," she said, and picked up a marble figurine from off an inlaid table and hurled it toward him.

He caught it, fumbling, and set it on the ledge at his side.

"Your reflexes are good," she replied. "Very well, I'll play with you."

"Will you have dinner with me tonight?"

"Why?"

"Why not? I don't know anyone here."

"All right. Eight o'clock."

"I'll pick you up then."

"Till then."

"Till then."

He turned, and headed back toward the town and his hotel.

Of course, they took the tournament. They won hands down. And Stain and Galatea danced that night and drank champagne, and she asked him as he held her, both of them all in black, "What do you do, Stain?"

"Nothing but enjoy myself," he said. "I'm retired."

"In your thirties?"

She sighed and softened within his arms.

"What do *you* do?" he asked.

"I, too, am retired. I enjoy my hobbies. I do as I would."

"What does that come to?"

"Whatever I please."

"I've brought you a Hylagian orchid to wear in your hair, or anywhere else you may choose. I'll give it to you when we return to the table."

"They're very expensive," she said.

"Not so if you raise them yourself."

"And you do?"

"*My* hobby," he replied.

At their table, they finished their champagne and smoked and she studied the flower and her companion. The club was done all in silver and black, and the music was soft—and as the dancers seated themselves it lost all semblance of a theme. Her smile was the candle of their table, and he ordered them a dessert and liqueurs to accompany it, and she said, "Your poise defies description."

"Thank you, but yours is superior."

"What did you do, before you retired?"

"I was a paymaster. What of yourself?"

"I dealt in accounts receivable, for a large concern."

"Then we have something else almost in common."

"So it would seem. What will you do now?"

"I'd like to continue seeing you, for so long as I am in town."

"How long might that be?"

"For so long as I might wish, or you desire."

"Then let us finish our sherbet; and since you wish me to have the trophy, we will take it home."

He brushed the back of her hand, lightly, and for an instant their eyes met, and a spark that might have been electric leapt between them and they smiled at precisely the same instant.

After a time, he took her home.

The bat-thing quivered and dipped, on the way to the council of its people.

As it passed by a mountaintop, there came a flash of light. Though its speed was virtually inconceivable and its movement unpredictable, it knew that it would fall in an instant; and it did, as the thunder roared above it.

He held her very closely and their lips met. They stood in the foyer of her big old remodeled house on the outskirts of Cyborg City on Ankus, of the Ceti System, and one of her mechanical servants had taken their cloaks and another the double-handled golden tennis trophy, and the front door had closed behind them and the night lights had come on dim as they had entered.

"You'll stay awhile," she said.

"Fine."

And she led him into a long, sunken living room filled with soft furniture, with a fresco upon one wall. They faced it as he seated himself on the green divan, and he stared at the wall as he lit two cigarettes and she handed him a final drink and joined him there.

"Lovely," he said.

"You like my fresco?"

"I hadn't noticed it."

". . . And you haven't tasted your drink."

"I know."

Her hand came to rest upon his arm, and he put his drink aside and drew her to him once again, just as she put hers to rest.

"You are quite different from most men," she said.

". . . And you from most women."

"Is it growing warm in here?"

"Very," he said.

Somewhere it is raining. Controlled or artificial—somewhere it is always raining, any time you care to think about it. Always remember that, if you can.

A dozen days had passed since the finale of the Cyborg City Mixed Open. Every day Stain and Galatea moved together somewhere. His hand upon her elbow or about her waist, she showed him Cyborg City. They laughed often, and the sky was pink and the winds were gentle and in the distance the cliffs of Ankus wore haloes of fog prismatic and crowns of snow and ice.

Then he asked her of the fresco as they sat in her living room.

"It represents the progress of human thought," she said. "That figure—far to the left, contemplating the birds in flight—is Leonardo Da Vinci, deciding that man might do likewise. High at the top and somewhat to the left, the two figures ascending the ziggurat toward the rose are Dante and Virgil, the Classic and the Christian, joined together and departing the Middle Ages of Earth into a new freedom—the place where Leonardo might contemplate. That man off to the right is John Locke. That's the social contract in his hand. That man near the middle—the little man clutching the figure-eight—is Albert Einstein."

"Who is the blinded man far to the left, with the burning city at his back?"

"That is Homer."

"And *that* one?"

"Job, on a heap of rubble."

"Why are they all here?"

"Because they represent that which must never be forgotten."

"I do not understand. I have not forgotten them."

"Yet the final five feet to the right are blank."

"Why?"

"There is nothing to put there. Not in a century has there been anything worth adding. Everything now is planned, prescribed, directed—"

"And no ill comes of it, and the worlds are managed well. Do not tell me how fine were the days of glorious discontent, days through which you never lived yourself. The work done then has not gone to waste. Everything is appreciated, used."

"But what new things have been added?"

"Size, and ease of operation within it. Do not preach to me of progress. Change is not desirable for its own sake but only if it offers improvement. I could complete your fresco for you—"

"With a gigantic machine guarded by the Angel of Death! I know!"

"You are wrong. It would end with the Garden of Eden."

She laughed.

"Now you know the story of my fresco."

He took her hand. "You may be right," he said. "I don't really know. I was only talking about how things seem to me."

"And *you* may be right," she said. "*I* don't really know ... I just feel there should be something to counterbalance that wonderfully flexible mechanism which guides us so superbly that we are becoming the vegetables in that garden you would draw me."

"Have you any suggestions?"

"Have you read any of my papers?"

"I'm afraid not. I fool around with my own garden and I play tennis. That's about it."

"I have proposed the thesis that man's intelligence, extruded into the inanimate, has lost all that is human. Could you repair the machine that mixes our drinks, if it ceased to function?"

"Yes."

"Then you are very unusual, Most people would call in a robot which specializes in small appliance repairs."

Stain shrugged.

"Not only have we given up this function of intelligent manipulation— but divorced from us and existing elsewhere, it turns and seeks to suppress what remains of it within ourselves."

"What do you mean?"

"Why has life become a horizontal line, rather than an upward curve? One reason is that men of genius die young."

"This I cannot believe."

"I purposely published my most important papers recently and I was visited by the Angel of Death. This proved it to me."

He smiled.

"You still live, so this could not be so."

She returned his smile, and he lit two cigarettes and said, "On what subjects were the papers?"

"The Preservation of Sensibility."

"An innocuous-seeming subject."

"Perhaps."

"What do you mean 'perhaps'? Perhaps I misunderstand you."

"It would seem that you do. Sensibility is a form of esthetic consciousness cultivated by intelligence. This is lacking today and I proposed a method whereby it might be preserved. The fruits of my work were then threatened.

"And what may these be?"

She tilted her head slightly, studied his face, then, "Come with me, and I will show you," she said, and she rose and led him into her library. As he followed her, he removed from an inner pocket his black gauntlets and drew them onto his hands. Then he jammed his hands into his side pockets to cover them and entered the room at her back.

"Simule," she called out, and the tiny creature that sat before a reading machine upon her desk leapt into her extended hand, ran up her right arm and sat upon her shoulder.

"What is it?" he questioned.

"The answer," she said. "Pure, mechanistic intelligence can be countered by an infinitely mobile and easily concealed organic preserver of sensibility. This is Simule. He and others like him came to life in my laboratory."

"Others?"

"There are many, upon many worlds already. They share a mass mind. They learn constantly. They have no personal ambition. They wish only to learn and to instruct any who wish to learn from them. They do not fear the death of their bodies, for they continue to exist thereafter as a part of the mind they all share. They—or it—are—or is—lacking in any other personal passion. The Simule could never represent a threat to the human races. I know this, for I am their mother. Take Simule into your hand, consider him, ask him anything. Simule, this is Stain; Stain, this is Simule."

Stain extended his right hand, and the Simule leaped into it. Stain studied the tiny, six-legged creature, with its disquietingly near-human face. Near. Yet not quite. It was unmarked by the physical conversions of those abstract passion-producers men call good and evil, which show in some form upon every human countenance. Its ears were large, doubtless for purposes of eavesdropping, and its two antennae quivered upon its hairless head as it raised a frail limb as if to shake hands. An eternal smile played upon its lips, and Stain smiled back. "Hello," he said, and the Simule replied in a soft, but surprisingly rich voice, "The pleasure is mine, sir."

Stain said, "What is so rare as a day in June?" and the Simule replied, "Why, the lady Galatea, of course, to whom I now return," and leaped and was upon her suddenly extended palm.

She clutched the Simule to her breast and said, "Those gauntlets—!"

"I put them on because I did not know what sort of creature the Simule might be. I feared it might bite. Please give him back that I might question him further—"

"You fool!" she said. "Point your hands in another direction, unless you wish to die! Do you not know who I am!"

Then Stain knew.

"I did not know," he said.


In Shadowhall in Morgenguard the Angel of Death stands within ten thousand transport cubicles. Morgenguard, who controls the destinies of all civilized worlds, briefs his agents for anything from ten seconds to a minute and a half—and then, with a clap of thunder, dispatches them. A second later—generally—there is a flash of light and a brief report, which is the word "Done," and there then follows another briefing and another mission.

The Angel of Death is, at any given moment, any one of ten thousand anonymous individuals whose bodies bear the mark of Morgenguard, after this fashion:

Selected before birth because of a genetic heritage which includes heightened perception and rapid reflexes, certain individuals of the Homo sapiens variety are given a deadly powerful education under force-fed conditions. This compensates for its brevity. At age fourteen, they may or may not accept employment in the service of Morgenguard, the city-sized machine created by the mutual efforts of all civilized peoples over a period of fifteen years and empowered to manage their worlds for them. Should any decline, these individuals generally proceed to excel in their chosen professions. Should they accept, a two-year period of specialized training follows. At the end of this time, their bodies have built into them an arsenal of weapons and numerous protective devices and their reflexes have been surgically and chemically stimulated to a point of thoughtlike rapidity.

They work an eight-hour day, five days a week, with two daily coffee breaks and an hour for lunch. They receive two vacations a year and they work for fourteen years and are retired on full salary at age thirty, when their reflexes begin to slow. At any given moment, there are always at least ten thousand on duty.

On any given workday, they stand in the transport cubicles in

Shadowhall in Morgenguard, receive instructions, are transported to the worlds and into the presence of the individuals who have become superfluous, dispatch these individuals and depart.

He is the Angel of Death. Life lasts long, save for him; populations would rise up like tidal waves and inundate worlds, save for him; criminals would require trials and sentencing, save for him, and of course history might reflect unnecessary twistings and turnings, save for the Angel of Death.

One dark form might walk the streets of a city and leave that city empty of life at its back. Coming in lightning and departing in thunder, no world is foreign, no face unfamiliar, and the wearer of the black gauntlets is legend, folklore and myth; for to a hundred billion people, he is but one being with a single personality.

All of which is true. Quite, quite true.

And the Dark Angel cannot die.

Should the near-impossible occur, should some being with speed and intrepidity be standing accidentally armed at the moment his name on the roll yonder and up is being shouted, then the remains of the stricken Dark Angel vanish as, with a simultaneous lightning-and-thunder effect, another takes his place, rising, as it were, out of ashes.

The few times that this had occurred, the second has always finished the job.

But this time things were different; and what little remained of seven agents of Morgenguard had lain in cubicles, smoldered, bled, been dead.

"You are the Dark Angel, the Sword of Morgenguard," she said. "I did not mean to love you."

"Nor I you, Galatea, and were you only a mortal woman, rather than a retired Angel yourself—the only being whose body would throw back the charge upon me and destroy me, as it did the others—please believe that I would not raise my hand against you."

"I would like to believe that, Stain."

"I am going now. You have nothing to fear of me."

He turned and headed toward the door.

"Where are you going?" she asked him.

"Back to my hotel. I will be returning soon, to give a report."

"What will it say?"

He shook his head and left.

But he knew.

He stood in Shadowhall within the thing called Morgenguard. He was the Angel of Death, Emeritus, and when the old familiar voice crackled over the loudspeaker and said, "Report" he did not say, "Done." He said,

"Extremely confidential," for he knew what that meant.

There came a flash of lightning, and he stood in a larger hall before a ten-story console, and he advanced toward it and heard the order repeated once more.

"One question, Morgenguard," he said, as he halted and folded his arms upon his breast. "Is it true that you were fifteen years in the building?"

"Fifteen years, three months, two weeks, four days, eight hours, fourteen minutes and eleven seconds," Morgenguard replied.

Then Stain unclasped his arms, and his hands came together upon his breast.

Morgenguard may have realized in that instant what he was doing; but then, an Angel's body has built into it an arsenal of weapons and numerous protective devices and his reflexes have been surgically and chemically stimulated to a point of thoughtlike rapidity; also, Stain had been recalled from retirement because he was one of the ten fastest who had ever served Morgenguard.

The effect was instantaneous. The clap of thunder was not Morgenguard's doing, for he did not remove Stain in time.

The Dark Angel might never strike itself. The seven who had approached the lady Galatea had suffered from a recoil-effect from her own defense system. Never before had the power of the Dark Angel been turned upon himself, and never in the person of one. Stain had worked it out, though.

Death and destruction meeting automatic defense meeting recoil meeting defense recoil defense recoil breakthrough, and a tremendous fireball blooming like an incandescent rose rose within the heart of the city-sized machine Morgenguard.

*Right or wrong, Simule will have some years to grow,* he knew, in that instant, and—

—and somewhere the sun is shining, and its heart is the moebius-burn of the Phoenix Action/Reaction. Somewhere the sun is always shining, any time you care to think about it. Try to remember that, if you can. It is very important.

She remembers. Her name is Galatea. And we remember.

We always remember. . . .

# PROLOGUE TO
# *THE TRUMPS OF DOOM*

*He started out walking, into the dim labyrinth. There seemed to be a faint tune in the air . . .*

*It was almost too easy. A turning, a twisting, a doubling back . . .*

*And then he faced a rough, slanted wall, looked up and saw the shaft. He commenced climbing.*

*It was no longer easy. A swaying sensation began—faint, then distinct—as if he were mounting into the uppermost branches of a tall tree. His way brightened and then dimmed, repeatedly, in no perceptible pattern. After a time, his eyes ached. Images doubled, wavered . . .*

*When the way grew suddenly level he doubted his vision, till his extended hand assured him that there was indeed a choice of passages.*

*He leaned and moved his head into each of these. The faint musical sound seemed slightly louder in the one to the left, and he followed it. Of that, at least, he was certain.*

*Now his way rose and fell. He climbed up, he climbed down. The brightening and dimming continued, only now the brightness was brighter and the dimness dimmer.*

*And the sensations of external movement had not abated. The floor of the tunnel seemed to ripple beneath his feet, the walls and roof to contract and expand. He stumbled, caught himself. Stumbled again . . .*

*At the next turning the sounds grew slightly louder, and he realized that they were not a tune, but rather a totally random concatenation of noises.*

*He climbed. He descended. The passageway shrank, and finally he crawled.*

*The sensations of movement increased. At times he seemed to be spinning; other times, it fell as if he were falling into an enormous abyss.*

*The flashes of light now drove nails of pain into his skull. He began to hallucinate. Faces and figures. Flames. Or were they hallucinations?*

*He felt the first faint pulsation upon his left wrist . . .*

*How long had he been moving? His clothes were already in tatters and he bled, painlessly, from a dozen scrapes and lacerations.*

*He descended a well and emerged somehow upward onto a floor. Mad laughter rang about him, ceasing only when he realized it to be his own.*

*The sounds grew even louder, until it felt as if he negotiated a gallery of demonic bells—wild, out of phase, their vibrations beating against him.*

*Thinking became painful. He knew that he must not stop, that he must not turn back, that he must not take any of the lesser turnings where the sounds came softer. Any of these courses would prove fatal. He reduced this to one imperative: Continue.*

*Again, a pulsing at his wrist, and a faint, slow movement.*

*He gritted his teeth when he saw that he must climb once more, for his limbs had grown heavy. Each movement seemed as if it were performed underwater— slowly, requiring more than normal effort.*

*A screen of smoke offered frightening resistance. He drove himself against it for an age before he passed through and felt hi's movements become easy once again. Six times this occurred, and each time the pressure against him was greater.*

*When he crawled out, drooling and dripping blood, on the other side of the chamber from which he had entered, his eyes darted wildly and could not fix upon the small, dark figure which stood before him.*

*"You are a fool," it told him.*

*It took some time for the words to register, and when they did he lacked the strength to reply.*

*"A lucky fool," it went on, darkness flowing about it like wings. (Or were they really wings?) "I had not judged you ready to essay the Logrus for a long while yet."*

*He closed his eyes against this speaker, and an image of the route he had followed danced within his mind's seeing, like a bright, torn web folding in a breeze.*

*". . . And a fool not to have borne a blade and so enchanted it—or a mirror, a chalice or a wand to brace your magic. No, all I see is a piece of rope. You should have waited, for more instruction, for greater strength. What say you?"*

*He raised himself from the floor, and a mad light danced within his eyes. "It was time," he said. "I was ready."*

*"And a cord! What a half-ass—Uck!"*

*The cord, glowing now, tightened about his throat.*

*When the other released it, the dark one coughed and nodded.*

*"Perhaps—you knew—what you were doing—on that count . . ." it muttered. "Is it really time? You will be leaving?"*

*"Yes."*

*A dark cloak fell upon his shoulders. He heard the splash of water within a flask.*

*"Here."*

*As he drank, the cord wrapped itself about his wrist and vanished.*

*"Thanks, Uncle," he said, after several swallows.*

*The dark figure shook its head.*

*"Impulsive," it said. "Just like your father."*

# BLUE HORSE, DANCING MOUNTAINS

I took a right at the Burning Wells and fled smokeghosts across the Uplands of Artine. I slew the leader of the Kerts of Shem as her flock harried me from high-towered perches among the canyons of that place. The others abandoned the sport, and we were through, beneath a green rain out of a slate-colored sky. Onward and down then, to where the plains swirled dust devils that sang of sad eternities in rock that once they were.

At last the winds fell off and Shask, my deadly mount, blue stallion out of Chaos, slowed to a stop before vermilion sands.

"What is the matter?" I asked.

"We must cross this neck of the desert to reach the Dancing Mountains," Shask replied.

"And how long a journey might that be?"

"Most of the rest of the day," he said. "It is narrowest here. We have paid in part for this indulgence already. The rest will come in the mountains themselves, for now we must cross where they are very active."

I raised my canteen and shook it.

"Worth it," I said, "so long as they don't really dance in Richter terms."

"No, but at the Great Divide between the shadows of Amber and the shadows of Chaos there is some natural shifting activity in play where they meet."

"I'm no stranger to shadow-storms, which is what that sounds like—a permanent shadow-storm front. But I wish we could just push on through rather than camp there."

"I told you when you chose me, Lord Corwin, that I could bear you farther than any other mount by day. But by night I become an unmoving serpent, hardening to stone and cold as a demon's heart, thawing come dawn."

"Yes, I recall," I said, "and you have served me well, as Merlin said you might. Perhaps we should overnight this side of the mountains and cross tomorrow."

"The front, as I said, shifts. Likely, at some point, it would join you in the foothills or before. Once you reach the region, it matters not where we spend the night. The shadows will dance over us or near us. Dismount now, please, unsaddle, and remove your gear, that I may shift."

"To what?" I asked as I swung to the ground.

"I've a lizard form would face this desert best."

"By all means, Shask, be comfortable, be efficient. Be a lizard."

I set about unburdening him. It was good to be free again.

Shask as blue lizard was enormously fast and virtually tireless. He got us across the sands with daylight to spare, and as I stood beside him contemplating the trail that led upward through the foothills, he spoke in a sibilant tone: "As I said, the shadows can catch us anywhere around here, and I still have strength to take us up for an hour or so before we camp, rest, and feed. What is your choice?"

"Go," I told him.

Trees changed their foliage even as I watched. The trail was maddeningly irregular, shifting its course, changing its character beneath us. Seasons came and went—a flurrying of snow followed by a blast of hot air, then springtime and blooming flowers. There were glimpses of towers and metal people, highways, bridges, tunnels: gone in moments. Then the entire dance would shift away and we would simply be mounting a trail again.

At last, we made camp in a sheltered area near to a summit. Clouds collected as we ate, and a few rumbles of thunder rolled in the distance. I made myself a low lean-to. Shask transformed himself into a great dragonheaded, winged, feathered serpent, and coiled nearby.

"A good night to you, Shask," I called out, as the first drops fell.

"And-to-you-Corwin," he said softly.

I lay back, closed my eyes, and was asleep almost immediately. How long I slept, I do not know. I was jarred out of it, however, by a terrific clap of thunder which seemed to occur directly overhead.

I found myself sitting up, having reached out to and half drawn Grayswandir, before the echoes died. I shook my head and sat listening. Something seemed to be missing and I could not determine what.

There came a brilliant flash of light and another thunderclap. I flinched at them and sat waiting for more, but only silence followed.

Silence. . . .

I stuck my hand outside the lean-to, then my head. It had stopped raining. That was the missing item—the splatter of droplets.

My gaze was attracted by a glow from beyond the nearby summit. I pulled on my boots and departed the shelter. Outside, I buckled on my sword belt and fastened my cloak at the neck. I had to investigate. In a place like this, any activity might represent a threat.

I touched Shask—who indeed felt stony—as I passed, and made my way to where the trail had been. It was still there, though diminished in width, and I set foot upon it and climbed upward. The light source for which I was headed seemed to be moving slightly. Now, faintly, in the distance, I seemed to hear the sound of rainfall. Perhaps it was coming down on the other side of the peak.

As I advanced, I became convinced that it was storming not too far away. I could now hear the moaning of wind within the splashing.

I was suddenly dazzled by a flash from beyond the crest. A sharp report of thunder kept it company. I halted for only a moment. During that time, amid the ringing in my ears, I thought that I heard the sound of a cackling laugh.

Trudging ahead, I came at last to the summit. Immediately, the wind assailed me, bearing a full load of moisture. I drew my cloak closed and fastened it down the front as I made my way forward.

Several paces then, and I beheld a hollow, below and to my left. It was eerily illuminated by dancing orbs of ball lightning. There were two figures within it—one seated on the ground, the other, cross-legged, hanging upside down in the air with no apparent means of support, across from him. I chose the most concealed route I could and headed toward them.

They were lost to my sight much of the way, as the course I had taken bore me through areas of fairly dense foliage. Abruptly, however, I knew that I was near when the rain ceased to fall upon me and I no longer felt the pressures of the wind. It was as if I had entered the still eye of a hurricane.

Cautiously, I continued my advance, winding up on my belly, peering amid branches at the two old men. Both regarded the invisible cubes of a three-dimensional game, pieces hung above a board on the ground between them, squares of their aerial positions limned faintly in fire. The man seated upon the ground was a hunchback, and he was smiling, and I knew him. It was Dworkin Barimen, my legendary ancestor, filled with ages and wisdom and godlike powers, creator of Amber, the Pattern, the Trumps, and maybe reality itself as I understood it. Unfortunately, through much of my dealing with him in recent times, he'd also been more than a little bit nuts. Merlin had assured me that he was recovered now, but I wondered. Godlike beings are often noted for some measure of nontraditional rationality. It just seems to go with the territory. I wouldn't put it past the old bugger to be using sanity as a pose while in pursuit of some paradoxical end.

The other man, whose back was to me, reached forward and moved a piece that seemed to correspond to a pawn. It was a representation of the Chaos beast known as a Fire Angel. When the move was completed the lightning flashed again and the thunder cracked and my body tingled. Then Dworkin reached out and moved one of his pieces, a Wyvern. Again, the thunder and lightning, the tingling. I saw that a rearing Unicorn occupied the place of the King among Dworkin's pieces, a representation of the palace at Amber on the square beside it. His opponent's King was an erect Serpent, the Thelbane—the great needlelike palace of the Kings of Chaos—beside it.

Dworkin's opponent advanced a piece, laughing as he did so. "Mandor," he announced. "He thinks himself puppet-master and king-maker."

After the crash and dazzle, Dworkin moved a piece. "Corwin," he said. "He is free again."

"Yes. But he does not know he is in a race with destiny. I doubt he will make it back to Amber in time to encounter the hall of mirrors. Without their clues, how effective will he be?"

Dworkin smiled and raised his eyes. For a moment, he seemed to be looking right at me. "I think his timing is perfect, Suhuy," he said then, "and I have several pieces of his memory I found years ago drifting above the Pattern in Rebma. I wish I had a golden piss-pot for each time he's been underestimated."

"What would that give you?" asked the other.

"Expensive helmets for his enemies."

Both men laughed, and Suhuy rotated 90 degrees counterclockwise. Dworkin rose into the air and tilted forward until he was parallel to the ground, looking down on the board. Suhuy extended a hand toward a female figure on one of the higher levels, then drew it back. Abruptly, he moved the Fire Angel again. Even as the air was burned and beaten Dworkin made a move, so that the thunder continued into a roll and the brightness hung there. Dworkin said something I could not hear over the din. Suhuy's response to the probable naming was, "But she's a Chaos figure!"

"So? We set no rule against it. Your move."

"I want to study this," Suhuy said. "More than a little."

"Take it with you," Dworkin responded. "Bring it back tomorrow night?"

"I'll be occupied. The night after?"

"I will be occupied. Three nights hence?"

"Yes. Until then—"

"—good night."

The blast and the crash that followed blinded me and deafened me for several moments. Suddenly, I felt the rain and the wind. When my vision cleared, I saw that the hollow was empty. Retreating, I made my way back over the crest and down to my camp, which the rain had found again, also. The trail was wider now.

I rose at dawn and fed myself while I waited for Shask to stir. The night's doings did not seem like a dream.

"Shask," I said later, "do you know what a hellride is?"

"I've heard of it," he replied, "as an arcane means of traveling great distances in a short time, employed by the House of Amber. Said to be hazardous to the mental health of the noble steed."

"You strike me as being eminently stable, emotionally and intellectually."

"Why, thank you—I guess. Why the sudden rush?"

"You slept through a great show," I said, "and now I've a date with a gang of reflections if I can catch them before they fade."

"If it must be done . . ."

"We race for the golden piss-pot, my friend. Rise up and be a horse."

# THE SALESMAN'S TALE

Glad I'd planned on leaving Merlin in the Crystal Cave for a long while. Glad he didn't stay the entire time.

As I interrupted our trumped conversation by kicking over my glass of iced tea and shouting "Shit! I spilled it—" I turned over the Trump of Doom in my good hand.

Junkyard Forest. Nice sketch, that. Though it didn't matter what it depicted, which is why I'd had Merlin fan the cards face down and had drawn one at random. That was for show, to confuse the Pattern. All of them led to places within spitting distance of the Crystal Cave—which had been the real reason for their existence in the first place. Their only purpose had been to draw Merlin into the Cave's orbit, at which point a blue crystal warning system was to have alerted me. The plan was for me to get there in a hurry and find a way to make him a prisoner. Unfortunately, I hadn't gotten the message when he'd drawn the Sphinx to escape from mom. Her neurotoxins had canceled a necessary trigger signal from his nervous system—just one of the many ways she's messed up my plans without half-trying. Didn't matter, though, in the long run. I got Merlin there, anyway. Only . . . everything changed after that.

"Luke! You fool!" The Pattern's message blasted through me like the closing number at a rock concert.

But the Junkyard Forest had already come clear, and I was trumping out, before the Pattern realized that tea rather than my blood was flowing upon it.

I rose to my feet as the Pattern faded, and I moved forward amid the rusty sawblade bushes, the twisted girder trees, the gaily colored beds of broken bottles. I began to run, blood spilling from the slashed palm of my left hand. I didn't even take the time to bind it. Once the Pattern recovered from its shock and discovered itself undamaged, it was going to begin scanning Shadow for me, for the others. They'd be safe within the ambit of the other Pattern, and that left me. The walls of the Crystal Cave had the effect of blocking every paraphysical phenomenon I'd been able to test them for, and I'd a hunch they'd screen me from the Pattern's scrutiny as well. It was just a matter of my getting there before it shadow-shuffled this far.

I increased my pace. I'd stayed in shape. I could run. Past rusting cars and swirls of bedsprings, broken tiles, shattered crates . . . Down alleys of ashes, up trails of bottlecaps and pulltabs . . . Alert. Waiting. Waiting for the world to spin and waver, to hear the voice of the Pattern announce, "Gotcha!"

I rounded a bend and caught a glimpse of blue in the distance. The

Junkyard Forest—result of an ancient Shadow-storm—ended abruptly as I entered upon a downward slope, to be succeeded within paces by a wood of the more normal variety.

Here, I heard a few birdcalls as I passed, and the humming of insects, above the steady striking of my feet upon the earth. The sky was overcast, and I could tell nothing of temperature or wind because of my activity. The shimmering mound of blue grew larger. I maintained my pace. By now, the others should be safe, if they'd made it at all. Hell! By *now* they should be well out of harm's way. Just a little while in this time-stream was a much longer time back on the main drag. They could be sitting around eating and joking by now. Even napping. I bit back a curse to save breath. That also meant that the Pattern could have been searching for even longer than it seemed . . .

Larger, even larger now, the blue ridge. I decided to see how well my finishing spurt had held up, and I went into high gear and held it there.

The earth and air were vibrated by what seemed a rumble of thunder. It could be a reaction of the irate design on having finally located me. It could also just be a rumble of thunder.

I kept pumping, and moments later, it seemed, I was braking so as not to smash up against that crystal base. No lightning bolts yet, and I scrambled for hand and toeholds—never having tried climbing this face of it before—as my lungs worked like a bellows and a light rain began to fall, mingling with a layer of my perspiration. I left bloody smears on the stone, but that should soon wash away.

Achieving the summit, I rushed to its opening on all fours and entered feet first, hanging, then dropping into the dark interior, despite the presence of a ladder. Haste was all. Not until I stood within that shadowy blueness, still puffing, did I feel at all safe. As soon as I caught my breath I allowed myself to laugh. I had done it. I had escaped the Pattern.

I walked about the chamber beating upon my thighs and slapping the walls. A victory such as this tasted good, and I would not let it pass unmarked. I hustled back to the larder, located a bottle of wine, opened it, and took a drink. Then I repaired to a side cavern which still contained a sleeping bag, seated myself upon it, and continued to chuckle as I reenacted in my mind our experience there at the primal Pattern. My lady Nayda had been so magnificent. So had Merlin, for that matter. Now . . .

I wondered whether the Pattern really held grudges. That is, how long would it be before it was safe to me to go forth without feeling in imminent peril?

No real way to tell. Unfortunate. Still, the Pattern must have too much to occupy it to behave in any manner similar to those people who hung about in its vicinity—*i.e.*, Amberites. Mustn't it? I took another drink. I might be here for a long time.

I would use a spell to alter my appearance, I decided. When I left here I would have dark hair and a beard (over the beginnings of a real beard), gray eyes, a straight nose, higher cheekbones, and a smaller chin. I would seem taller and a lot thinner. I would switch from my usual bright ones to dark garments. Not just some light, cosmetic spell either. It would have to be a strong one, with depth and substance to it.

Musing upon this, I got up and went in search of food. I found some tinned beef and biscuits, and I used a small spell to heat a can of soup. No, that was not a violation of the physical laws of the place. The crystal walls block sendings in and out, but my spells came in with me and operated as normal in the interior.

Eating, I thought again of Nayda, of Merlin, and of Coral. Whatever was happening to them—good or bad—time was favoring them in getting it done. Even if I stayed here for but a short while developments back home would be incommensurate with time's apparent lapse here. And what kind of time did the Pattern really keep? All of them, I supposed—that is to say, its own—but I also felt it to be especially keyed to the mainline of its flow in Amber. In fact, I was almost sure of it, since that's where the action was. So if I wanted to be back in action quickly I should just stay here long enough for my hand to heal.

But really, how badly could the Pattern want me? How much would I actually matter to it? What was I in its view? King of a minor Golden Circle realm. Assassin of one Prince of Amber. Son of the man who had once sought to destroy it . . . I winced at that, but reflected that the Pattern had let me live my entire life up to now without reprisal for dad's actions. And my part in the current business had been minimal. Coral had seemed its main concern, and then Merlin. Perhaps I was being ultra-cautious. Likely, it had dismissed me from its main considerations the moment I had vanished. Still, I wasn't going to step out of here without that disguise.

I finished eating and sipped at the wine. And when I did step out? What exactly would I be about then? Numerous possibilities tumbled through my mind. I also began yawning and the sleeping bag looked very good. Lightning flashed, blue wave through the walls. Then the thunder came, like surf. Tomorrow then. Tomorrow I would plan . . .

I crawled inside and got comfortable. In a moment, I was gone.

I've no idea how long I slept. On rising, I made the rounds to establish a security habit, ran through a vigorous routine of exercises, cleaned myself up, then ate a leisurely breakfast. I felt better than I had the day before, and my hand had already commenced healing.

Then I sat and stared at the wall, probably for hours. What was my best course of action?

I could rush back to Kashfa and the kingship, I could hunt after my friends, I could simply go underground, lie low, and investigate until I learned what was going on. It was a question of priorities. What was the most important thing I could do for everybody concerned? I thought about it till lunchtime and then I ate again.

Afterwards, I took up my small sketchpad and a pencil and I began recalling a certain lady, feature by feature. I fiddled with it all afternoon, to pass the time, though I knew I had her right. When I knocked off for dinner the next day's activities had already taken shape in my mind.

The next morning my injury was considerably diminished, and I conjured myself a mirror upon a smooth surface of the wall. Using an oil lamp so as not to waste an illumination spell, I conjured that tall, dark, lean figure upon my own form, cast those aquiline features upon my own—complete with beard—and I looked upon my work and saw that it was good. I transformed the appearance of my garments then, also, to keep the new me company—this latter a single spell. I'd have to fetch real garments as soon as I could. No use wasting a high-powered working on something that trivial. I did this all first thing, because I'd wanted to wear the guise all day, let it soak in, see whether there were any hidden weaknesses to my working. Then I wanted to sleep in it, for the same reason.

That afternoon I took up the sketchpad again. I studied my pervious day's work, then turned to a fresh page and executed a Trump. It felt exactly right.

The next morning, following the usual routine, I reviewed myself in the mirror again, was satisfied, and mounted the ladder to emerge from the cave. It was a damp, cool morning with a few blue breaks in the cloud cover high overhead. Could rain again. But what the hell did I care? I was on my way out.

I reached for my pad, then paused. I was reminded of other Trumps I had dealt with over the years, and of something else. I withdrew my deck of cards. Uncasing them, I moved slowly through until I came to the sad one—dad's. I had kept his card for sentiment's sake, not utility. He looked just as I remembered him, but I hadn't sought it for purposes of reminiscence. It was because of the item he wore at his side.

I focussed on Werewindle, by all accounts a magical blade, in some way related to Corwin's Greyswandir. And I recalled Merlin's telling me how his father had summoned Greyswandir to him in Shadow, following his escape from the dungeons of Amber. There was some special affinity between him and that weapon. I wondered. Now that the pace had quickened and new adventures were looming, it would probably be advisable to face things prepared with the appropriate steel. Though dad was dead, Werewindle was somehow alive. Though I could not reach my father, might I somehow reach his blade, its whereabouts, of last report, somewhere in the Courts of Chaos?

I focused my attention upon it, calling it with my mind. It seemed that I felt something, and when I touched it the spot it occupied on the card seemed to be growing cold. I reached. Farther. Harder.

And then there was clarity and nearness and the feeling of a cold, alien intelligence regarding me.

"Werewindle," I said softly.

If there can be the sound of an echo in the absence of a prior sound this is what I heard.

"Son of Brand," came a reverberation.

"Call me Luke."

There was silence. Then, "Luke," came the vibration.

I reached forward, caught hold of it, and drew it toward me. The scabbard came with it. I drew back.

I held it in my hands then and I drew it. It flowed like molten gold around the design it wore. I raised it, extended it, executed a cut. It felt right. It felt perfect. It felt as if enormous power lay behind its every movement.

"Thanks," I said, and the echo of laughter came and went.

I raised my pad and opened it to the appropriate page, hoping it was a good time to make the call. I regarded the lady's delicate features, her unfocused gaze that somehow indicated the breadth and depth of her vision. After a few moments, the page grew cold beneath my fingertips, and my drawing took on a 3-dimensional quality, seemed faintly to stir.

"Yes?" came her voice.

"Your Highness." I said. "However you may perceive these things, I want you to know that I have intentionally altered my appearance. I was hoping that—"

"Luke," she said, "of course I recognize you—your own Majesty now," her gaze still unfocused. "You are troubled."

"Indeed I am."

"You wish to come through?"

"If it is appropriate and convenient."

"Certainly."

She extended her hand. I reached forward, taking it lightly in my own, as her studio came clear, banishing gray skies and crystal hill. I took a step toward her and I was there.

Immediately, I dropped to my knees, unclasped my swordbelt and offered her my blade. In the distance, I could hear sounds of hammering and sawing.

"Rise," she said, touching my shoulder. "Come and be seated. Have a cup of tea with me."

I got to my feet and followed her to a table in the corner. She took off her dusty apron and hung it on a peg on the wall. As she prepared the tea I regarded the small army of statues which lined one wall and bivouacked in random cluster about the enormous room—large, small, realistic, impressionistic, beautiful, grotesque. She worked mainly in clay, though a few smaller ones were of stone; and there were furnaces at the room's far end, though these were cold now. Several metal mobiles of unusual shape were suspended from ceiling beams.

When she joined me again she reached out and touched my left hand, locating the ring she had given me.

"Yes, I value the Queen's protection," I said.

"Even though you are now a monarch yourself, from a country on friendly terms with us?"

"Even so," I said. "So much so, in fact, that I wish to reciprocate in part."

"Oh?"

"I'm not at all certain that Amber is aware of recent events to which I have been party or of which I have knowledge, which may affect her welfare. That is, unless Merlin has been in touch recently."

"Merlin has not been in touch," she said. "If you have information vital to the realm, though, perhaps you ought to give it to Random direct. He's not here just now, but I could reach him for you via Trump."

"No," I said. "I know he doesn't like me at all or trust me, as his brother's killer and a friend of the man who has sworn to destroy Amber. I am sure he would love to see me deposed and some puppet on the throne of Kashfa. I suppose I must have things out with him one day, but this isn't the day. I've too much else going on just now. But the information transcends local politics. It involves Amber and the Courts of Chaos, the Pattern and the Logrus, the death of Swayvill and Merlin's possible succession to the throne in the Courts—"

"You're serious!"

"You bet. I know he'll listen to you. And he'll even understand why I told you. Let me avoid him this way. There are big events in the offing."

"Tell me," she said, raising her cup.

So I did, including everything Merlin had told me, up through the confrontation at the primal Pattern and my flight to the Crystal Cave. We went through the entire pot of tea in the process, and when I was finished we just sat for a time in silence.

Finally, she sighed.

"You have charged me to deliver major intelligence," she said.

"I know."

"Yet I feel it is but a small part of much greater developments."

"How's that?" I asked.

"A few small things I have heard, known, guessed at, and perhaps dreamed—and a few, I suppose, I simply fear. Hardly a coherent shape. Yet enough, perhaps, to query the powers of the earth I work with. Yes. Now that I have thought it I must try it, of course. At a time such as this."

She rose slowly, paused, and gestured high.

"That shall be the Tongue," she said, and a draft stirred one of the mobiles causing it to produce many tones.

She crossed the studio to the righthand wall—small figure in gray and green, chestnut hair down to the middle of her back—and ran her fingers lightly over the sculpted figure that stood there. Finally, selecting a broad-faced statue with a narrow torso, she began pushing it toward the center of the room.

I was on my feet and moving in an instant.

"Let me do that for you, Your Highness."

She shook her head.

"Call me Vialle," she said. "And no, I must position them myself. This one is named Memory."

She placed it below and somewhat to the northwest of the Tongue. Then she moved to a knot of figures and selected a thin one with slightly parted lips which she placed to the south on Tongue's compass.

". . . And this is Desire," she stated.

Quickly locating a third—a tall, squinting figure—she placed it to the northeast.

"Caution," she went on.

A lady, her right hand boldly extended, went to the west.

"Risk," she continued.

To the east she positioned another lady, both arms spread wide.

"Heart," she said.

To the southwest went a high-domed, shaggy-browed philosopher. "Head," she said.

. . . And to the southeast a smiling lady—impossible to say whether her hand was raised in greeting or to deliver a blow.

"Chance," she finished, fitting her into the circle which had come to remind me both of Stonehenge and of Easter Island.

"Bring two chairs," she said, "and place them here and here."

She indicated positions to the north and south of her circle.

I did as she'd said, and she seated herself in the northern-most chair, behind a final figure she had placed: Foresight. I took my place back of Desire.

"Be silent now," she instructed.

Then she sat still, hands in her lap, for several minutes.

Finally, "At the deepest level," she said, "what threatens the peace?"

From my left, Caution seemed to speak, though the Tongue chimed his words overhead.

"A redistribution of ancient powers," he said.

"In what manner?"

"That which was hidden becomes known and is moved about," answered Risk.

"Are both Amber and the Courts involved?"

"Indeed," answered Desire, from before me.

"'Ancient powers,'" she said. "How ancient?"

"Before there was an Amber, they were," stated Memory.

"Before there was a Jewel of Judgement—the Eye of the Serpent?"

"No," Memory responded.

She drew a sudden breath.

"Their number?" she said.

"Eleven," Memory replied.

She grew pale at that, but I held my silence as she had instructed.

"Those responsible for this stirring of ashes," she said then, "what do they wish?"

"A return to the glory of days gone by," Desire stated.

"Could this end be realized?"

"Yes," Foresight replied.

"Could it be averted?"

"Yes," said Foresight.

"At peril," Caution added.

"How might one begin?"

"Query the guardians," Head stated.

"How bad is the situation?"

"It has already begun," Head answered.

"And the danger is already present," said Risk.

"So is opportunity," said Chance.

"Of what sort?" Vialle inquired.

There came a sound from across the room as my scabbard and blade slid to the floor from where I had leaned them against the wall. Vialle stared.

"My weapon," I said, "just slipped."

"Name it."

"It was my father's sword, called Werewindle."

"I know of it." Then, "This man, Luke," she said, "there is something about his blade and its sister weapon that figures in all of this. I do not know their stories, though."

"Yes, they are connected," said Memory.

"How?"

"They were created in a similar fashion at near to the same time, and they partake of the powers of which we have spoken," Memory replied.

"Will there be a conflict?"

"Yes," said Foresight.

"On what scale?"

Foresight was silent. Chance laughed.

"I do not understand."

"The laughter of Chance is uncertainty," Head responded.

"Will Luke figure in the conflict?"

"Yes," Foresight answered.

"Should he seek the guardians?"

"He must try," said Heart.

"And if he fails?"

"A Prince approaches even now who knows more of these matters," said Head.

"Who is that?"

"A prisoner freed," Head replied.

"Who?"

"He wears a silver rose," said Head. "He bears the other blade."

Vialle raised her head.

"Have you any questions?" she asked me.

"Yes. But I doubt I'd get an answer if I asked whether we'll win."

Chance laughed as Vialle rose.

She let me help move the statues back into place. Then, seated once more, I said to her, "'Seek the guardians?'"

"There is a custodian—possibly two," she replied. "A self-exiled Prince of Amber and his sister have guarded a portion of this power for a long while. It would seem in order to see that they still live, still discharge the duty."

"Self-exiled? Why?"

"Personal reasons, involving the late King."

"Where are they?"

"I do not know."

"Then how could we find them?"

"There is a Trump."

She rose and moved to a small chest of drawers. Opening one, she withdrew a boxed set of cards. Slowly, she counted down from the top of the deck and removed one.

When she returned she presented me with the card, portrait of a slim man with hair the color of rust. "His name is Delwin," she said.

"You think I should just call him and ask whether he still has whatever he had?"

"State quickly that you are not of Amber," she told me, "but give your lineage. Ask whether his stewardship of the spikards remains intact. Try to find out where he is, or to go through and discuss it face to face if you can."

"Right," I said, not wanting to tell her that I had spoken—very briefly—with him before in seeking allies in my war against Amber. He'd dismissed me out of hand, but I didn't want to stir Vialle's memories of those days. So I simply said, "Okay. I'll give it a try."

I decided to fast-talk him at first, to give him time to think, to realize that I was not alone, and not to let slip anything of our earlier exchange. My altered appearance should help in this, too.

I reached for contact.

First, the coldness, then a feeling of personality suddenly alert.

"Who is it?" I felt the question even before the likeness took on depth and life.

"Luke Reynard, otherwise known as Rinaldo," I answered, as the card was suddenly animated and I felt his scrutiny, "King of Kashfa and B.S. in Business Management, University of California at Berkeley." Our gazes locked. He seemed neither belligerent nor friendly. "I wanted to know whether your stewardship of the spikards remains intact."

"Luke—Rinaldo," he said, "just what is your concern in this, and how did you come to learn of the matter?"

"While I am not of Amber," I replied, "my father was. I know it is soon to become a matter of concern in that place because of Merlin—son of Corwin—apparently being in direct line for the succession to the throne in the Courts of Chaos."

"I know who Merlin is," Delwin sated. "Who is your father?"

"Prince Brand."

"And your mother?"

"The Lady Jasra, formerly Queen of Kashfa. Now, might we talk about this matter a little?"

"No," Delwin said. "We may not."

He moved his hand as if to break the contact.

"Wait!" I said. "Do you have a microwave oven?"

He hesitated.

"A what?"

"It's a box-like device that can warm a meal in a matter of minutes. I've worked out a general spell to allow one to operate in most of Shadow. Wake up in the middle of the night with a taste for a steaming hot tuna casserole? Take one out of the freezer, unwrap it, and pop it in. What's a freezer? Glad you asked. It's another box, with eternal winter inside. Store meals in there, take one out and zap it in the mike whenever the fancy hits. And yes, I can supply the freezer, too. You don't want to talk spikards, let's talk business. I can give you a deal on these devices, in quantity, that will meet or beat the price of anyone else capable of supplying them—and I don't think it would be an easy thing to find another supplier. But that's not all I can do for you—"

"I'm sorry," said Delwin. "No solicitors either."

His hand moved again.

"Wait!" I cried. "I'll make you an offer you can't refuse!"

He broke the connection.

"Come back," I willed after his image, but it went 2-dimensional and warmed to room temperature again. "Sorry," I said to Vialle. "I gave it my best shot, but he wasn't buying any."

"To tell the truth, I didn't think you'd hold him even that long. But I could tell he was interested in you until you mentioned your mother. Then something changed."

"Wouldn't be the first time," I said. "I've a mind to try him again later."

"In that case, keep the Trump."

"I don't need it, Vialle. I'll make my own when the time comes."

"You are an artist and a Trump master?"

"Well, I do paint. Fairly seriously sometimes."

"Then you must see all of my works while you wait. I'd value your opinion."

"My pleasure," I said. "You mean while I wait—"

"—for Corwin."

"Ah, just so. Thank you."

"You can be the first to use one of the new rooms. We've been doing a lot of reconstruction and remodeling since the Logrus and the Pattern had their confrontation."

"I heard about it," I said. "Very well. I wonder when he'll arrive?"

"Soon, I feel," she said. "I'll summon a servant to get you settled now. Another will bring you to dine with me later, and we can discuss art."

"That will be fine."

I wondered where all of this was going to lead. It seemed that the big picture was about to change drastically again.

Glad Delwin wasn't interested in the microwave oven, though. The spell would have been a bitch to work out.

# COMING TO A CORD

It is no fun being tied to a bedpost when you are feeling under the weather. I phased back and forth between visibility and invisibility uncontrollably. On the other wrist, I felt my ability to communicate beginning to return. My increased sentience had remained with me ever since my strange journey with Merlin in the place between shadows. But there was a shock on my return to this reality. Slowly now, I was recovering from it, though some of the symptoms were slower in going than others. Consequently, it took me much longer than it normally would have to unknot myself.

I am Frakir, strangling cord to Merlin—Lord of Amber and Prince of Chaos. Normally, too, he would never have abandoned me like this, in the blasted apartment of Brand, late Prince of Amber and would-be Lord of the Universe. But he was under a mild spell Brand had actually left about for his son Rinaldo. However, Merlin has such a strong affinity with Rinaldo—also known as Luke—by virtue of their long association, that the spell latched onto him. He must have shaken it by now, but that still left me in an awkward position, with him doubtless back in the Courts.

I did not feel like waiting around with all the rebuilding and redecorating going on. They could decide to chuck the bed, with me attached, and go for all new stuff.

I finished unknotting myself. At least, Merlin had used no magic when he'd tied me there. On the other hand, it was a tight knot, and I squirmed for a long while to get myself unlooped. Finally, the thing was loosened and I was able to undo it. Once I had freed myself from its subtle geometries, I slithered down the bedpost to the ground. At least this left me in a position to slip away, should a gang of furniture movers suddenly appear. In fact, it suddenly seemed a good idea to get out of the fast traffic lane now.

I moved away from the bed—out of Brand's room and into Merlin's—wondering what had been the secret of that ring he'd found and put on—the spikard thing. That it was extremely powerful and drew its energies from many sources was obvious to a being such as myself. That it seemed a thing of the same order as the sword Werewindle was also readily apparent, despite their varied forms to the eye of a human. Suddenly, it occurred to me that Merlin might not notice this, and I began to think that it might be necessary he should.

I crossed his room. I can move like a snake when I would. I have no ability to transport myself magically like almost everyone else I know, so I figured it were best to find someone who did. My only problem was that, in keeping with the family's general policy of personal secrecy on everything from magic to souffle recipes, many of them did not even know I existed.

. . . And for that matter I didn't know the location of their apartments, save for Merlin's, Brand's, Random and Vialle's, and Martin's—which Merlin sometime visited. Random and Vialle's would be hard to reach, with all the work that was going on. So I headed off in the direction of Martin's rooms and slithered under the door when I got there. He had rock posters on most of the walls, as well as the speakers for a magically powered CD player. He, alas, was absent, and I had no idea when he might return.

I went back out into the hall and slithered along it, listening for a familiar voice, checking under doors, into rooms. This went on for some time before I heard Flora say, "Oh, bother!" from behind a door up the hall. I headed in that direction. She was one of the ones privy to my existence.

Her door was closed, but I was able to make my way beneath it into a highly decorated sitting room. She seemed in the process of mending a broken fingernail with some sort of goo.

I crossed the room to her side, maintaining my invisibility, and wrapped myself about her right ankle.

*Hello,* I said. *This is Frakir, Merlin's friend and strangling cord. Can you help me?*

Following a moment of silence, she said, "Frakir! What's happened? What do you need?"

*I was inadvertently abandoned,* I explained, *while Merlin was under the influence of a peculiar spell. I need to get in touch with him. I've realized something he may need to know. Also, I want to get back on his wrist.*

"I'll give his Trump a try," she said, "though if he's in the Courts I'll probably not be able to reach him."

I heard her open a drawer, and moments later I heard her fumbling with cards. I tried to tune in on her thoughts as she manipulated them, but I could not.

"Sorry," she said, after a time. "I can't seem to get through to him."

*Thanks for trying,* I told her.

"When did you get separated from Merlin?" she asked.

*It was the day the Powers met in the back hall,* I said.

"What sort of spell did Merlin get caught up in?"

*One that was hanging fairly free in Brand's quarters. You see, Merlin's and Brand's room being next door to each other, he'd entered out of curiosity when the wall fell during the confrontation.*

"Frakir, I don't think that was an accident," she said. "One Power or the other probably arranged for things to be so."

*Seems likely when one thinks about it, Princess.*

"What do you want to do now? I'll be glad to help," she said.

*I'd like to find a way to get back to Merlin,* I said. *He's had a general aura of danger about him for some time—to which I am particularly sensitive.*

"I understand," she said, "and I'll find a way. It may take a few days, but I'll figure out something."

*All right. I'll wait,* I said. *I've no real choice in the matter.*

"You're welcome to stay with me till that happens."

*I'll do that,* I said. *Thanks.*

I found a comfortable-looking table and wrapped myself about one of its legs. I went into stasis then, if one needs a word for it. It is not sleep, as there is no loss of consciousness. But there is no thinking in the conventional sense either. I just sort of spread out my awareness and am, until I am needed.

How long I lay coiled in this position, I have no way of telling. I was alone in the sitting room, though I was aware of Flora's breathing next door.

Suddenly, she shrieked. This time, I just loosened myself and dropped to the floor.

As I began hurrying toward the room I heard another voice. "Sorry," it said. "I am pursued. I had no choice but to drop in without invitation."

"Who are you?" she asked.

"Well, I'm a sorcerer," he said. "I was hiding in your mirror, as I have every night for a long while. I have this crush on you and I like to watch you as you go about your business."

"A Peeping Tom—a voyeur!" she said.

"No," he said. "I think you're a really nice-looking lady, and I like watching you. That's all."

"There are many legitimate ways by which you could have gained an introduction," she said.

"True, but that may might have led to horrible complications in my life."

"Oh, you're married."

"Worse than that," he said.

"What, then?"

"No time now. I can feel its approach," he said.

"What's approach?"

"The guisel," he said. "I sent one to slay another sorcerer, but he disposed of it and sent one of his own after me. Didn't know he was that good. I don't know how to dispose of the things, and it will be oozing through that mirror in a matter of minutes, to destroy us all most nastily. So, this place being Amber and all, is there some hero available who might be anxious to earn another merit badge?"

"I think not," she replied. "Sorry."

Just then the mirror began to darken.

"Oh, it's coming!" he cried.

I had felt the menace it exuded some time before. But then, that is my job.

But now I got a glimpse of the thing. It was big, and wormlike, eyeless, but possessed of a shark-like mouth, a multitude of short legs, and vestigial wings. It was twice again the length of a human, and black, having crisscrossing red and yellow stripes. It slithered across our reflected room, rearing as it came on.

"You imply," Flora said, "in your quest of a hero, that it will make it through that interface and attack us."

"In a word," said the strange little man, "yes."

*When it does*, I said to Flora, *throw me at it. Wherever I hit I'll stick—and I'll go for the throat.*

"All right," she said, "and there's one other thing."

*What's that?* I asked.

"Help! Help!" she cried.

It began crawling out through the silver, flower-bordered mirror. Flora unwound me from her ankle and threw me at the thing. It had no real neck, but I wrapped myself about its upper extremity below the mouth and began tightening immediately.

Flora continued to call out, and from somewhere up the hall I heard the sound of heavy footfalls.

I tightened and tightened my grip, but the creature's neck was like rubber.

The sorcerer was moving to exit the room when the door burst open and the tall and husky, redhaired form of Luke entered.

"Flora!" he said, and then he saw the guisel and drew his blade.

On my recent journey with Merlin in the space between shadows I had gained the ability to converse at complex levels. My perceptions—which seem quite different—also became more acute. They showed me nothing special about Luke, the sorcerer, or the guisel, but Werewindle now burned of an entirely different light. I realized then that it was not merely a blade.

As Luke moved to position himself between Flora and the guisel, I heard the sorcerer say, "What is the blade?"

"'Tis called Werewindle," Luke replied.

"And you are . . . ?"

"Rinaldo, King of Kashfa," Luke said.

"Your father—who was he?"

"Brand—Prince of Amber."

"Of course," the sorcerer said, moving again toward the door. "You can destroy that thing with it. Command it to draw energy while you're using it. It has a virtually limitless supply to draw upon."

"Why?" Luke asked.

"Because it isn't really a sword."

"What is it then?"

"Sorry," the sorcerer said, regarding the guisel, which was now moving toward us. "Out of time. Got to find another mirror."

I could tell that he was, unaware of my presence, really teasing Luke, because I had figured it out for myself and knew that it would take only a moment to tell him, if one could speak.

Then I was disengaging and dropping as fast as I could, for Luke was swinging Werewindle, and I'd no desire to be severed. I really did not know what would happen if this were to occur—if both segments would wind up as wise, witty, and conscious as myself; or, perhaps, whether I would be destroyed in the process. And having no desire to learn this information firsthand, flight seemed most prudent.

I hit the floor before the blow fell. A section of the guisel's head also dropped, still writhing. I squirmed toward Luke's nearest ankle. Flora picked up a heavy chair and brought it down on the thing's back with considerable force, despite her broken fingernail. And she swung it a couple of more times, with some effect, while Luke was in the process of cutting it in half.

I found my way to where I was headed, crawled up, and caught hold.

*Can you hear me, Luke?* I tried then.

"Yes," he replied. "What are you?"

*Merlin's strangling cord, Frakir.*

Luke swung at the hind section then as it whipped toward him, tiny legs clawing. Then he whirled and halved the attacking forepart. Flora struck its rear end again with the chair.

*I know what the sorcerer knew,* I said.

"Oh, what's that?" he asked, slicing off another section and slipping on its gooey exudations as he retreated.

*You might well be able to draw enough energy through Werewindle to destroy a world.*

"Really?" he said, struggling to regain his feet as a section of the creature thrust itself upon him. "All right."

He touched it with the point of his blade and it withdrew from him as if shocked. Then he rose to his feet.

"You're right," he said. "There's something to it." He touched the attacking segment again and it vanished in a burst of blue fire. "Flora! Get back!" he cried.

She did, and he proceeded to incinerate the section that had been about to attack her. Then another that came at him.

"I'm getting the hang of it," he said, turning to get another segment. "But I'm not quite sure why it works this way."

*It's not just a sword,* I said.

"What is it, then?"

*Long before there was Werewindle, it was the spikard Rawg.*

"Spikard? Like that strange ring Merlin picked up?"

*Exactly.*

With rapid moves then, Luke disposed of the rest of the guisel.

"Thanks, Frakir," he said, "for telling me how the thing worked. I'd better try a quick search for that sorcerer now, though I've a hunch he disappeared into the nearest mirror."

*I'd guess that, too.*

"What was his name?"

*He didn't say.*

"It figures."

"Flora," he continued, "I'm going to look for that sorcerer. I'll be back in a bit. Good show."

She gave him a smile and he departed. Needless to say, the sorcerer did not turn up.

"Wonder where he came from, beyond the mirror," Luke asked.

*I've no idea, I replied. I think I might be more interested in the person who sent that thing after him.*

Luke nodded.

"What now?" he asked.

*I guess we tell Flora that her Peeping Tom has hit the road, I said. You're a sorcerer. Any way of fixing her mirrors so he can't pull that routine again?*

"I think so," Luke said, moving to the nearest window and looking out. "I'll fix them in just a bit. What about you?"

*I'd like to get back to Merlin.*

"I can't send you through by Trumps if he's in the Courts—and I suspect he is."

*What about Werewindle?*

"I still don't know exactly how it works. I'm going to have to practice some with it."

*Uh—why are you here?* I asked.

"Had to talk to Vialle about a number of things," he said, "and she told me that Corwin might be by soon—and she offered me room and board if I wanted to wait for him for a few days."

*Well, if you can wear me till he gets here maybe I can persuade him to take me with him. I've a feeling he'll be seeing Merlin again soon.*

"I might, too, but it's hard to say at this point."

*Okay. We can work it out when the time comes.*

"What do you think is going on, anyway?"

*Some horrible Wagnerian thing, I told him, full of blood, thunder, and death for us all.*

"Oh, the usual," Luke said.

*Exactly,* I replied.

# HALL OF MIRRORS

Neither of us realized there had been a change until a half-dozen guys tried an ambush.

We had spent the night in the Dancing Mountains, Shask and I, where I'd witnessed a bizarre game between Dworkin and Suhuy. I'd heard strange tales about things that happened to people who spent the night there, but I hadn't had a hell of a lot of choice in the matter. It had been storming, I was tired, and my mount had become a statue. I don't know how that game turned out, though I was mentioned obliquely as a participant and I'm still wondering.

The next morning my blue horse Shask and I had crossed the Shadow Divide 'twixt Amber and Chaos. Shask was a Shadow mount my son Merlin had found for me in the royal stables of the Courts. At the moment, Shask was traveling under the guise of a giant blue lizard, and we were singing songs from various times and places.

Two men rose on either side of the trail from amid rocky cover, pointing crossbows at us. Two more stepped out before us—one with a bow, the other bearing a rather beautiful-looking blade, doubtless stolen, considering the guy's obvious profession.

"Halt! and no harm'll happen," said the swordsman.

I drew rein.

"When it comes to money, I'm pretty much broke right now," I said, "and I doubt any of you could ride my mount, or would care to."

"Well now, maybe and maybe not," said the leader, "but it's a rough way to make a living, so we take whatever we can."

"It's not a good idea to leave a man with nothing," I said. "Some people hold grudges."

"Most of them can't walk out of here."

"Sounds like a death sentence to me."

He shrugged.

"That sword of yours looks pretty fancy," he said. "Let's see it."

"I don't think that's a good idea," I said.

"Why not?"

"If I draw it, I may wind up killing you," I said.

He laughed.

"We can take it off your body," he said, glancing to his right and left.

"Maybe," I said.

"Let's see it."

"If you insist."

I drew Grayswandir with a singing note. It persisted, and the eyes of the swordsman before me widened as it went on to describe an arc calcu-

lated to intersect with his neck. His own weapon came out as mine passed
through his neck and continued. His cut toward Shask and passed through
the animal's shoulder. Neither blow did any damage whatsoever.

"You a sorcerer?" he asked as I swung again, delivering a blow that
might have removed his arm. Instead, it passed harmlessly by.

"Not the kind who does things like this. You?"

"No," he answered, striking again. "What's going on?"

I slammed Grayswandir back into the scabbard.

"Nothing," I said. "Go bother someone else."

I shook the reins, and Shask moved forward.

"Shoot him down!" the man cried.

The men on either side of the trail released their crossbow bolts, as did
the other man before me. All four bolts from the sides passed through
Shask, three of the men injuring or killing their opposite numbers. The one
from ahead passed through me without pain or discomfort. An attempted
sword blow achieved nothing for my first assailant.

"Ride on," I said.

Shask did so and we ignored their swearing as we went.

"We seem to have come into a strange situation," I observed.

The beast nodded.

"At least it kept us out of some trouble," I said.

"Funny. I'd a feeling you would have welcomed trouble," Shask said.

I chuckled.

"Perhaps, perhaps not," I replied. "I wonder how long the spell lasts?"

"Maybe it has to be lifted."

"Shit. That's always a pain."

"Beats being insubstantial."

"True."

"Surely someone back at Amber will know what to do."

"Hope so."

We rode on, and we encountered no one else that day. I felt the rocks
beneath me when I wrapped myself in my cloak to sleep that night. Why
did I feel them when I didn't feel a sword or a crossbow bolt? Too late to ask
Shask whether he had felt anything, for he had turned to stone for the night.

I yawned and stretched. A partly unsheathed Grayswandir felt normal
beneath my fingers. I pushed it back in and went to sleep.

Following my morning ablutions, we rode again. Shask was taking
well to hellrides, as well as most Amber mounts did. Better, in some ways.
We raced through a wildly changing landscape. I thought ahead to Amber,
and I thought back to the time I'd spent imprisoned in the Courts. I had
honed my sensitivity to a very high degree through meditation, and I began
to wonder whether that, coupled with other strange disciplines I'd under-
taken, could have led to my intangibility. I supposed it might have contrib-

uted, but I'd a feeling the Dancing Mountains were the largest donor.

"I wonder what it represents and where it came from?" I said aloud.

"Your homeland, I'd bet," Shask replied, "left especially for you."

"Why did you read it that way?"

"You've been telling me about your family as we rode along. I wouldn't trust them."

"Those days are past."

"Who knows what might have happened while you were away? Old habits return easily."

"One would need a reason for something like that."

"For all you know, one of them has a very good one."

"Possibly. But it doesn't seem likely. I've been away for some time, and few know—I'm free at last."

"Then question those few."

"We'll see."

"Just trying to be helpful."

"Don't stop. Say, what do you want to do after we get to Amber?"

"Haven't made up my mind yet. I've been something of a wanderer." I laughed.

"You're a beast after my own heart. In that your sentiments are most unbeastlike, how can I repay you for this transport?"

"Wait. I've a feeling the Fates will take care of that."

"So be it. In the meantime, though, if you happen to think of something special, let me know."

"It's a privilege to help you, Lord Corwin. Let it go at that."

"All right. Thanks."

We passed through shadow after shadow. Suns ran backward and storms assailed us out of beautiful skies. We toyed with night, which might have trapped a less adroit pair than us, found a twilight, and took our rations there. Shortly thereafter, Shask turned back to stone. Nothing attacked us that night, and my dreams were hardly worth dreaming.

Next day we were on our way early, and I used every trick I knew to shortcut us through Shadow on our way home. Home . . . It did feel good to be headed back, despite Shask's comments on my relatives. I'd no idea I would miss Amber as much as I had. I'd been away far longer on countless occasions, but usually I had at least a rough idea as to when I might be heading back. A prison in the Courts, though, was not a place from which one might make such estimates.

So we tore on, wind across a plain, fire in the mountains, water down a steep ravine. That evening I felt the resistance begin, the resistance which comes when one enters that area of Shadow near to Amber. I tried to make it all the way but failed. We spent that night at a place near to where the Black Road used to run. There was no trace of it now.

The next day the going was slower, but, more and more, familiar shadows cropped up. That night we slept in Arden, but Julian did not find us. I either dreamed his hunting horn or heard it in the distance as I slept; and though it is often prelude to death and destruction, it merely made me feel nostalgic. I was finally near to home.

The next morning I woke before sunup. Shask, of course, was still a blue lizard curled at the base of a giant tree. So I made tea and ate an apple afterward. We were low on provisions but should soon be in the land of plenty.

Shask slowly unwound as the sun came up. I fed him the rest of the apples and gathered my possessions.

We were riding before too long, slow and easy, since there would be some hard climbing up the back route I favored. During our first break I asked him to become once more a horse, and he obliged. It didn't seem to make that much difference, and I requested he maintain it. I wanted to display his beauty in that form.

"Will you be heading right back after you've seen me here?" I asked.

"I've been meaning to talk to you about that," he responded. "Things have been slow back in the Courts, and I'm no one's assigned mount."

"Oh?"

"You're going to need a good mount, Lord Corwin."

"Yes, I'm sure."

"I'd like to apply for the job, for an indefinite period."

"I'd be honored," I said. "You're very special."

"Yes, I am."

We were atop Kolvir that afternoon and onto the grounds of Amber Palace within hours after that. I found Shask a good stall, groomed him, fed him, and left him to turn to stone at his leisure. I found a nameplate, scratched Shasko's name and my own upon it, and tacked it to his door.

"See you later," I said.

"Whatever, Lord. Whatever."

I departed the stables and headed for the palace. It was a damp, cloudy day, with a chill breeze from the direction of the sea. So far, no one had spotted me.

I entered by way of the kitchen, where there was new help on duty. None of them recognized me, though they obviously realized that I belonged. At least, they returned my greeting with due respect and did not object to some fruit I pocketed. They did ask whether I cared to have something sent to one of the rooms, and I answered "yes" and told them to send a bottle of wine and a chicken along with it. The afternoon head chef— a red-haired lady named Clare—began studying me more closely, and more than once her gaze drifted toward the silver rose on my cloak. I did not want to announce my identity just then, and I thought they'd be a little afraid to guess ahead at it, at least for a few hours. I did want the time to rest a bit and just enjoy the pleasure of being back. So, "Thanks," I said, and I went on my way to my quarters.

I started up the back stairs the servants use for being unobtrusive and the rest of us for being sneaky.

Partway up, I realized that the way was blocked by sawhorses. Tools lay scattered about the stairs though there were no workmen in sight, and I couldn't tell whether a section of old stair had simply given way or whether some other force had been brought to bear upon it.

I returned, cut around to the front, and took the big stairway up. As I made my way, I saw signs of exterior repair work, including entire walls and sections of flooring. Any number of apartments were open to viewing. I hurried to make sure that mine was not among their number.

Fortunately, it was not. I was about to let myself in when a big red-haired fellow turned a corner and headed toward me. I shrugged. Some visiting dignitary, no doubt. . . .

"Corwin!" he called out. "What are you doing here?"

As he drew nearer, I saw that he was studying me most intently. I gave him the same treatment.

"I don't believe I've had the pleasure," I said.

"Aw, come on, Corwin," he said. "You surprised me. Thought you were off by your Pattern and the '57 Chevy."

I shook my head.

"Not sure what you're talking about," I said.

He narrowed his eyes.

"You're not a Pattern ghost?" he said.

"Merlin told me something about them," I said, "after he effected my release at the Courts. But I don't believe I've ever met one."

I rolled up my left sleeve.

"Cut me. I bleed," I said.

As he studied my arm, his gaze appeared more than a little serious. For a moment, I thought he'd actually take me up on it.

"All right," he said then. "Just a nick. For security purposes."

"I still don't know who I'm talking to," I said.

He bowed.

"Sorry. I am Luke of Kashfa, sometimes known as Rinaldo I, its king. If you are who you say you are, I am your nephew. My dad was your brother Brand."

Studying him, I saw the resemblance. I thrust my arm farther forward.

"Do it," I said.

"You're serious."

"Dead right."

He drew a Bowie knife from his belt then and looked into my eyes. I nodded. He moved to touch my forearm with its tip and nothing happened.

That is to say, something happened, but it was neither desired nor wholly anticipated.

The point of his blade seemed to sink a half-inch or so into my arm. It kept going then, finally passing all the way through. But no blood came.

He tried again. Nothing.

"Damn!" he said. "I don't understand. If you were a Pattern ghost, we'd at least get a flare. But there's not even a mark on you."

"May I borrow the blade?" I asked.

"Sure."

He passed it to me. I took it in my hand and studied it. I pushed it into my arm and drew it along for perhaps three-quarters of an inch. Blood oozed.

"I'll be damned!" Luke said. "What's going on?"

"I'd say it's a spell I picked up when I spent a night in the Dancing Mountains recently," I replied.

"Hm," Luke mused. "I've never had the pleasure, but I've heard stories of the place. I don't know any simple ways to break its spells. My room's off toward the front." He gestured southward. "If you'd care to stop by, I'll see what I can figure out about it. I studied Chaos magic with my dad, and with my mother, Jasra."

I shrugged.

"This is my room right here," I said, "and I've a chicken and a bottle of wine on the way up. Let's do the diagnosis in here, and I'll split the meal with you."

He smiled.

"Best offer I've had all day," he said. "But let me stop back at my room for some tools of the trade."

"All right. I'll walk you back, so I'll know the way in case I need it."

He nodded and turned. We headed up the hall.

Turning the coner, we moved from west to east, passing Flora's apartments and moving in the direction of some of the better visitors' quarters. Luke halted before one room and reached into his pocket, presumably after the key. Then he halted.

"Uh, Corwin?" he said.

"What?" I responded.

"Those two big cobra-shaped candle holders," he said, gesturing up the hall. "Bronze, I believe."

"Most likely. What of them?"

"I thought they were just hall decorations."

"That's what they are."

"The last time I looked at them, they kind of bracketed a small painting or tapestry," he said.

"My recollection, too," I said.

"Well, there seems to be a corridor between them now."

"No, that can't be. There's a proper hallway just a little beyond—" I began.

Then I shut up because I knew. I began walking toward it.

"What's going on?" Luke asked.

"It's calling me," I said. "I've got to go and see what it wants."

"What is it?"

"The Hall of Mirrors. It comes and goes. It brings sometimes useful, sometimes ambiguous messages to the one it calls."

"Is it calling us both, or just you?" Luke said.

"Dunno," I replied. "I feel it calling me, as it has in the past. You're welcome to come with me. Maybe it has some goodies for you, too."

"You ever hear of two people taking it at once?"

"No, but there's a first time for everything," I said.

Luke nodded slowly.

"What the hell!" he said. "I'm game."

He followed me to the place of the snakes, and we peered up it. Candles flared along its walls, at either hand. And the walls glittered from the countless mirrors which hung upon them. I stepped forward. Luke followed, at my left.

The mirror frames were of every shape imaginable. I walked very slowly, observing the contents of each one. I told Luke to do the same. For several paces, the mirrors seemed simply to be giving back what was before them. Then Luke stiffened and halted, head turning to the left.

"Mom!" he said explosively.

The reflection of an attractive red-haired woman occupied a mirror framed in green-tinged copper in the shape of an Ouroboros serpent.

She smiled.

"So glad you did the right thing, taking the throne," she said.

"You really mean that?" he asked.

"Of course," she replied.

"Thought you might be mad. Thought you wanted it," he said.

"I did once, but those damned Kashfans never appreciated me. I've got the Keep now, though, and I feel like doing a few years' research here—and it's full of sentimental values as well. So as long as Kashfa stays in the family, I wanted you to know I was pleased."

"Why—uh—glad to hear that, Mom. Very glad. I'll hang onto it."

"Do," she said, and vanished.

He turned to me, a small ironic smile flickering across his lips.

"That's one of the rare times in my life when she's approved of something I've done," he said. "Doubtless for all the wrong reasons, but still . . . How real are these things? What exactly did we see? Was that a conscious communication on her part? Was—"

"They're real," I said. "I don't know how or why or what part of the other is actually present. They may be stylized, surreal, may even suck you in. But in some way they're really real. That's all I know. Holy cow!"

From the huge gold-framed mirror, ahead and to my right, the grim visage of my father Oberon peered forth. I advanced a pace.

"Corwin," he said. "You were my chosen, but you always had a way of disappointing me."

"That's the breaks," I said.

"True. And one should not speak of you as a child after all these years. You've made your choices. Of some I have been proud. You have been valiant."

"Why, thank you—sir."

"I bid you do something immediately."

"What?"

"Draw your dagger and stab Luke."

I stared.

"No," I said.

"Corwin," Luke said. "It could be something like your proving you're not a Pattern ghost."

"But I don't give a damn whether you're a Pattern ghost," I said. "It's nothing to me."

"Not that," Oberon interjected. "This is of a different order."

"What, then?" I asked.

"Easier to show than to tell," Oberon replied.

Luke shrugged.

"So nick my arm," he said. "Big deal."

"All right. Let's see how the show beats the tell."

I drew a stiletto from my boot sheath. He pulled back his sleeve and extended his arm. I stabbed lightly.

My blade passed through his arm as if the limb were made of smoke.

"Shit!" Luke said. "It's contagious!"

"No," Oberon responded. "It is a thing of very special scope."

"That is to say?" Luke asked.

"Would you draw your sword, please?"

Luke nodded and drew a familiar-looking golden blade. It emitted a high keening sound, causing all of the candle flames in the vicinity to flicker. Then I knew it for what it was—my brother Brand's blade, Werewindle.

"Haven't seen that in a long while," I said, as the keening continued.

"Luke, would you cut Corwin with your blade, please?"

Luke raised his eyes, met my gaze. I nodded. He moved the blade, scored my arm with its point. I bled.

"Corwin—If you would. . . ?" Oberon said.

I drew Grayswandir and it, too, ventured into fighting song—as I had only heard it do on great battlefields in the past. The two tones joined together into a devastating duet.

"Cut Luke."

Luke nodded and I sliced the back of his hand with Grayswandir. An incision line occurred, reddening immediately. The sounds from our blades rose and fell.

I sheathed Grayswandir to shut her up. Luke did the same with Werewindle.

"There's a lesson there somewhere," Luke said. "Damned if I can see what it is, though."

"They're brother and sister weapons, you know, with a certain magic in common. In fact, they've a powerful secret in common," Oberon said. "Tell him, Corwin."

"It's a dangerous secret, sir."

"The time has come for it to be known. You may tell him."

"All right," I said. "Back in the early days of creation, the gods had a series of rings their champions used in the stabilization of Shadow."

"I know of them," Luke said. "Merlin wears a spikard."

"Really," I said. "They each have the power to draw on many sources in many shadows. They're all different."

"So Merlin said."

"Ours were turned into swords, and so they remain."

"Oh?" Luke said. "What do you know?"

"What do you deduce from the fact that they can do you harm when another weapon cannot?"

"Looks as if they're somehow involved in our enchantments," I ventured.

"That's right," Oberon said. "In whatever conflict lies ahead—no matter what side you are on—you will need exotic protection against the oddball power of someone like Jurt."

"Jurt?" I said.

"Later," Luke told me. "I'll fill you in."

I nodded.

"Just how is this protection to be employed? How do we get back to full permeability?" I asked.

"I will not say," he replied, "but someone along the way here should be able to tell you. And whatever happens, my blessing—which is probably no longer worth much—lies on both of you."

We bowed and said thanks. When we looked up again, he was gone.

"Great," I said. "Back for less than an hour and involved in Amber ambiguity."

Luke nodded.

"Chaos and Kashfa seem just as bad, though," he said. "Maybe the state's highest function is to grind out insoluble problems."

I chuckled as we moved on, regarding ourselves in dozens of pools of light. For several paces nothing happened, then a familiar face appeared in a red-framed oval to my left.

"Corwin, what a pleasure," she said.

"Dara!"

"It seems that my unconscious will must be stronger than that of anyone else who wishes you ill," she said. "So I get to deliver the best piece of news of all."

"Yes?" I said.

"I see one of you lying pierced by the blade of the other. What joy!"

"I've no intention of killing this guy," I told her.

"Goes both ways," Luke said.

"Ah, but that is the deadly beauty of it," she said. "One of you must be run through by the other for the survivor to regain that element of permeability he has lost."

"Thanks, but I'll find another way," Luke said. "My mom, Jasra, is a pretty good sorceress."

Her laughter sounded like the breaking of one of the mirrors.

"Jasra! She was one of my maids," she said. "She picked up whatever she knows of the Art by eavesdropping on my work. Not without talent, but she never received full training."

"My dad completed her training," Luke said.

As she studied Luke, the merriment went out of her face.

"All right," she said. "I'll level with you, son of Brand. I can't see any way to resolve it other than the way I stated. As I have nothing against you, I hope to see you victorious."

"Thanks," he said, "but I've no intention of fighting my uncle. Someone must be able to lift this thing."

"The tools themselves have drawn you into this," she said. "They will force you to fight. They are stronger than mortal sorcery."

"Thanks for the advice," he said. "Some of it may come in handy," and he winked at her. She blushed, hardly a response I'd have anticipated, then she was gone.

"I don't like the tenor this has acquired," I said.

"Me neither. Can't we just turn around and go back?"

I shook my head.

"It sucks you in," I told him. "Just get everything you can out of it—that's the best advice I ever got on the thing."

We walked on for perhaps ten feet, past some absolutely lovely examples of mirror making as well as some battered old looking glasses.

A yellow-lacquered one on Luke's side, embossed with Chinese characters and chipped here and there, froze us in our tracks as the booming voice of my late brother Eric rang out:

"I see your fates," he said with a rumbling laugh, "And I can see the killing ground where you are destined to enact them. It will be interesting, brother. If you hear laughter as you lie dying, it will be mine."

"You always were a great kidder," I said. "By the way, rest in peace. You're a hero, you know."

He studied my face.

"Crazy brother," he said, and he turned his head away and was gone.

"That was Eric, who reigned briefly as king here?" Luke asked.

I nodded. "Crazy brother," I said.

We moved forward and a slim hand emerged from a steel-framed mirror patterned with roses of rust.

I halted, then turned quickly, somehow knowing even before I saw her who I would behold.

"Deirdre . . ." I said.

"Corwin," she replied softly.

"Do you know what's been going on as we walked along?"

She nodded.

"How much is bullshit and how much is true?" I asked.

"I don't know, but I don't think any of the others do either—not for sure."

"Thanks. I'll take all the reassurances I can get. What now?"

"If you will take hold of the other's arm, it will make the transport easier."

"What transport?"

"You may not leave this hall on your own motion. You will be taken direct to the killing ground."

"By you, love?"

"I've no choice in the matter."

I nodded. I took hold of Luke's arm.

"What do you think?" I asked him.

"I think we should go," he said, "offering no resistance—and when we find out who's behind this, we take him apart with hot irons."

"I like the way you think," I said. "Deirdre, show us the way."

"I've bad feelings about this one, Corwin."

"If, as you said, we've no choice in the matter, what difference does it make? Lead on, lady. Lead on."

She took my hand. The world began to spin around us.

Somebody owed me a chicken and a bottle of wine. I would collect.

I awoke lying in what seemed a glade under a moonlit sky. I kept my eyes half-lidded and did not move. No sense in giving away my wakefulness.

Very slowly, I moved my eyes. Deirdre was nowhere in sight. My right-side peripheral vision informed me that there might be a bonfire in that direction, with some folks seated around it.

I rolled my eyes to the left and got a glimpse of Luke. No one else seemed to be nearby.

"You awake?" I whispered.

"Yeah," he replied.

"No one near," I said, rising, "except maybe for a few around a fire off to the right. We might be able to find a way out and take it—Trumps, Shadowwalk—and thus break the ritual. Or we might be trapped."

Luke put a finger into his mouth, removed it, and raised it, as if testing the wind.

"We're caught up in a sequence I think we need," he said.

"To the death?" I said.

"I don't know. But I don't really think we can escape this one," he replied.

He rose to his feet.

"Ain't the fighting, it's the familiarity," I said. "I begrudge knowing you."

"Me, too. Want to flip a coin?" he asked.

"Heads, we walk away. Tails, we go over and see what the story is."

"Fine with me." He plunged his hand into a pocket, brought out a quarter.

"Do the honors," I said.

He flipped it. We both dropped to our knees.

"Tails," he said. "Best two out of three?"

"Naw," I said. "Let's go."

Luke pocketed his quarter, and we turned and walked toward the fire.

"Only a dozen people or so. We can take them," Luke said softly.

"They don't look particularly hostile," I said.

"True."

I nodded as we approached and addressed them in Thari:

"Hello," I said. "I'm Corwin of Amber and this is Rinaldo I, King of Kashfa, also known as Luke. Are we by any chance expected here?"

An older man, who had been seated before the fire and poking at it with a stick, rose to his feet and bowed.

"My name is Reis," he said, "and we are witnesses."

"For whom?" Luke said.

"We do not know their names, There were two and they wore hoods. One, I think, was a woman. We may offer you food and drink before things begin. . . ."

"Yeah," I said. "I'm out a meal because of this. Feed me."

"Me, too," Luke added, and the man and a couple of his cohorts brought meat, apples, cheese, bread, and cups of red wine.

As we ate, I asked Reis, "Can you tell me how this thing works?"

"Of course," he said, "they told me. When you're finished eating, if you two will move to the other side of the fire, the cues will come to you."

I laughed and then I shrugged.

"All right," I said.

Finished dining, I looked at Luke. He smiled.

"If we've got to sing for our supper," Luke said, "let's give them a ten-minute demonstration and call it a draw."

I nodded.

"Sounds good to me."

We put aside our plates, rose, moved to the fire, and passed behind it.

"Ready?" I said.

"Sure. Why not?"

We drew our weapons, stepped back, and saluted. We both laughed when the music began. Suddenly, I found myself attacking, though I had decided to await the attack and put my first energies into its counter. The movement had been thoughtless, though quite deft and speedy.

"Luke," I said as he parried, "it got away from me. Be careful. There's something odd going on."

"I know," he said as he delivered a formidable attack. "I wasn't planning that."

I parried it and came back even faster. He retreated.

"Not bad," he said, as I felt something loosened in my arm. Suddenly I was fencing on my own again, voluntarily, with no apparent control but with fear that it might be reasserted at any moment.

Suddenly, I knew that we were fairly free and it scared me. If I weren't sufficiently vicious, I might be taken over again. If I were, someone might slip in an unsolicited move at the wrong moment. I grew somewhat afraid.

"Luke, if what's happening to you is similar to what's been happening to me, I don't like this show a bit," I told him.

"Me neither," he said.

I glanced back across the fire. A pair of hooded individuals stood among the others. They were not overlarge and there was a certain whiteness within the cowl of the nearer.

"We've more audience," I said.

Luke glanced back; it was only with great difficulty that I halted a cowardly attack as he turned away. When we returned to hard combat, he shook his head.

"Couldn't recognize either of them," he said. "This seems a little more serious than I thought."

"Yeah."

"We can both take quite a beating and recover."

"True."

Our blades rattled on. Occasionally, one or the other of us received a cheer.

"What say we injure each other," Luke said, "then throw ourselves down and wait for their judgment on whatever's been accomplished. If either of them come near enough, we take them out just for laughs."

"Okay," I said. "If you can expose your left shoulder a bit, I'm willing to take a midline cut. Let's give them lots of gore before we flop, though. Head and forearm cuts. Anything easy."

"Okay. And 'simultaneity' is the word."

So we fought. I stood off a bit, going faster and faster. Why not? It was kind of a game.

Suddenly, my body executed a move I had not ordered it to. Luke's eyes widened as the blood spurted and Grayswandir passed entirely through his shoulder. Moments later, Werewindle pierced my vitals.

"Sorry," Luke said. "Listen, Corwin. If you live and I don't, you'd better know that there's too much crazy stuff involving mirrors going on around the castle. The night before you came back, Flora and I fought a creature that came out of a mirror. And there's an odd sorcerer involved—has a crush on Flora. Nobody knows his name. Has something to do with Chaos, though, I'd judge. Could it be that for the first time Amber is starting to reflect Shadow, rather than the other way around?"

"Hello," said a familiar voice. "The deed is done."

"Indeed," said another.

It was the two cowled figures who had spoken. One was Fiona, the other Mandor.

"However it be resolved, good night, sweet prince," said Fiona.

I tried to rise. So did Luke. Tried also to raise my blade. Could not. Again, the world grew dim, and this time I was leaking precious bodily fluids.

"I'm going to live—and come after you," I said.

"Corwin," I heard her say faintly. "We are not as culpable as you may think. This was—"

"—all for my own good I'll bet," I muttered before the world went dark, growling with the realization that I hadn't gotten to use my death curse. One of these days. . . .

I woke up in the dispensary in Amber, Luke in the next bed. We both had IVs dripping into us.

"You're going to live," Flora said, lowering my wrist from taking my pulse. "Care to tell me your story now?

"They just found us in the hall?" Luke asked. "The Hall of Mirrors was nowhere in sight?"

"That's right."

"I don't want to mention any names yet," I said.

"Corwin," Luke said. "Did the Hall of Mirrors show up a lot when you were a kid?"

"No," I said.

"Hardly ever, when I was growing up either," Flora said. "It's only in recent years that it's become this active. Almost as if the place were waking up."

"The place?" Luke said.

"Almost as if there's another player in the game," she responded.

"Who?" I demanded, causing a pain in my gut.

"Why, the castle itself, of course," she said.

# THE SHROUDLING AND THE GUISEL

I awoke in a dark room, making love to a lady I did not recall having gone to bed with. Life can be strange. Also oddly sweet at times. I hadn't the will to destroy our congress, and I went on and on with what I was doing and so did she until we came to that point of sudden giving and taking, that moment of balance and rest.

I made a gesture with my left hand and a small light appeared and glowed above our heads. She had long black hair and green eyes, and her cheekbones were high and her brow wide. She laughed when the light came on, revealing the teeth of a vampire. Her mouth held not a trace of blood, making it seem somehow impolite for me to touch my throat seeking after any trace of soreness. "It's been a long time, Merlin," she said softly.

"Madame, you have the advantage of me," I said.

She laughed again. "Hardly," she answered, and she moved in such a fashion as to distract me entirely, causing the entire chain of events to begin again on my part.

"Unfair," I said, staring into those sea-deep eyes, stroking that pale brow. There was something terribly familiar there, but I could not understand it.

"Think," she said, "for I wish to be remembered."

"I . . . Rhanda?" I asked.

"Your first love, as you were mine," she said smiling, "there in the mausoleum. Children at play, really. But it was sweet, was it not?"

"It still is," I replied, stroking her hair. "No, I never forgot you. Never thought to see you again, though, after finding that note saying your parents no longer permitted you to play with me . . . thinking me a vampire."

"It seemed so, my Prince of Chaos and of Amber. Your strange strengths and your magics. . . ."

I looked at her mouth, at her unsheathed fangs. "Odd thing for a family of vampires to forbid," I stated.

"Vampires? We're not vampires," she said. "We are among the last of the shroudlings. There are only five families of us left in all the secret images of all the shadows from here to Amber—and farther, on into that place and into Chaos."

I held her more tightly and a long lifetime of strange lore passed through my head. Later I said, "Sorry, but I have no idea what a shroudling is."

Later still she responded, "I would be very surprised if you did, for we have always been a secret race." She opened her mouth to me, and I saw by spirit-light a slow retraction of her fangs into normal-seeming dentition. "They emerge in times of passion other than feasting," she remarked.

"So you do use them as a vampire would," I said.

"Or a ghoul," she said. "Their flesh is even richer than their blood."

"Their?" I said.

"That of those we would take."

". . . And who might they be?" I asked.

"Those the world might be better off without," she said. "Most of them simply vanish. Occasionally, with a feast of jokers, only parts of some remain."

I shook my head.

"Shroudling lady, I do not understand," I told her.

"We come and go where we would. We are an undetected people, a proud people. We live by a code of honor which has protected us against all your understanding. Even those who suspect us do not know where to turn to seek us."

"Yet you come to me and tell me these things."

"I have watched you much of my life. You would not betray us. You, too, live by a code."

"Watched me much of my life? How?"

But we distracted each other then and that moment came to a close. I would not let it die, however. Finally, as we lay side by side, I repeated it. By then, however, she was ready for it.

"I am the fleeting shadow in your mirror," she said. "I look out, yet you see me not. All of us have our pets, my love, a person or place of hobby. You have always been mine."

"Why do you come to me now, Rhanda?" I asked. "After all these years?"

She looked away.

"Mayhap you will die soon," she said after a time, "and I wished to recall our happy days together at Wildwood."

"Die soon? I live in danger. I can't deny it. I'm too near the Throne. But I've strong protectors—and I am stronger than people think."

"As I said, I have watched," she stated. "I do not doubt your prowess. I've seen you hang many spells and maintain them. Some of them I do not even understand."

"You are a sorceress?"

She shook her head. "My knowledge of these matters, while extensive, is purely academic," she said. "My own powers lie elsewhere."

"Where?" I inquired.

She gestured toward my wall. I stared. Finally, I said, "I don't understand."

"Could you turn that thing up?" she asked, nodding toward the spirit-light.

I did so.

"Now move it into the vicinity of your mirror."

I did that also. The mirror was very dark, but so was everything else there in Mandor's guest house, where I had elected to spend the night following our recent reconciliation.

I got out of bed and crossed the room. The mirror was absolutely black, containing no reflection of anything. "Peculiar," I remarked.

"No," she said. "I closed it and locked it after I entered here. Likewise, every other mirror in the house."

"You came in by way of the mirror?"

"I did. I live in the mirrorworld."

"And your family? And the four other families you mentioned?"

"We all of us make our homes beyond the bounds of reflection."

"And from there you travel from place to place?"

"Indeed."

"Obviously, to watch your pets. And to eat people of whom you disapprove?"

"That, too."

"You're scary, Rhanda." I returned to the bed, seating myself on its edge. I took hold of her hand and held it. "And it is good to see you again. I wish you had come to me sooner."

"I have," she said, "using the sleep spells of our kind."

"I wish you had awakened me."

She nodded. "I would like to have stayed with you, or taken you home with me. But for this part of your life you are a certified danger bringer."

"It does seem that way," I agreed. "Still . . . Why are you here now, apart from the obvious?"

"The danger has spread. It involves us now."

"I actually thought that the danger in my life had been minimized a bit of late," I told her. "I have beaten off Dara's and Mandor's attempts to control me and come to an understanding of sorts with them."

"Yet still they will scheme."

I shrugged. "It is their nature. They know that I know, and they know I am their match. They know I am ready for them now. And my brother Jurt . . . we, too, seem to have reached an understanding. And Julia . . . we have been reconciled. We—"

She laughed. "Julia has already used your 'reconciliation' to try to turn Jurt against you again. I watched. I know. She stirs his jealousy with hints that she still cares more for you than for him. What she really wants is you removed, along with the seven in the running with you—and the others who stand ready. She would be queen in Chaos."

"She's no match for Dara," I said.

"Ever since she defeated Jasra, she's had a high opinion of herself. It has not occurred to her that Jasra had grown lazy and lost by a trick, not by a matter of power. She would rather believe her own strength greater than it is. And that is her weakness. She would be reunited with you to put you off-guard as well as to turn your brother against you once again."

"I am forewarned, and I thank you—though there are really only six others in the running for the Throne. I was number one, but a half dozen pretenders have recently turned up. You said seven. There's one I don't know about?"

"There is the hidden one," she said. "I do not know his name to tell you, though I know you saw him in Suhuy's pool. I know his appearance, Chaotic and human. I know that even Mandor considers him a worthy antagonist when it comes to scheming. Conversely, I believe Mandor is the main reason he removed himself to our realm. He fears Mandor."

"He inhabits the mirrorworld?"

"Yes, though he is not yet aware of our existence there. He found it by a near-impossible accident, but he simply thinks he has made a marvelous discovery—a secret way to go nearly anywhere, to see nearly anything without detection. Our people have avoided his awareness, using curves he cannot perceive let alone turn. It has made him considerably more formidable in his path to the Throne."

"If he can look out—even listen—through any mirror without being detected; if he can step out, assassinate someone, and escape by the same route—yes, I can understand it."

The night suddenly seemed very cold. Rhanda's eyes widened. I moved to the chair where I had thrown my garments and began dressing myself.

"Yes, do that," she said.

"There's more, isn't there?"

"Yes. The hidden one has located and brought back an abomination to our peaceful realm. Somewhere, he found a guisel."

"What is a guisel?"

"A being out of our myth, one we had thought long exterminated in the mirrorworld. Its kind nearly destroyed the shroudlings. A monster, it took an entire family to destroy what was thought to be the last of them."

I buckled my sword belt and drew on my boots. I crossed the chamber to the mirror and held my hand before its blackness. Yes, it seemed the source of the cold.

"You closed them and locked them?" I said. "All of the mirrors in this vicinity?"

"The hidden one has sent the guisel through the ways of the mirrors to destroy nine rivals to the Throne. It is on its way to seek the tenth now: yourself."

"I see. Can it break your locks?"

"I don't know. Not easily, I wouldn't think. It brings the cold, however. It lurks just beyond the mirror. It knows that you are here."

"What does it look like?"

"A winged eel with a multitude of clawed legs. It is about 10 feet long."

"If we let it in?"

"It will attack you."

"If we enter the mirror ourselves?"

"It will attack you!"

"On which side is it stronger?"

"The same on either, I think."

"Well, hell! Can we enter by a different mirror and sneak up on it?"

"Maybe."

"Let's give it a shot. Come on."

She rose, dressed quickly in a blood-red garment, and followed me through a wall to a room that was actually several miles distant. Like most of the nobles of Chaos, brother Mandor believes in keeping a residence scattered. A long mirror hung on the far wall between the desk and a large Chaos clock. The clock, I saw, was about to chime a nonlinear for the observer. Great. I drew my blade.

"I didn't even know this one was here," she said.

"We're some distance from the room where I slept. Forget space. Take me through."

"I'd better warn you first," she said. "According to tradition, nobody's ever succeeded in killing a guisel with a sword, or purely by means of magic. Guisels can absorb spells and lashes of force. They can take terrible wounds and survive."

"Any suggestions then?"

"Baffle it, imprison it, banish it. That might be better than trying to kill it."

"OK, we'll play it as it's dealt. If I get into real bad trouble, you get the hell out."

She did not reply but took my hand and stepped into the mirror. As I followed her, the antique Chaos clock began to chime an irregular beat. The inside of the mirror seemed the same as the room without, but turned around. Rhanda led me to the farthest point of reflection, to the left, then stepped around a corner.

We came into a twisted, twilit place of towers and great residences, none of them familiar to me. The air bore clusters of wavy, crooked lines here and there. She approached one, inserted her free hand, and stepped through it, taking me with her. We emerged on a crooked street lined with twisted buildings.

"Thank you," I said then, "for the warning and for the chance to strike."
She squeezed my hand.

"It is not just for you, but for my family, also, that I do it."

"I know that," I said.

"I would not be doing this if I did not believe that you have a chance against the thing. If I did not, I would simply have warned you and told you what I know. But I also remember one day . . . back in Wildwood . . . when you promised to be my champion. You seemed a real hero to me then."

I smiled as I recalled that gloomy day. We had been reading tales of chivalry in the mausoleum. In a fit of nobility I led her outside as the thunder roiled, and I stood among the grave markers of unknown mortals—Dennis Colt, Remo Williams, John Gaunt—and swore to be her champion if ever she needed one. She had kissed me then, and I had hoped for some immediate evil circumstance against which to pit myself on her behalf. But none occurred.

We moved ahead, and she counted doors, halting at the seventh. "That one," she said," leads through the curves to the place behind the locked mirror in your room."

I released her hand and moved past her.

"All right," I said, "time to go a-guiseling," and I advanced. The guisel saved me the trouble of testing the curves by emerging before I got there.

Ten or 12 feet in length, it was, and eyeless as near as I could tell, with rapid-beating cilia all over what I took to be its head. It was very pink, with a long, green stripe passing about its body in one direction, and a blue one in the other. It raised its cilia-end three or four feet above the ground and swayed. It made a squeaking sound. It turned in my direction. Underneath it had a large, angled mouth like that of a shark; it opened and closed it several times and I saw many teeth. A green, venomous-seeming liquid dripped from that orifice to steam upon the ground.

I waited for it to come to me, and it did. I studied the way it moved—quickly, as it turned out—on the horde of small legs. I held my blade before me in an en garde position as I awaited its attack. I reviewed my spells.

It came on, and I hit it with my Runaway Buick and my Blazing Outhouse spells. In each instance, it stopped dead and waited for the spell to run its course. The air grew frigid and steamed about its mouth and midsection. It was as if it were digesting the magic and rushing it down entropy lane. When the steaming stopped, it advanced again and I hit it with my Demented Power Tools spell. Again, it halted, remained motionless, and steamed. This time I rushed forward and struck it a great blow with my blade. It rang like a bell, but nothing else happened, and I drew back as it stirred.

"It seems to eat my spells and excrete refrigeration," I said.

"This has been noted by others," Rhanda responded.

Even as we spoke, it torqued its body, moving that awful mouth to the top, and it lunged at me. I thrust my blade down its throat as its long legs clawed at or caught hold of me. I was driven over backwards as it closed its mouth, and I heard a shattering sound. I was left holding only a hilt. It had bitten off my blade. Frightened, I felt after my new power as the mouth opened again.

The gates of the spikard were opened; and I struck the creature with a raw force from somewhere in Shadow. Again, the thing seemed frozen as the air about me grew chill. I tore myself away from it, bleeding from dozens of small wounds. I rolled away and rose to my feet, still lashing it with the spikard, holding it cold. I tried using the blade to dismember it, but all it did was eat the attack and remain a statue of pink ice.

Reaching out through Shadow, I found myself another blade. With its tip, I traced a rectangle in the air, a bright circle at its center. I reached into it with my will and desire. After a moment, I felt contact.

"Dad! I feel you but I can't see you!"

"Ghostwheel," I said, "I am fighting for my life, and doubtless those of many others. Come to me if you can."

"I am trying. But you have found your way into a strange space. I seem to be barred from entering there."

"Damn!"

"I agree. I have faced this problem before in my travels. It does not lend itself to ready resolution."

The guisel began to move again. I tried to maintain the Trump contact but it was fading. "Father!" Ghostwheel cried as I lost hold. "Try—" Then he was gone. I backed away. I glanced at Rhanda. Dozens of other shroudlings now stood with her, all of them wearing black, white, or red garments. They began to sing a strange, dirgelike song, as if a dark sound-track were required for our struggle. It did seem to slow the guisel, and it reminded me of something from long ago.

I threw back my head and gave voice to that ululant cry I had heard once in a dream and never forgotten.

My friend came.

Kergma—the living equation—come sliding in from many angles at once. I watched and waited as he/she/it—I had never been certain—assembled itself. Kergma had been a childhood playmate, along with Glait and Gryll.

Rhanda must have remembered the being who could go anywhere, for I heard her gasp. Kergma passed around and around her body in greeting, then came to me and did the same.

*"My friends! It has been so long since you called me to play! I have missed you!"*

The guisel dragged itself forward against the song of the shroudlings as if beginning to overcome its power. "This is not a game," I answered. "That beast will destroy us all unless we nail it first," I said.

*"Then I must solve it for us. Everything that lives is an equation, a complex quantum study. I told you that long ago."*

"Yes. Try. Please."

I feared blasting the thing again with the spikard while Kergma worked on it, lest it interfere with his calculations. I kept my blade and spikard at ready as I continued to back away. The shroudlings retreated with me, slowly.

*"A deadly balance,"* Kergma said at last. *"It has a wonderful life equation. Use your toy to stop it now."*

I froze it again with the spikard. The shroudlings' song went on.

At length Kergma said, *"There is a weapon that can destroy it under the right circumstances. You must reach for it, however. It is a twisted blade you have wielded before. It hangs on the wall of a bar where once you drank with Luke."*

"The Vorpal Sword?" I said. "It can kill it?"

*"A piece at a time, under the proper circumstances."*

"You know these circumstances?"

*"I have solved for them."*

I clutched my weapon and struck the guisel again with a force from the spikard. It squeaked and grew still. Then I discarded the blade I held and reached—far, far out through Shadow. I was a long time in finding what I sought and I had a resistance to overcome, so I added the force of the spikard to my own and it came to me. Once again, I held the shining, twisted Vorpal Sword in my hands.

I moved to strike at the guisel with it, but Kergma stopped me. So I hit it again with a lash of force from the spikard.

*"Not the way. Not the way."*

"What then?"

*"We require a Dyson variation on the mirror equation."*

"Show me."

Walls of mirrors shot up on all sides about me, the guisel, and Kergma, but excluding Rhanda. We rose into the air and drifted toward the center of the sphere. Our reflections came at us from everywhere.

*"Now. But you must keep it from touching the walls."*

"Save your equation. I may want to do something with it by and by."

I struck the dormant guisel with the Vorpal Sword. Again, it emitted a bell-like tone and remained quiescent.

*"No,"* Kergma said. *"Let it thaw."*

So I waited until it began to stir, meaning that it would be able to attack me soon. Nothing is ever easy. From outside, I still heard the faint sounds of singing.

The guisel recovered more quickly than I had anticipated. But I swung and lopped off half of its head, which seemed to divide itself into tissue-thin images which then flew away in every direction.

"Caloo! Callay!" I cried, swinging again and removing a long section of tissue from its right side, which repeated the phenomenon of the ghosting and the flight. It came on again and I cut again. Another chunk departed from its twisting body in the same fashion. Whenever its writhing took it near a wall, I intervened with my body and sword, driving it back toward the center and hacking at or slicing it.

Again and again it came on or flipped toward the wall. Each time my response was similar. But it did not die. I fought it till but a tip of its writhing tail moved before me.

"Kergma," I said then," we've sent most of it down infinite lines. Now, can you revise the equation? Then I'll find sufficient mass with the spikard to allow you to create another guisel for me—one that will return to the sender of this one and regard that person as prey."

"*I think so,*" Kergma said. "*I take it you left that final piece for the new one to eat?*"

"Yes, that was my thinking."

And so it was done. When the walls came down, the new guisel—black, its stripes red and yellow—was rubbing against my ankles like a cat. The singing stopped.

"Go and seek the hidden one," I said, "and return his message."

It raced off, passing a curve and vanishing.

"What have you done?" Rhanda asked me. So I told her.

"The hidden one will now consider you the most dangerous of his rivals," she said, "if he lives. Probably he will increase his efforts against you, in subtlety as well as violence."

"Good," I said. "That is my hope. I'd like to force a confrontation. He will probably not feel safe in your world now either, never knowing when a new guisel might come ahunting."

"True," she said. "You have been my champion," and she kissed me.

Just then, out of nowhere a paw appeared and fell upon the blade I held. Its opposite waved two slips of paper before me. Then a soft voice spoke: "You keep borrowing the sword without signing for it. Kindly do that now, Merlin. The other slip is for last time." I found a ballpoint beneath my cloak and signed as the rest of the cat materialized. "That'll be $40," it said then. "It costs 20 bucks for each hour or portion of an hour, to vorp."

I dug around in my pockets and came up with the fees. The cat grinned and began to fade. "Good doing business with you," it said through the smile. "Come back soon. The next drink's on the house. And bring Luke. He's a great baritone."

I noticed as it faded that the shroudling family had also vanished.

Kergma moved nearer. *"Where are the others—Glait and Gryll?"*

"I left Glait in a wood," I replied, "though he may well be back in the Windmaster's vase in Gamble's museum in the Ways of Sawall by now. If you see him, tell him that the bigger thing has not eaten me—and he will drink warm milk with me one night and hear more tales yet. Gryll, I believe, is in the employ of my Uncle Suhuy."

*"Ah, the Windmaster . . . those were the days,"* he said. *"Yes, we must get together and play again. Thank you for calling me for this one,"* and he slid off in many directions and was gone, like the others.

"What now?" Rhanda asked me.

"I am going home and back to bed." I hesitated, then said, "Come with me?"

She hesitated too, then nodded, "Let us finish the night as we began it," she said.

We walked through the seventh door and she unlocked my mirror. I knew that she would be gone when I awoke.

CPSIA information can be obtained at www.ICGtesting.com
Printed in the USA
LVOW040008111212

310789LV00002B/101/A